THE SILVER SKULL

SWORDS OF ALBION

THE SILVER SKULL

SWORDS OF ALBION

MARK CHADBOURN

an imprint of **Prometheus Books**
Amherst, NY

Inquiries should be addressed to
Pyr
59 John Glenn Drive
Amherst, New York 14228–2119
VOICE: 716–691–0133
FAX: 716–691–0137
WWW.PYRSF.COM

13 12 11 10 09   5 4 3 2 1

Library of Congress Cataloging-in-Publication Data

Chadbourn, Mark.
 The silver skull / by Mark Chadbourn.
  p. cm. — (Swords of Albion ; bk. 1)
 ISBN 978–1–59102–783–6 (pbk. : alk. paper)
 1. Great Britain—History—Elizabeth, 1558–1603—Fiction. I. Title.

PR6053.H23S55 2009
823'.914—dc22

2009026408

Printed in the United States on acid-free paper

For Elizabeth, Betsy, Joe, and Eve

ACKNOWLEDGMENTS

Credit must go to four hundred and thirty years of authors responsible for the primary, secondary, and tertiary texts that provided the research and resources for this work.

On the matter of dates: at the time of this story, England still used the old Julian calendar while the rest of Europe had adopted the new Gregorian calendar, with which we are all familiar today. To avoid any confusion, I have used the Gregorian dates for all events.

Spies are men of doubtful credit,
who make a show of one thing and speak another.

—Mary, Queen of Scots

# PROLOGUE

Far beneath the slow-moving Thames, a procession of flickering lights drew inexorably towards London from the east. The pace was funereal, the trajectory steady, purposeful. In that hour after midnight, the spectral glow under the black waters passed unseen by all but two observers.

"There! What are they, sir?" In the lantern light, the guard's fear was apparent as he peered over the battlements of the White Tower, ninety feet above the river.

Matthew Mayhew, who had seen worse things in his thirty years than the guard could ever dream in his worst fever-sleep, replied with boredom, "I see the proud heart of the greatest nation on Earth. I see a city safe and secure within its walls, where the queen may sleep peacefully."

"There!" The guard pointed urgently.

"A waterman has met with disaster." Mayhew sighed. With a temper as short as his stature, the Tower guards had learned to handle him with care and always praised the fine court fashions he took delight in parading.

The guard gulped the cold air of the March night. "And his lantern still burns on the bottom? What of the other lights? And they move—"

"The current."

The guard shook his head. "They are ghosts!"

Mayhew gave a dismissive snort.

"There are such things! Samuel Hale saw the queen's mother walking with her head beneath her arm in the Chapel of Saint Peter ad Vincula. Why, the Tower is the most haunted place in England! The Two Princes, Margaret Pole, Lady Jane Grey . . . all seen here, Master Mayhew. Damned by God to walk this world after their deaths."

Mayhew studied the slow-moving lights, imagining fish in the deep with their own candles to guide their way through the inky dark.

The guard's fear made his lantern swing so wildly the shadows flew across the Tower.

Steadying the lantern, Mayhew said, "When this great fortress was built five hundred years gone, King William had the mortar tempered with the blood of beasts. Do you know why that was?"

"No, no. I—"

"Suffice it to say," Mayhew interrupted wearily, "that you are safe here from all supernatural threat."

The guard calmed a little. "Safe, you say?"

"England's defences are built on more than the rock of its people."

The lights veered away from the centre of the river towards the Tower of London where it nestled inside the old Roman walls, guarding the eastern approach to the capital. Mayhew couldn't prevent a shiver running up his spine.

"Complete your rounds," he said sharply, overcompensating in case the guard had seen his weakness. "We must ensure that the White Tower remains secure against England's enemies."

"And the prisoner you are charged to guard?"

"I will attend to him." Mayhew pressed a scented handkerchief against his nose to block out the stink of the city's filth caught on the wind. Sometimes it was unbearable. He hated being away from the court where the virtues of life were more apparent, hated the boredom of his task, and at that moment hated that he was caught on the cold summit of the White Tower when he should have been inside by the fire.

He cast his eye around the fortress where pools of darkness were held back by the lanterns strung along the walkways among the wards. The only movement came from the slow circuit of the night watch.

The Tower of London was an unassailable symbol of England. Solid Kentish ragstone formed the bulk of the impregnable White Tower, protected by its own curtain wall and moat, with a further curtain wall and thirteen towers guarding the Inner Ward beyond. Finally, there was the Outer Ward, with another solid wall, five towers, and three bastions. Everything valuable to the nation lay within the walls—the Crown jewels, the treasury, the Royal Mint, the armoury, and England's most dangerous prisoners, including Mayhew's personal charge.

As he made his way down the stone steps, he was greeted by the clatter of boots ascending and the light of another lantern. William Osborne appeared, his youthful face and intelligent grey eyes unsettled. Mayhew contemptuously wondered if he now regretted giving up his promising career in the law to join the Queen's Service out of love for his country, not realising what would be asked of him.

"What is it?" Mayhew demanded.

"A disturbance. At the Traitors' Gate."

Where the river lights were heading, Mayhew thought. "The gate remains secure, and well guarded?" he asked.

Osborne's face loomed white in the lamplight. "There are six men upon it, as our Lord Walsingham demanded."

"And yet?"

Osborne's voice quavered with uncertainty. "The guards say the restraining beam moves of its own accord. Bolts draw without the help of human hand. Is this what we always feared?"

Pushing past him with irritation, Mayhew snapped, "You know as well as I that the Tower is protected. These guards are frighted like maidens." For all his contempt at his colleague's words, Mayhew's chest tightened in apprehension.

Walsingham said it could never happen, he reminded himself. *He told the queen . . . Burghley . . .*

Trying to maintain his decorum, he descended to the ground floor with studied nonchalance and stepped out into the Inmost Ward. The whitewashed walls of the Tower glowed in the lantern light.

"Listen!" Osborne's features flared in the gloom as he raised his lantern to illuminate the way ahead.

The steady silence of the Tower was shattered by a cacophony of roars and howls, barks, shrieks, and high-pitched chattering. In the Royal Menagerie, the lions, leopards, and lynxes threw themselves around their pens, while the other exotic beasts tore at the mud of their enclosures in a frenzy.

"What do they sense?" There was a querulous tremble in Osborne's voice.

Scanning the Inmost Ward for any sign of movement, Mayhew relented. "You know."

Osborne winced at his words. "Are you not afraid?"

"This is the work we were charged to do, for queen and country. Raise the alarm. Then we must take ourselves to the prisoner."

Within moments, guards raced to their positions under Osborne's direction. Venturing to the gate, they peered beyond the curtain wall to where the string of lanterns kept the dark at bay.

"Nothing," Osborne said with relief, his voice almost lost beneath the screams of the animals.

Mayhew kept his attention on Saint Thomas's Tower in the outer curtain wall. Beyond it was the river, and beneath it lay the water entrance that had become known as Traitors' Gate, after the enemies of the Crown who had been transported through it to imprisonment or death. The guards had disappeared inside, but there was no clamour.

After five minutes, Osborne's relief was palpable. "A false alarm, then. Perhaps it was only Spanish spies. With the country on the brink of war, they must be operating everywhere. Yes?"

A guard emerged from Saint Thomas's Tower, pausing for a moment on the threshold. Mayhew and Osborne watched him curiously. With an odd, lurching gait, he picked a winding path towards them.

"Is he drunk?" Mayhew growled. "His head will be on the block by noon if he has deserted his post."

"I . . . I do not . . ." The words died in Osborne's throat as the guard's path became more erratic. His jerky movements were deeply upsetting, as if he had been afflicted by a palsy.

Mayhew cursed under his breath. "I gave up a life at court for this."

As the guard neared, they saw his hands continually went to his head as if searching for a missing hat. Despite himself, Mayhew reached for the knife hidden in the folds of his cloak.

"I am afraid," Osborne whispered.

"Do you hear music?" Mayhew cocked his head. "Like pipes playing, caught on the breeze?" As he breathed deeply of the night air, he realised the foul odour of the city had been replaced by sweet, seductive scents that took him back to his childhood. A tear stung his eye. "That aroma," he noted, "like cornfields beneath the summer moon." He inhaled. "Honey, from the hive my grandfather kept."

"What is wrong with you?" Osborne demanded. "This is no time for dreams!"

Mayhew's attention snapped back to the approaching guard. As he entered a circle of torchlight, Mayhew saw for the first time that something was wrong with the guard's face. Revolted yet fascinated, he tried to see the detail behind the guard's pawing hands. The skin was unduly white and had the texture of sackcloth. When the hands came away, Mayhew was sickened to glimpse large dark eyes that resembled nothing so much as buttons, and a row of stitches where the mouth had been. An illusion, he tried to tell himself, but he was left with an impression of the dollies the old women sold in Cheapside at Christmastime.

"God's wounds!" Osbourne exclaimed. "What has happened to him?"

Before Mayhew could answer, a blur of ochre and brown burst from the shadows with a terrible roar, slamming the guard onto the turf. Claws revealed bones and organs, and tearing jaws sprayed viscera around the convulsing form. But the most chilling thing was that the guard did not utter a sound.

He could not, Mayhew thought.

The lion's triumphant roar jolted Mayhew and Osborne from their shock.

"The beasts have escaped the Menagerie!" Mayhew thrust Osborne back towards the White Tower, where they ordered the guards who remained within to bar the door and defend it with their lives.

On the steps, Osborne rested one hand on the stone and bowed his head, fighting the waves of panic that threatened to consume him.

Mayhew eyed him contemptuously. "When you volunteered to become one of Walsingham's men, you vowed to deal with the great affairs of state with courage and fortitude. Now look at you."

"How can you be so hardened to this terror?" Osborne blinked away tears of dread. "When I stepped away from my quiet halls of study, it was to give my life in service to England and our queen, and to protect her from the great Catholic conspiracy . . . and the . . . the Spanish . . ." He swallowed. "The threats on her life from those who wish to turn us back to the terrible rule of Rome. Not this! I never foresaw that my soul would be placed at risk, until it was too late."

"Of course not," Mayhew sneered. "If the common herd knew the real reason why England has established a network of spies the envy of all other nations, they would never rest in their beds. Do not fail me. Or the queen."

Osborne steadied himself. "You are right, Mayhew. I act like a child. I must be strong."

Mayhew clapped him on the shoulder with little affection. "Come, then. We have work to do."

They had only climbed a few steps when a tremendous crash resounded from the great oak door through which they had entered the Tower. Flashing a wide-eyed stare at Mayhew, Osborne took the steps two at a time. As they raced along the ringing corridors, Osborne asked breathlessly, "What is coming, Mayhew?"

"Best not to think of that now."

"What did they do to the guard? I knew him. Carter, a good man, with a wife and two girls."

"Stop asking foolish questions!"

The scream of one of the guards at the door below echoed through the Tower, cut short mercifully soon.

"Let nothing slow your step," Mayhew urged.

In the most secure area of the White Tower, they came to a heavy oak door studded with iron. The walls were thicker than a man's height. After Mayhew gave three sharp bursts of a coded knock, a hatch opened to reveal a pair of glowering eyes.

"Who goes?" came the voice from within.

"Mayhew and Osborne, your Lord Walsingham's men."

While Osborne twitched and glanced anxiously over his shoulder, the guard searched their faces, until, satisfied, he began to draw the fourteen bolts that the queen herself had personally insisted be installed.

"Hurry," Osborne whined. Mayhew cuffed him across his arm.

Once inside, Osborne pressed his back against the resealed door and let out a juddering sigh of relief. "Finally. We are safe."

Mayhew didn't hide his contempt. Osborne was too weak to survive in their business; he would not be long for the world and there was little point in tormenting him further by explaining the obvious.

Six guards waited by the door, and another twenty in the chambers within. Handpicked by Walsingham himself for their brutality and their lack of human compassion, their faces were uniformly hard, their hands rarely more than an inch from their weapons. At any other time they would have been slitting the throats of rich sots in the stews of Bankside, yet here they were in the queen's most trusted employ.

"The cell remains secure?" Mayhew asked the captain of the guard. His face boasted the scars of numerous fights.

"It is. It was examined 'pon the hour, as it is every hour."

"Take us to it."

"Who attempts to breach our defences?" the captain asked. "Surely the Spanish would not risk an attack."

When Mayhew did not respond, the captain nodded and ordered two of the guards to accompany the spies. A moment later they were marching past rooms stacked high with the riches of England, gold seized from the New World or looted from ships from the Spanish Main to the Channel.

Beyond the bullion rooms, one of the guards unlocked a stout door and led them down a steep flight of steps to another locked door. Inside was a low-ceilinged chamber warmed by a brazier in one corner and lit by sputtering torches on opposite walls. Two guards played cards at a heavy, scarred table. On the far side of the room was a single door with a small barred window.

"I do not see why he could not have been kept with the other prisoners," Osborne said.

"No, of course you do not," Mayhew replied.

"The Tower's main rooms have held two kings of Scotland and a king of France, our own King Henry VI, Thomas More, and our own good queen. What is so special about this one that he deserves more secure premises than those great personages?" Osborne persisted.

"You have only been assigned to this task for two days," Mayhew replied. "When you have been here as long as I, you will understand."

Crossing the room, Mayhew peered through the bars in the door. As his eyes adjusted to the gloom within, he made out the form of the cell's occupant hunched on a rough wooden bench, the hood of his cloak, as always, pulled over his head so his features were hidden. He was allowed no naked flame for illumination, no drink in a bowl or goblet, only in a bottle, and he was never allowed to leave the secure area of the White Tower where he had been imprisoned for twenty years.

"Still nothing to say?" Mayhew murmured, and then laughed at his own joke. He passed the comment every day, in full knowledge that the prisoner had never been known to speak in all his time in the Tower.

Yet on this occasion the light leaking through the grille revealed a subtle shift in the dark shape, as though the prisoner was listening to what Mayhew said, perhaps even considering a response.

Mayhew's deliberations were interrupted by muffled bangs and clatters in the Mint above their heads, the sound of raised voices, and then a low, chilling cry.

"They are in," he said flatly, turning back to the room.

Osborne had pressed himself against one wall like a hunted animal. The four guards looked to Mayhew hesitantly.

"Help your friends," he said. "Do whatever is in your power to protect this place. Lock the door as you leave. I will bolt it."

Once they had gone, he slammed the bolts into place with a flick of his wrist that showed his disdain for their security.

"You know it will do no good," Osborne said. "If they have gained access to the Mint, there is no door that will keep them out."

"What do you suggest? That we beg for mercy, or run screaming, like girls?"

"Pray," Osborne replied, "for that is surely the only thing that can save us. These are not men that we face, not Spaniards, or French, not the Catholic traitors from within our own realm. These are the Devil's own agents, and they come for our immortal souls."

Mayhew snorted. "Forget God, Osborne. If He even exists, He has scant regard for this vale of misery."

Osborne recoiled as if he had been struck. "You do not believe in the Lord?"

"If you want atheism, talk to Marlowe. He makes clear his views with every action he takes. But I learn from the evidence of my own eyes, Osborne. We face a threat that stands to wipe us away as though we had never been, and if there is to be salvation, it will not come from above. It will be achieved by our own hand."

"Then help me barricade the door," Osborne pleaded.

With a sigh and a shrug, Mayhew set his weight against the great oak table, and with Osborne puffing and blowing beside him, they pushed it solidly against the door.

When they stood back, Mayhew paused as the faint strains of the haunting pipe music reached him again, plucking at his emotions, turning him in an instant from despair to such ecstasy that he wanted to dance with wild abandon. "That music," he said, closing his eyes in awe.

"I hear no music!" Osborne shouted. "You are imagining it."

"It sounds," Mayhew said with a faint smile, "like the end of all things." He turned back to the cell door where the prisoner now waited, the torch-light catching a metallic glint beneath his hood.

"Damn your eyes!" Osborne raged. "Return to your bench! They shall not free you!"

Unmoving, the prisoner watched them through the grille. Mayhew did not sense any triumphalism in his body language, no sign that he was assured of his freedom, merely a faint curiosity at the change to the pattern that had dominated his life for so many years.

"Sit down!" Osborne bellowed.

"Leave him," Mayhew responded as calmly as he could manage. "We have a more pressing matter."

Above their heads, the distant clamour of battle was punctuated by a muffled boom that shook the heavy door and brought a shower of dust from the cracks in the stone. Silence followed, accompanied by the cloying scent of honeysuckle growing stronger by the moment.

Drawing their swords, Mayhew and Osborne focused their attention on the door.

A random scream, becoming a sound like the wind through the trees on a lonely moor. More noises, fragments of events that painted no comprehensive picture.

Breath tight in their chests, knuckles aching from gripping their swords, Mayhew and Osborne waited.

Something bouncing down the stone steps, coming to rest against the door with a thud.

A soft tread, then gone like a whisper in the night, followed by a long silence that felt like it would never end.

Finally the unbearable quiet was broken by a rough grating as the top bolt drew back of its own accord. His eyes frozen wide, Osborne watched its inexorable progress.

As soon as the bolt had clicked open, the one at the foot of the door followed, and when that had been drawn the great tumblers of the iron lock turned until they fell into place with a shattering *clack*.

"I . . . I think I can hear the music now, Mayhew, and there are voices in it," Osborne said. He began to recite the Lord's Prayer quietly.

The door creaked open a notch and then stopped. Light flickered through the gap, not torchlight or candlelight, but with some troubling quality that Mayhew could not identify, but which reminded him of moonlight on the Downs. The music was louder now, and he too could hear the voices.

A sound at his back disrupted his thoughts. The prisoner's hands were on the bars of the grille and he had removed his hood for the first time that Mayhew could recall. In the ethereal light, there was an echo of the moon within the cell. The prisoner's head was encompassed by a silver skull of the finest workmanship, gleaming so brightly Mayhew could barely look at it. Etched on it with almost invisible black filigree were ritual marks and symbols. Through the silver orbits, the prisoner's eyes hung heavily upon Mayhew, steady and unblinking, the whites marred by a tracing of burst capillaries.

The door opened.

CHAPTER 1

Even four hours of soft skin and full lips could not take away her face. Empty wine bottles rattling on the bare boards did not drown out her voice, nor did the creak of the bed and the gasps of pleasure. She was with him always.

"They say you single-handedly defeated ten of Spain's finest swordsmen on board a sinking ship in the middle of a storm," the redheaded woman breathed in his ear as she ran her hand gently along his naked thigh.

"True."

"And you broke into the Doge's palace in disguise and romanced the most beautiful woman in all of Venice," the blonde woman whispered into his other ear, stroking his lower belly.

"Yes, all true."

"And you wrestled a bear and killed it with your bare hands," the redhead added.

He paused thoughtfully, then replied, "Actually, that one is not true, but I think I will appropriate it nonetheless."

The women both laughed. He didn't know their names, didn't really care. They would be amply rewarded, and have tales to tell of their night with the great Will Swyfte, and he would have passed a few hours in the kind of abandon that always promised more than it actually delivered.

"Your hair is so black," the blonde one said, twirling a finger in his curls.

"Yes, like my heart."

They both laughed at that, though he wasn't particularly joking. Nathaniel would have laughed too, although with more of a sardonic edge.

The redhead reached out a lazy hand to examine his clothes hanging over the back of the chair. "You must cut a dashing figure at court, with these finest and most expensive fashions." Reaching a long leg from the bed, she traced her toes across the shiny surface of his boots.

"I heard you were a poet." The blonde rubbed her groin gently against his hip. "Will you compose a sonnet to us?"

"I was a poet. And a scholar. But that part of my life is far behind me."

"You have exchanged it for a life of adventure," she said, impressed. "A fair exchange, for it has brought you riches and fame."

Will did not respond.

The blonde examined his bare torso, which bore the tales of the last few years in each pink slash of a rapier scar or ragged weal of torture, stories that had filtered into the consciousness of every inhabitant of the land, from Carlisle to Kent to Cornwall.

As she swung her leg over him to begin another bout of lovemaking, they were interrupted by an insistent knocking at the door.

"Go away," Will shouted.

The knocking continued. "I know you are deep in doxie and sack, Master Swyfte," came a curt, familiar voice, "but duty calls."

"Nat. Go away."

The door swung open to reveal Nathaniel Colt, shorter than Will and slim, but with eyes that revealed a quick wit. He studiedly ignored the naked, rounded bodies and focused his attention directly on Will.

"A fine place to find a hero of the realm," he said with sarcasm. "A tawdry room atop a stew, stinking of coitus and spilled wine."

"In these harsh times, every man deserves his pleasures, Nat."

"This is England's greatest spy," the redhead challenged. "He has earned his comforts."

"Yes, England's greatest spy," Nathaniel replied acidly. "Though I remain unconvinced of the value of a spy whose name and face are recognised by all and sundry."

"England needs its heroes, Nat. Do not deny the people the chance to celebrate the successes of God's own nation." He eased the women off the bed with gentle hands. "We will continue our relaxation at another time," he said warmly, "for I fear my friend is determined to enforce chastity."

His eyes communicated more than his words. The women responded with coquettish giggles as they scooped up their dresses to cover them as they skipped out of the room.

Kicking the door shut after them, Nathaniel said, "You will catch the pox if you continue these sinful ways with the Winchester Geese."

"The pox is not God's judgment, or all the aristocracy of England would be rotting in their breeches as they dance at court."

"And 'twould be best if you did not let any but me hear your views on our betters."

"Besides," Will continued, "Liz Longshanks' is a fine establishment. Does it not bear the mark of the Cardinal's Hat? Is this land on which this stew rests not in the blessed ownership of the bishop of Winchester? Everything has two faces, Nat, neither good nor bad, just there. That is the way of the world, and if there is a Lord, it is His way."

Ignoring Nathaniel's snort, Will stretched the kinks from his limbs and lazily eased out of the bed to dress, absently kicking the empty bottles against the chamber pot. "And," he added, "I am in good company. That master of theatre, Philip Henslowe, and his son-in-law Edward Alleyn are entertaining Liz's girls in the room below."

"Alleyn the actor?"

"Whoring and acting go together by tradition, as does every profession that entails holding one face to the world and another in the privacy of your room. When you cannot be yourself, it creates certain tensions that must be released."

"You will be releasing more tensions if you do not hurry. Your Lord Walsingham is on his way to Bankside, and if he finds his favoured tool deep in whores, or in his cups, he will be less than pleased." Nathaniel threw Will his shirt to end his frustrated searching.

"What trouble now, then? More Spanish spies plotting against our queen? You know they fall over their own swords."

"I am pleased to hear you take the threats against us so lightly. England is on the brink of war with Spain, the nation is torn by fears of the enemy landing on our shores at every moment, we lack adequate defences, our navy is in disarray, we are short of gunpowder, and the great Catholic powers of Europe are all eager to see us crushed and returned to the old faith, but the great Will Swyfte thinks it is just a trifling. I can rest easily now."

"One day you will cut yourself with that tongue, Nat."

"There is some trouble at the White Tower, though I am too lowly a worm to be given any important details. No, I am only capable of dragging my master out of brothels and hostelries and keeping him one step out of the Clink," he added tartly.

"You are of great value to me, as well you know." Finishing his dressing, Will ran a hand through his hair thoughtfully. "The Tower, you say?"

"An attempt to steal our gold, perhaps. Or the Crown jewels. The Spanish always look for interesting ways to undermine this nation."

"I cannot imagine Lord Walsingham venturing into Bankside for bullion or jewels." He ensured Nathaniel didn't see his mounting sense of unease. "Let us to the Palace of Whitehall before the principal secretary sullies his boots in Bankside's filth."

A commotion outside drew Nathaniel to the small window, where he saw a sleek black carriage with a dark red awning and the gold brocade and ostrich feathers that signified it had been dispatched from the palace. The chestnut horse stamped its hooves and snorted as a crowd of drunken apprentices tumbled out of the Sugar Loaf across the street to surround the carriage.

"I fear it is too late for that," Nathaniel said.

Four accompanying guards used their mounts to drive the crowd back, amid loud curses and threats but none of the violence that troubled the constables and beadles on a Saturday night. Two of the guards barged into the brothel, raising angry cries from Liz Longshanks and the girls waiting in the downstairs parlour, and soon the clatter of their boots rose up the wooden stairs.

"Let us meet them halfway," Will said.

"If I were you, I would wonder how our Lord Walsingham knows exactly which stew is your chosen hideaway this evening."

"Lord Walsingham commands the greatest spy network in the world. Do you think he would not use a little of that power to keep track of his own?"

"But you are in his employ."

"As the queen's godson likes to say, 'treason begets spies and spies treason.' In this business, as perhaps in life itself, it is best not to trust anyone. There is always another face behind the one we see."

"What a sad life you lead."

"It is the life I have. No point bemoaning." Will's broad smile gave away nothing of his true thoughts.

The guards escorted him out into the rutted street, where a light frost now glistened across the mud. The smell of ale and woodsmoke hung heavily between the inns and stews that dominated Bankside, and the night was filled with the usual cacophony of cries, angry shouts, the sound of numerous simultaneous fights, the clatter of cudgels, cheers and roars from the bull- and bear-baiting arenas, music flooding from open doors, and drunken voices singing clashing songs. Every conversation was conducted at a shout.

As Will pushed through the crowd towards the carriage, he was recognised by some of the locals from the inns he frequented, and his name flickered from tongue to tongue in awed whispers. Apprentices tentatively touched his sleeve, and sultry-eyed women pursed their lips or thrust their breasts towards him, to Nathaniel's weary disdain. But many revealed their fears about the impending invasion and offered their prayers that Will was off to protect them. Grinning, he shook hands, offered wry dismissals of the Spanish threat, and raised their spirits with enthusiastic proclamations of England's strength; he played well the part he had been given.

At the carriage, the curtain was drawn back to reveal a man with an ascetic demeanour and a fixed mouth that appeared never to have smiled, his eyes dark and implacable. Francis Walsingham was approaching sixty, but his hair and beard were still black, as were his clothes, apart from a crisp white ruff.

"My lord," Will said.

"Master Swyfte. We have business." Walsingham's eyes flickered towards Nathaniel. "Come alone."

Will guessed the nature of the business immediately, for Nathaniel usually accompanied him everywhere and had been privy to some of the great secrets of state. Will turned to him and said, "Nat, I would ask a favour of you. Go to Grace and ensure she has all she needs."

Reading the gravity in Will's eyes, Nathaniel nodded curtly and pushed his way back through the crowd. It was in those silent moments of communication that Will valued Nathaniel more than ever; more than a servant, Nathaniel had become a trusted companion, perhaps even a friend. But friends did not keep secrets from each other, and Will guarded the biggest secret of all. It ensured his path was a lonely one.

Walsingham saw the familiar signs in Will's face. "Our knowledge and our work are a privilege," he said in his modulated, emotionless voice.

"We have all learned to love the lick of the lash," Will replied.

Walsingham held the carriage door open for Will to climb into the heavy perfume of the court—lavender, sandalwood, and rose from iron containers hanging in each of the four corners of the interior. They kept the stink of the city at bay, but also served a more serious purpose that only the most learned would recognise.

Hands reached in through the open window for Will to touch. After he had shaken and clasped a few, he drew the curtain and let his public face fall away along with his smile.

"They love you, Master Swyfte," Walsingham observed, "which is as it should be. Your fame reaches to all corners of England, your exploits recounted in inn and marketplace. Your heroism on behalf of queen and country is a beacon in the long dark of the night that ensures the good men and women of our land sleep well in their beds, secure in the knowledge that they are protected by the best that England has to offer."

"Perhaps I should become one of Marlowe's players."

"Do you sour of the public role you must play?"

"If they knew the truth about me, there would be few flagons raised to the great Will Swyfte in Chichester and Chester."

"There is no truth," Walsingham replied as the carriage lurched into motion with the crack of the driver's whip. "There are only the stories we tell ourselves. They shape our world, our minds, our hearts. And the strongest stories win the war." His piercing eyes fell upon Will from the dark depths beneath his glowering brow. "You seem in a melancholy mood this night."

"My revels were interrupted. Any man who had his wine and his women dragged from his grasp would be in a similar mood."

A shadow crossed Walsingham's face. "Be careful, William. Your love of the pleasures of this world will destroy you."

His disapproval meant nothing to Will. He did not fear God's damnation; mankind had been left to its own devices. There was too much hell around him to worry about the one that might lie beyond death.

"I understand why you immerse yourself in pleasure," Walsingham continued. "We all find ways to ease the burden of our knowledge. I have my God. You have your wine and your whores. Through my eyes, that is no balance, but each must find his own way to carry out our work. Still, take care, William. The devils use seduction to achieve their work, and you provide them with a way through your defences."

"As always, my lord, I am vigilant." Will pretended to agree with Walsingham's assessment of his motivations, but in truth the principal secretary didn't have the slightest inkling of what drove Will, and never would. Will took some pleasure in knowing that a part of him would always remain his own, however painful.

As the carriage trundled over the ruts, the carnal sounds and smells of Bankside receded. Through the window, Will noticed a light burning high up in the heart of the City across the river, the warning beacon at the top of the lightning-blasted spire of Saint Paul's.

"This is it, then," he said quietly.

"Blood has been spilled. Lives have been ruined. The clock begins to tick."

"I did not think it would be so soon. Why now?"

"You will receive answers shortly. We knew it was coming." After a pause, he said gravely, "William Osborne is dead, his eyes put out, his bones crushed at the foot of the White Tower."

"Death alone was not enough for them."

"He did it to himself."

Will considered Osborne's last moments and what could have driven him to such a gruesome end.

"Master Mayhew survived, though injured," Walsingham continued.

"You have never told me why they were posted to the Tower."

Walsingham did not reply. The carriage trundled towards London Bridge, the entrance closed along with the City's gates every night when the Bow Bells sounded.

Echoing from the river's edge came the agonised cries of the prisoners chained to the posts in the mud along the banks, waiting for the tide to come in to add to their suffering. Above the gates, thirty spiked decomposing heads of traitors were a warning of a worse fate to those who threatened the established order.

As the driver hailed his arrival, the gates ground open to reveal the grand, timber-framed houses of wealthy merchants on either side of the bridge. The carriage rattled through without slowing and the guards hastily closed the gates behind them to seal out the night's terrors.

The closing of the gates had always signalled security, but if the City's defences had been breached there would be no security again.

"A weapon of tremendous power has fallen into the hands of the Enemy," Walsingham said. "A weapon with the power to bring about doomsday. These are the days we feared."

 CHAPTER 2

In the narrow, ancient streets clustering hard around the stone bulk of the Tower of London, the dark was impenetrable, threatening, and there was a sense of relief when the carriage broke out onto the green to the north of the outer wall where lanterns produced a reassuring pool of light.

Standing in ranks, soldiers waited to be dispatched by their commander in small search parties fanning out across the capital. Robert Dudley, the earl of Leicester, strutted in front of them, firing off orders. Though grey-bearded and with a growing belly, he still carried the charisma of the man who had entranced Elizabeth and seduced many other ladies of the court.

A crowd had gathered around the perimeter of the green, sleepy-eyed men and women straggling from their homes as word spread of the activity at the Tower. Will could see anxiety grow in their faces as they watched the grim determination of the commanders directing the search parties. Fear of the impending Spanish invasion ran high, and in the feverish atmosphere of the City tempers were close to boiling over into public disturbance. Spanish spies and Catholic agitators were everywhere, plotting assassination attempts on the queen and whipping up the unease in the inns, markets, and wherever people gathered and unfounded rumours could be quickly spread.

Ignoring the crowd's calls for information about the disturbance, Walsingham guided Will to the edge of the green where a dazed, badly bruised, and bloody Mayhew squatted.

"England's greatest spy," Mayhew said, forming each word carefully, as he nodded to them.

"Master Mayhew. You have taken a few knocks."

"But I live. And for that I am thankful." Hesitating, he glanced at the White Tower looming against the night sky. "Which is more than can be said for that fool Osborne."

"You were guarding the weapon," Will surmised correctly.

"A weapon," Mayhew exclaimed bitterly. "We thought it was only a man. A prisoner held in his cell for twenty years."

Walsingham cast a cautionary glare and they both fell silent. "There will be time for discussion in a more private forum. For now, all you need know is that a hostile group has freed a prisoner and escaped into the streets of London. The City gates remain firmly closed . . ." He paused, choosing his words carefully. "Although we do not yet know if they have some other way to flee the City. The prisoner has information vital to the security of the nation. He must be found and returned to his cell."

"And if he is not found?" Will enquired.

"He *must* be found."

The intensity in Walsingham's voice shocked Will. Why was one man so important—they had lost prisoners before, though none from the Tower— and how could he also be considered a weapon?

"Your particular skills may well be needed if the prisoner is located," Walsingham said to Will before turning to Mayhew. "You must accompany me back to the Palace of Whitehall. I would know the detail of what occurred."

Mayhew looked unsettled at the prospect of Walsingham's questioning, but before they could leave, the principal secretary was summoned urgently by Leicester, who had been in intense conversation with a gesticulating commander.

"They call your name." Mayhew nodded to the crowd. "Your reputation has spread from those ridiculous pamphlets they sell outside Saint Paul's."

"It serves a purpose," Will replied.

"Would they be so full of admiration if those same pamphlets had called you assassin, murderer, corruptor, torturer, liar, and deceiver?" Mayhew's mockery was edged with bitterness.

"Words mean nothing and everything, Matthew. It is actions that count. And results."

"Ah, yes," Mayhew said. "The end results justify the means. The proverb that saves us all from damnation."

Will was troubled by Mayhew's dark mood, but he put it down to the shock of the spy's encounter with the Enemy. His attention was distracted by Walsingham, who, after listening intently to Leicester, summoned Will over. "We may have something," he said with an uncharacteristic urgency. "Accompany Leicester, and may God go with you."

At speed, Leicester, Will, and a small search party left the lights of the green. Rats fled their lantern by the score as they made their way into the dark, reeking streets to the north, some barely wide enough for two men abreast.

"On Lord Walsingham's orders, I attempted to seek the path the Enemy took from the Tower," Leicester said, as they followed the lead of the soldier Will had seen animatedly talking to Leicester. "They did not pass through the Traitors' Gate and back along the river, the route by which they gained access to the fortress. None of the City gates were disturbed, according to the watch. And so I dispatched the search parties to the north and west." He puffed out his chest, pleased with himself.

"You found their trail?"

"Perhaps. We shall see," he replied, but sounded confident.

In the dark, Will lost all sense of direction, but soon they came to a broader street guarded by four other soldiers, from what Will guessed was the original search party. They continually scanned the shadowed areas of the street with deep unease. Will understood why when he saw the three dead men on the frozen ruts, their bodies torn and broken.

Kneeling to examine the corpses, Will saw that some wounds looked to have been caused by an animal, perhaps a wolf or a bear, others as if the victims had been thrown to the ground from a great height. They carried cudgels and knives, common street thugs who had surprised the wrong marks.

"Were these men killed by the Enemy?" Leicester asked, his own eyes flickering towards the dark.

Ignoring the question, Will said, "Three deaths in this manner would not have happened silently. Someone must have heard the commotion, perhaps even saw in which direction the Enemy departed. Search the buildings."

As Leicester's men moved along the street hammering on doors, bleary-eyed men and women emerged, cursing at being disturbed until they were roughly dragged out and questioned by the soldiers.

Will returned to the bodies, concerned by the degree of brutality. In it, he saw a level of desperation and urgency that echoed the anxiety Walsingham had expressed; here was something of worrying import that would have consequences for all of them.

His thoughts were interrupted by a cry from one of Leicester's men who was struggling with an unshaven man in filthy clothes snarling and spitting like an animal. Three soldiers rushed over to help knock him to the frosty street.

"He knows something," the man's captor said, when Will came over.

"I saw nothing," the prisoner snarled, but Will could see the lie in his furtive eyes.

"It would be in your best interests to talk," Leicester said, but his exhortation was delivered in such a courtly manner that it was ineffectual. The man spat and tried to wrestle himself free until he was cuffed to the ground again.

Leicester turned to Will and said quietly, "We could transport him back to the Tower. I gather Walsingham has men there who could loosen his tongue."

"If we delay, the Enemy will be far from here and their prize with them," Will said. "The stakes are high, I am told. We cannot risk that." He hesitated a moment as he examined the man's face and then said, "Let me speak with him. Alone."

"Are you sure?" Leicester hissed. "He may be dangerous."

"He is dangerous." Will eyed the pink scars from knife fights that lined the man's jaw. "I am worse."

Leicester's men manhandled the prisoner back into his house, and Will closed the door behind him after they left. It was a stinking hovel with little furniture, and most that was there looked as if it had been stolen from wealthier premises. The prisoner hunched on the floor by the hearth, pretending to catch his breath, and then threw himself at Will ferociously. Sidestepping his attack, Will crashed a fist into his face. Blood spurted from his nose as he was thrown back against a chair, but it did not deter him. He pulled a knife from a chest beside the fireplace, only to drop it when Will hit him again. As he scrambled for the blade, Will stamped his boot on the man's fingers, shattering the bones. The man howled in pain.

Dragging the man to his feet, Will threw him against the wall, pressing his own knife against his prisoner's throat. "England stands on the brink of war. The queen's life is threatened daily. A crisis looms for our country," Will said. "This is not the time for your games."

"This is not a game!" the man protested. "I dare not speak! I fear for my life!"

Will pressed the tip of his knife a shade deeper for emphasis. "Fear me more," he said calmly. "I will whittle you down a piece at a time—fingers, nose, ears—until you choose to speak. And you will choose. Better to speak now and save yourself unnecessary suffering."

Once the rogue had seen the truth in Will's eyes, he nodded reluctantly.

"You saw what happened out there?" Will asked.

"I was woken by the sounds of a brawl. From my window, I saw a small group of cloaked travellers set upon by a gang of fifteen or more."

"Cutthroats?"

The man nodded.

"Fifteen? At this time? They cannot find much regular trade in this area to justify such a number."

"It seemed they knew the travellers would be passing this way. They lay in wait. Some of them emerged only after the battle had commenced."

This information gave Will pause, but his prisoner was too scared to be telling anything but the truth. "Who were these cutthroats?"

The man shook his head. "I did not recognise them. But if they find I spoke of them they will be back for me!"

"I would think they now have more important things on their minds. What happened?"

"They surprised the travellers." He hesitated, not sure how much he should say. "The travellers . . ." He swallowed, looked like he was about to be sick. "They turned on the cutthroats. I had to look away. I saw no more."

"The faces of the travellers?"

He shook his head. "They moved too fast. I . . . I saw no weapons. Only the slaughter of three victims. It was madness! The other cutthroats fled—"

"And the travellers continued on their way?"

"One of them was different . . . his head glowed like the moon."

"What do you mean?"

The man began to stutter and Will had to wait until he calmed. "I do not know . . . it was a glimpse, no more. But his head glowed. And in the confusion, two of the cutthroats grabbed him and made good their escape into the alleys. He went with them freely, as though he had been a prisoner of the travellers."

"And the travellers gave pursuit?"

"Once they saw he was missing . . . a minute, perhaps two later. By then, their chances of finding him would have been poor."

The frightened man had no further answers to give. Out in the street, Will summoned Leicester away from his men's ears.

"The prize the Enemy stole from the Tower was in turn taken from them by a band of cutthroats," Will told him. "Put all your men onto the streets of London. This threat may now have gone from bad to worse."

CHAPTER 3

ill clung on to the leather straps as the sleek black carriage raced towards the Palace of Whitehall, a solitary ship of light sailing on the sea of darkness washing against London's ancient walls.

Lanterns hung from the great gates and along the walls. From diamond-pane windows, candles glimmered across the great halls and towers, the chapels, wings, courtyards, stores, meeting rooms, and debating chambers, and in the living quarters of the court and its army of servants. At more than half a mile square, it was one of the largest palaces in the world, shaped and reshaped over three hundred years. Hard against the Thames, it had its own wharf where barges were moored to take the queen along the great river and where vast warehouses received the produce that kept the palace fed. Surrounding the complex of buildings were a tiltyard, bowling green, tennis courts, and formal gardens, everything needed for entertainment.

The palace looked out across London with two faces: at once filled with the sprawling, colourful, noisy pageantry of royalty, of a court permanently at play, of music and masques and arts and feasting, of romances and joys and intrigues, a tease to the senses and a home to lives lost to a whirl that always threatened to spin off its axis; and a place of grave decisions on the affairs of state, where the queen guided a nation that permanently threatened to come apart at the seams from pressures both within and without. Whispers and fanfares, long, dark shadows and never-extinguished lights, conspiracies and open rivalries. The palace was a puzzle that had no solution.

The carriage came to a halt under a low arch in a cobbled courtyard so small that the buildings on every side kept it swathed in gloom even during the height of noon. Few from the court even knew it existed, or guessed what took place behind the iron-studded oak door beside which two torches permanently hissed. The jamb too was lined with iron, as was the step.

The door swung open at Will's knock and admitted him to a long, windowless corridor lit by intermittent pools of lamplight. The silent guard closed the door and slid six bolts home. Will's echoing footsteps followed him up one flight of a spiral staircase into the Black Gallery, a large panelled hall. Heavy drapes covered the windows, but it was lit by several lamps and a few flames danced along a charred log in the glowing ashes of the large stone fireplace.

A long oak table filled the centre of the hall, covered with maps, and at the far end sat Mayhew, one louche leg over the arm of his chair. His head was tightly bound in a bloodstained cloth and his left arm was in a sling. He was taking deep drafts of wine from a goblet, and appeared drunk.

Will always found Mayhew difficult. He was hard, in the manner of all spies forced to operate in a world of deceit, and had little patience for his fellows, more concerned with the latest courtly fashions. He liked his wine, too, when he was not working, but he was a sullen, sharp-tongued drunk.

Walsingham emerged at the sound of Will's voice, his features drawn. He listened intently as Will told him about the attack on the Enemy and their loss of the mysterious prisoner from the Tower, but he passed no comment.

"The queen has been informed?" Will asked once he had finished his account.

"I advised her myself," Walsingham replied. "She is fully aware of the magnitude of what lies ahead."

"Which is more than I am." Will expected a terse response, but the principal secretary was distracted by the sound of slamming doors and rapidly marching feet.

Through a door at the far end of the hall, two guards escorted a man wearing a purple cloak and hood that shrouded his features. The guards retreated as the new arrival strode across the room to the fire.

"I can never get warm these days," he said, holding out aged hands to the flames. "It is one of the prices I pay."

The man threw off his hood to reveal a bald pate and silvery hair at the back falling over his collar. As he turned to face the room, fierce grey eyes shone with a coruscating intellect and a sexual potency that belied his sixty-odd years.

"Dee!" Mayhew visibly started in his chair, slopping wine in his lap.

Dr. John Dee cast a disinterested eye over Mayhew. "You have not aged well," he said, before slipping off his cloak and throwing it over a chair.

To the outside world, Dee was a respected scholar and founding fellow of Trinity College in Cambridge who had been an advisor and tutor to the queen, whose *General and Rare Memorials Pertaining to the Perfect Arte of Navigation* had established a vision of an English maritime empire and defined the nation's claims upon the New World. Few knew that Dee had been instrumental in helping Walsingham establish the extensive spy network, providing intelligence and guidance as well as designing many of the tools the spies used to ply their dangerous trade.

But Will had heard other rumours: that Dee had turned his back upon his studies of the natural world for black magic and scrying and attempts to commune with angels. Will had presumed this had contributed to Dee's fall from favour—for five years he had been absent from the court in Central Europe. The last any of them had heard of him was in Bohemia a year ago.

"No word must be uttered of Dr. Dee's appearance here. He has been engaged on official business in Europe under my orders and will return there shortly," Walsingham stressed, in full understanding of what was passing through Will and Mayhew's minds.

"It appears there are secrets kept even from the gatekeepers to the world of secrets," Will noted.

"That is the way of things, Master Swyfte." Walsingham poked the fire absently, sending showers of sparks up the chimney.

"It was fortuitous that I arrived at this time to deliver the information I had secured." Filled with pent-up energy that revealed no hint of fragility, Dee prowled the room. "Events set in motion one year past are now coming to fruition. The Enemy are about to play their hand, and we must divine their secrets quickly before it is too late. Time is short. The queen's life and all of England are at stake."

Will carefully studied the way Walsingham held himself as he moved around the room. To the unfamiliar eye, there was an unruffled indifference to his seemingly detached state, but Will had observed the spymaster carefully since the day he had been brought from his chambers at Cambridge University to be inducted into the ranks of the secret service network. Although he had been overcome by grief and haunted by images of his loss, Will had seen from the first that Walsingham was a man whose deep thoughts were revealed in only the subtlest signs: the relaxation of the taut muscles around his mouth, the tension of a finger, a stiffness in his back. Walsingham was a man forged in the crucible of the secret war they fought, and a symbol of the toll that battle took. Though he hid it well, his mood at that moment was grim.

"Where is the weapon now?" Dee asked.

Once Will had spoken his piece, Mayhew added, "The operation was well planned and efficiently executed." He cast a furtive eye towards Walsingham. "When I was given my post, I was told the Tower was under special protection, even beyond the protection that keeps England safe."

"It is," Dee replied. "And how those defences were breached remains a mystery."

"That need not concern us now," Walsingham interrupted. "Master Swyfte, you are charged with finding the weapon before it can be used and bringing it back to our control, or destroying it, whichever course is necessary. But first you must be apprised of the facts of the matter."

Sifting through the charts on the table, he came to one of the New World and traced his finger along the coastline until he came to the name San Juan de Ulúa in the Spanish territories, the main port for the shipment of silver back to Spain.

"A poor harbour by English standards," Walsingham said. "Little more than a shingle bank to protect it from the storms. Twenty years ago, on December 3, 1568, John Hawkins put in for repairs to his storm-damaged trading fleet, including two of the queen's galleons."

"Into a Spanish port?" Mayhew said, surprised.

"Hawkins paid his taxes and more besides. In the past the Spanish had always left him alone once their coffers were full. But on this occasion their own spies had told them there was more to Hawkins's visit than the repair of rigging and the patching of hulls." Walsingham looked to Dee.

"Since I first arrived at court," Dee began, "I have been advising the queen on the threat that has faced England since the Flood. Every moment of my life has been directed towards finding adequate defences to protect the Crown, the people, the nation."

"And you have succeeded. England has never been safer," Will noted.

"We can never rest, for the Enemy are wise as snakes, and all of their formidable resources are continually directed towards recapturing the upper hand they once enjoyed. And so we too search for new defences, new weapons." In Dee's eyes, the gleam of the candles suggested an inner fire raging out of control.

"My enquiries into the secrets of this world pointed me towards a weapon of immeasurable power that the Spanish were attempting to unlock in the hills not far from San Juan de Ulúa," Dee continued. "So fearful were they of the weapon that the king had insisted it be tested far away from the homeland. A weapon that had brought devastation to the great rulers in the far Orient. A weapon that had surfaced during the Crusades and had been fought over by the Knights Templar and the enemies of Christendom." Dee looked from one to the other, now incandescent with passion. "With a weapon like that, England would be a fortress. The Enemy would retreat to their lakes and their underhills and their lonely moors and we would be safe. Finally."

"What is the nature of the weapon?" Will asked.

"Therein lies the greatest mystery of all." Kneading his hands, Dee paced the room. A tremor ran through him. "It is a mask, a silver skull etched with the secret incantations of the long-forgotten race that first created it. A mask that must be bonded with a mortal to unleash its great power. But all we have are stories, fragments, hints. The nature of that power is not known. All that is known for sure is that nothing can stand before it and survive."

"So Hawkins was charged with seizing the weapon from the Spanish," Will surmised.

"That, at least, was England's fervent hope," Walsingham replied. "While his fleet was being repaired, Hawkins, Francis Drake, and a small group of men slipped secretly into the interior. Five men gave their lives to secure the skull from the Spanish, but before Hawkins could reach his ships, the viceroy, Don Martin Enriquez, took his fleet into the harbour and launched an attack while the English guard was down. Hawkins, Drake, and a small crew escaped in two ships, but the remainder of the English party were tortured and killed by the viceroy as he attempted to discover what we knew about the skull." A shadow passed over Walsingham's face that was like a bellow of rage against his usual detachment. "One of the few survivors, Job Hortop, told how the Spanish dogs hanged Hawkins's men from high posts until the blood burst from the ends of their fingers, and flogged them until the bones showed through their flesh. But not a man spoke of the skull. Heroes all."

Nodding in agreement, Mayhew bowed his head for a moment.

"Hawkins and Drake returned in two storm-torn ships with just fifteen men," Walsingham said. "Eighty-five stout fellows had starved to death on the journey home. But the skull was ours."

Several elements of the story puzzled Will. "Then why did we not use this great weapon to drive back the Enemy, and our other, temporal enemies. Spain would not be so bold if it knew we held such a thing," he asked.

"Because the skull alone is not enough," Dee replied sharply to the note of disbelief in Will's voice. "The stories talk of three parts—a Mask, a Key, and a Shield. All are necessary to use the weapon effectively, though its power can be released without direction and with great consequences for the user by the Mask and Key alone."

Mayhew refilled his goblet, his hands shaking. "And the Key and the Shield?"

"The last twenty years were spent in search of them, to no avail," Walsingham replied. "They were for a time in the hands of the Knights Templar, this we know for sure."

"And those warrior monks fought the Enemy long before us," Dee stressed. "The Templars must have known of the importance of these items and hid them well."

"Then who was the prisoner in the Tower?" Will enquired.

"Some Spaniard who had been cajoled into trying to make the Mask work. What he cannot have realised is that, once bonded, the Mask cannot be removed until death," Dee said. "You are a slave to it, as it is to you."

Will finally understood. "And so he was locked away in the Tower for twenty years while you attempted to find the other two parts."

"We could not risk the weapon falling into the hands of the Enemy in case they located the Key," Walsingham said, "and brought devastation down upon us all."

"But after twenty years, the Enemy chose this night to free the prisoner from the Tower," Will pressed. "Why now, unless the Key is already in their hands?"

Walsingham and Dee exchanged a brief glance.

"What do you know?" Will demanded.

"The Enemy's plans burn slowly," Dee replied. "They do not see time like you or I, defined by the span of a man's life. Their minds move like the oceans, steady and powerful, over years and decades, and longer still. Yet we knew some great scheme was in motion, just not its true nature."

"When the defences of the nation were first put in place, all was quiet for many years." Walsingham stood erect, his hands clasped behind his back.

"The hope grew that finally we would be safe. But then there came the strange and terrible events surrounding the execution of the traitor Mary, Queen of Scots, one year ago and we glimpsed the true face of the terror that was to come."

CHAPTER 4

18th February 1587

*A*ll through the bitter winter's night, Robert, earl of Launceston, had ridden, and finally in the thin, grey morning light his destination fell into view on the rain-soaked Midlands terrain. His fingers were frozen on the reins, his breeches sodden and mud-splattered, and his bones ached from the cold and exhaustion.

Launceston was hardly used to such privation, but he could not refuse his orders to be the eyes and ears of Lord Walsingham for the momentous event about to take place. Though thirty-eight, he looked much older. His skin had an unnatural, deathly pallor that many found repulsive and had made him something of an outcast at court, his nose long and pointed, his eyes a steely grey.

When Walsingham called on him, it was usually to have a throat slit in the middle of the night, a Spanish agent agitating for Elizabeth's overthrow or assassination, sometimes a minor aristocrat with unfortunate Catholic sympathies. He had forgotten how many he had killed.

At least this time he would only be watching a death instead of instigating it.

Just beyond Oundle, Fotheringhay Castle rose up out of the flat, bleak Northamptonshire landscape on the north side of the meandering River Nene. On top of the motte was the grand stone keep, surrounded by a moat, with ramparts and a ditch protecting the inner bailey where the great hall lay alongside some domestic buildings. The gatehouse stood on the other side of a lake crossed by a bridge. Lonely. Well defended. Perfect for what lay ahead.

As he drew towards the castle, Launceston feared he had missed the event. Mary's execution had been scheduled for the cold dark of seven a.m. and the hour was already approaching ten, but he could hear music from the courtyard and the distant hubbub of an excited crowd.

Encouraging his horse to find its last reserves, he pressed on through the deserted Fotheringhay village, across the bridge, and the drawbridge, and into the courtyard.

"A ghost!"

"An omen!"

When they saw his ghastly features peering from the depths of his hood, a shiver ran through the crowd of more than a hundred who had come to see history made. He hated them all, common, witless sheep, but to be fair, he disliked his own kind at the court just as much.

As they slowly realised he was only a man, they returned their attention to the grey bulk of the great hall. Some waved placards with Mary drawn as a mermaid, a crude insult suggesting she was a prostitute. She had no friends there on the outside, but the long wait had reduced the baying to a harsh murmur. The air of celebration was emphasised by a band of musicians, playing an air that usually accompanied the execution of witches. It could have been considered another insult, except Launceston knew that Walsingham had personally requested the playing of the dirge.

Dismounting, he strode towards the hall where his way was barred by the captain of the sheriff's guard in breastplate and helmet, halberd raised. "Launceston," he said, "here at the behest of your Lord Walsingham, and our queen, God save her. I am not too late?"

"The traitor has been at her prayers for three hours," the captain replied. "She has read her will aloud to her servants, and prepared for them her final instructions. My men have been instructed to break down the door to her quarters if she delays much longer."

Launceston pushed his way into the great hall where two hundred of the most respected men in the land waited as witnesses. They had been carefully selected for their trustworthiness, their numbers limited so that whatever happened in that hall, only the official version would reach the wider population.

Though logs blazed in the stone hearth, it provided little cheer. Black was the abiding colour in the room, on the drapes surrounding the three-foot-high platform that would provide a clear view of the proceedings to the audience, on the high-backed chair at the rear of the dais, on the kneeling cushion and the executioner's block. It was there too in the clothes and masks of the executioner and his assistant. Bulle, the London hangman, was ox-like, tall and erect, his hands calmly resting on the haft of his double-headed axe.

Launceston could feel the stew of conflicting emotions, the sense of relief that the traitorous whore's lethal machinations would finally be ended, the anxiety that they were embarking on a dangerous course into uncharted waters. Spain, France, and Rome watched and waited. The killing of one of royal blood was not to be taken lightly, espe-

cially one so many Catholics believed to be the rightful ruler of England. Her execution was the right course of action; Mary would always be a threat to England as long as she lived.

A murmur ran through the assembled group, and a moment later the sheriff, carrying his white wand of office, led Mary into the hall accompanied by the earls of Shrewsbury and Kent. Six of her retinue trailed behind.

Launceston had never seen her before, but in that instant he understood why she loomed so large over the affairs of several states. She exuded a rapacious sexuality that was most evident in the flash of her unflinching eyes. A glimpse of her red hair beneath her kerchief was made even more potent by the shimmering black velvet of her dress. She would not be hurried, her pace steady as she clutched on to an ivory crucifix. A gold cross hung at her neck, and a rosary at her waist.

Launceston was surprised to find himself captivated like every other man in the room. The blood of two men lay upon her, yet that only served to increase her magnetism; she appeared to be a woman who could do anything, who could control any man. She climbed onto the platform and sat in the chair, levelling her gaze slowly and dispassionately across all present.

Walsingham's brother-in-law, Robert Beale, the clerk to the Privy Council, caught Launceston's eye and nodded before reading the warrant detailing Mary's crime of high treason for her constant conspiracies against Elizabeth, and calling for the death sentence. The earl of Shrewsbury asked her if she understood.

Mary gave a slight smile that Launceston found unaccountably chilling. "I thank my God that He has permitted that in this hour I die for my religion," she intoned slyly.

No one in the room was prepared to listen to a Catholic diatribe, and the dean of Peterborough stood up to silence her. Mary suddenly began to sob and wail and shout in Latin, raising her crucifix over her head.

Launceston had the strangest impression that he was seeing two women occupying the same space; this Mary was devout, believing herself to be a martyr to her religion, not sexually manipulative, not threatening, or cunning. The change troubled him for it did not seem natural, and he was reminded of the coded warning Walsingham had given him before his departure: "Do not trust your eyes or your heart."

After she had pleaded passionately for England to return to the true faith, she changed again, her eyes glinting in the firelight, her lips growing cruel and hard.

As Bulle the executioner knelt before her and made the traditional request that she forgive him her death, she replied loudly, "I forgive you with all my heart, for now,

I hope, you shall make an end of all my troubles." It was a stately comment, but Mary twisted it when she added in a whisper that only a few could hear, "But not your own." As she looked around the room, she made it plain that she was speaking about England.

Bulle went to remove Mary's gown, but she stopped him with a flirtatious smile and summoned her ladies-in-waiting to help. "I have never put off my clothes before such a company," she said archly.

A gasp ran through the room as her black gown fell away. A bodice and petticoat of crimson satin flared among the dark shapes. It was a bold, almost brash statement, and in it Launceston once again saw two opposing faces: crimson was the colour of the martyr, but it was also the colour of sex, and Launceston could see the effect it had upon some of the elderly men around. Though forty-four, Mary was still a beautiful, alluring woman. She flaunted the swell of her bosoms and displayed her cleavage, as though she was available for more than death.

"Death is not the end," she said. "For me. And there are worse things than death by far, as you will all come to know."

With a flourish of her petticoat, she knelt, pausing briefly at the level of Bulle's groin before placing her head upon the block. Launceston had the briefest sensation that she was looking directly at him. With another disturbing smile, she stretched out her arms in a crucified position and said, "In manus tuas, Domine."

Bulle's mask hid whatever he thought of this display, if anything. He swung the heavy woodcutter's axe above his head and brought it down. It thudded into the block so hard Launceston was sure he could feel the vibrations. Mary made no sound, did not move, continued to stare at the assemblage, still smiling. Bracing himself, Bulle wrenched the axe free and brought it down again. The head lolled forwards, hanging by one piece of gristle that Bulle quickly cut.

Stooping to pluck the head by the hair as he had been ordered, Bulle called out, "God save the queen." All apart from Launceston responded, "Amen."

But Mary had played one last trick on her executioner. Her auburn hair was a wig that now flapped impotently in Bulle's hand, the grey-stubbled head still rolling around the platform.

His breath tight in his chest, Launceston kept his gaze upon it, aware a second before the others that the eyes still swivelled in their sockets.

The head came to rest at an angle and Mary surveyed her persecutors. "Two queens now you have plucked in your arrogance," she said, a slight smile still lying on her lips, "and the third that will fall shall be your own."

The knights and gentlemen cried out in terror, making the sign of the cross as they pressed away from the platform. Even the sheriff's guards lowered their halberds and shied away.

"Against you in the shadows, the powers align," Mary continued. "Death, disease, destruction on a scale undreamed of—all these lie in your days ahead, now that long-buried secrets have come to light. Soon now, the thunderous tread of our marching feet. Soon now, the scythe cutting you down like wheat. The shadows lengthen. Night draws in, on you and all your kind."

Two hundred men were rooted as their worst fears were confirmed and a mood of absolute dread descended on the great hall. As Mary's eyes continued to swivel, and her teeth clacked, Bulle fell to his knees, his axe clattering noisily on the platform. Launceston thrust his way through the crowd to Beale and shook him roughly from his daze.

"Yes, of course," Beale stuttered, before hailing two men who waited at the back of the crowd. Launceston recognised them as two of Dr. Dee's assistants. Rushing to the platform, they pulled from a leather bag a pair of cold-iron tongs which one of them used to grip the head tightly. Mary snarled and spat like a wildcat until the other assistant used a poker to ram bundles of pungent herbs into her mouth. When the cavity was filled, the snarling diminished, and the eyes rolled slower and finally stopped as the light within them died.

A furore erupted as the terrified crowd shouted for protection from God, or demanded answers, on the brink of fleeing the room in blind panic.

Leaping to the platform, Launceston asked the captain of the guard to lock the doors so none of the assembled knights and gentlemen could escape. Grabbing Bulle's dripping axe, he hammered the haft down hard on the dais, once, twice, three times, until silence fell and all eyes turned towards him.

"What you have seen today will never be repeated, on peril of your life." His dispassionate voice filled every corner of the great hall. "To speak of this abomination will be considered an act of high treason, for diminishing the defences of the realm and putting the queen's life at risk from a frightened populace. One word and Bulle here will be your final friend. Do you heed my words?"

Silence held for a moment, and then a few angry mutterings arose.

"Lest you misunderstand, I speak with the full authority of the queen, and her principal secretary Lord Walsingham," Launceston continued. "Nothing must leave this room that gives succour to our enemies, or which turns determined Englishmen to trembling cowards. I ask again: do you heed my words?"

In his face they saw the truth of what he said, and gradually acceded. When he was satisfied, Launceston handed the axe back to Bulle and said, "Complete your business."

Still trembling, the earl of Kent stood over Mary's headless corpse and stuttered in a voice so frail few could hear, "May it please God that all the queen's enemies be brought into this condition. This be the end of all who hate the Gospel and Her Majesty's government."

With tentative fingers, Bulle plopped the head onto a platter and held it up to the window three times so the baying crowd without could be sure the traitorous pretender to the throne was truly dead.

Immediately, the doors were briefly unlocked so Henry Talbot, the earl of Shrewsbury's son, could take the official news of Mary's death to the court in London. As he galloped through the towns and villages, shouting the news, a network of beacons blazed into life across the country and church bells were rung with gusto.

At Fotheringhay, Launceston spoke to each of the knights and gentlemen in turn, studying their eyes and letting them see his. Then he oversaw the removal of Mary's body and head to the chapel, where prayers were said over them as Dee's assistants stuffed the remains with more purifying herbs and painted defensive sigils on the cold flesh. Everything she had worn, and everything her blood had touched, was burned.

Few beyond that great hall knew the truth: that terrible events had been set in motion, like the ocean, like the falling night, and soon disaster would strike, and blood and terror would rain down on every head.

CHAPTER 5

After Walsingham had finished speaking, silence fell across the Black Gallery, interrupted only by the crackle and spit of the fire in the hearth.

"The Enemy has been planning the assault on the Tower for more than a year," Mayhew said eventually.

Will now understood the depths of the worry he had seen etched into Walsingham's face earlier that night. "*Long-buried secrets have come to light*," he repeated. "Then we must assume they have the Key, or the Shield, or both, and are now able to use the weapon."

"We have spent the last twelve months attempting to prepare for the inevitable," Walsingham said, "listening in the long dark for the first approaching footstep, watching for the shadow on the horizon, every hour, every minute, vigilant."

"And now all our souls are at risk," Mayhew said. Upending the bottle he'd been steadily draining, he was disgusted to find it empty. "So that traitorous witch Mary was in the grip of the Enemy. Is no one safe from their sly control?" he added. "How much of the misery she caused was down to her, and how much to whatever rode her?"

"We will never know," Walsingham replied. "The past matters little. We must now concern ourselves with the desperate situation that unfolds."

"It is the nature of these things that the waiting seems to go on forever and then, suddenly, there is no time at all when the wave engulfs us," Dee added. "Yet fortune has given us a gift. The Enemy has lost the weapon almost as soon as it fell into their hands."

"For now. But they will be scouring London, even as we do. If time has been bought for us, it will not be long." With one hand on the mantelpiece as he peered into the embers, Will turned over Walsingham's account of Mary's execution. "You said the thing in Mary's head spoke of *two queens* plucked in arrogance."

"Elizabeth's father provided ample candidates," Mayhew said. "That is of little import. Of more concern are the actions of the Catholic sympathisers and our enemies across the water. Will Spain seize upon our distraction with this crisis to launch an attack upon England?"

"Philip of Spain is determined to destroy us at all costs and will use any opportunity that arises," Walsingham replied. "He makes a great play of English *heresy* for turning away from his Catholic faith, but his hatred is as much about gold. He is heartily sick of our attacks on his ships, and our constant forays into the New World, the source of all his riches."

"But war can still be averted?" Mayhew said hopefully.

Walsingham gave a derisive snort. "The spineless fools at court who nag Elizabeth believe so. They encourage her in peace negotiations that drag on and on. In the face of all reason, our lord treasurer, Burghley, is convinced that peace will continue. He will still be advocating gentle negotiation when the Spanish are hammering on his door. Leicester opposes him as much as possible, but if Burghley wins the queen's ear, all is lost."

"War was inevitable when Elizabeth signed the treaty to defend the Dutch against any further Spanish demands upon their territories. Philip saw it as a declaration of war on Spain," Will noted.

"Now the duke of Parma sits across the channel with seventeen thousand men, waiting for the moment to invade England. And in Spain, Philip amasses a great fleet, and plots and plans," Walsingham continued. "The invasion *will* come. It is only a matter of when. And the Enemy has chosen this moment to assail us from within. Destabilised, distracted, we are ripe for an attack."

"Spain and the Catholic sympathisers are in league with the Enemy," Mayhew spat. "We will be torn apart by these threats coming from all directions."

"No, this business is both greater and more cunning than that." Will turned back to the cluttered table. "In this room, we know there is a worse threat than Catholics and Spain. Our differences with them may seem great, but they are meagre compared to the gulf between us and the true Enemy, whose manipulations set brother against brother when we should be shoulder to shoulder. Religious arguments mean nothing in the face of the threat that stands before us."

Will could see Dee agreed, but Mayhew cared little, and Walsingham was steadfast in the hatred of Catholics that had been embedded in him since his early days at the defiantly Protestant King's College at Cambridge.

"There are threats and there are threats. Some greater and some lesser, but threats nonetheless, and we shall use whatever is at our disposal to defeat them." Walsingham's voice was stripped of all emotion and all the more chilling for it. "Barely a day passes without some Catholic plot on Elizabeth's life coming to light. We resist them resolutely. We listen. We watch. We extract information from those who know. And when we are ready we act, quickly, and brutally, where necessary."

An entire world lay behind Walsingham's words, and Will fully understood its gravity. Elizabeth had chosen her spymaster well. Walsingham was not hampered by morals in pursuit of his aims; he believed he could not afford to be so restricted. The tools of his trade were not only ciphers, secret writing, double and triple agents, and dead-letter boxes, but also bribery, forgery, blackmail, extortion, and torture. Sometimes, in unguarded moments, the cost was visible in his eyes.

"This war with our long-standing Enemy has blown cold for many years, but if it has now turned hot, we shall do what we always do: trap and eradicate them at every level," Walsingham continued.

Will watched the evidence of Walsingham's cold, monstrous drive and wondered what had made him that way. The war shaped them all, and never for the better.

"We must move quickly, and find this Silver Skull before the Enemy does," Walsingham stressed. He turned to Will and said, "All of England's resources are at your disposal. Do what you will, but keep me informed at every step. Take Mayhew here, and Launceston." He considered his options and added, "Also Tom Miller, a stout fellow, if simple, who has just joined our ranks. He has yet to be inducted in the ways of the Enemy, so take care in bringing him to understanding."

Will attempted to hide his frustration. Putting an agent into the field without time to educate them in the true nature of the Enemy was cruel and dangerous. More than one spy had been driven out of their wits and into Bedlam after the heat of an encounter.

"And John Carpenter," Walsingham concluded.

Will flinched.

"I know there has been business between the two of you, but you must put it behind you for the sake of England, and our queen."

"I would prefer Kit."

"Marlowe is your good friend and true, but he wrestles with his own demons and they will be the end of him. We need a steady course in this matter."

Will could see Walsingham's mind would not be changed. He turned to Dee and asked, "Have you developed any new tricks that might aid me?"

"Tricks, you say!" Dee's eyes flared, but he maintained his temper. "I have a parcel of powder which explodes in a flash of light and heat and smoke when exposed to the air. A new cipher that even the Enemy could not break. And a few other things that will make your life more interesting. I will present them to you once I have apprised Lord Walsingham of my findings in Bohemia."

Briefly, Will wondered what matter Dee could be involved in that was as pressing as the search for the Silver Skull. But the thought passed quickly; the burden he had been given was large enough and it would take all his abilities to shoulder it.

"There are many questions here," Will said. "Who took the prisoner from the Enemy and why? Were they truly rogues, or were they Spanish spies, and the Silver Skull is now in the hands of a different enemy?"

"And can we possibly find one man in a teeming city before the Enemy reaches him first?" Mayhew added sourly.

"Let us hear no more talk like that, Master Mayhew," Will said. "Time is short and we all have a part to play." As Mayhew grunted and lurched to his feet, Will turned to Walsingham. "Fearful that their hard-won prize might slip through their fingers, the Enemy will be at their most dangerous at this time."

The log in the hearth cracked and flared into life, casting a ruddy glow across Walsingham's face. "The next few hours will decide if we march towards hell or remain triumphant," he replied. "Let nothing stand in your way, Master Swyfte. God speed."

CHAPTER 6

Wrapped in a heavy woollen cloak against the chill, Grace Seldon waited in the shadowy courtyard outside the Black Gallery. Whatever danger lay nearby, it would not deter her; it would *never* deter her. Surely Will understood that by now.

Beside her, Nathaniel shifted anxiously. "You will have me whipped and my wages docked for this, Grace. Go back to your room before you are seen."

Easing off her hood, she tied back her chestnut ringlets with a blue ribbon, but her fumbling fingers only emphasised her irritation. "Because I have a slender frame and a face that does not curdle cream, every man treats me like a delicate treasure to be protected at all times."

"Will is only concerned—"

"Will is always concerned for me!" she snapped. "We have both seen our fair share of tragedy and are stronger for it. I will not swoon at the first sign of threat."

Nathaniel continued to look uncomfortable at her refusal to comply with the order he had been given.

"Besides," she continued, "you know as well as I that Will would no more punish you than hurt a dog."

"I thank you for putting me on a level with a cur, Mistress Seldon," Nat said tartly, "but if I am not whipped, I will have to endure a day of his lectures and I do not know which I prefer."

"You are right there," she muttered to herself, adding, "If he sent you to ensure I was well cared for, then it is because there is great danger."

"Yes, that is the nature of his business." Nathaniel sighed. "You make my work very difficult, Grace."

Will emerged from the Black Gallery alongside a man who lurched drunkenly. Nathaniel made to restrain her, but she dodged past him. Half stumbling in her haste, her hands went to Will's chest, and he caught her at the waist.

"Grace." His eyes flickered towards Nathaniel, who pretended to scrub a spot from his shirt.

"You would deny me the opportunity to wish you well as you embark on one of your dangerous missions?" she said sharply.

"This is not the time for one of our lively debates, Grace."

"Did you think I would lock myself away because you told me to?"

He sighed. "No, Grace. You would never do anything I told you to do. I know that."

"What, then?"

"These are dangerous times. I would see you safe, that is all."

"From whom?"

"From yourself, mostly," he said with exasperation. "Your capacity for recklessness exceeds that of any other person I know."

"You say reckless. I say fearless. I am not afraid. Of anything."

"As always, this conversation goes nowhere, and I have urgent matters that require my attention—"

Calming herself, she chose the words she knew would stop him walking away. "I could not say farewell to Jenny and I have regretted it ever since. I will not be denied this by you."

He hesitated, softened. "I am not your sister."

In the subtle attenuation of his smile, she recognised the ghost of his true feelings. "You wear your masks well," she said quietly, so no one else could hear, "but I know the true you, as you know me. You are not my sister. Because you live still, and Jenny is dead—"

The blaze in his eyes scared her a little.

"Dead, Will. I spent long months yearning for answers, like you, but I have slowly come to an accommodation. I still need to know who took her, and why, and then I can rest. Then we both can. On that warm, starlit night in Arden, by the churchyard, with the owls hooting and the bats flitting, you told me you had been given the tools to discover the truth, and you vowed to me that the answers we both sought would be forthcoming. I ask now, though you always say one thing with your mouth and another with your eyes: is this mission the one that will allow us to find peace?"

"No." A moment, then: "Perhaps." Frustration laced his words. "Jenny is in my every thought and every deed, Grace, but these things are not as easy as you would believe. Now—"

She caught his arm to stop him leaving, and though he feigned irritation, she could see his affection, though whether it was for her alone or for her long-gone sister she did not know. The drunken man watched their encounter intently, and then, out of embarrassment or boredom, dragged open the carriage door and lurched inside.

"Let me accompany you," she pleaded.

"And do what?" he said incredulously. "Carry my sword? Distract the enemy so I could more easily strike the killing blow?" His mockery was faint, but her cheeks still reddened. "No, Grace," he continued, softening, "you must stay safe from harm's way."

"You wish to protect me because you could not protect my sister," she said defiantly.

"I could say the same of you." He gave a confident smile, a slight bow, and walked towards the carriage.

"A fine pair we are," she called after him, flushed with the heat of her frustration. "Both trapped in a dead woman's snare and neither able to release us."

As Will climbed into the carriage without looking back, Nathaniel hurried over. "Make haste back to your room, Grace—I must depart with Will. These times are too dangerous to be abroad at night, even in the Palace of Whitehall."

Nathaniel hurried to the carriage and soon the iron-clad wheels were rattling across the cobbles. Grace watched it leave with mounting defiance. She would never go as Jenny went. Nor would she lose Will the same way, if it was in her power to prevent it.

CHAPTER 7

To some, it was a monument to the globe-spanning power of the Spanish empire. Others saw a tribute to the power of God, a tomb, a menacing fortress, one man's grand folly. San Lorenzo de El Escorial, twenty-eight miles northwest of the Spanish capital of Madrid, was all of them. Within the vast mountain of worked stone, its vertiginous walls punctuated by more than twelve thousand windows, seven towers reaching to the heavens, lay both a palace and a monastery, temporal and ecclesiastical power in perfect union.

Cold, empty, echoing, the sprawling complex was a perfectly sombre reflection of the man who directed its construction: King Philip II. At a cost of three and a half million ducats, it took twenty-one years to build, with a floor plan that also had a secret face. Many believed its design was chosen in honour of its patron, Saint Lawrence, but the truth was that it had been constructed to echo the Temple of Solomon, as described by the historian Flavius Josephus.

Now Philip retreated behind its forbidding walls, cutting himself off from advisors and family so that his relationship with his God could be so much more potent. A distant, deeply introspective man who rarely spoke, Philip preferred to dress in black to show his contempt for material things. Always extremely devout, as the years passed he had become hardened, listening so intently for God's voice that he was ripe for direction from much closer quarters than heaven.

Inside the monastic palace, Spain's riches from the New World and the Indies provided great works of art—statues, paintings, and frescoes—the finest furniture, the most lavish building materials—coral, marble, jasper, alabaster. Yet the long corridors and lofty halls rang with an abiding silence that was only intermittently interrupted by the soft, steady step of cowled monks or the deliberate murmur of priests. No hands of friends touched Philip, no warm words eased his frozen thoughts.

He lived, and died slowly, for his religion. His extensive library, which could have held the greatest literature of civilisation, contained only religious works. In the great church at the heart of the complex, second only to Saint Peter's in Rome, were seven thousand relics of saints in the reliquary in the Royal Basilica, not just shards of bone, but heads and entire bodies, magic symbols designed to ward off the evils of the world and point the way along the road to salvation.

As dawn broke across the mountains, Philip could be found where he spent a good deal of his day, kneeling in prayer before the altar. Lean, with a soft, gentle face, his dark eyes revealed only lonely depths. At sixty-one, his arthritic joints ached, but he forced himself to continue his devotions before struggling to the secret door beside the altar that led to his private rooms.

The sound of no other feet echoed here. It was Philip's sanctuary away from the rigours of the world, austere, chill, dominated by an office with a table before a blank wall where he spent the rest of each day and much of the night, signing the constant stream of papers from his government and planning the great enterprise that had dominated so much of his thoughts in recent times. The suite was silent and still and empty.

Padding across the cold flags before the fire blazing in the hearth, he smelled her before he saw her: the unusual heady aroma of sharp lime and perfumed cardamom, with a hint of Moorish spice just beneath. Heat rose instantly in his belly. He felt embarrassed by his body's earthy passion, which suggested troubling unexplored depths of his mind that he always thought well sealed. How did she do that to him, when nothing else in the world could stimulate him?

"Come out," he whispered.

As he turned slowly, he caught a flash of a reflection in the ornate mirror she had installed on the wall: a hollow-cheeked, bone white face with red-rimmed eyes glaring at him with such malignancy he was overcome with terror. But it was gone in the blink of an eye, an illusion caused by his troubled mind.

Light shimmering off the glass blinded him, and when his eyes cleared, she stood before him, ageless, a beauty that burned like the sun and was as mysterious as the moon, dark brown hair cascading over bare shoulders, her eyes filled with a sexual promise that made his breath catch in his throat. She wore only a thin dress tied just above the curve of her breasts, clinging to her hips, her thighs, as she moved, barefoot, towards him.

"Malantha," he said. "I would not wish for you to be found here. It would not be seemly."

"No one will ever find me here. I am yours alone." Her unblinking eyes held him in her gravity.

When her cool fingers touched his cheek, he jolted as if burned. She continued up into his hair, and then down the nape of his neck, her eyes never leaving his, never blinking. Deep inside, at that moment lost to all conscious thought, he hated what she did to him, but could not get enough of it. Later he would be filled with so much revulsion he would vomit.

"You do not want me here?" she asked, knowing the answer.

"You know that I do. Since you came into my life, you have haunted my every waking hour, my every dream. I hear your honeyed words when you are not around. I feel your hand in mine when you are not at my side. How could I not want you with me?"

She appeared to sense the furious competition of desire and loathing, but all it brought was the faintest smile. She leaned in closely, her warm breath playing against his ear. "The Enterprise of England. How goes it?"

"The monetary cost is high, but I have support for my God-given endeavour from across Europe. Emperor Rudolf has agreed to send troops, but no coin. The Doge stands beside us, though may not say so publicly. The English continue with their peace negotiations, blind to our true intentions."

"And the Armada?"

Philip smiled. "Formidable. Our success is assured. One hundred and thirty ships. Thirty thousand men. Near three thousand cannon."

"And England will be defeated?"

"Broken on the rack of Spanish might. The English will attack our ships no more, nor steal our gold and silver, and the true religion will return to that land. It did not have to be this way. If Mary had not been executed. If Elizabeth had married me—"

Malantha pressed a finger to his lips. "If Elizabeth had married you, you would not be here with me."

"Yes . . . yes . . ." he stuttered. Her scent, her beauty, filled his senses, speaking of other lands far from Spain.

"The English are devils," she breathed in his ear. "They cannot be trusted. They think themselves higher than all others, but there are things that are higher by far."

"Yes. God."

She smiled.

"I will do all in my power to break the English."

He was happy that his words pleased her. Releasing the tie on her dress, she let it fall from her, presenting her body to him for a moment before pushing him back to a divan and climbing astride him. Her skin was luminous, her scent heady. Pressing her breasts against his chest, she kissed him on the lips in a way that no one else had kissed him, deep and slow, with the subtle probing of her tongue. Her groin gently rubbed against his, up and down, up and down. Every sensation was so potent, his thoughts broke up and he was cast adrift in the moment.

He perceived only flashes—of her removing his clothes, working down his body with her lips, using her hands and her mouth, and then climbing astride him once more to slide him inside her—before he was overwhelmed.

When he awoke later, he was alone, as he always was in the aftermath, but fragments of memory mixed with dreams. He thought he recalled Malantha standing naked in front of the ornate mirror, and speaking to it. The mirror was smoky, but reflected flashes of sunlight.

She was saying, "All proceeds well. Spain readies its forces. The pieces move into place."

And then another voice came back, decadent and sly, and spoke briefly about something being lost and something else being found, and another object close to being found.

Though Malantha used the term *brother*, her voice was laced with the sexual flirtation he knew so well. "And how is life in the night-dark city, Cavillex?" she enquired.

"Here they call us the Unseelie Court," the voice came back drolly.

"Unseelie?"

"Unholy," the voice explained.

Her laughter filled his senses and it all slipped away from him once again.

A dream, nothing more.

CHAPTER 8

"These are dark times." Still drunk, Mayhew stared out of the carriage window with a dazed expression that revealed a depth of troubles. The White Tower was silhouetted against the rosy sky, the first rays of the sun gleaming across the rooftops as London slowly stirred.

"Take charge of your tongue, Master Mayhew," Will cautioned. "A man in his cups says the strangest things."

Mayhew flashed Will an apologetic look for speaking out of turn with Nathaniel in the carriage.

"Worry not about me," Nat said tartly. "I have no interest in the affairs of Lord Walsingham's great men."

Returning his gaze to the waking street, Mayhew sniffed, and said, "You should watch your servant. A sharp tongue and an independent mind are dangerous flaws."

"Nat keeps me honest, Matthew, and I will hear no word against him," Will replied. He watched the first market traders spill onto the street, bleary-eyed and yawning. Soon there would be a deafening throng heading for Cheapside, the broadest of the capital's streets, where the market sprawled along the centre from the Carfax to Saint Paul's. There, it was possible to buy produce from all over London and the rapidly expanding villages just beyond the city walls: pudding pies from Pimlico and bread from Holloway or Stratford, root vegetables and sweet cakes, horses and hunting dogs, and peacocks and apes from the foreign traders.

The danger was apparent with each face Will saw. London was the boom town of Europe. The population had more than doubled since Elizabeth came to the throne, and the city elders struggled to cope with the problems caused by the influx: the overcrowding, the crime, the beggars, the filth, the disease. Larger now than the great cities of Bristol and Norwich, London bloated beyond the city walls, eating up all the villages that lay beyond. In that thick, seething mass of life, an emboldened Enemy could bring death on a grand scale.

What was the nature of the missing weapon? Was it truly as dangerous as Walsingham feared?

"You have your directions?" he asked Mayhew.

"I will wait among the rabble on Cheapside for the others to join me while you attend your secret assignation. We question the market traders about the gangs who prey on the innocent near the Tower, and meet again at noon to exchange what we have learned."

"Very good, Master Mayhew. I like a man whose brain stays sharp even after wine."

Mayhew didn't attempt to hide his displeasure. As Will stretched an arm out of the window and banged a hand on the roof of the carriage, the driver brought the horses to a halt with a loud, "Hey, and steady there!"

Half stumbling, Mayhew clambered out of the carriage without a backward glance and weaved his way towards the shade at the side of the street.

"Master Mayhew has a choleric disposition," Nathaniel noted. "And he likes his wine more than you do."

"Life is a constant struggle between virtue and vice, Nat. We cannot all be as worthy as you. Master Mayhew has served the queen well across the years, but what has been asked of him has taken its toll. Do not judge him harshly."

Will banged the carriage roof again and the wheels lurched into motion. After a pause, Nathaniel enquired with an air of studied disinterest, "This business is truly pressing?"

"You know I cannot say more."

"Yes. Better I remain in ignorance than be dragged into duplicitous affairs that could cost me my sanity or my life. The view from the poles above the gatehouse tower at London Bridge is not one to which I aspire." He paused. "But still. An assistant's work is better carried out with a little light."

"You do your job well enough, Nat. I have no complaints. I would not add to your burdens."

Nathaniel shrugged, but Will could see the curiosity burning inside him. It was difficult to move so close to the secrets without peering too deeply into the shadows; Will understood that urge well and had learned to control it within himself. But to know more about Will's work truly would be dangerous to Nat's life and his sanity. The less he knew, the safer he would be. In his ignorance, Nathaniel did not understand, of course, thinking the only threat was a few Spanish agents, but for all his barbed comments he remained an obedient assistant, and had worked much harder than Will had anticipated when he promised Nathaniel's father that he would employ him, and keep him well.

The carriage turned north away from the cobbles of Cheapside into the rutted, narrow tracks that formed the majority of the city's streets. Soon the choking stink of the city swept in through the open windows, the dung and the rotting vegetables and household waste deposited morning, noon, and night from doors and windows of the ramshackle hovels into the narrow thoroughfares. Even the mayor's order to burn each home's rubbish three times a week appeared to have little effect. Nathaniel coughed and spluttered and clutched his hand to his mouth and nose, futilely banging the pomanders hanging within the carriage to try to extricate more scent.

The heat of the day was already growing by the time they arrived at Bishopsgate. The Bull Inn was a three-story stone building with rows of tiny windows looking out from dark, low-ceilinged rooms. Without breaking its pace, the carriage rushed through the arch into the cobbled yard at the back where plays were regularly performed. In one corner, members of the resident acting troupe intoned loudly and performed tumbles, though many of them were still clearly hungover. A pair of carpenters lazily erected a temporary trestled stage.

Nathaniel waited with the carriage, and after a brief exchange with the vintner, Will made his way to a small back room set aside for "private affairs," usually gambling or the plotting of criminal activity. Smelling of stale beer and sweat, it was uncomfortably warm. While two men snored loudly in drunken sleep on the floor, a third wrote at a table.

Dark eyes that appeared old and sad stared out of a young, pale face framed by long black hair. A small moustache and close-clipped chin hair attempted to give him some appearance of maturity, though his sensitive face still made him look much younger than his twenty-four years.

"Kit," Will said. "I thought I might find you hiding here."

Lost to his imagination, Christopher Marlowe blinked blankly until his thoughts returned to the room and he recognised Will. He smiled shyly.

"Will, good friend. I am currently not in my Lord Walsingham's favours and thought it best to lay low to avoid his wrath. He has a cold face, but a terrible fire within."

"As have we all, Kit. For good reason."

Understanding, Marlowe nodded and motioned to a stool. "Shall we drink as we did at Corpus Christi on that night when you inducted me into this business of fools and knaves—" He caught himself. "I am sorry, Will. My bitterness sometimes gets the better of me. This is not the life that was promised me, and there is no going back, but you have always been good to me."

"No apologies are necessary, Kit." Will pulled up a stool. Pain lay just beneath the surface of Marlowe's face and Will knew he was complicit in embedding it there. "We are all lost souls."

"True enough. Beer, then. Or wine? Some breakfast?" Marlowe laid down his quill and pushed his beer-spattered work to one side.

"Information is all I require."

Marlowe sighed. "Work, then. One day we shall drink like brothers. I see from your face this is a grave matter."

"The gravest. All England is at stake."

"The Spanish. Those stories of a fleet of warships, an invasion planned—"

Will shook his head. "The true Enemy."

"Ah." Marlowe's eyes fell and for a moment he pretended to arrange his work materials. "*Tamburlaine* the second is all but done. I have drained myself with tales of endless war and strife." He smiled. "What is it, coz?"

"Last night, from the Tower, the Enemy stole a magical item whose origins are lost to antiquity—a Silver Skull, attached now to an unwitting victim."

Filled with the intellectual curiosity that Will admired so much, Marlowe leaned across the table. "I have never heard of such a thing."

"It is one of the mysteries of ancient times, a great weapon once guarded by the Templar Knights." Will smiled. "Our Lord Walsingham and our ally Doctor Dee saw fit to keep knowledge of it well away from the likes of you and me."

"And that is why they are our masters! I would only have sold it for beer and a night of pleasure! And what is the purpose of this Silver Skull?"

"Our betters have spent nigh on two decades trying to divine that very thing, but its mysteries remain untouched."

"Yet if the Enemy has need of it, it must be a great threat indeed to our well-being," Marlowe said.

Will nodded slowly. "Within a short time of the Enemy taking the Skull, they lost it. Stolen by a gang of thieves and spirited away, like magpies caught by a shiny bauble. The Enemy searches for it even as we speak, and so do we. Whosoever finds it first wins everything."

"And so this thing is an act of God, waiting to be unleashed on the dumb populace."

"Our Lord Walsingham and Dee fear the Enemy knows the key to its use. But more, who is to say one of those rogues could not stumble by accident across it and unleash death in the twinkle of an eye? All our lives hang by a thread while the Skull remains beyond our grasp."

Leaning back against the wall, Marlowe swung one scuffed boot onto a stool and pondered. "I have many questions, about how the Enemy plans to use the Skull when England's defences against them still stand, and the timing of this act—"

"And I have no answers. There is mystery here. But we are out of time." As one of the drunken men on the floor stirred, Will leaned across the table and lowered his voice. "You are our eyes and ears in the underworld, Kit. You know of things that lie far beneath the notice of men of good standing. Who would have the Skull? Where would it be now?"

The brightness faded from Marlowe's face. "Walsingham did not send you."

"No."

"Even in this hour of need he cannot bring himself to deal with me!" A flicker of fear rose in his eyes. "He does not trust me, Will. And in our world what is not trusted often meets a bloody end."

"It will pass, Kit."

Angrily, Marlowe put the toe of his boot under the stool and flicked it across the room where it crashed against the wall. The man who had stirred looked up with bloodshot eyes.

"Out!" Marlowe yelled at him. "Fetch me the ordinary! I am hungry." When the man had lurched away to find the vintner for the Bull's daily stew, Marlowe rounded on Will. "As children we walked in summer fields and dreamed of the wonders that lay ahead. Yet we sold those dreams, and our lives, to defend England against something that can never be defeated, which waits, quiet and patient and still, until we let our guard slip, as it always will, and then we are torn apart in a gale of knives and teeth, unmourned even by our own. Mistrusted by our own! Look at what this business has made us, Will! See what we have become! We cannot trust those closest to us. We fear death from Enemy and friend alike. We are alone, waiting for that moment when it all ends. Where is the comfort in this world?"

"There is little for the likes of us, Kit. We live our blighted lives so others can sleep soundly in their beds. You know that." Will watched the hopelessness play out across his friend's face and it troubled him. He had seen it many times before on others and in every case it ended the same way, an insidious despair that found its roots in the very nature of their Enemy, spreading like bindweed until every part of a person was choked by it. He had seen men kill themselves, others throw themselves into danger with no care for their lives, and revelling when they met their end. More simply setting in motion their own demise through their quiet actions. "If this matter was not so grave I would not have troubled you, Kit. Time away from this business . . . a lost week or more in one of your dens of iniquity will help you regain your equilibrium."

"Yes, of course, Will," Marlowe lied. "I am tired, that is all. Forgive me."

Though he feared the repercussions, Will pressed his friend for information. Marlowe was right: their business allowed little softness or compassion. The war was everything, and everyone was a victim.

Marlowe ran a hand through his hair as he steadied himself. "A gang of rogues near the Tower over night? No. There are no gulls there for them to prey upon. They would be near the stews or ordinaries, the baiting rings and taverns and theatres."

"They came upon the Enemy as they slipped away."

Marlowe shook his head; it still did not make sense to him. "The villains of London are an army, with generals and troops who march to order and follow detailed plans and strategy. They do not wait for their next meal, for they would starve."

"You say they knew the Enemy would be passing by?"

"Perhaps. As we have spies everywhere, so do they. A guard at the Tower, sending word as the Enemy took their moment. A Silver Skull would be a valuable prize, even if they did not know its true worth. I pity the poor sod who wore it for they will have cut it free by now." Marlowe made a slitting motion across his throat. "Who was he?"

Will shook his head. "This was not a random occurrence, then."

Marlowe shook his head slowly too.

"Then who is the general? Who could place an agent in the Tower?"

"The gangs of London are countries within a country. They have their own spies, yes, and their own forces to keep them secure. They even have their own land where a criminal can find refuge, and no one—not even the queen's own men—can touch them. In Damnation Alley and the Bermudas and Devil's Gap. By the brick kilns in Islington, and Newington Butts and Alsatia. Cutpurses and cutthroats, pickpockets and tricksters, the coney-catchers and head-breakers. Who would dare such an act? Why, all of them, Will."

Glancing through the window to where Nathaniel waited by the carriage, Will saw the inn yard now bright as the sun moved high in the sky. "Time is short, Kit. You run with these rogues. Give me a name. If you were to point a finger at a likely culprit, who would it be?"

His shoulders hunched as if carrying a great weight, Marlowe thought for a moment and then said, "There is one they call the King of Cutpurses. Laurence Pickering. Every week he holds a gathering at his house in Kent Street for all the heads of the London gangs, where they exchange information and drink and carouse with doxies. If Pickering is not behind this, he would know who is."

"I have not heard of this man."

"Few have. He has faces behind faces, and no one is quite sure which one is the real one, or if that is his true name. But I know one thing—he is the cousin of Bulle, the Tyburn hangman. Bulle himself admitted it when he was cup-shotten one night."

"Bulle?"

Marlowe raised an eyebrow at Will's sudden interest. "Why is that brute important?"

The image of Bulle hacking away at the neck of Mary, Queen of Scots, was still fresh in Will's mind, as was Walsingham's account of what happened after her death. "Because there are no random occurrences in this world, Kit. And Kent Street is where I should find this Pickering?"

"No. That is the front he presents to the world so he can pass himself off as an upstanding man. If he has something of value, it will be in one of the fortresses his kind have built for themselves, secure from any lawful pursuit." Marlowe turned over the possibilities in his mind and then announced,

"Alsatia, below the west end of Fleet Street, next to the Temple. There is no safer place in London for the debauched and the criminal."

Will understood. "It has the privilege of sanctuary. Only a writ of the lord chief justice or the lords of the Privy Council carries any force there."

"And even then, not much. No warrant would ever be issued in Alsatia. I told you, Will—a country within a country. The citizens of Alsatia are, to a man and woman, criminal, and they will turn upon and attack any who come to seize one of their own. Have caution. If there is another way to achieve your ends, take it. You will not emerge from Alsatia with your life."

Will held his arms wide. "If we took no risks, Kit, how would we know we are alive?"

Marlowe laughed quietly. "How secure I feel knowing the remarkable Will Swyfte is abroad to keep the land safe." With a surprising display of emotion, he leaned across the table and grasped Will's hand. "Take care, Will. You have been a good friend to me, and my life would be worse if you were not in it." Tears stung Marlowe's eyes. His tumbling emotions were a clear sign of the tremendous stress he was under.

"You should know that taking care of myself is my greatest attribute. I will not be led gracefully towards the dark night, not while there is wine to be drunk and women to romance."

Marlowe was one of the few men who could see through Will's words, but he was kind enough not to say anything.

Rising, Will nodded his goodbye, adding, "Heed my words, Kit. Take time to find yourself."

"If this business ever let me, I would." He gave a lazy, sad smile, but when Will was at the door, he added, "I have an idea for a play in which a man sells his soul to the Devil for knowledge, status, and power. What do you think of that, Will?" His eyes were haunted and said more than his words.

Will did not need to answer. As he left the room, Will wondered, as he did with increasing regularity, if he would see his friend alive again. But his mind was already turning to the trial that lay ahead—an assault on the most notorious and dangerous part of London: Alsatia, the Thieves' Quarter.

HAPTER 9

As the black carriage rattled at speed through the archway and out of the Bull Inn's yard, Grace stepped from the shadows by the east wall and dropped her hood, ignoring the lecherous stares from the carpenters at work on the temporary stage. Her own carriage waited a little further along Bishopsgate. She didn't have to follow Will's carriage to know his destination: Marlowe had been one of his few confidants since Will had recruited him after the reports of a brilliant, and more importantly daring and transgressional, student at Cambridge.

Her heart beat fast as she skipped across the cobbles. Will would be angry if he knew she was following him, but she had recognised the glint in his eye at the Palace of Whitehall: he felt that the business in which he was engaged had something to do with Jenny's disappearance. His work remained a mystery to her, as it should, but she could not find peace until she understood the truth of what had happened to her sister and she feared Will would never tell her even if he uncovered it, under some misguided sense of duty to ensure her protection. Marlowe would tell her everything; she had always been able to wrap him around her finger.

Good Kit, she thought. *Too gentle and sensitive for the demands placed upon you.*

The actors delivered their speeches in declamatory fashion, something about lost love and fairies stealing hearts under cover of the night. It distracted her briefly, so she did not see the four men arrive in the shade beneath the archway. Their well-polished boots were expensive Flemish leather, their cloaks thick and unblemished, their hoods pulled low to mask their features, gloves tight on their hands.

They had followed Grace at a distance from the palace, where they had observed her meeting with Will from the shadows.

Blood was on their minds, and righteous vengeance in their hearts.

The end was drawing near.

CHAPTER 10

ill's carriage raced towards Saint Paul's, past the crowd thronging through Cheapside market. Rival apprentices spilled dangerously close to the wheels as they beat each other furiously. Blood flowed across the street and respectable gentlemen darted wildly to avoid randomly thrown blows.

Amid the cacophony, traders loudly competed with each other to ensnare the attention of passersby, focusing most of their attention on the smartly dressed servants from the grand four-story homes of the goldsmiths that lined the street.

Old Saint Paul's, with its blasted spire towering five hundred feet above the rooftops, was the heart of the City and a stone anchor in a rapidly changing world. In the bustling, sun-drenched church precinct, Will found Walsingham, like a black crow, his beady eyes flickering over the men that Leicester marshalled before the puzzled eyes of the booksellers, merchants, lawyers, and servants looking for work. Beside him, Dee hid his identity with a deep hood.

Mayhew had assembled the members of Will's team nearby: Launceston, his ghastly complexion and saturnine disposition unsettling many in the churchyard; John Carpenter, whose handsome features were marred by a jagged scar that ran from temple to mouth on his left side; and one who was clearly Tom Miller, the new recruit, as big as a side of beef with hands that could encompass a child's head and an expression of edgy confusion.

Mayhew and the others passed among the crowd swarming around the church, questioning cutpurses, cutthroats, beggars, and coney-catchers, who were as numerous as the respectable tradesmen who sought business around Saint Paul's, and those who had come simply to parade their expensive, highly fashionable cloaks and doublets.

Nathaniel cast a perceptive eye over the proceedings as he followed Will from the carriage. "These are dark times indeed for so many of the great and good to be gathered in public away from the security of their halls of privilege."

"The people should be comforted that these men are active in the defence of the nation."

"England's greatest spy is not comfort enough?" Nathaniel replied archly. "The talk in the taverns and ordinaries is all of a Spanish invasion. Since Mary's death, people are afraid. They see Spanish agents everywhere. Swarthy-skinned men are attacked in the street, and foreigners threatened over their meals. Will all this activity calm them, or frit them more?"

As Walsingham approached with a grave expression, Will said, "Fetch the items we discussed in the carriage. And hurry. From our Lord Walsingham's face, I fear that time is shorter still."

When Nathaniel had departed, Walsingham drew Will in conspiratorially. "The Enemy is abroad. Stories circulate hereabouts of a fearsome black dog with eyes like hot coals that leaves claw-marks in stone."

"Are we to be afraid of a dog, then?" Will replied. "We could toss it a bone and be done with it."

"I am pleased to see your spirits remain high, Master Swyfte, for we appear to be no closer to discovering the rogues who have taken the Silver Skull."

"Do not give up hope yet." Will told Walsingham what he had learned from Marlowe without disclosing the source of his information.

Glowering at the passing crowd, Walsingham was clearly concerned by Will's suggestion. "Alsatia is a dangerous place. There will be bloodshed if we send in an army, and no guarantee this Pickering will not escape with his prize."

"Then we do not send in an army," Will replied. "A few men, moving secretly, can achieve more, and quicker."

Walsingham nodded in agreement. "Even so, you will be strangers in a place where most are known to each other. And I am told they speak their own tongue down there—the thieves' cant. One wrong word could be your undoing."

"The quicker we are in, the quicker out."

Realising there was no alternative, Walsingham gave his approval before summoning over Dee. "The doctor has some gifts that may aid you."

From the depths of his hood, Dee's eyes glimmered. "Two items for now," he whispered. From a leather bag, he withdrew a handful of small muslin packages like the bundles of herbs a cook would drop in a stew. "Take care with these," he said, depositing the packages gently in Will's cupped hands. "Hold the loose knot at the top and shake them open. But be careful to look away. They will release a flash of light that will blind, and a loud noise to disorient the senses."

With a shrug, Will deposited them in the pouch at his belt.

Annoyed that Will was not more impressed, Dee delved into his bag once more for a leather forearm shield with two fastening buckles. When he touched a hidden catch, a seven-inch blade burst from a hidden compartment.

"There will come a time when you will be separated from your sword," he said, "but you will never be separated from this weapon. You can wound and kill at close quarters, and with stealth."

Will gave the weapon a cursory examination. "What, no codpieces that burst into flames? I could have had sport with that."

Snorting, Dee turned to Walsingham. "We place the security of England in the hands of a coxcomb!"

As Dee stalked away, Walsingham sighed. "Now you have offended him, and now I will have to deal with his foul temper. Since he started communing with angels, Dee has been like a devil, filled with fire and brimstone."

As he prepared to gather his crew to depart, Will scrutinised Miller who awkwardly accompanied Mayhew and the others in their questioning. "The new fellow. He seems . . . slow."

"He is more quick-witted than he appears. He is a miller's son, shaped by hard labour. His strength will be an asset to you."

"And his lack of understanding of the Enemy and their guiles may be the death of us. Who does he think we fight?"

"Spanish agents." Walsingham was unmoved by Will's concerns, even though he knew the risks involved.

Hiding his irritation, Will noted the innocence in Miller's face. "If we encounter the Enemy, the shock may prove too great for him."

"Then you must provide a quick lesson."

"Quick lessons do not work. You know that. It takes time to accept that the world is not the way any of us are brought up to believe. The mind and heart are both fragile things, easily broken, repaired with the greatest difficulty, if at all."

"That is the way God made us, Master Swyfte. He is your charge now. I have faith you will see him right."

Walsingham returned to Leicester, who swaggered along the ranks of his men, enjoying the eyes of the public upon him. Urgently summoning Mayhew and the others, Will led them from the churchyard, past the shop where the fashionable London men bought their pouches of the New World tobacco, to a quiet spot beyond the bookstalls.

An incandescent rage appeared to be permanently burning just beneath Carpenter's skin. Unconsciously tracing a fingertip down the pink scar tissue on his face, he said, "Why did Walsingham see fit to throw us together?"

"I think he feels you will keep my feet on the ground, John."

"That I will do."

Turning his attention to Miller, Will shook his hand. "Tom. Lord Walsingham has only good words for you. I am Will Swyfte."

"I know you." A hint of awe laced the young man's words.

Snorting derisively, Carpenter pretended to inspect Saint Paul's Cross where a wild-eyed, grey-haired man prepared to deliver a sermon.

"You will have heard about some of our work," Will continued, "but know this: you may well see things across the course of this day that you find . . . puzzling . . . troubling—"

"Frightening," Mayhew interjected, staring at his boots.

"There is an explanation, and you will get it when our work is done," Will continued. "Till then, anything you see that makes little sense must be put from your mind. Do you understand?"

Baffled, Miller nodded.

"Let me put it another way," Launceston said in his precise, aristocratic tones, "if you fail to keep a steady course, and place us in danger, I will slit your throat as surely as I would an enemy's, and leave you where you fall for the rats to feast on."

Miller turned almost as white as Launceston.

"Steady now," Will said. "We must not go bragging about the speed and size of our blades. For I would win. Listen with care, for we have a matter to test even the greatest swords of Albion."

By the time Will finished explaining the task that lay ahead, Nathaniel had returned with a large, foul-smelling sack. From it, he distributed various items of clothing.

"What is this?" Mayhew clutched a hand to his mouth. "Foul vinegar rags stolen from the backs of three-day-dead beggars?"

"Master Mayhew, you are known around London as a man of exquisite taste for the finery of your dress," Will said. "But if you walk into Alsatia as a gallant, flashing that costly silk lining of your cloak, you will find yourself a honeypot for bees with a deadly sting."

In the cramped carriage on the road to Fleet Street, they quickly changed into the stinking rags, with much complaining from Mayhew and stoic acceptance from Launceston. Miller was eager, but Carpenter made a show of the mass of scar tissue that covered his back and left arm, casting sullen glares towards Will.

When they were done, Nathaniel said, "I have never seen . . . nor smelled . . . a more convincing group of foul beggars. You wear it well."

"I hear the buzzing of a gnat, Master Swyfte." Launceston sniffed. "I will swat it if I see it."

The carriage trundled to a halt next to a tiny alley where rats ran and clouds of flies swarmed in shafts of sunlight. "From here there is danger every step of the way," Will said. "We will be surrounded by people who would gladly slit our throats for a shiny button, but they are the least of our worries. The Enemy races to reach the Silver Skull before us." Will glanced down the alley to where it wound away into shadow. "And they come like the night. We must watch each other's backs." Will cast an eye towards Carpenter, who pretended not to notice. "Good luck, boys. We go for queen and country, and wine and a warm embrace when we are done. Let nothing keep us from our just rewards."

Leaping from the carriage, he plunged straight into the alley.

The boundaries of Alsatia were clearly demarcated by a piercing whistle from an unseen watchman somewhere near the rooftops. Heads held low by the weight of a harsh life, furtive eyes cast down, Will and the other beggars limped and stumbled in a tight knot, faces smeared with dirt they had scraped up on the way.

While the rest of London was filled with colour, noise, and life, on the boundaries Alsatia was eerily still. Stone tenements blackened by smoke and the accumulation of centuries of filth rose up four stories high. Overhanging upper floors on some of the newer buildings meant that little sun reached the rutted, puddled, narrow streets where a thin, grey light leached the colour from everything. Smoke blew back and forth along the byways like a constant fog from the blocked chimneys of the many who could not afford the services of a sweep.

On the fringes, the houses appeared deserted, the stink of excrement drifting from shattered windows and ragged doors. But as they progressed towards the heart of the quarter, life began to appear, in ones and twos at first, talking in hushed tones in the entrances to alleys, or slumped on doorsteps watching with mean eyes. The clothes were brown and grey and muddy-green, rough cloth, hard worn, wide-brimmed felt hats that could hide the features, pale skin and stubble, filthy fingernails. The women hung out of windows, faces lashed pink by the elements, hair prematurely grey. The doxies barely bothered to dress after each short, grunting encounter, pendulous breasts hanging out of torn, filthy dresses, makeup applied so half-heartedly it appeared to be the work of children, turning each one into a rouge and cream grotesque, a pastiche of sexual attraction. It did not appear to deter the men. The doxies carried out their trade on the street, against a wall, or on their backs in hallways, doors thrown wide, skirts pulled high, their faces implacable as the men thrust into them, sweating and cursing.

"Animals," Launceston said under his breath.

The stink grew more intense with each step. Rubbish was piled as high as a man on either side of every door, scraps of rotting meat, and bones, and vegetables, and the dung of animals, and the contents of chamber pots. Every heap was alive with rats. They carpeted the streets, swarming away from approaching feet to return a moment later. Clouds of flies filled the air, and white maggots glistened in the half-light.

As Will led the way, the piercing whistles followed them, but their tone was merely observational and not insistent.

Gangs of men flowed past them, ready for an afternoon's work seeking out the country gulls and foreign visitors who would be more amenable to the nip and foist relieving them of their gold-stuffed purses. They would prowl Saint Paul's, all the bowling alleys and ordinaries, the brothels, baiting rings, and theatres, seeking out their likely marks.

Everywhere was the glint of knives and cold, hard eyes. Will felt their gazes on his back, heard the rustle of whispers in his wake, but it passed as he knew it would; earning a dishonest living took precedence over the searching of a few beggars.

"Do you hear that?" Mayhew brought them to a slow halt, cocking his head to listen to some sound that escaped the rest of them. All they heard was the wind beneath the eaves, the occasional frightened shout in the distance, and the murmur of plotting voices every now and then.

"What do you hear?" Will caught sight of Mayhew's oddly troubled face.

"Music?" He strained to catch it. "The playing of some flute just beneath the wind, or behind it, or part of it?"

"Why bother yourself with that, you fool?" Carpenter growled. "They make merry here like the rest of us."

"No, I have heard it before." Mayhew appeared to be trying to recall a fading dream. "At . . . the Tower?"

Miller had picked up on Mayhew's unease. "Why should a flute trouble you so?"

"'Tis nothing," Will interrupted. "Do not jump at shadows. There are harder dangers to concern you."

As they arrived at a crossroads, they all became aware of an eerie stillness lying across the area. It was as deserted as the first part of Alsatia they had entered. The cold wind had dropped and dense, choking smoke billowed all around.

It was Launceston who noted the most unnerving aspect. "The rats have fled," he said.

A hint of the flute-playing Mayhew had heard rose up and disappeared. Peering down each of the streets in turn, Will tried to discern the origin of the music.

Miller dabbed at his nose where a trickle of blood ran down to his upper lip. "What is this?" he asked, his eyes widening.

Will urged him to be silent. The flute-playing ebbed away to be replaced by the faint tread of boots upon the baked mud, drawing nearer. The dim sound drifted through the smoke and reflected from wall to wall so it was difficult to identify the source.

On a deeper level than their five senses, they understood the nature of what approached. Launceston slapped a cold hand on Miller's shoulder to steady him.

Turning slowly, Will stopped for the briefest moment at each street. "Which way, which way?" he muttered to himself.

Then, along the route to the west, almost lost to the swirling smoke, two hot coals nearly a yard off the ground moved towards them. The moment he glimpsed that almost insignificant blaze of colour in that shadowy place, several sounds came to Will from the same direction: a low, growling breath, barely audible but which made his stomach clench and the hairs on his neck tingle; the pad of a paw, the slap of a tensing leather leash as something strained against it; and then the measured tread of boots.

Will propelled Miller down the street that led to the south, the others following at his heels. They only came to a halt when the strained atmosphere had evaporated and there was no sign of pursuit.

Miller had grown pale. "Who was that?" he asked. "A ghost?"

"No spectre would haunt this foul place," Will replied. "Not when there are peaceful churchyards and castle towers sheltered from the elements." His grin took the edge off Miller's anxiety. "A man with a dog, no more. Probably for the fighting pit. But we could not risk it smelling us out. Even with these foul rags, we are sweeter to the nose than anyone else in this place."

Calming a little, Miller moved his fingers unconsciously to the dried blood under his nose, but before any errant thoughts could resurface, Launceston gave him a rough shove and they were back on their journey.

They had not gone far when Launceston appeared at Will's shoulder. In a low voice that none of the others could hear, he said, "Bringing that youth was a mistake. The knowledge of what we face, revealed in one shattering blow, will destroy him, and us along with him if we are not careful."

"Then we protect him until he can be prepared for the truth." Launceston was right, and in ideal circumstances Miller would have gone through the same slow stabilising process of induction and revelation as the rest of them. But Will understood Walsingham's urge to circumvent procedure: these were desperate times, and they were always short-handed compared to the force arrayed against them. "This is the hand we have been dealt. We must play it as best we can," he said firmly.

In the icy flash of the glance Launceston levelled at Miller, Will saw the earl would not shy from taking matters into his own hands if Miller placed them, or their mission, at risk. None of them were strangers to shedding blood, but killing came particularly easy to Launceston. Marlowe had once said something was missing inside him. Will would need to pay careful attention.

As they pressed deeper into Alsatia, the residents felt safer from the unwanted scrutiny of the law-keepers. Dice was played noisily on doorsteps, or cards on ramshackle tables at the side of the street. Disabled men and women abandoned by society tried to scrape a living begging, and sometimes the criminals would take pity and toss them a coin.

Outside a tavern, amid heaps of vomit and reeking lakes of urine, people sprawled drunkenly across the street with no one to move them on. The noise from the open doors and windows of the tavern was deafening, inebriated conversations delivered at a bellow against a backdrop of fiddle music and ferociously contested gambling.

Occasionally brawls would begin, but they were swiftly broken up by men armed with cudgels who kept the order among the unruly class. They were likely in the pay of the gangs, Will guessed, ready to be sent to the defence of any member of the community being dragged out to face justice.

One man lay facedown, his skull split open and his blood flowing into the mud and the urine. Will saw the hands of his own men going instinctively to their swords, knowing what they would face if they were found out. The close call with the Enemy and his dog had unnerved them all.

As Will prepared to enter the tavern to search for information, an uproar echoed from the end of the street where men and women ran towards the entrance to one of the tenements.

"Someone is in danger," Will guessed from the tone of the cries. "Let us investigate."

CHAPTER 11

As Will and the others were taking their first steps into Alsatia, Grace was already progressing into the filthy, smoke-filled streets. Marlowe had always liked her, and it had not taken a great effort to worm Will's destination out of him. Although he would not speak directly of the nature of Will's business in the Thieves' Quarter, his occasional unguarded comment told Grace her instincts were correct: there was some connection to Jenny's disappearance. Marlowe warned her of the dangers awaiting a young woman alone in Alsatia—it was not the court, it was certainly not Warwickshire— but the drive to discover the truth about her sister overrode all else.

But as she stood on a street where a man at a table took receipt of purses, jewellery, silk handkerchiefs, and occasionally coats and boots, she cursed her ignorance. She thought she would be able to find Will easily—he was often recognised and hailed by upstanding men and women—but here there was no trace of his passing, and she was lost, and her perfumed handkerchief could not keep the foul smells from her nose. And now a group of four men were casting surreptitious glances her way, and muttering among themselves. She was not naive; she recognised the hunger in their eyes.

At least a woman alone was no threat and she was not troubled by the majority of the other unsavoury characters she saw. But as she attempted to retrace her steps to the London she knew, the men began to follow her.

Her heart beat faster, but she tried not to give in to panic, for she knew that would only attract more unwanted attention. Keeping her head down, she skipped a stinking puddle, unsure whether she should move down the centre of the street where everyone would see her or keep in the shadow of the tenements where she could be snatched in through one of the open doors. Opting for somewhere between the two, she kept up a fast pace, deciding that she hated that place more than anywhere she had been in her life. Every face had either a hint of cruelty or the stain of life's crushing ills. She saw no hope anywhere. The desolation made her yearn for Will; he had kept his own hope alive in the face of, as she saw it, all reason. He truly believed Jenny still lived. More than anything she didn't want that hope crushed, but she feared the worst. Soon he might find out the truth, and what then for him?

That thought prompted a stark memory: on the fourth day after Jenny's disappearance when a black carriage had arrived at the home of Will's family just as night fell, a waning moon casting a silver light over the Warwickshire cornfields. A mysterious visitor, armed guards at the door, and then Will emerging at dawn to tell her, "There is a great secret to the way the world works. Nothing is as it seems."

Will appeared to dread that was true, but as Grace glanced back at the four men loping in her wake, elbowing each other and flashing lascivious grins while their eyes remained furtive and hard, she fervently hoped that was the case.

The street to her right was wider and had more traffic. Grace took it in the hope that the men would leave her alone under the gaze of others. But she had not gone more than twenty paces when a rough hand grabbed her arm.

The youngest of the men, with sandy hair and a ruddy complexion covered with pox scars, said, "Walk with us, lady. These are rough parts and you need strong arms to keep you safe."

"I fear that cure will be worse than the disease," Grace said. "Leave me. I would walk alone."

She tried to throw off his hand, but he only held her tighter, and then the other three men were moving to surround her.

"Aid me!" Grace called to the people moving along the street. A man with grey hair and hollow cheeks only winked at the men and moved on. A fat woman threw back her head and laughed, and her friend pointed and made a sexual gesture at the men, who laughed and called back rudely.

"You will get no help round these parts," the pox-scarred man said.

Grace launched a sharp kick at his shins, and as he yelped and staggered back towards his associates, she ran. Along the street, jeers and encouragement to pursuit rose up loudly. Catching her quickly, the men bundled her through the open door of one of the tenements.

Grace careered across the mud floor to come to rest against a damp wall. The place was bare apart from a table and a chair, and a fire stoked with cheap coal smoked into the room.

Laughing as they loosened their hose, the four men ranged across the room, blocking her escape.

"Come near me and I will tear out your eyes," she hissed. The men only laughed harder.

Sliding up the wall, Grace hooked her fingers like claws as her attackers approached. Through the filthy window, she glimpsed movement: more of the jeering locals coming to witness her degradation, she guessed.

But when the door clattered open, it was four cloaked men who burst in. Grace had as little time to react as her attackers before a drawn sword was thrust into the heart of the pox-scarred man, and just as quickly withdrawn and slashed across the throat of another. Grace had only ever seen one person exhibit that degree of skill with the blade.

"Will," she murmured with relief.

The remaining two attackers had only a second to plead for their lives before they too were run through. Sickened by the cold efficiency of the kills, Grace turned away, but she was also troubled that a part of her was triumphant.

When she turned back, her saviour stood before her. She went to throw her arms around Will, only for an unfamiliar face to be revealed when the hood was thrust back: aristocratic, with an aquiline nose and dark eyes that were as charismatic as Will's, a waxed moustache and chin hair, swarthy skin.

"Greetings, mistress," he said. "I am Don Alanzo de las Posadas, and you will now accompany me."

"Spanish spies," Grace gasped.

Don Alanzo gave a curt bow.

CHAPTER 12

Passing through the flow of drunks from the tavern, Will and the others joined the rear of the crowd at the entrance to the tenement. As people jostled for a view of the mysterious spectacle, Will eased his way past sharp shoulders and elbows until the laughter and quizzical shouts gave way to sudden silence. A moment of confusion ended in panic, shrieks, and barked warnings, as those near the front tried to drive back into the flow of the ones joining the crowd.

When Will broke through the flow with renewed urgency, at first he couldn't see anything out of the ordinary. Slumped across the step against the door jamb, the local children had placed a scarecrow, straw protruding from the sleeves and neck of worn clothes, head lolling on the chest beneath a wide-brimmed felt hat. Yet something about the well-stuffed shape held him fast.

A moment later, the scarecrow shifted.

"A game!" Miller chuckled under his breath. "I have seen this before, in my village. A child hides inside it!"

"Away," Will urged as gently as he could, trying to push Miller back against the weight of the crowd behind him.

The scarecrow lurched to its feet, stumbling and swaying on the step, straw hands going to a face that was at once twisted knots of straw and hazel switches and also completely human. Terrified eyes rolled insanely. Twig fingers clawed at the place where the mouth should have been, and a mad mewling came from deep inside it. With a pleading arm, the scarecrow reached out to the crowd, but as it staggered around the arc, everyone moved back, unnerved, trying to believe it was some joke, knowing in their hearts what they were really seeing.

Miller's eyes widened. Grabbing his shoulder in an attempt to drag him away, Launceston urged through clenched teeth, "Get him out of here!" But Miller threw Launceston and Will off, and stepped towards the scarecrow.

Flailing desperately, its puppetlike movements drove the crowd to silence until an old woman whispered, "The Devil has been here."

That was enough. "The Devil! The Devil!" jumped from mouth to mouth as the mob fell apart in uproar.

One bull-necked, bald-headed man was not convinced. Stepping forwards, he tore open the scarecrow's jacket and ripped at the straw beneath. The scarecrow's desperate mewling grew louder.

Golden straw rained across the street as the frenzied search for the hidden occupant tore through the insides. Finally his fingers scraped the back of the jacket and the expression of dumb realisation that crept across his face was devastating to see.

"There is nothing in it," he croaked. "It is the Devil's work."

Falling to its knees, the scarecrow futilely clawed up the straw and stuffed it back inside. Its mewling was now a loud whine that set the teeth on edge.

"It is one of Pickering's men," someone else said, "taken by Old Nick for his sins."

The horror that gripped the crowd broke out in anger and cruelty. With cudgels and boots they attacked the scarecrow as it flopped and flailed and emitted muffled whines on the ground. From one of the tenements, the bald-headed man emerged with a burning stick pulled from the hearth. Faces torn by fear, the crowd parted with a desperate hope that here would be an end to it. Dragging the scarecrow to its feet, the bald man thrust the blazing stick into the scarecrow's gaping belly. The straw caught immediately. With roaring flames engulfing the figure in a second, greasy black smoke billowed up between the tenements. Women clutched their ears to keep out the mewling noise as the scarecrow at first ran back and forth, then staggered, and finally fell to its knees and grew silent as the blaze consumed it.

Finally, nothing remained but black ashes, half-burned boots, and remnants of clothing. Kicking through the ashes with a fury that revealed his secret fear, the bald man searched for any blackened bones, and only calmed when he saw there were none.

As their anger dissipated, a deep unease fell on the silent crowd. Miller tore off the hood of his cloak, tears of fear streaking his pallid face.

"What happened to him?" he croaked.

Will and Launceston did their best to bundle him away, but the damage had already been done.

"Strangers." A pointing finger was levelled at Miller.

"Strangers," another repeated.

"They did it."

Hands tore at Will's cloak. Carpenter's sword was revealed, and Mayhew had his hood ripped from his head.

"Strangers!"

It did not matter whether they were agents of the law or responsible for the terrifying event that had just unfolded, Will saw that he and the others were a vent for the crowd's churning emotions. Throwing off the men attempting to grip his arms, he drew his sword and carved an arc around him with the tip of the blade.

The others were not so quick. "The Devil!" quickly gave way to "Spies!" and "The law!" followed rapidly by the call to arms of "Clubs!" which was soon ringing out loudly along the street. Men rushed from the tavern and the buildings all around, armed with whatever they could pick up to defend their illicit livelihoods, quickly joined by women and children who were just as ferocious.

A cudgel clattered across Mayhew's temple, sending a gout of blood spattering in a wide arc. Stunned, he staggered back until Carpenter caught him, his sword now drawn. But the crowd surged in such numbers that there was no room to use his blade, and soon he was swamped in bodies, fists and sticks and bottles raining down on him.

The mob was kept at bay by Will's flashing sword, but he could not see a way out. Overhead, the whistles rang out from the rooftops, and more people ran to the disturbance by the minute from all around the area. There was no point reasoning with them; the normally febrile emotions of the criminal class in defending their territory against suspicious intruders were now infused with the fear engendered by the scarecrow and burning as furiously as that thing had done.

Worse, the whistles had drawn the attention of the underworld security force. Daggers were being drawn and razors pulled from the lining of cloaks. The people of Alsatia would only be sated when five torn bodies were found on the edge of the Thames at daybreak.

Miller, Launceston, Mayhew, and Carpenter were lost to Will beneath the roiling sea of bodies, but he could hear the thwack of wood on flesh and the slap of boots and fists.

With a flourish, he plucked one of Dee's packages from his pouch and unfurled it, shielding his eyes with his arm. As the powder within met the air, the resounding bang made his ears ring and the flash burned through his closed lids, but it brought turmoil to the already anxious crowd. With yells and shrieks, the attackers surged back. Dazed and covered in blood, Miller quickly found his equilibrium as Will dragged him from the mud. Mayhew, Launceston, and Carpenter staggered towards him, similarly bloody and bruised.

As their eyes and nerves recovered, the mob circled warily. Will knew it would only be a matter of moments before they rediscovered their courage, and the sheer weight of numbers would bring him down.

"Follow my lead," he said quietly to the others, "and do not tarry, for if you fall behind they will be like wolves upon you."

Spinning, he kicked open the door at his back and raced into the smoky, damp-smelling shadows. A woman sat next to the hearth, sharpening a knife on a leather strap, a filthy, naked child playing at her feet. She glared at Will hatefully as he flashed her a smile and said, "Apologies. We shall not be staying for dinner."

The roaring mob thundered in pursuit. Will ran through the tenement and out of the back door onto another street with Launceston, Miller, Mayhew, and Carpenter at his back.

"Fool!" Launceston snapped at Miller. "If we survive this, I will take it out of your hide."

"Master Miller has prevented our day from becoming too dull," Will said, "and tedium is the most unforgivable crime of all. You will thank him for this later."

They ran west along the street, the mob slowed by the narrow passage of the tenement. But as the whistles blasted urgently from the rooftops, more streamed from alleys into the street ahead, trying to block their way.

"They will not rest until we are dead," Carpenter said. "They fear we are taking the secrets of their crimes away with us."

Gripping his sword tightly as he ran, Mayhew said fiercely, "I will take a hundred of them with me when I go! Damn the Spanish and the Enemy— sometimes I wonder if the real enemies are within." He ducked his head low as bottles and stones rained down around them. "Perhaps what we do is wrong. This rabble is not worth protecting."

As the mob drew in from all sides, Will saw it would be pointless trying to fight; they faced an army as ferocious in the defence of their beliefs as any foreign force. "We must find a place to hide," he said, "at least till night falls, and we can move on under cover of darkness."

"Hide where?" Carpenter snapped. "They will ransack any filthy hovel we choose to make our castle. Look—they are everywhere!"

"And did you accept defeat so easily when we fled across the snows of Muscovy with Feodor's men at our heels?" Will said. "Or did I dream us hiding like foxes in the roots of a tree?"

"I wish it had been a dream," Carpenter spat. "At least then I would not have these scars to itch morning, noon, and night."

Will could feel Carpenter's eyes on his back, and knew his associate wished his gaze was a dagger.

With a bellow, a man wearing a butcher's leather apron erupted from a door, swinging a bloodstained cleaver directly towards Will's head. Ducking beneath the arc, Will brought the pommel of his sword crashing against the back of the assailant's head. That was enough to deter him, but Launceston stepped in swiftly and slit the butcher's throat. Gurgling, and attempting to stem the arterial spurt, he plunged to the ground.

"A warning to the others," Launceston said before Will could speak.

The shouts of the mob grew louder, but their advance slowed. They were wary now, but just as murderous.

Will scanned the ranks moving in along both ends of the street before kicking his way into another tenement. "Bar the door behind us!" he called as he ran to open the rear door onto the next street.

Mayhew and Carpenter jammed what little furniture they could find in front of the door, and then made for the back door before Will summoned them to follow him up the stairs.

"Has the Devil taken your mind?" Carpenter shouted. "We will be trapped up there!"

"Follow him," Launceston said with cold insistence. "He is no fool."

Launceston and Mayhew propelled a dazed Miller up the stairs after Will. At the bottom, Carpenter hesitated for a moment until the sound of the mob drew towards the door and then he reluctantly followed.

Just as they reached the top of the creaking stairs, the front door burst open and the torrent of angry voices flooded through the tenement and out of the back door.

"They will be back the moment they find we are not in the street," Carpenter snapped, exasperated, "and this is the first place they will search."

"But they will not find us," Will said, "for we shall be disappeared."

Forcing his way through a door into a room filled with detritus and a bedroll on the bare boards in one corner, Will enjoyed the confusion for a moment and then pointed up to where a hatch led to the loft space. Mayhew and Launceston boosted him up, and then Will helped the others scramble into the dusty dark space filled with the flapping of nesting birds and the scurrying of rats along the rafters. Here and there, missing tiles allowed shafts of sunlight to punch through into the gloom.

Below, the muffled sounds of the mob washed around the tenement.

"You are still a fool," Carpenter raged. "They will find us here in time."

"Why, if I did not know better I would think you wanted us to fail," Will replied.

Keeping his head low, Will loped along a rafter to the end of the loft where a crawlspace led through to the loft of the adjoining tenement.

"The houses are all connected," Mayhew noted.

"The builders left the ways so they could move swiftly from roof to roof to finish their work. Now, follow."

Will crawled through the space into the next loft and continued along the row of tenements to the end house where they made their way down to the ground floor. While the hubbub continued further along the street, they took advantage of the billowing smoke to slip across to the opposite tenement and make their way rapidly up the stairs and into the loft space of the next row.

They finally came to rest halfway along the row where the roof was missing enough shingles to give them a view across Alsatia.

"We are surrounded by an army of cutthroats who will kill us the moment we emerge," Mayhew said, peering at the crowd milling along the street. "We are trapped here."

"We wait until nightfall and try again." Will hated wasting time when they were in danger of losing the Silver Skull at any moment, but after the disturbance all of Alsatia would be on watch for hours.

Launceston leaned in close and nodded towards Miller, who huddled in a corner, head bowed. "The boy was a mistake," he whispered. "It is not his fault, but that matters not now. Look at him. He will break at any moment. That makes him a danger to what we do here." Pausing, Launceston attempted to show a modicum of compassion, but all Will saw was cold efficiency. "We should dispatch him now and be done with it."

"Let me talk to him," Will said. "We all recall our introduction to this world. He may find his feet quickly."

"Or he may not. And what then?"

In Miller Will saw the innocence that the rest of them hardly remembered, the pleasant days of his rural upbringing, and he regretted the toll taken by the hard business of life. When he went over, Miller didn't look up.

"Was that the Devil's work?" Miller's voice was a ghostly rustle. The country burr was clear, and Will realised the youth had been suppressing it, probably to appear more sophisticated to his new associates.

"Not in the way you mean. But it is certainly devilish."

"I heard stories of these things, in the tavern, and around Swainson's hearth one winter night, but . . ." He chewed his lip, drawing blood. "They were just stories. Not real. But that . . . That should not be!" Finally, he looked up at Will with wide eyes stung by tears.

"You are right. It should not."

"They burned him alive! Whatever happened, the poor soul was still inside somewhere. And they burned him!"

"People do terrible things when they are scared. We are taught to see the world a certain way. A clockwork place, where the sun rises in the morning and sets at dusk, and all happens as it should. Tick-tock. But the world is not like that."

As Miller wiped away his tears, Will saw a hint of defiance that gave him hope. Perhaps that was what Walsingham had recognised. "What is it like, then?" Miller asked.

"It is a place where night can fall at noon, and cows give blood not milk. Where mothers can find strange creatures in the cribs where their babies lay only a moment before. Where mortal men do not rule and never have." He cast an eye towards Launceston, Carpenter, and Mayhew, who whispered conspiratorially on the far side of the loft. "I will tell you the truth of these matters," he said quietly, squatting next to Miller. "Listen carefully, and then I will answer any questions you have, as much as I can. But you must not cry, or rail to the heavens, or give any sign of fear. You must accept these things like the man that our Lord Walsingham saw when he chose you to defend our queen and country. Do you understand?"

Miller nodded.

"Good man. These secrets would have been revealed to you at the Palace of Whitehall over time, and they would have been allowed to settle on you, so they did not disturb your mind. But there was no time for that, and so you must hear them now, hard, and cold, and painful."

"Tell me. Make sense of what I saw."

"Sense? No, there is no sense to any of this, but I will help you understand as best I can. The stories that you heard at Swainson's hearth are true. Every story that you laughed off in the light of day but feared deep in your heart at night is true."

"The Devil—"

"Yes, by other names. Devils. A race of them. For as long as we have walked on this Earth, they have preyed on us, for sport, out of cruelty, for malign purposes. They have transformed us, like that poor wretch you saw in the street, tormented our nightmares, twisted our limbs, stolen our children, driven our old men to their graves, slaughtered our young men, and drunk their blood, and bathed in it. No forest was ever safe for us, no lonely moor, no quiet, moonlit pool or river's edge or mountaintop, for they would come from under hill and mound and treat us like cattle, or worse, like rats, forced to play for the mouser's enjoyment before one swipe of claw bares innards to the light."

Will paused to allow his words to sink in. Disbelief, and the hint of a smile flickered on Miller's face. It was the first sign, Will knew from long experience, and it would pass. There would be worse to come, not just then, but for many nights after, if not a lifetime.

"You have had an education of the history of this land?" Will asked.

"A little."

"Then let me tell you of the true history, the secret history. England has always been at war—"

"Always?"

"Not with the Spanish, or the French, the Scots or the Welsh or the Irish."

"With this race of devils?" Miller's disbelief had already started to turn.

"I dress it up in fine clothes to call it a war," Will continued, "but really we have been in rags, 'pon our knees. The Enemy did what they wanted with us. Killed, stole, tormented. And we could not fight back, for they were too powerful."

"They have magic?"

"They can do things we cannot. They have guile and secret knowledge. Magic? It seems that way at times, but I am just a humble spy and do not understand such things." Will spoke calmly and carefully, smiling to make his words appear simpler than they were. "In truth, they are more dangerous than wolves, they see like eagles, swim like fish, are stronger than bears, more cunning than snakes. They are there and gone in the twinkling of an eye. Most importantly, they value our lives not a whit. In their eyes, we are as far beneath them as the sheep of the field are beneath us."

"And this Enemy . . . you say they have been attacking us forever? Then why have I not seen nor heard of them?"

"You have, in stories, in whispers. They are always known by other names. You called them the Devil yourself. But our kings and queens have always ruled that their existence should be kept a secret from the common man as much as is possible. For if the good men and women of England knew the terrors that could pluck them from their lives at any moment, they would be driven mad with fear, and all we have tried to build here would fall into an abyss."

In the street below, the clamour had ebbed away as the mob returned to their plots and plans. But even in the silence there was little peace.

"Tell me what they do," Miller said.

"I will tell you some of what they do," Will replied. "A flavour, but there is no time to tell you all." *And I would not see your hope extinguished*, Will thought. "In Chanctonbury Ring, in Sussex, the Devil appears every Midsummer Eve, the local people say, and plucks one poor wretch from his hearth to take beneath the clump.

"In Tolleshunt Knights in Essex, not far from your quiet home, these people of the dark engaged in carnal displays on the banks of the bottomless pool in the place known as the Devil's Wood. One year, a local landowner attempted to build a house there, and the unholy crew ripped out his heart, screaming that his soul was lost.

"At Wandlebury Camp, near Cambridge, a night rider will appear under the full moon to challenge all-comers. The wounds he inflicts bleed anew on the anniversary of the night they were inflicted. In the Lickey Hills in haunted Worcestershire, the local folk tell how the Devil and his chief huntsman Harry-ca-nab hunt wild boars, and if they cannot find their game they hunt the locals."

For nearly an hour, Will detailed the atrocities, the blood-soaked fields, the devastated lives and stolen children, the changelings, the disappeared, the hunted and the haunted and the corrupted. His litany of misery covered every quarter of England, and reached back as far into the past as historians had documented. It was as he had been told in the days after he had been recruited by Walsingham, and Miller's reaction was the same, the disbelief shading to shock, then to a creeping, cold devastation at the realisation that there was no safe place.

Stretching his legs, Will watched the clouds blowing across the afternoon sky as he completed the first part of his account. "In Atwick, in Yorkshire, no one dares drink at the local spring. In York . . . at Alderley Edge . . . at Kirkby Lonsdale and Castleton Fell . . ." His words dried up, but the silence that followed said enough.

"My grandfather disappeared in the marshes at Romney, following a mysterious light. We never found his body," Miller began hesitantly.

"They are everywhere, Tom Miller. In every part of this country, and beyond too, I would wager. We have all been touched by them, though we might not realise it. They may exist on the edges of what we see, but they are always there. They have always been there."

"What are they?" Miller asked. "Are they—?"

With a reassuring smile, Will held up a hand to silence him. "The farmers do not speak their name, lest they answer. They call them the Fair Folk or the Good Neighbours. You know who they are."

"My mother said they helped."

"Some did. But there is a cruel group among them who find us game for hunting, or sport when they are bored." As he looked out past the broken tiles, across the smoky city, Will could feel the eyes of Launceston, Mayhew, and Carpenter on his back, all waiting to see how Miller would deal with the news. He had revealed to him the problem and brought him down; now it was time to uncover the solution. "But no more," he added.

"But . . . the scarecrow in the street. They do not leave us alone," Miller said, puzzled.

"No. There are other accounts, but fewer now. Mere skirmishes, to let us know they still exist. The hot war we fought with their kind has blown cold." Will struck a defiant tone as he turned back to Miller. "We found a way to fight back."

"Against a power like that? How?"

"Your thanks should go to Doctor Dee. When Elizabeth came to the throne in 1558 and received the truth of these matters passed down across the years through royal channels, she decided it was time to take a stand. The people of England could no longer be the plaything of an outside power. Determined to end generations of suffering, she turned to her teacher, advisor, and confidant Doctor Dee, and brought him close, charging him with the task. Through his esoteric studies, Dee came upon a solution, and after a night in which it is said storms tore England apart and ghosts walked in every churchyard, England's defences were secured."

"How did Doctor Dee achieve such a thing?"

"In this business of secrets, Dee keeps his closer than any. Whatever he did . . . whatever price he paid . . . it changed everything overnight. The Enemy could no longer attack us with impunity. They retreated to their distant homes, seething that those they considered so lowly had now risen up to challenge their rule."

"If we have locked them out, how do they return to torment us?" Miller asked.

"Over time, they still find a way through here or there, a quick blow, but it is nothing like before. Yet in their absence they are even more dangerous. Their loss of power has wounded them. Always arrogant, they refuse to accept they now have equals and are determined to bring us once again to our knees. Now, instead of seeing us as sport, they see us as a threat, and they are determined to destroy us for all time. And so they plot, and bide their time, and search for a way through our defences. We must be ever vigilant, for we do not know where or when their decisive blow will come. And it will come, sooner or later. Their intellect, and their anger, burn hot. They have been spurned, and they will want a vengeance that will clear us from the world."

"And this business with the Silver Skull?"

Will was pleased to see that Miller's unease had dissipated a little. His brow was furrowed as he turned over the information, weighing options, realising, Will hoped, that there was no need to be fatalistic.

"They have never launched such a bold attack before, which suggests this artefact is of the greatest importance to them. And the only thing they consider important now is our destruction."

"So . . . so . . . we do not fight the Spanish?"

"We do. We are in a bitter struggle with our Earthly enemies for our continued existence as a nation. That is how it always has been, though our lot was made more difficult by Henry's decision to break with Rome. But now the Enemy stirs and manipulates our Catholic opponents. Indeed, not just Spain, or France, but all the foreign monarchs. We should stand shoulder to shoulder against a common foe, but religion is a formidable wedge. Catholic? Protestant? It means nothing to me. We are all brothers in our skin. But the Enemy is skilled at finding weaknesses and exploiting them to their own advantage."

Cleaning his nails with his knife, Launceston came over. Will could see he had softened in his opinion of Miller now that the youth had not lost his head. "At times it appears the whole world is against us, with the Enemy manipulating all to crush us. But we have risen up off our knees and now that we have gained freedom, we shall not let it go again. We will do whatever it takes to survive."

"And this is our job, then?" Miller asked.

"This is the true reason for our network of spies," Will agreed. "Yes, we have agents in the foreign courts and we continually gather information against our Earthly enemies, but the real reason for our existence is the true Enemy."

"We operate in the shadows, always presenting two faces to the world," Launceston continued, "but the true nature of our fight, and the Enemy we face, must never be revealed. For the people of England would lose hope if they knew the scale of the forces ranged against us."

"After Dee's defences were secured, the first plans for a secret service to oppose the Enemy's renewed attention were laid by Elizabeth's chief minister William Cecil, Lord Burghley, and in 1566 he summoned our Lord Walsingham to enact the strategy that we now see through today."

Miller clutched his temples. "My head is spinning. I can no longer tell what is truth or fiction. This all seems like a dream. A nightmare."

"A nightmare indeed," Launceston replied, "and we continue to take those bad dreams back to the Enemy's door. We have fought them to a standstill in the twenty-two years since Lord Walsingham came to court, and there have been casualties on both sides. The battle will continue, cold, and hard, and fought forever in the shadows. I cannot see an end to it."

"We cannot defeat them?" Miller asked.

"They are like the sea," Launceston replied.

"But if our defences ever crack, they would wash us away in the flood," Will said. "We cannot let that happen. Our guard must not fall for an instant. You see now the importance of the work we do?"

"It is all down to us?" Miller's voice had grown thin and reedy.

"England and our queen demand the best of us," Will said. "We shall not let them down."

Outside, a flock of birds rose suddenly into the sky, cawing discordantly as they swooped across the rooftops. It was a strangely desolate sound that touched them all.

"I would be alone with my thoughts for a while," Miller said quietly. "You have given me much to ponder."

Once again, Launceston fixed an incisive eye on the youth.

"Take your moment," Will said, "but when night falls the time for thinking will have passed. Then we act."

CHAPTER 13

ranches tore at Will's face and brambles ripped at his ankles as he crashed through the trees in search of the watcher. It was cool in the twilit world, the trees so densely packed in the ancient forest that he could barely see more than ten feet ahead. After a moment, he came to a halt against a twisted oak and listened intently. Only the sighing of the wind reached his ears.

After a moment's hesitation, he picked his way back along the trail he had made. It would be too dangerous to go any deeper. Near-impenetrable in parts, the Forest of Arden sprawled for mile upon mile across the Warwickshire countryside and was home to bands of cutthroats and robbers.

In the high summer heat, Jenny sat on the grassy slope falling away from the forest's edge, the whole of their world spread before her. She greeted him with a wry smile. "Starting at shadows again," she teased.

Will was caught by a moment of pure clarity. Her dress, the blue of forget-me-nots, the tumble of her brown hair across her shoulders, features more delicate than all the other village girls, green eyes more intelligent, the faintly quizzical nature of her smile. Some element, or combination of elements, brought forth an acute awareness of the tumble of time: from the moment the tomboy pushed him into the pond on the green when he was ten, through the fights and the arguments, the slow surfacing of respect, emotions and perceptions shifting and coalescing across the seasons. At no point would he ever have predicted it would lead here, now. But it had.

"Some of the girls hereabouts dream of a valiant protector who would fling themselves into danger at the slightest provocation." He sniffed archly.

"Then you should seek them out."

Lounging languorously next to her, he feigned aloofness, but his gaze was continually drawn back to the trees and the shadows that lay among them. Someone had been watching them.

"Though I am now filled with confusion," she mused. "I thought I was stepping out with a poet. Who, in recent times, had also found fame in the debating chambers

of the university at Cambridge. A scholar, and a dreamer. A writer of beautiful sonnets mapping the landscape of his heart."

"A man can be many things, Jenny."

"You would not hurt a fly," she said, laughing. She toyed absently with the locket at her throat.

"What do you keep in there?"

"A fresh rose petal every day during the summer. To remind me of my one true love."

"He is a lucky man."

"He is. I hope he knows it."

Excitement and nervousness fought within him. Everything was changing quickly. Good fortune had brought the patron to his door, and it now seemed certain his poetry would be published. At first there would only be a small stipend, but his future appeared assured and he could finally consider marriage.

With his hands behind his head, he pretended to watch the clouds, while eyeing her surreptitiously. Was this the right time to ask her?

She cuffed him on the arm. "I can see you watching me," she said.

"Making sure you are safe."

"I need no man to keep me safe." She arched one eyebrow at him. "You should know that by now, Will Swyfte."

He did. She was strong-willed and independent, fearless in the way she lived her life, and she kept the men of the village at bay with a quick wit that left them slack-jawed. Many of the locals found her hard to handle, but those were just the qualities that had drawn Will to her.

He weighed telling her of his intentions, and then decided it would wait until the afternoon. He wanted to ensure the moment was perfect, shaped like a sonnet to capture the emotion for all time, and soon she would be away to help Grace prepare lunch for their mother.

"When does your father return from his business in Kenilworth?" he asked.

She eyed him curiously. "Why do you ask?"

"No reason."

"Well, Master Without-Reason, I must be away to my chores. Let us meet again in an hour. And I will give you my opinion on your latest sonnet, should you require it."

"As always."

She surprised him with a kiss on the forehead. "My heart is yours," she whispered. And then she was gone.

He spent the next few minutes planning the proposal in his head, and then fell asleep beneath a rowan tree, confident in the knowledge that there would be no bigger day in his life.

When he awoke, it was afternoon and the countryside was held beneath a languid heat. Afraid he was late, he hurried down the baked track towards Jenny's house. The wind stirred the golden sea of corn into gentle waves that rippled around the hedgerows, where clouds of butterflies fluttered over the meadow fescue and birdsfoot trefoil. Birdsong and the drone of bees wove a languorous accompaniment to a day for lazy walks, not momentous events.

Across the field, he could just make out the thatched roof, and beyond it the dense, dark wall of the Forest of Arden stretching as far as the eye could see. Jenny's mother would undoubtedly be tending the garden with Grace at her side after the morning's chores had been completed. And Jenny would be free to spend the afternoon with him.

His thoughts of a lifetime with Jenny, and of writing, of love and art, were interrupted by the sound of her voice calling his name. On the far side of the field, she pushed her way through the corn towards him, smiling and waving, the blue of her dress sharp against the gold. Her face was filled with the joy of seeing him. There was something so perfect in that image he was sure it would stay with him always.

Climbing the stile, he set off across the field to meet her halfway. Before he had taken ten paces into the crop, the black clouds of a summer storm swirled out of nowhere in a sudden blast of wind. Puzzled by the strange phenomenon, he paused to watch the clouds sweeping towards the sun, wondering why the image troubled him so.

Within a moment, it had grown almost as dark as night. Disoriented by the buffeting gale, Will was shocked by a crack of thunder directly overhead, and then the clouds dissipated as quickly as they had arrived.

With the sun blazing once more, he returned his attention to the cornfield and prepared to hurry on to Jenny. Yet she was nowhere to be seen. He came to a slow halt and looked around the rolling, golden waves.

Playing a game, he thought with a smile. No one took such joy in teasing him. "You cannot hide from me," he called. "I will find you."

She had ducked down below the level of the corn and was circling to surprise him from behind.

Calling her name, he ploughed a furrow through the swaying gold, but when he reached the point where he had last seen her, he came to another puzzled halt. Her trail was clear through the corn to her house. But there was no sign of any other path leading off. He knelt down to examine the stems of the corn, but none had been bent or broken.

His heart began to beat faster, still without truly realising why. Jenny was playful, and clever, he told himself, trying to find an answer to the puzzle.

He searched around the area, but when he glanced back he saw a confusion of his own furrows crisscrossing the corn. It was impossible to move without leaving a trail. But Jenny had left none.

He called her name loudly. He tried to call brightly, but he could hear the edge of desperation in his voice.

Only the sighing of the wind returned, as it had in the forest. A feeling of unaccountable dread descended on him. Jenny was gone.

Turning slowly, he tried to find answers that would not come, and after a moment he heard himself whispering, "I will find you."

CHAPTER 14

The Bow Bells rang out and the City gates were slammed shut as night fell. From the ragged gap in the roof, Will heard the bellman set out to patrol the streets, calling the hour followed by his familiar refrain:

Remember the clocks,
Look well to your locks,
Fire and your light,
And God give you good night,
For now the bell ringeth.

"Now?" Carpenter prompted.

"Now," Will replied. His dream-memory, and the feeling of loss and grief that accompanied it, was still heavy on him.

In the street, the chill of the spring dark had done little to dampen the stink. As they waited in a doorway for a pair of smartly dressed coney-catchers to pass on their way to finding a gull or two at the theatre, Launceston whispered, "Let us hope Pickering has not disposed of the Silver Skull, or the Enemy has not located it while we hid like mice. If the boy had not acted so weak we would not be in this position."

"But we are, so let us hear no more of it," Will replied.

He eyed Miller, who waited with Mayhew, now even more subdued since night had fallen. His eyes continually flickered from side to side as if searching for an imminent attack.

Will wished he could have sent Miller back to Walsingham, but in his current state it was unlikely he would get out of Alsatia alive. Knowing they would have to carry their liability with them, he had assigned Mayhew to watch over him, and subdue him at the first sign of panic; at least Mayhew could be trusted not to kill Miller, unlike Launceston.

The dark cloaked them as they moved along the streets, the only illumination the glimmer of candles and lamps through dirty glass. At the tavern, they hid in an alley where they could observe the door. When a drunk reeled out across the ruts, Will and Carpenter caught him beneath the arms, clamping one hand over his mouth, and steered him into the alley, where a knife at the throat helped loosen his tongue. Once they had the location of a house where Pickering's men took daily delivery of prizes stolen by their cutpurses, they left the drunk unconscious.

Dodging down alleys and racing from doorway to doorway to avoid scrutiny, it took them five minutes to find the house. Of all the run-down tenements in Alsatia, at first glance it was one of the worst, windows covered with planks, no signs of life within. A second glance revealed an incongruously heavy door with a large lock, and in the shadowed doorway of the next property, the dark shape of a sentry, arms folded, unmoving.

"Master Carpenter?" Will whispered.

Drawing a weighted knife, Carpenter measured the distance and then let the blade fly. It thudded into the guard's throat and he pitched forwards into the street.

Mayhew gaped at the fallen body. "God's loaves! Where did you learn that trick?"

"Why should I not have natural skill?" Carpenter snarled, adding sullenly, "It was taught me by one of the natives brought back from the New World."

At the door, Launceston kept watch while Carpenter retrieved his throwing knife and Mayhew dropped to his knees and unfurled a roll of purple velvet on the step. A set of locksmith's tools was revealed.

"A steerpointe three-chamber." He sniffed. "The lock of kings. A grand addition to such a hovel."

"Pickering lives cheek by jowl with the greatest thieves in all of England, and there is no honour among them. Of all places, this needs the best protection," Will replied. "You can open it?"

With a theatrical sigh, Mayhew's skillful fingers swiftly manipulated three of the tools in the keyhole until the lock turned.

Aside to Miller, Will said, "It is time to put all doubts behind you, Tom. We face only mundane foes here. Pickering will have guarded his riches with the strongest arms in Alsatia. We will have to fight to reach him. Are you ready?"

"You need not doubt me, Will," Miller replied.

Easing the door open a crack, Will slipped in, drawing his sword. The hall was dark, but he was instantly caught by the scent of lavender pomanders, and bowls of spice to keep the smell of the street at bay. From high above them came the dim sound of revelry.

Putting a finger to his lips, Will beckoned the others in. He had expected there to be at least one guard on the other side of the door and was uneasy to find the hall deserted.

A blast of chill, smoky air reached him. Further along the hall, the door leading to the cellars hung open, and muffled noises came from the dark below. Carpenter made to climb the stairs until Will motioned to him to stop. The cellars would offer a secure place to store riches or prisoners.

Cautiously, he approached the open door. Rough stone steps led down past glistening, damp walls to where a ruddy glow was visible through the smoke, as though a furnace roared beneath. The voices were louder, but still indistinct, yet something in the tone made Will uneasy. Sword at the ready, he edged down a step at a time, covering his mouth against the smoke. As he moved below the level of the hall, he crouched down until he could peer into the room.

The smoke came from the open door of a blazing stove, burning clothes, purses, and other indecipherable objects spilling around its feet. What Will perceived to be the next bundle for the fire was revealed by the shifting smoke to be a body, tossed against one wall, leaking blood. Growing still, Will waited for the smoke to uncover the rest of what the cellar had to offer.

The murmur of voices continued, a susurration ebbing and flowing, but now it was joined by a low, throaty rumble. Near the fiery maw of the stove, Will saw two hot embers suspended in the smoke. They moved slowly.

From the shifting grey appeared a black dog, bigger than a calf, heavyset with muscle, its implacable eyes surveying the cellar. A leather leash stretched from its thick neck to a dark shape hunched over another.

Will waited.

The dog's growl grew louder as it sensed his presence.

Finally the smoke shifted to reveal a lithe, strong figure, brown hair falling across his shoulders, wearing a shirt and breeches of a timeless cut in deep forest shades, brown leather boots to his knees, an oddly shaped knife at his belt, and the hilt of a sword curved at the end into a dragon's head. With the dog's leash held loosely in his hand, to Will he resembled a hunter. Though Will couldn't see his face, the stranger's presence burned as hot as a furnace.

In front of the Hunter lay another of Pickering's guards, his eyes flickering on the brink of death. His stomach had been torn open by the dog. The Hunter held the poor wretch up with one powerful hand wrapped in the folds of his shirt and was clearly questioning him in a low tone.

When the timbre of the dog's growl changed, the Hunter paused. Slowly, he turned his head towards Will. Slipping back before he was seen, Will was sure he caught a fleeting glimpse of eyes as glittering and intense as the dog's red glare.

Easing back into the hall, he closed the cellar door and sealed it with the iron key protruding from the lock, although he knew at best it would only slow the Hunter for a moment.

Miller instantly read Will's face. "What is down there?"

"Nothing of note," Will lied. "They are burning the leftovers of Pickering's ill-gotten gains." As he moved past Miller, he whispered to the others, "Time is slipping through our fingers, men. We must find what we came for and be gone in a twinkling."

Leading the way up the tight stairs, Will slowed as he neared the second floor to peer around the turn where two men waited halfway along the landing. They were rough, unshaven, in poor clothes, their numerous scars detailing their violent life.

Withdrawing, Will rapped on the wall. A second later the shadows of the men loomed across the top of the stairs. Miller burst forth, and before the guards could raise the alarm, he cracked their heads together and they fell to the boards unconscious.

On the third floor, four more men waited, arguing noisily as they drank ale, too many to eliminate without a fight.

Bounding from the top of the stairs, Will took them by surprise. His sword went to the throat of the nearest, while Carpenter, Miller, and Mayhew attacked the others, but not before shouts rose up. Launceston ran one of the guards through, and Mayhew rammed his knife under the ribs of another, withdrawing it with a flourish to slash his victim across the throat. Miller's solid punch broke the jaw of the remaining guard.

A clatter on the stairs signalled the arrival of a guard from the fourth floor who let out a cry of shock before scampering back up. Before he had climbed half the flight, Carpenter's throwing knife was embedded in his back.

"How many guards above?" Will asked his prisoner. The tip of his blade brought a droplet of blood on the guard's throat.

"He was the last," the man croaked.

"Pickering is up there?"

"He is making merry with his copesmates for his bene fortune."

"He speaks the thieves' cant," Carpenter said. "Prick him some more until he recalls the queen's English."

"The meaning is clear." Will brought his sword hilt up hard against the guard's head and knocked him unconscious.

From below came the faint rattle of the cellar door. The others didn't notice, but Will was acutely aware that the Hunter would soon stand between them and their only route out of the building. He would face that conundrum when he came to it.

Will took the remaining steps two at a time. The sound of festivities emanating from the room at the top was so loud Will understood why no one from within had investigated the disturbance. A woman's exclamation of surprise. The smash of a broken bottle. Music and raucous cheers.

"Some wine would be good now," Mayhew said.

"You can have all the wine in the Palace of Whitehall if we recover the Silver Skull from this den of thieves." Will peered through the keyhole.

Men in gaudy costumes and masks sat at tables around the outside of a large room, the roughness of what features were visible at odds with the delicacy of their outfits: gold and silver, black and red diamonds, green velvet, purple silk. The masks had long beaks like birds, or resembled devils or farmyard animals. Piled high on the tables were chicken and pork, cheese and bread and honeycakes, and numerous jugs of wine and ale, on the finest tableware Will had seen outside of the queen's dining hall. In the space among the tables, a buxom, half-naked woman frolicked with a jester.

From his narrow view, Will estimated twenty men were present, all of them undoubtedly the hardest, most violent cutthroats who had sealed with blood their ascension to the ranks of Pickering's inner circle.

On the edge of his view was a grand, high-backed chair that resembled a throne. In it sat a fat, ruddy-faced man with a booming laugh. His manner was confident, and the others appeared to be paying deference to him.

"We are about to step into a pit of vipers, outnumbered by four to one," Will said, "but we have surprise on our side. Cause as much disturbance as you can. I will seek out Pickering. The others will calm once I have a knife at his throat. Agreed?"

Nodding, the others drew their swords.

Kicking the door open, Will bounded onto the nearest table, booting a platter of meat into the throat of one of the guests. Amid the deafening outcry that erupted, knives were drawn and cudgels pulled from beside seats. Shrieking, the woman scrambled beneath the tables.

As two men pushed back their chairs to attack, Carpenter and Mayhew ran them through. By the time the other cutthroats had thrown off the effects of their drink and food, Miller and Launceston were among them. Blood spattered across the floorboards as the spies carved a swathe through the drunken underworld lords.

Leaping over the jester's head, Will avoided the fray and went directly for the King of Cutpurses. Leaping onto the table, and then, with one boot on the back of the throne, propelling himself behind Pickering, he turned fluidly to slide his dagger against his throat.

"Hold now, or your master dies," he shouted. Sheathing his sword, he tore off Pickering's mask to reveal a red-faced man, hair lank with sweat, piggy eyes roving fearfully.

Slowly, the cutthroats came to a halt, gazes flickering between Pickering and the door.

"Any attempt to leave this room will ensure you leave your life," Will continued.

Through the open door came the creak of the stairs and the advancing rumble of the dog's growl.

"Matthew." Will pulled a small pouch from his cloak and tossed it to Mayhew.

Slamming the door, Mayhew poured the contents of the pouch—salt and a mixture of herbs—along the floorboards from hinge to lock. "Now we shall not be disturbed," he said, gesturing to the protective concoction that Dee had created long ago.

"Now, Pickering, I presume?"

Rolling his eyes towards Will, Pickering looked so frightened he might faint.

"All we want is the Silver Skull," Will continued. "You have overreached yourself this time. This is not some purse from a poor country visitor or a necklace from some dowager fresh off the ship from Flanders. The price you pay for this prize will be your life."

Pickering opened and closed his mouth like a beached fish. Beyond the door, Will could hear the tramp of boots, the rise and fall of the dog's throaty rumble setting his teeth on edge. All eyes flickered uneasily towards the door.

Spinning Pickering around roughly, Will pressed the knife harder against his throat. "Speak, now!"

"I . . . I . . ." Pickering stuttered, "I am not who you think I am!" His eyes darted towards his associates.

"He lies," Launceston said. "Cut him a little. It will loosen his tongue."

But Will could see the fat man was too scared to lie. He scanned the faces of the other cutthroats and saw puzzlement there. "So, even you did not know this was not your master." The stand-in tried to scramble away, but Will caught him and dragged him back. "So Pickering keeps his identity a secret even from those closest to him for protection from rivals and injured parties," Will continued. "Who is your master?"

"I do not know."

"He hired you."

"He wore a mask!"

Throwing the fat man to one side, Will stepped onto the table and walked slowly around the perimeter so he could study his prisoners. "Take off your masks," he ordered.

Reluctantly, they obeyed, revealing sullen, brutish eyes and unshaven jowls, scars and missing ears, teeth, and eyes.

"The court of the King of Cutpurses," Will mocked. "A poor king deserves a court like this." He watched for any sign of offence, but all eyes were downcast.

Outside the door, the dog's growl became a low howl that had a chilling, hungry quality. Everyone in the room started.

"What, you would feed us to your dog once we speak?" one of the men said. "We know nothing. That one there is Laurence Pickering." He pointed to the fat man. "He gave me ruff-peck and shrap every time I brought the lifts."

"Feeding to the dog? A good idea," Will said. "Matthew, John, what say we toss one out of the door at a time until we find the real Pickering?"

"A good idea," Mayhew replied. "Our dog has a frightful hunger."

Laughter rose up from the back of the group of cutthroats. Unable to see who had made the sound, Will jumped from the table and advanced. The cutthroats moved away from him.

In the middle of the room, Will scanned the faces slowly for any clue to the man who had laughed. A faint click reached his ears, and a second later the boards fell away beneath his feet.

CHAPTER 15

As Will surfaced from a deep, dark pool, the first thing he saw was the ruddy, grinning face of Pickering's jester filling his entire vision. "Life is an illusion," the jester hummed with a slight sibilance. "Laugh now, for there will be none of it when you are gone."

When the jester tumbled away with an insane giggle, Will was overwhelmed by the colours, sounds, and smells of his surroundings. Fiddle music soaring over a hundred drunken, clamouring voices. Woodsmoke and roasting pig, fat sizzling and spattering in the darting flames. Lanterns dancing on the awnings of stalls, the brightly coloured canvas glowing in reds, greens, and golds, banners on the tall poles flapping in the breeze. Jugglers and fire-eaters moved among the crowd, alongside the vendors selling hot pies and sausages. The Thieves' Fair had transformed a dirty courtyard constantly thrown into shade by the crumbling tenements into a sea of colour and life that raised the spirits of people dragged down by day-to-day survival.

Will turned his attention to Miller, who was bound to a wooden frame beside him. Beyond, Carpenter, Mayhew, and Launceston hung from a beam by their wrists, toes just resting on the cobbles. Their faces bloomed with bruises and cuts from a harsh beating.

"Tom, are you well?" Will called.

"No bones broken. When you fell through the trapdoor, they rushed us, and beat us with their cudgels. We took several of them with us as we went down, but that only inflamed them more."

Around the market, the thieves' strong-arm men patrolled with cudgels clutched in meaty fists. Glowering eyes watched every face for sign of trouble. Sizing up the force, Will reckoned they were a formidable barrier to any way out of that enclosed space.

"What now, Will? They mean to do us in, I fear," Miller said in a low voice.

"Keep steady. An opportunity will present itself."

"I am not afraid. Better to go this way, looking a man in the eye, than facing up to those things that should not exist in any sane world."

Miller held himself defiantly, despite the bonds. Will had decided he liked him, and admired the way he fought to keep his equilibrium in the face of knowledge that filled him with dread, but the fatalistic note in his voice was a concern.

"Tom, you must trust me," Will said. "I have stared into some dark and dismal holes in my short but exhilarating life, and yet here I am."

A commotion on the far side of the fair caught their eye as a torchlight procession made its way among the stalls. Cheers rose in its wake. When the parade drew near, Will saw the torches were held by young women in fine dresses, coquettishly flirting with the men they passed. They were accompanied by five men in the masks and costumes worn at the feast. At the head of the procession was a tall, wiry man in a robe embroidered with so much silver and gold thread it gleamed like a lantern in the reflected torchlight. He wore a white mask with a long, cruel bird's beak that arced down at the end and several peacock feathers sprouting from an elaborate headdress. It was flamboyant and unthreatening, but through the eyeholes Will glimpsed an aloof, menacing persona.

"Is that him?" Miller whispered. "Laurence Pickering?"

"We forced him to step out of the shadows," Will replied. "But he still wears his mask."

As Pickering led the procession forwards, Will saw more prisoners trailing behind them, bound with ropes and covered in blood and bruises, and at the back a cloaked figure who walked accompanied by two guards, but unbound. The prisoners appeared Spanish in dress and features, and from the way the crowd assailed them with threatening gestures and the occasional missile, Will guessed that was correct.

Pickering came to a halt in front of Will and looked him up and down silently.

"Life is an illusion," Will said wryly. "Laugh now, for there will be none of it when you are gone."

"You are far from the fields you know. This is my court now." Pickering rolled the words around his mouth like pebbles. A note of at least rudimentary education shaped his tone, which was a dangerous thing for a man brought up among the rough criminal class of London where the skill of cutting purses and handling a knife or a razor were taught at the mother's apron.

"You appear to lead a grand life. I am surprised your fame has not spread further afield," Will said.

"I do not seek attention. Indeed, I detest it. I am a private man—"

"And the work you do does not thrive in the full light of the sun."

Pickering hardly blinked, which added a strange, detached manner to his demeanour as though he were examining another species. "I would not appreciate more of your kind crawling around here like beetles on a dung-heap. And that is why I cannot allow you to return to your masters to tell them what you know."

"You think very highly of yourself. I have no interest in you, whatever title you give yourself, nor in your society of rogues. All I require is the return of an item that belongs to Her Majesty's government."

"I think not. I know your kind. Your pride has been hurt." Pickering motioned to the wooden frame and the taut bonds. "You would have to return to teach one such as me a lesson."

"I have far better things to do."

Pickering flinched as though Will had slapped him. "I am king here. I rule. I command men and women to do my bidding. I have riches at my disposal. I may act upon any whim. I have my own army. Your kind would prefer I did not exist. You think I—and all these good men and womenfolk—are the dirt beneath your feet. But you cannot dismiss me. And especially now, for I hold your life in my hands." Pickering fought to hide a quaver in his voice. Will gave a knowing smile that only angered the King of Cutpurses more.

Raising one hand imperiously, he snapped his fingers. From behind the prisoners, two of Pickering's men brought out a tall figure in a black robe. The Silver Skull glowed like the moon. With great bearing and dignity, hands clasped calmly in front of him, he looked directly into Will's face.

"Fine workmanship indeed, but that is little silver for a man of your standing," Will said. "Why, I would give you the same amount in gold to buy back that entertaining mask."

"You think me a fool too," Pickering noted. "The value of the thing lies beyond the silver."

Will looked deeply into the shadowy eyeholes of Pickering's mask. "And what did your cousin Bulle the hangman tell you of this thing?"

"I know that it is more than a mask. That some think it has a great power hidden within it. And I know interest in it reaches far beyond our shores."

Will's attention fell on the Spanish prisoners who glowered among the armed guards. "That is an interesting way to negotiate a sale with Spain."

"Do you take me for a traitor?" Pickering snapped. "Again, you show your contempt for me. I am as good a man as you, a true Englishman."

"Then I admit I am confused."

"It was my intention to arrange an exchange with the Spanish, and then to steal their gold. However, they proved their untrustworthiness and attempted to trick me first. Like you, they did not give me the respect I deserved, and so paid the price." He turned to examine the Spanish spies. "Or will do before the hour is out."

Since he had awakened, Will had been testing the bonds, but they were fastened with the thieves' reek-wort knot, considered to be unbreakable. "English gold would be much more rewarding," he said.

"And that will be my next port of call. Once you are dead, and there is no one to trace this business to me."

"You will not escape so easily. You have woken the beast now." Will's hard smile only emphasised the weight of his words.

"Do you fear death?" Pickering asked sharply.

"There are worse things than death. I have seen them."

"Will?" The female voice drifted out from the back of the prisoners, quizzical and slightly dazed. Will recognised it immediately.

"Grace?" He instantly regretted showing any sign of recognition, for Pickering immediately snapped those black, unblinking eyes towards him, and Will got the impression that beneath the mask he was smirking.

Pickering motioned for the guards to allow Grace to come forwards. Throwing back her hood, her eyes glistened with tears. "I am sorry, Will. I persuaded Kit to tell me where you had gone. The Spanish knew you and I were friends and they followed me here." She appeared dazed.

"Did they hurt you?" Will asked.

"No . . . no . . . They thought they could offer me in exchange if you acquired the item for which they were searching, but then we were all taken."

"Let her go," Will said quietly.

Pickering didn't answer, but Will could see he had no intention of freeing Grace. No one who had witnessed the role Pickering played could be allowed to leave Alsatia.

"Free her now," Will continued, "or, God help me, you will pay a price far in excess of anything you plan to do to us."

"You are in no position to make demands." Basking in the adulation of the cheering mass of criminals, Pickering stood for a moment with his arms raised to the sky. "Is it time for our entertainment?" he called across the fair. The crowd bayed its response. "Is it time for good sport?" Howls now, feverish eyes gleaming in the torchlight. "Let us celebrate our good fortune. We are the masters here. We can do anything."

Hammering their cudgels on the cobbles as they pressed in on every side, the mob appeared on the brink of rushing forwards to tear the prisoners limb from limb. The crowd parted as Pickering walked towards them in a parody of stateliness. At a snap of his fingers, four guards lifted the wooden frame from its mountings, and Will and the others were paraded through the fair behind the Spanish prisoners. Missiles rained down from all sides and the noise of bloodlust became deafening. Fearful, Grace eased herself close to Will's side, her hands pressed together in prayer.

On the far side of the fair, Pickering led the procession up the steps of a circular wooden arena about twenty feet across. The crowd eased around the perimeter, resting against a fence. "It is time for you to shake hands with Hob!" Pickering announced with a theatrical flourish.

In the pit below was a large brown bear, blind in one eye, patches of fur missing and covered in scars. From its roars and wild flailing it appeared half mad at the pain that had been inflicted upon it. In the centre of the small arena was a post used to tether the beast with a chain, but the bear had been set to roam free.

Pickering took his seat in a high-backed chair behind a long wooden table. A plate of hot pork and a flagon of ale were quickly laid before him by eager hands, and then the crowd began to chant. "Hob! Hob!"

Will watched the bear crash around the pit, swatting at the taunting spectators just out of reach of its claws. "I have danced with some ferocious partners, but that is the worst, no doubt," he mused.

Pickering pointed to one of the Spanish prisoners. A guard cut the man loose and before the prisoner could protest he was thrown into the pit. With a terrifying savagery, the bear tore him apart in a matter of seconds. Inflamed by the blood, the crowd cheered loudly.

Regally, Pickering waved for a second Spanish prisoner to be tossed to his death. He went silently and defiantly, with a proud bow to the Spaniard who was clearly his leader.

Sobbing, the third prisoner pleaded in babbling Spanish. It amused Pickering for a while until he became frustrated by his inability to understand and gestured for the prisoner to be sacrificed. With a scream, the Spanish agent plunged into the whirl of snapping jaws and raking claws.

Grimly, Will watched the spectacle. The bear moved awkwardly, the result of an injury to its left back leg. The blind eye also hampered its movements.

"My time is being wasted! Commit me now before I die of boredom!" he called.

Falling silent, the crowd looked to Pickering. Under their scrutiny, he flinched, fearful of losing face. "I accept your offer," he responded quickly. "But the bear appears to be winning this bout. Shall we make more competition?" The crowd cheered its response.

As Will was released, Pickering ordered the final Spanish prisoner to be set free too. Rubbing his wrists, the prisoner approached Will and said, "Don Alanzo de las Posadas." He bowed.

"Will Swyfte."

Pausing, Don Alanzo fixed Will with a quizzical eye. "England's greatest spy?"

"If my assistant, Nathaniel, were here, he would have a quick reply. But . . . I have been called worse names."

Don Alanzo bowed again. "And I am the world's greatest swordsman."

"And a spy too. We have much in common. Though I would be forced to challenge your title, in another place, at another time."

"For now, we are associates in battle." Don Alanzo turned to the bear pit. "Though I would have preferred more equal competition."

"We could give the bear a sword?" As he stepped towards the edge of the pit, Will whispered to Don Alanzo. "Stay on his left side."

Before Pickering's men could throw them in, Will and Don Alanzo jumped into the gore-splattered pit. In the enclosed space, the bear's roars were magnified, and the baying of the crowd faded into the background. The bear lunged with a massive swinging paw. Will ducked beneath it, the claws tearing chunks from the wooden planks covering the walls. Taking Will's advice, Don Alanzo danced into the bear's blind zone.

"Do you have a plan?" he called.

"Yes. Not to die."

"I expected something more detailed from someone with such an impressive reputation."

"Your patience will be amply rewarded." Will had a brief but shockingly evocative flash back more than a year to a snowy landscape and another bear threatening to end his life, but the image was lost as he fought to stay ahead of the claws.

The bear was fast, but its age and injuries had taken a toll on its stamina. Even so, Will's concealed sword was too small to cause any real harm to the beast, and he was afraid the weapon would only serve to enrage it further. Will and Don Alanzo continued to dart left, forcing the beast to flail around in a continual circle. Every time it attempted an attack, they put the central tethering post between them and the bear. Its frustration only made it waste more energy, and once again it began to lash out towards the crowd, who were hanging over the restraining fence, bellowing their frustration. Will caught sight of Pickering's beaked mask as he leaned forwards, his posture rigid. Will flashed a grin and bowed, which provoked Pickering to berate his guards angrily. They moved closer to the edge of the pit, but there was nothing they could do.

As they continued their baiting, Don Alanzo lost his footing in the grue and skidded into the bear's path. Driven into a frenzy by frustration, the bear roared and dropped its head low, throwing all its weight into a ferocious attack. Don Alanzo sprawled before it, unable to move.

Reacting instinctively, Will swung himself around the central pole and kicked both feet into the side of the bear's head. As it lumbered and half skidded in surprise, Will dragged Don Alanzo out of its path.

"Best not toy with him," Will said.

Barely had he scrambled halfway across the pit when the bear returned furiously, its jaws torn wide. Will flung himself to one side. The teeth snapped air a mere inch beyond his heel. Angered by Will's blow, the bear had found a new reserve of speed and strength, and it was all Will and Don Alanzo could do to keep away from its jaws and claws.

Each lunge came closer, and at the last Will ran, placed one foot on the wall of the pit, and propelled himself onto the bear's back, clutching an arm around its throat. The bear's roar was deafening as it attempted to swat him off. Writhing on its back, he ducked this way and that as the claws came within a hairbreadth of his face. But with each twist, he exerted more pressure on the bear's throat until its swats became feebler and it began to stumble. Finally, it fell to all fours and Will rolled off its back.

Don Alanzo levelled an unsettled stare at him. "You are insane."

"We only know we live when our heart beats faster," Will gasped. "Now, I think we are done here. Shall we be away?"

Before the bear had recovered, Will cupped his hands for Don Alanzo to propel himself to the top of the central pole. Half slipping, he steadied himself on the top and then leapt to the edge of the pit. Two of Pickering's men rushed him, but he ducked beneath their grasping hands, turned, and thrust both of them into the pit. As they shrieked in terror, he reached an arm down and hauled Will to safety.

In their brief glance was a mutual admission that the truce was over, and as Will turned to his men, Don Alanzo disappeared into the melee. Three of Pickering's men came at Will with cudgels and daggers. As they neared, confident in their numbers, Will activated the sheath Dee had given him. The blade burst out of its hidden compartment along his forearm, and with one fluid swing he slashed the throat of the first man and planted the knife edge into the heart of the next. Startled, the third man fell before an elbow rammed into his face.

The crowd roared its anger. Bounding to his men, Will slashed the restraining ropes. As they quickly freed themselves and turned to fight, Will fought his way through the crowd to where Pickering was rapidly disappearing into the throng. Before he gave pursuit, Will put his weight against the long table and heaved one end into the pit. The bear hesitated for only a second, and then launched itself up the table.

Chaos erupted across the fair as the bear crashed over the edge of the pit and into the crowd. The screams and shrieks were drowned out by roars as it tore through flesh and bone.

With grim determination, Will rammed his way through the fleeing people, throwing bodies right and left. Two conflicting targets fought for his attention: the Silver Skull and Grace, both of whom had been standing behind Pickering, held tight by his men. Now they were both lost in the swell.

In the confusion, stalls were overturned, their owners fighting furiously with their former customers. Shattered lanterns sent flames leaping to canvas and wood and then up into a blazing column that only added to the panic; in the city, fire was the greatest threat.

Through the whirling bodies, Will glimpsed a gleam of silver bobbing towards the other side of the courtyard. As he neared, he saw Don Alanzo leading the Silver Skull through the throng towards one of the alleys heading off the courtyard. Will cuffed a wild-eyed drunk who stumbled into his path and tossed him onto a stall, but Don Alanzo had now been lost to the torrent of people.

Above the hubbub, Pickering's barking orders rolled out. His men drew their attention from the bear, the fires, and the fights towards Don Alanzo, and Will.

Troubled that he could no longer see Grace, Will redoubled his efforts to break through the flow. When he finally emerged from the crowd, he caught a fleeting glimpse of Don Alanzo and the Silver Skull disappearing into the maze of alleys, but the cry of "Clubs!" was already rising up from Pickering's men as they surged towards him.

Will sprinted across the cobbles, but he had not got far when the chilling howl of a hunting dog echoed over Alsatia.

The Hunter was close and drawing closer.

CHAPTER 16

With her hood pulled low to hide her face, Grace sheltered behind the wreckage of a stall from the yelling crowd of cutthroats and customers washing back and forth between fire and the rampaging bear. Knots of Pickering's men beat paths through the mass. Certain they were searching for her, Grace regretted foolishly calling out Will's name; now Pickering would try to use her to control Will.

With frenzied roars, the lunging bear was surrounded by several men with staffs. Shrill screams echoed as raking claws tore one open from throat to groin, but within a minute the others forced the beast over the edge and back into the pit. A cheer went up, and as the bear's rage subsided, the panic receded. Grace knew she had to secure her escape while there was still some tumult to obscure her passing.

Keeping low, she edged around the stall until she glimpsed a path to one of the four alleys leading off the courtyard. Before she could move, a heavy hand fell on her shoulder.

Her startled cry was stifled by a hand over her mouth, and her head turned to reveal Miller's kind face. Grace recognised him instantly as one of the men who had been held prisoner alongside Will.

"Mistress, we must get you out of this danger," he said.

"Please," she begged, "Will is in great danger. You must help him."

"Will can take care of himself."

"No," she pressed. "I saw him in pursuit of Don Alanzo. The Spaniard will lead him into a trap—the Don has other allies in London. And the King of Cutpurses has dispatched his murderous crew on Will's heels. You must help him!"

Grace's pitiful expression moved Miller. "Very well. But stay here. I will fetch the others to help you—"

"Go!" she interrupted. "I will call if I need them."

With a nod, Miller threw his great frame in the direction Grace indicated. Glancing around, Grace spied Launceston, Mayhew, and Carpenter, who had now claimed cudgels and knives and were carving a path through Pickering's men with cold efficiency. They were too occupied to help her.

Determination blazed inside her. She would not be beaten down, nor afraid. Jenny's death had convinced her that life was hard, and easily cut short, and that living in fear only diminished it further. Setting her jaw, she waited for the path to the alley to clear again, and then leapt from her hiding place and ran.

Few women were there, and most of them were doxies or members of the criminal gang, but she moved swiftly without drawing attention to herself. For a while she was caught up in a hectic attempt to put out the blazes, but eventually the alley appeared in reach. Yet as her heart beat faster in anticipation, in the corner of her eye she caught sight of a bird mask fixed upon her, and for the briefest moment, she was caught in Pickering's unblinking stare. With no men close to hand, Pickering gave pursuit himself. Barging through the crowd, he closed the gap so quickly Grace knew that even if she reached the alley, he would be upon her soon after.

The clatter of his hobnails upon the cobbles rang at her back. With her breath burning in her chest, she slipped into the dark of the alley and only when her eyes adjusted did she realise it was occupied. Her startled cry faded at a familiar face.

"Kit!" she cried. "And Nathaniel!"

With a small group of the queen's men at their backs, Marlowe and Nathaniel advanced on the courtyard. Marlowe had his sword drawn, but Grace fell into his arms in relief.

"Thank God," she gasped. Glancing back, she saw Pickering come to a halt when he saw the new arrivals, and then turn and rush back into the crowd.

"Nat urged me to bring help when Will did not return by the appointed hour," Marlowe said. He turned to the men. "Seal off this courtyard. Let no man escape, for we will have an army of rogues at our back if word gets out that we are here."

"Will pursues a Spanish spy, and another of your men has gone to help," Grace said. "You must aid him—"

The words died in her throat as the howl of the hunting dog rose up again, this time laced with an insistent bloodlust. It had located its prey.

CHAPTER 17

The twisting routes among the tenements were impenetrably dark, the buildings too high to allow the moonlight to reach the ground. Only the occasional glimmer of candlelight gleamed in the black windows. Will's footsteps echoed off the walls like stones dropped on ice. From somewhere ahead of him, a similar noise resounded, and from behind came the tramp of many boots as Pickering's men fanned out through the maze of byways. Their lanterns flickered like fireflies as they searched doorways and side alleys.

At a crossroads, he realised the footsteps ahead had slowed. Keeping close to a wall, he edged forwards until whispering voices emerged from the gloom, speaking Spanish. Another voice responded, mellifluous but with an unsettling note of menace.

Tracing the low conversation along an alley to another courtyard large enough to be filled with silvery moonlight, Will found Don Alanzo and the Silver Skull with the Hunter. Beside him, his dog's red eyes sparked.

Keeping well to the shadows where he could not be seen, Will spied on the scene, but within an instant the dog's hackles rose and it released a low, threatening growl. Peering directly at Will, the Hunter gave a knowing smile.

Will expected the Hunter to set his dog loose, but instead he removed an item from the pouch at his belt and kept it hidden in his palm.

Stepping out from the shadows, Will said, "You keep dishonourable company, Don Alanzo."

Don Alanzo eyed the Hunter. "A mercenary from Flanders."

"More than that. And worse." Will strode forwards, keeping his right arm and Dee's blade hidden behind his back.

"Leave here, Will Swyfte, as quickly as you can," Don Alanzo said. "I offer this advice as a courtesy. In return for you saving my life in the bear pit, I now save yours."

Don Alanzo's words could have been glib arrogance regarding his skills as a swordsman, but Will heard a powerful note of truth in them. "I cannot leave without the Silver Skull," Will responded. "I have been entrusted with the task of returning it to the Tower."

"Him," Don Alanzo snapped. "Not it. There is a man beneath this mask, and he has been held prisoner in this Godforsaken country for twenty years. You claim to be the civilised defenders of the true way, righteously holding back the conspiracy of barbarians beyond your borders, but you commit atrocities without a second thought. You persecute good Catholics—"

"Because you persecute us. You and your allies will not be happy until England is a memory."

"Arrogance finds a good home in this country. You believe any action you take is justified, and so you are capable of anything, without even a glimmer of guilt. You are blind to the blood on your hands and the brutality that lurks behind every sneering face in your court. You have turned away from God and Rome, but your sins run deeper by far."

"The one that stands beside you is more dangerous than any Englishman, and capable of worse things by far. He smiles and calls you friend, but he plays you like a lute."

"That may well be," Don Alanzo replied. "But for now we have a common enemy, and so we walk shoulder to shoulder."

Will knew there was no point arguing with Don Alanzo, but before he could act, Miller emerged from the alley on the other side of the courtyard. Signalling to Will that he was going to attack, he was brought up sharp by the sight of the Hunter and his dog. In a single moment of hesitation, all Miller's fears played out across his face, followed by a furious internal battle as the man Walsingham had recognised put those concerns to one side. Gripping his dagger tightly, Miller attacked.

Though he didn't make a sound, he'd barely got halfway across the courtyard before the Hunter sensed his presence. Will watched a smile flicker across the Hunter's lips, but it was too late to call out. The Hunter didn't turn until Miller was almost upon him, and then he whirled fluidly and grabbed Miller's wrist before he could plunge the dagger home.

As Will raced to help, the Hunter let slip the leash and his dog bounded forwards, its deep, rumbling growl turning the pit of Will's stomach. Will held the blade before him, but the dog didn't attack; it simply marked a line between the Hunter and Will and moved back and forth along it, holding Will at bay with the snap of its huge jaws every time he tried to pass it.

The Hunter didn't attempt to hurt Miller. Still smiling, he pulled Miller towards him by the wrist with a slow, relentless ease, even though the terrified farm boy used all his strength to resist. When he was close, the Hunter leaned in and whispered in Miller's ear.

Instantly, Miller grew still, his eyes widening. The Hunter pulled back, his smile now taking a different note, and he let go of Miller's wrist, which remained aloft for a second before his arm slumped to his side.

"Tom! Pay him no heed!" Will called, unable to round the snapping dog.

Miller appeared unable to hear. His shoulders slumped, he walked in a daze away from the Hunter, Don Alanzo, and the Silver Skull to the dark shadows on the edge of the courtyard, where he slid down the wall and came to rest with his head in his hands.

"I will extract a harsh price for any harm you have caused him," Will said.

Eyes glittering, the Hunter stared back, silently mocking.

As the dog returned to its master's side, the tension broke. Thirty of Pickering's men surged into the courtyard from different alleys. Turning slowly, Don Alanzo looked directly into each face as if searching for something he couldn't find. Despite the overwhelming force, he appeared completely at ease.

Turning back to Will, he said, "This is my final warning. Move away from here and do not look back."

His words were filled with such a powerful gravity that Will walked slowly backwards until rough hands grabbed his arms and held him tight. He continued to study Don Alanzo and the Hunter, trying to anticipate what was to come; but if one thing convinced him of the extent of the potential threat, it was their complete calmness in the face of cudgels and knives.

"This Spaniard is an Abraham-man," the leader of Pickering's men said in the thieves' cant. The ragged scar that ran from his left temple to his right cheek only emphasised his expression of mocking contempt. "Or he's been too long in the boozing ken. You know I cut bene whids—he carries no sword and there are thirty of us good copesmates! Let us have him!"

He beckoned the others with a hand missing two fingers and advanced on Don Alanzo and the Silver Skull. Will still expected the Hunter to unleash his dog, but instead the Hunter opened the palm of his hand to reveal a blue jewel as big as a coin which shimmered with the reflected light of the moon.

"See, lads! They offer us their riches to buy their lives. We shall have that . . . and their lives!" The scarred man gave a mocking laugh.

As the scarred man stepped forwards, the Hunter calmly fitted the jewel into an almost-invisible indentation on the Silver Skull's forehead. A loud click brought the scarred man to a suspicious halt. The Hunter whispered in the Silver Skull's ear. He wrung his hands in anguish, and tried to turn away, but the Hunter caught his arm in a tight grip. Don Alanzo whispered in the Skull's other ear in a manner that appeared to be calming. After a moment, the Silver Skull began to shake, and Will was convinced that beneath the mask he was trying to control deep sobs. Then, with a desperate resignation, he raised one hand to his temple and half bowed his head as though in deep thought.

The actions were strange enough to bring the band of thugs to a puzzled halt.

As Will studied the Silver Skull, a barely perceptible change came over the mask, perhaps a slight change in the quality of the moonlight it reflected, or a barely audible noise as though it were a tuning fork vibrating.

The scarred man flinched, his hand involuntarily going to his throat. He coughed once and spluttered. When it passed, his mocking smile returned. But only for a moment. Within seconds he was reeling, tearing at his face and arms and fighting for breath, eyes wide with panic.

The rest of Pickering's men were rooted in horror. The hands holding Will fell away, and he stepped quickly back through their ranks into the shadows at the edge of the alley.

The scarred man's skin blackened as if burned by an invisible fire. It spread quickly across his face, then down his arms, and his skin cracked like a muddy track beneath the hot sun. Blisters erupted everywhere, covering every part of him within seconds, forcing his eyes shut and deforming his lips. One by one the blisters burst to release foul yellow pus. As blood streamed from the corners of his eyes, his nose, his ears, his flesh began to liquefy, and he fell to his knees in a growing puddle, clawing at the areas where sticky bone was now visible.

Watching his death throes, Pickering's men crossed themselves or whispered prayers, but the spectacle kept them fixed.

Finally, the scarred man pitched forwards onto the cobbles and lay still. Will had observed something similar, in a village not far from Darmstadt when the plague had struck. But there the death had been slow, over days, not a matter of seconds. Yet he could see now what the Silver Skull was: an engine of disease, powered by the will of the one who wore it. All it required to operate was the key: the jewel the Hunter had fitted to it.

His impression was proved correct when first one, then ten, then all of Pickering's men began to experience the initial symptoms. In no time at all, the disease had leapt among them, driving them to their knees in an agonising death.

With horror, Will realised why the Enemy was so determined to gain the Skull: if thirty men could be brought down so quickly, where was the end of it? A street? A city? An entire country? Perhaps even the greatest army could be wiped away in the blink of an eye. With the Skull under their control, all Dee's defences amounted to nothing, and England was left naked and on the brink of becoming a charnel pit.

A tingling began in the tips of his fingers and his throat began to close. The Silver Skull looked directly at him. Before the disease rushed through Will, Don Alanzo caught the Skull's arm and guided him away with a gentle tug. The Hunter and his dog were nowhere to be seen. Don Alanzo gave Will a slight bow, the scales now balanced, and moved quickly away across the courtyard into the dark beyond, with the Skull beside him.

Will attempted to give pursuit, but his head was swimming and his legs were like jelly, even at the merest touch of the Skull's power. By the time he had recovered, Don Alanzo and the Skull had disappeared into the maze of Alsatia, and within moments, the whinny of a horse was followed by the crack of a whip and the rattle of carriage wheels.

Miller stumbled over, unscathed, a deep-seated horror burned into his eyes. "Will, I failed you," he croaked.

"You did what you could, as do we all. Come." As they headed back, Will added, "Whatever he said to you, ignore it. They lie. That is what they do."

Miller did not respond.

At the scene of the Thieves' Fair, Will was surprised to find that Marlowe and a group of the queen's men had rounded up the collection of rogues in one corner of the courtyard, where they were being held at sword point. Several bodies of those who had resisted lay on the cobbles as a lesson to the others.

Grace ran over and grasped Will's hand tightly. "You are safe," she said with relief. "I prayed for your return."

"You should not be here Grace," he scolded. "But I am glad to see you well." He motioned to Nathaniel to take Grace to one side.

"She only wished for knowledge of her sister," Nathaniel said quietly. "Do not treat her harshly."

The weight of what he had witnessed lay heavily on Will. With the weapon in the Enemy's hands, time was rapidly running out. He sought out Marlowe and said, "Kit, I thank you for coming to my aid. Now, bring me Pickering, the King of Cutpurses. I have some hard questions for him."

Marlowe motioned to Pickering's costume topped by the bird mask lying in a heap on the cobbles. "Mistress Seldon tells me this was his disguise."

"Then once again he hides among his people." Will eyed the sullen mass of rogues.

"If you do not know his looks, then you will never find him among that rabble, Will."

Will considered his options, and then said, "Bring the men to me one at a time."

As the pageant of glowering men trailed past, Will studied the size, the gait, and most importantly the eyes: Pickering's unwavering stare was unforgettable. Many he dismissed immediately, too squat, too large, too grey. A few he spent a moment considering. But there was one who at first appeared wrong, until Will realised he was feigning a limp and walking with his left shoulder stooped. He kept his gaze down, until Will forced him to look up. The unblinking black eyes were coldly familiar.

"The King of Cutpurses," Will said wryly. "Your nobility is about to be tested."

Pickering responded only with a defiant stare.

Will turned to Marlowe. "Take him to the Tower."

CHAPTER 18

"A lady, in Alsatia, amid the greatest rogues of London? What did you expect?" Will said angrily as he marched down the Long Corridor from the State Rooms to the wing set aside by Walsingham.

"And this is where I hear your lecture about recklessness again, I suppose?" Grace responded without flinching.

He could see her temper was hot and she would fight him every step of the way, as always. "You risked a great many things, including death."

"If you kept me informed, I would not have to take risks."

"So it is my fault?" he blazed.

"Stop treating me like a little girl."

"Then trust me. If I discover anything about Jenny, I will tell you."

She grew sullen. "It is not simply about Jenny, and you know that."

His own anger drained away as he saw clearly the young girl who raced to him through the garden whenever he visited Jenny. "You cannot protect me in the work I do," he said.

"And you cannot bring Jenny back by protecting me. Nor can you erase the pain of her loss. But we cannot help ourselves, can we? We are both cursed to repeat our mistakes, trying to save the one person who reminds us of that time when all was right with the world."

She looked away sharply. He knew it was because tears had sprung to her eyes, but she would not show him what she perceived to be a weakness. Much of what she said was true, he knew, but Grace was more to him than a symbol of what had been lost. In the midst of his own grief, he had been devastated to see the effect of Jenny's disappearance on her. It had torn out her heart at first, and then replaced her happiness with a slow-burning bitterness. He cared for her deeply, and he would not have her suffer any more.

Grace saw him wrestling with her account of his motivations and softened. "Jenny haunts us both. The manner of her passing . . . here one moment and then gone, no body to bury or grieve, no truthful account, only guesses and hints and what-might-have-beens . . . Neither of us can find rest while there are so many questions still to answer, and no likely answers forthcoming." She bit her lip and looked away out of the window to where the servants carried cuts of ham to the kitchens from the back of a wagon.

"This is not the life either of us would have chosen, but it is the one we have," he said. "You have accepted that Jenny is gone for there is no evidence to show otherwise. That is sensible. I believe she is still alive because there is no evidence to show she is dead. Less sensible, perhaps, but it is all I am capable of doing. Whatever happened that day is lost to us. For now. But I have seen . . ." He caught himself. "I do not believe the world is as simple as most people accept. There are spaces in it for strange things to happen."

"For Jenny still to be alive?" she mocked.

"Perhaps."

"You hold on to a ghost and it slowly sucks the life from you. You will never find peace, or happiness, while you look back, and while you grip tightly to fantasies, and ask question upon question. You are here, now. You must take some joy . . . some love . . . or all will be wasted."

"I only ever wanted my Jenny. She was right for me. There will be no other."

Grace turned away from him, pretending to examine the servants once again.

"Whatever happened to her, she is still with me every day," he continued, "here and here." He touched his temple and his breastbone. "I would not give up that to dull what pain I feel."

"If one of us is the child here, wishing and hoping, it is not I," she said brusquely. "I will continue to search for answers in my own way. And if you continue to keep secrets from me, I will be forced to go to even greater lengths."

Watching her march back along the corridor, head down, cheeks burning, Will felt a deep sadness for what she had lost, and a determination that she would, at least, have a happier life ahead. If he failed Grace, he failed Jenny; he failed in everything.

Putting aside his emotions, he made his way to the Tryst Rooms, where Henry had attempted to woo Ann Boleyn, away from the scrutiny of his wife. They were now set aside for Walsingham's use, and lay on the second floor above the hall that Dee had christened the Black Gallery.

Nursing their wounds, Mayhew sat gloomily in one corner, drinking wine despite the earliness of the hour, while Launceston and Carpenter ate bread and sausage as they turned over the previous night's events.

"Where is Tom?" Will asked.

"Away brooding," Launceston replied.

"I would not have him on his own after what he saw."

Mayhew let out a theatrical sigh. "We cannot mollycoddle the boy. He must learn to deal with these things, as we all have."

"He did not have the benefit of a slow admission to the secrets of the world, as we have," Will replied. "Find him and bring him here."

Cursing quietly, Mayhew levered himself from his chair and sloped out.

Carpenter pushed his plate away and growled, "At least the failure of this mission left no one dead. Or scarred."

"There are no failures, and no victories either, you know that. Just a constant shifting back and forth, with casualties on both sides. That is the true tragedy of our war: it will never be won."

"Defeatist." Carpenter sniffed. Then: "I presume Walsingham will want to hold someone accountable for our failure to recover the Silver Skull."

"Again, John, no failure, however much you want to apportion blame. This struggle continues. We have reached a turn in the road, and we must embark on another direction."

"Yet we still do not know what this Silver Skull does," Launceston said, "or why it is so important to the Enemy. Perhaps it is simply meant to distract us from the real threat."

"All will become clear in time," Will replied. So far he had only told Walsingham what he had witnessed of the Skull's capabilities, and Miller had been sworn to silence, although the disease-powers appeared to be the last thing on his mind.

Nathaniel appeared at the door to the Tryst Rooms and summoned Will over. "Lord Walsingham is ready for you now," he said. "Should I be prepared for fanfares and fawning crowds?"

"Not this time, Nat. This matter is still a tangled web, which requires some unpicking."

Nathaniel held the door open. "A case not concluded in time for an ordinary in the tavern? Your reputation is in danger."

"We all have our bad days, and I fear this one will get worse before it gets better."

They took Walsingham's black carriage and followed the cluttered, noisy streets east to the Tower. As was often the case, Nathaniel pretended to show no interest in the matter under investigation while asking oblique, circuitous questions in an attempt to assuage his curiosity. And as was usual, Will pretended not to notice, and batted them away with an insouciant manner. It was a game between friends, but with serious intent: in his ignorance, Nathaniel rattled the cage door, but Will had made it his business never to let him realise what beast lurked within.

The carriage was admitted through the main gates of the Tower into a furious hive of activity, the like of which Will had not seen before. Soldiers brought weapons from the Tower's armoury, while other groups escorted bruised and battered prisoners to the cells for interrogation.

Will ordered Nathaniel to stay with the carriage, and then sought Walsingham out in his rooms in the White Tower. In a room filled with charts and documents, Will found him making plans for England's defences with a small army of advisors. The atmosphere was strained, the advisors failing to grasp the urgency of Walsingham's requests. By their reckoning, an invasion was weeks away, at the earliest, and his suggestion that disaster could strike within hours or days filled them with incredulity. Will realised he had never seen Walsingham lose his temper, but there was a frightening intensity about him that Will had witnessed before on occasion; in those times he appeared capable of anything.

Once the advisors had been dismissed, Walsingham led Will along the corridors and down the winding stairs into the bowels of the White Tower.

"It would be easier if you could guide them with more than hints and innuendo," Will said.

"That is our burden," Walsingham replied. "Only a very few understand the true nature of the war we fight. The rest must accept our guidance on faith alone."

"No sign of Don Alanzo or the Silver Skull?"

"Our informants watch all the highways out of London, and the ports of Kent and Norfolk, Sussex and Dorset. They have vanished like the mist."

"You have informed the queen?"

"Of only the most basic details. One must walk a line between providing an adequate summation of the threat facing the nation and leaving the monarch paralysed by fear." Walsingham waited for the guards to unlock a large, iron-studded door before continuing. "We have struggled with the outbreak of disease many times during Elizabeth's reign. The thought that such devastation could be unleashed by an enemy in the blink of an eye, in one of our cities, perhaps even in London itself, is beyond the comprehension of most minds. But we know the depths to which the Enemy will go to destroy us. And the Spanish, of course, would seize upon such internal chaos to launch an invasion from without. We are in a state of high alert— England's future hangs by a thread. Never have matters been so critical."

"Then we cannot afford to delay here," Will said. "Pickering is our only link to the Skull, and the Enemy's plans."

At the foot of the stairs, in the deepest part of the White Tower, they were confronted by another oaken door flanked by two guards, who unlocked it and closed it swiftly behind them. The room beyond was vast and unpleasantly gloomy. A handful of torches at large intervals created a permanent twilight that obscured many of the workings of that place. Occasional moans or cries emerged from the shadows, like the haunting voices of lost souls, and there was a heavy stink of excrement, urine, and blood.

A tall man in his early forties, fair-haired, with bright eyes and an easy smile, walked out of the dark to greet them. He clasped his hands before him with an expression of continual glee. Jeremiah Kemp, England's torturer-in-chief, enjoyed his work.

A constant succession of Catholic spies, and potential spies, criminals, traitors, and informants passed through his doors, Jesuit priests, minor aristocrats, lawyers, farmers, gentlewomen, and wealthy merchants. Kemp treated them all with equal care and attention.

"Welcome, my Lord Walsingham, Master Swyfte," he said with a shy smile and a deep bow. "All is ready for you."

"Pickering?" Walsingham asked.

"He has been softening. Please come and see." Kemp led them past every imaginable device of human torture to one of the wooden posts that supported the ceiling of that underground chamber. From near the top of the pillar, Pickering hung from an iron bar supported by staples in the wood, his hands fastened into iron gauntlets attached to the bar. It was a deceptively simple instrument. The weight of the suspended body caused the flesh in the arms to swell, creating the agonising sensation that blood was about to burst from the end of every finger.

His face drawn and badly bruised, Pickering watched them with dazed eyes.

"Are you ready to confess?" Walsingham asked him.

"I am but a lowly thief," Pickering croaked. "I know nothing of these matters of state." His weak voice sounded truthful, but Will caught the briefest shadow flicker in his eyes.

"You like games?" Will asked. "Chess?"

Pickering eyed him hatefully.

"The pawns are removed from the game early. There is little to be gained by extending their lives."

"Unless they are clever pawns, with aspirations to rise to be the true power on the board." Pickering's eyes gleamed.

Will nodded. "Then we know where we stand." Turning to Kemp, he said, "Let us introduce our guest to the Duke of Exeter's Daughter."

"Certainly, Master Swyfte." Kemp clapped his hands to summon the guards to bring Pickering down from his perch. Though he had only been on the pillar for a short while, his legs were too weak to support his weight.

The guards dragged him to the end of the chamber where the rack stood before a row of candles, a wooden bed stained with bodily fluids, a ratchet system for turning at one end.

"The Duke of Exeter was an inventive man when he was the constable of the Tower, and he devised this method to ensure full truth and honesty from those he entertained," Will said. "You are aware how this works?"

Pickering shook his head, but his expression suggested his imagination was already hard at work.

"The arms and legs are fastened thusly. This winch is turned, which extends the rack here, and here, and so the guest's limbs are stretched. I am told the pain is very great indeed, in the joints in particular. If the turning of the winch is continued, the limbs are dislocated, and eventually torn free."

"I will tell all you wish to know," Pickering said.

"Unfortunately, it is already too late for that," Will replied. "The moment has long since passed for caution. We can no longer risk wasting time on dissembling and half-truths in the hope that you might find some small advantage for yourself."

Pickering's face drained of blood as he realised what Will was saying. "You will torture me, even though I will tell you what you want to know?"

"Every act we perform in this dark room destroys our humanity a little more," Will said. "We strip our souls by degrees. But we are small men, all of us, and meaningless in the vast sweep of the nation's life. When we are gone, we shall be forgotten, but for now we have a part to play. The men and women of England deserve to live free, and earn their crust, and laugh and play, and sleep easy every night, free from fear. I gladly sacrifice my life to buy that liberty for them." He paused. "And I would gladly sacrifice your life for the same."

Walsingham nodded to the guards. Pickering's feeble struggles were quickly overpowered, but his mounting cries reverberated off the stone walls. Calming a little once he was strapped to the rack by his wrists and ankles, he began to babble everything he thought his captors wanted to hear.

Will stood back until the rack had been tightened to the point where every incremental turn of the winch pulled a cry of agony from Pickering. "You are inhuman!" he screamed.

"We are," Will said. "No good man should ever submit another to these deprivations. It would behoove neither of us to say you brought this upon yourself. Nor should we consider it a punishment, for I pass no judgment on you. But at this point all men and women in England are at risk of the worst death imaginable. I weigh my own soul, and your agonies, against that. Now, let us proceed slowly and carefully, so there is no room for doubt. You are the cousin of Bulle, the Tyburn hangman. Is that true?"

"Yes, yes, yes!"

Walsingham watched Will, curious to see where the line of questioning would take him.

"I am always troubled by seemingly random connections," Will stated. "This business began with the execution of Mary, Queen of Scots, at the hands of Bulle. Now his cousin is involved in the next stage. By chance?" Will shook his head. "What did Bulle learn at Fotheringhay?"

It took a moment for Pickering to stifle his sobs, and then he began, "Mary . . . Mary delayed her execution for hours, through pleas, and prayers, and lies, and deceit."

"That is true," Walsingham said.

"There was nothing to gain by delaying her execution. She was not afraid to die."

"Why, then?" Will pressed.

"She was waiting. For . . . for news of the discovery of the Key to the Silver Skull."

"No news could reach her in Fotheringhay," Walsingham said. "Guards were at the door of her chamber continually. All letters in and out were carefully scrutinised." He nodded to Kemp to turn the winch another notch.

When Pickering's screams had died, the King of Cutpurses cried with a raw throat, "What I say is true. She did receive news by . . ." He looked from face to face fearfully. "You will not believe me, but it is true!"

"Go on," Will said.

"By a mirror. A magic mirror!" He screwed his eyes shut and waited for the pain to lance through his joints. Kemp poised with one hand on the winch.

"A magic mirror," Will mused. "That is how the Enemy communicates?"

"Their own mirrors? Or all mirrors?" Walsingham queried aloud. "Should we remove every looking glass from the Palace of Whitehall? Are they spying on us as we look into our own faces?"

"'Tis true," Pickering gasped, relieved. "That is how Bulle told it to me. He spied upon Mary through the secret passage that ran behind her chamber."

"He knew of that?" Walsingham asked.

"He bribed the captain of the sheriff's guard," Pickering continued, still desperately eager to please. "Many of the women brought to execution offered their bodies to Bulle in return for their freedom, or at the least a quick end. He took them regardless. This time, he thought . . . perhaps—"

"With a queen?" Walsingham said, disgusted.

"Mary was renowned for her skills between the sheets," Pickering noted.

"So, while Bulle spied on Mary in the hope that he could steal favours from her, he saw her speaking at the mirror?" Will enquired.

"Yes! As my cousin told it to me, the glass grew cloudy, as if the smoke of a great fire billowed within it. From his vantage point, he could not see any face within it, but he could hear a voice."

"What kind of voice?" Walsingham asked.

"A man. Or something that purported to be a man. It told Mary that the key had been recovered . . . from the crypt beneath the Holy Rood—"

"The palace in Edinburgh." Will wondered how long the Enemy's plan had been in motion; when had they first seized control of Mary to manipulate their way into the Palace of Holyroodhouse to search for the key? Months ago? Years? Had she always been under their control, as they slipped into the spaces and the weaknesses between human prejudices?

"And then the voice proceeded to tell Mary about the plot to steal the Silver Skull from the Tower, and the time and the date."

"And Bulle passed this information on to you, for you to find some way to gain financial advantage from a blow against England itself," Will said sharply. "You did not pass this on to the authorities. You sought only your own personal gain. That is treason in and of itself." He nodded to Kemp to tighten the winch another notch.

Pickering's shrieks ended in a series of juddering sobs. "I did not seek to harm my country or my queen!" he wailed. "I simply saw an opportunity."

"As all men of business do," Will said sardonically.

"I planned to return the Skull to the authorities—"

"Once you had played England and Spain off against each other, and grown fat on the proceeds. What else did Bulle tell you?"

"Nothing."

"Nothing that you remember?"

"No."

Will gave the nod to Kemp, who tightened the rack another notch. Briefly, Pickering blacked out from the pain, and when he finally came round, Will said, "Jog your memory, while your limbs are still attached."

Babbling incoherently, Pickering eventually attempted to run through everything his cousin had told him, one drunken night in the Bear in Alsatia. It was only after two more turns of the winch that he recalled something new.

"The voice said . . . they still search . . . beneath the palace," he gasped.

"For what?"

"I do not remember! I . . . I . . ." Kemp moved a hand onto the winch. "A shield! Yes, my cousin said a shield!"

"A shield," Walsingham repeated.

"Thank you for your time," Will said to Pickering. "You have been most helpful. Now, I believe Master Kemp has some further questions for you on other matters."

From a brown leather bag, Kemp removed a sheaf of documents an inch thick. Pickering began to sob gently.

As Will and Walsingham made their way back to the light, Walsingham mused, "The Shield. The third and final item required for the Silver Skull's operation. It lies—or lay—beneath the Palace of Holyroodhouse. The Enemy searched at the time of Mary's execution, but do they now have the object they sought?"

"If the Enemy had the Shield, the Hunter would have used it in Alsatia," Will replied. "As it was, the Skull's power was only released briefly, the display stopped before it could do harm to all present. It was a warning to us . . . mockery, perhaps . . . nothing more."

"My agents in Hertfordshire reported a black carriage moving north at great speed, all curtains drawn. It did not stop at the usual places," Walsingham said.

"Then I will be away to Edinburgh within the hour," Will announced. "There may still be hope if we act swiftly."

"Godspeed," Walsingham said. "But remember, Scotland and England may now have a steady relationship, but Dee's defences do not extend beyond the border. The Enemy has always thrived on the lonely moors and misty mountains of that northern land, aye, and in their cities too. One reason why King James is so keen to bring England into an even closer embrace. It is said he rankles nightly to his advisors about yawning churchyards, straw dolls in babies' cribs, and the threat that waits for him and all Scotsmen under the Hill of Yews. You must watch your back at all times."

"Nathaniel will do that for me. Our spies in Edinburgh are to be trusted?"

"As much as any. I will alert them to your arrival."

"No," Will said. "Let my arrival be a surprise. I will contact them when I reach the north."

In the carriage on the journey back to the Palace of Whitehall, Will ordered Nathaniel to pack his bags to accompany him on the journey to Edinburgh.

"Scotland." Nathaniel sighed. "I hear it is a place of hard, grey skies and a constant drizzle that dampens the spirit as much as the clothes."

"But you'll have the joy of my company, and such learned and witty discourse that many would pay for such a privilege." Will watched the faces pass the window, afraid that with every one he would see some sign of disease starting to flower.

"My heart sings already," Nathaniel replied.

In the courtyard next to the Black Gallery, the carriage pulled into a stream of activity, with several servants accompanying the court physician and bystanders whispering in doorways. Almost as ashen as Launceston's natural complexion, Mayhew dashed from the Black Gallery and tore open the carriage door.

"What is wrong?" Will enquired. "The queen—?"

Mayhew shook his head. "The boy."

He led Will at speed from the Black Gallery through the Tryst Rooms and into a loft where pigeons cooed. The physician was just leaving as they arrived, shaking his head as they passed.

Miller hung by the neck from one of the rafters.

Sickened, Will could not speak for a moment as he tried to comprehend the torments the youth must have suffered after his encounter with the Hunter. He cursed himself for not doing more to ease Miller's pain, and for failing to protect one in his charge.

"Cut him down," Will ordered.

"I searched for him as you said," Mayhew stuttered, "and could not find him anywhere until one of the servant girls came here for a tryst with her love and—"

"Cut him down!"

Mayhew hastily complied. Once the youth was laid on the dusty boards, Will collected him in his arms and carried him down to the Tryst Rooms. Although he had only known Miller for a matter of hours, he felt the death more personally than any he had experienced in recent months.

"We failed him," he said to Mayhew as he laid the body on a table.

"We did what we could," Mayhew replied. "The knowledge of the Enemy affects all of us in different ways. We cannot predict the outcome. We can only hope."

"We did not do all we could have," Will stated. "He was thrust into this battle too soon, without proper precautions."

"Desperate times—"

"Quiet!" Will snapped. "Many people killed this youth and they will all have to carry it on their conscience—our side, who engaged him in activities beyond him, those who stole the Silver Skull and ensured he would be forced into battle too soon, but most of all the Enemy . . . the Hunter." Will recalled the Hunter whispering in Miller's ear, the grinding expression of confusion, then the horror that bloomed in his face at whatever had been said. "He was murdered at that moment, though it took some time to take effect. But know this: there is a price to be paid here, and I will ensure it is extracted from that Hunter the next time we meet. So do I vow!"

Will studied Miller's face, which even in death contained the innocence that he had carried like a torch. He tried to recall the last time he had felt that warm innocence himself, but it had long since been driven out of him.

"Fetch me parchment and a quill," he said desolately. "I shall write to his father myself."

CHAPTER 19

"Can this thing not go any faster?" Will bellowed over the thunder of the carriage wheels on the rutted lane winding through the night-dark Scottish lowlands. Hanging out of the window, he clutched the rail on top of the carriage to stop himself being thrown clear.

"Not unless you want to risk pitching down the bank into the valley," the driver yelled back. Even so, he cracked his whip and the horses increased their pace, but the carriage immediately slewed onto one wheel, skidding sideways across the mud before crashing back with an impact that threatened to shatter the axle.

The road had been treacherous ever since they had left England behind, winding around the side of great hills still touched by snow on the top, or ploughing across valley bottoms beside sucking bogs. Horses would have been quicker, but the carriage allowed them to sleep while travelling, and to remain out of sight of prying eyes.

Glancing behind, Will could just make out the silhouettes of their pursuers against the star-dappled sky as they crested a ridge: three of them on horseback, riding as if hell were at their backs. Will had known the Enemy would attempt to prevent his journey at some point, but when the riders had appeared from the trees in the carriage's wake four miles back, their arrival had still felt like a winter storm.

Cloaks billowing behind them like bat wings, the riders moved inexorably closer. Recalling the maps he had memorised before their journey began more than seven days ago, he peered into the dark landscape flashing by to try to get his bearings. Away in the valley was the River Esk, and he could see the bulk of Rosslyn Castle rising up from the dense forest. That meant Edinburgh was only six miles away, but the riders would have caught them long before then.

He threw himself back inside the carriage where Nathaniel clung on for dear life. "Spanish or highwaymen?" Nathaniel asked.

"Being a poor fellow, you have nothing to offer either, so do not alarm yourself."

"I suppose you will be playing the hero at some point." He sniffed. "Have some regard for my life while you seek to bolster your own fame."

"Nat, you are first and foremost in my mind, as always."

The carriage careered to the left as the road followed the contours of the hill. Once again the left wheels lifted, this time so high it seemed the carriage was going over. Bags and cases flew around the interior, and Nathaniel crashed across the leather seats. As the wheels went down, it threw him back the other way.

"Damnation!" he shouted. "I could drive this carriage better myself!" Exhausted and hungry, his temper had deteriorated during the long journey from London, on which they had stopped only briefly to change horses and eat, sleeping in the carriage as it bounced north along the lanes of England.

"We will soon be in Edinburgh, Nat, where there will be all the wine, women, and hot food you desire."

"You think about yourself. All I want is a good bed and a long sleep."

Always a hairbreadth away from a disastrous crash, the carriage plunged on, around the steep sides of hills, through dense woodlands, where it felt as if they were floating in a sea of black, and then across the valley floor where the moon painted a silver trail ahead of them. Finally they began the ascent of the hills that rimmed Edinburgh.

The deafening storm of the horses' hooves had become the familiar music of their journey, so they were acutely aware when the note changed: the disturbing syncopation of more hooves had joined the steady beat.

From the space beneath the seat, Will removed a length of rope from among the tools the driver stored within the carriage and tied one end to his wrist, leaving the other to trail free.

"Nat, I ask this of you now: whatever happens, do not look out of the windows," Will said.

"Why? You are afraid I will see you fall like a jester upon your bony rump?"

"Heed me now, Nat. This is important."

Nathaniel recognised the tone in his master's voice and nodded. "Whatever you plan, take care."

"Those who take care never experience all the wonders life has to offer."

Will pushed his head outside where the wind tore at his hair and made him deaf. The nearest rider was just behind the rear wheels of the carriage and to one side. Though the face was lost to shadows, Will could see the fire of the eyes burning through the dark. He had noted the strange, shifting quality of the eyes' inner light before—sometimes green, sometimes gold, sometimes red like now—and though he had no idea what it meant, it confirmed their unnatural nature.

As the rider drew nearer still, he leaned down across his saddle and reached out an arm towards the wheel. Will couldn't see what he was holding, if anything, but as his fingers closed on the rapidly spinning wood, sparks danced around the iron sheath and the wheel began to wobble from side to side. Already leaping wildly, the carriage vibrated as if it would tear itself apart. Inside, Nathaniel cursed loudly.

Grimacing, the driver cast a glance back, his knuckles white on the reins. "The axle will break," he bellowed. "At this speed, we will all die."

Grasping the roof rail, Will hauled himself out of the window, placing one foot on the sill to push himself onto the roof. The carriage bounced so furiously that only the strength in his arm prevented him from being torn off.

The other two riders were close on the other side of the carriage, riding so effortlessly it appeared they were exerting no energy.

Gripping until his knuckles hurt, Will crashed repeatedly on the carriage roof, or was dragged back down the side by the ferocious winds buffeting him.

The carriage rattled into another area of dense woodland, the branches so low overhead that Will had to press himself against the carriage roof to avoid impact. The trees were so tight that the nearest rider was forced to break off from exerting his influence on the wheel and to drop behind the carriage.

Taking advantage of the brief respite, Will gained purchase with the toes of his boots and held himself fast within the area defined by the rail. With an effort, he tied the free end of the rope at his wrist to the rail, an anchor that would keep him from being thrown off the carriage. But he knew that if he fell it would drag him into the wheels.

When the carriage burst out of the wood, Will hooked his toes under the rail and carefully raised himself upright. The wind tore at him even more fiercely, and although the rope allowed him to steady himself, he had to keep shifting his weight to maintain his balance.

As the rider closed in on the wheel again, Will drew his sword. Gripping the rope with his left hand, he hung out over the void and sliced down. The rider dropped back to avoid the blow.

Within a second, the rider had drawn his own sword. Pulling his mount alongside, he launched a series of duelling strokes, attempting to slash through the rope that held Will fast.

Will adapted quickly to his new situation. The rope allowed him the kind of mobility he could never achieve on solid ground, so that he could lean out almost horizontally to the carriage or swing around in a half circle to strike from another angle. His sword became an arc of reflected moonlight flashing back and forth to parry every blow the rider made.

Recognising his inability to break through Will's defence, the rider dropped back a way before stepping up easily to balance on the saddle. Still clutching the reins in one hand, he drove the horse forwards before leaping for the carriage, slashing as he flew through the air.

Stumbling back on one knee, Will brought his sword up high to take the brunt of the attacker's blow. Even up close, the attacker's face was lost in shadow as if it drew all light from the vicinity.

Driving back upright, Will attempted to concentrate his attack before the Enemy swordsman could gain a foothold. Yet despite the carriage's velocity across the rutted road, his opponent kept his balance with ease. His sword darted towards Will's heart, his throat, the supporting rope, switching his attack rapidly as they roved round and round the carriage roof.

Just as Will thought he was gaining the upper hand, the carriage crashed over a fallen branch in the road and all four wheels left the ground. When it slammed back down, Will was thrown onto his back.

Seizing the moment, the Enemy swordsman thrust down with his sword. Will tore his head to one side at the last moment, the blade driving a fraction past his ear and through the carriage roof. Nathaniel's cry of surprise rang out.

Before the Enemy could withdraw his sword, Will thrust his weight onto his shoulders and jabbed his feet into his opponent's gut. The impact flipped the Enemy swordsman over the end of the carriage into the road.

Will had no time to catch his breath. One of the other riders was preparing to leap at the terrified driver, who lashed out frantically with his whip. The final rider was ready to jump onto the carriage roof from his saddle.

As Will threw himself towards the driver, another severe lurch knocked him off balance. When he next looked up, the Enemy was on the seat, fighting with the driver. Even with his whip, the driver didn't stand a chance. His attacker caught a hand in the neck of his cloak and wrenched him up with ease. Holding the screaming man over his head for a second, the Enemy flung him from the racing carriage.

At that moment, the third rider leapt onto the carriage roof.

Will didn't wait for him to land. With his sword, he slashed through the rope holding his wrist and in the same fluid movement propelled himself forwards. The momentum almost took him over the driver's seat and down among the horses' driving hooves, but at the last he caught the flailing reins. His head and shoulders dipped below the level of the seat, but Will brought his left foot up to kick the Enemy assailant from the seat. Plunging down the side of the carriage, he flew under the rear wheels.

Dragging himself up into the seat, Will gripped the reins with one hand to slow the horses, while turning with his sword raised to face the final rider, who was prowling towards him across the carriage roof.

They thrust and parried, but Will was hamstrung by his lack of mobility. The Enemy swordsman took full advantage of his uncanny balance, ducking and darting along the entire width of the roof.

In the full glare of the moon, the carriage crested the top of the hills and began the long descent towards Edinburgh. Will smelled smoke on the wind.

Slashing back and forth, the Enemy swordsman made the most of the carriage's sudden career downhill to press his attack on Will, who fought to stay upright on the seat.

At the last, the Enemy was distracted by a loud cry. Hanging half out of the window, Nathaniel brandished the long iron needle the driver used to repair the horses' bridles.

"Nat, inside!" Will yelled—too late.

As the swordsman fixed his gaze upon Nathaniel, a haunted expression slowly crossed Nathaniel's features.

Will thrust his sword into the distracted Enemy and used his weapon to lever the attacker off the side of the carriage. With relief, he turned all his attention back to the horses, refusing to slow the pace further until he was sure any Enemy survivors were far behind.

"Nat, inside, now!" he shouted, afraid his friend had already seen too much. After the devastation he felt at Miller's suicide, Will could not bear for Nathaniel to be infected by the same creeping despair. The words he had spoken to Nathaniel's father all those months ago were still heavy on him. He would keep Nathaniel safe.

After another mile, he reined in the horses and called for Nathaniel to sit with him. Will could see clearly in his assistant's subdued demeanour how greatly he had been affected.

"What was that, Will?" Nathaniel asked quietly once they had set off again.

"What kind of question is that, Nat?" Will replied lightly.

"The face—"

"Did not have the ruggedly handsome features of my own, but that is no reason to pour scorn on a poor, afflicted highway robber. Perhaps those same unsavoury features were what drove him to a life of crime. Why, perhaps we should pity him, Nat! Were he not now a bloody smear 'pon the road."

Will's tone eased Nathaniel a little. "I felt I saw my own face looking back, though frozen in death . . ." He gave a humourless laugh at how ridiculous that sounded.

"Exactly," Will affirmed. "An illusion. The mind plays strange tricks, especially when it is jolted free of its moorings by a runaway carriage ride."

"Then it was a highwayman I saw? Nothing more?"

"Nat—"

"Yes, I am a fool! I am sure you will find great humour at my expense when you are in your cups." Nathaniel feigned annoyance, but his relief was palpable.

Cracking the reins to urge the horses on, Will hid his own relief. At times, it felt like he was attempting to hold back a torrent that would wash away everything he held dear if he failed for a moment. Every word was a lie designed to create a world that did not exist. It was not surprising that the members of Walsingham's crew rarely survived long. Will was convinced many reached a point where they simply gave up, let themselves die, because they were worn down by the lies, and by the harshness of the reality that lay behind the fiction they created.

He put on a grin and showed it to Nathaniel. "Wine and women are within our grasp, Nat," he said. "Let us make haste so we can enjoy the night before it is gone!"

Nathaniel grumbled quietly, but sat back to watch the last of the countryside flash by.

Will let his own thoughts drift to what lay ahead. Whatever threat they had faced there on the road paled into insignificance compared to what waited for them in Edinburgh.

CHAPTER 20

Edinburgh was a slash of forbidding grey against the soaring, craggy-topped heights that ranged behind the city. Running along the top of a granite spine from the ancient fort of Castle Rock in the west down the gentle slope of the king's High Street to the Netherbow Port, the east gate to the city, it consisted of little more than one broad, mile-long street of large houses, kirks, and shops, and hard against it jumbled, stinking rat-runs of alleys and side streets, the wynds and closes, all of them poorly constructed, dark, narrow, and filthy, and packed to the brim with the poor. Often several generations of a family were crammed into a single room. Beyond Netherbow Port, the street continued through the burgh of Canongate to the king's Palace of Holyroodhouse.

During the time of Elizabeth's rule south of the border, Edinburgh's population had soared, like London's, by more than a quarter to nearly seventeen thousand people, all of them constrained within the walls of a city little more than a mile square in area. With no new room for building, the only way to go was up. Newer residents added precarious, poorly constructed stories on top of tenements—known as the "lands"—designed to carry less than half their new height. Barely a week passed without a new collapse, plunging the occupants to their deaths on the cobbles far below. From the top of these teetering towers, a constant rain of excrement and urine fell at morning and night, as the uppermost residents cried out "Guardez-l'eau!" and emptied their chamber pots from the windows.

All Edinburgh society mixed in the lands, from lawyers and judges to merchants, nobility, and commoners. There was no space to breathe; no peace.

After the unsettling dark of the wild Scottish countryside, Will was comforted by the candlelight and lanterns glinting as the carriage rattled through the city gates and onto the cobbles of the main street. The boom of the closing gates behind, too, was oddly reassuring.

Though filled with high art, scholarship, and religious thought, Will could see Edinburgh was a world away from London. It was a city of shadows, still attached to the old world while London was scrambling into the bright modern future. In the claustrophobic gloom among the dour stone buildings, the overcrowded, filthy streets were a breeding ground for disease and crime, where cutthroats and murderers preyed upon their own and hope was thin. It was the perfect hunting ground for the Enemy.

No Dee here to keep the people safe, he thought. *Only the harshness of daily life.*

Will was not blind to the irony that the city's brooding aspect reflected his own state of mind. Miller's death lay heavy upon him. He would never reveal it to Nathaniel, or anyone else, for that matter, but he felt the world slipping under his feet as it had after Jenny's disappearance, only this time the stew of emotions was infected with guilt and a sense of his own personal failure in defending Miller's life.

A cold anger seethed beneath the surface, demanding retribution, and answers. Nothing was going to stand in his way.

They left the carriage near Cowgate, where the noblemen, ambassadors, and rich clergy made their homes, and slipped quietly to the address Walsingham had given them, a three-hundred-year-old three-story house of solid stone with a fine oaken door and an iron knocker. Will gave the coded rap, and after a moment they were admitted by a man carrying a candle. He was in his early fifties, almost six foot six, thin and elegant, with a hooked nose and swept-back white hair.

"Alexander Reidheid?" Will said.

"Master Swyfte!" Reidheid shook his hand furiously. "It is an honour— such an honour!—to have the great hero of England in my home!"

Nathaniel sighed loudly.

"Lord Walsingham speaks highly of you," Will said. "He claims you know the comings and goings of every man in Edinburgh, and that your understanding of the subtle moods of this city is beyond peer."

"He flatters me." Reidheid's cheeks flushed, but he was pleased with the compliment.

Primping her hair, a woman of around twenty-five entered shyly. She was pretty, with delicate, upper-class features, brown hair in ringlets, and green eyes that flashed when she saw the guests.

"My daughter, Meg," Reidheid said. She curtsied as her father introduced

Will and Nathaniel. Will noticed Nathaniel about to register his tart weariness at another woman fawning over *England's great hero* when Meg's eyes skittered quickly across Will and settled on Nathaniel himself. Nathaniel was clearly taken aback by the attention and did not know how to respond.

"Perhaps Meg could show Nathaniel our quarters while we discuss more important matters," Will said. "And I would be grateful if your servant could also make arrangements to collect the body of our driver who met with misfortune on the way here. Nat will provide directions."

Shuffling with baffled discomfort at this new predicament, Nathaniel followed Meg to the rear of the house while Reidheid led Will into the drawing room where a fire roared in the grate.

"I apologise if you find the temperature unpleasant," he said. "Increasingly, I struggle to get warm. It appears to be an affliction that affects all our kind sooner or later, as though those damnable things suck the life and warmth from us."

"And you would have more experience of them here in Scotland than we south of the border." Will took a seat next to the fire, while Reidheid poured two crystal glasses of amber whisky.

"They torment the countryside as they have always done, haunting the glens and the lochs, and they move freely through our city. But here they have chosen to play a quiet game in recent years. They can pass for mortals, if they so choose, and they slip between the cracks of everyday life, causing mischief and misery in subtle ways and only intermittently."

"Their attention has been elsewhere," Will said, "on the search for a key to a great weapon, which had been hidden in the city. Now they hunt for the final thing they need to complete their plan."

Reidheid handed Will the glass. "*Uisge beatha*, in the native tongue. The Water of Life. It keeps me warm when there is no fire in the grate." He pulled his chair close to the hearth. "The poor and rich alike have long learned to protect their homes with salt and herbs and cold iron, and to watch where they walk after dark has fallen."

"You have seen new activity from them in recent days?"

"They call them the Unseelie Court here. It is an old name, coloured by centuries of torment." He sipped his whisky reflectively. "There is a place in Edinburgh not far from the castle that is known as the Fairy House. The local people understand it to be haunted, or cursed. It is said that anyone who ventures within never comes out. No one is ever seen inside, although the lights blaze intermittently. The downstairs rooms are said to be guarded by a demonic black dog."

"They have a house they call their own within the city?" Will ruminated. "And no one has raided it?"

"We have an uneasy relationship with the Unseelie Court in Edinburgh." There was a rueful note in Reidheid's voice. "A black carriage stood outside two days ago. No one was seen leaving it, or entering the house, and it left shortly after."

"No one would ever be seen. I need to explore the inside of this Fairy House."

Reidheid started. "I have watched that foul place for many days and nights. I can see no safe way in."

"Then it will have to be unsafe."

Nathaniel and Meg entered with a platter of cold beef, bread, and cheese and some ale. They were both quiet and respectful, but Will saw them exchange warm glances as they laid out the food on the table.

"I would also have access to the Palace of Holyroodhouse," Will said as he sliced the beef.

"An audience with the king will not be an easy thing to arrange—" Reidheid began.

"I do not want an audience. I want to prowl around his private rooms, poke my nose in his closets, go through his clothes, sift his jewels, rap on his walls, prise up his floorboards, and generally skulk around and make a nuisance of myself."

"It is the most heavily guarded residence in all of Edinburgh," Reidheid protested.

"Then I have two impenetrable buildings to penetrate."

"And you do like to penetrate the impenetrable," Nathaniel whispered to him.

"Father?" Meg began. "The king has a ball tomorrow night."

Reidheid considered this for a moment, then said, "Perhaps I could garner you an invitation. A visiting luminary. I am sure James will think you might brighten up the festivities and perhaps provide a welcome talking point for the members of the court who find these events overly familiar. Would that serve your purpose?"

"A palace swarming with people in which to lose myself?" Will nodded. "Perfect."

"And wine, and women," Nathaniel muttered.

Will loaded his plate and poured some ale from the pitcher before settling back by the fire. "Then let us make haste, for there is little of the night left."

"You intend to visit the Fairy House this night?" Reidheid asked incredulously. "You have not slept. Surely after some rest—"

"I have fire in my blood," Will replied, "and an urge to make the Enemy pay for the wrongs they have inflicted upon my friends. Sleep can wait."

CHAPTER 21

From the pitch of the roof, Will looked out across Edinburgh's jumbled mass sprawling around the winding, ancient ways, the grand stone houses glimmering with candlelight, the soaring backdrop of the great hills beyond. The wind tearing at his hair brought with it the salty aroma of the port at Leith two miles distant.

He stood atop one of the highest lands in the city, after picking his way past crowded apartments to bribe his way through the window of the topmost lodger. Balancing on the ledge with the dizzying drop to the cobbles far below, he briefly wondered if he was as mad as the lodger accused him of being, before hauling himself up and over the edge onto the slick tiles.

"I wish you could see this, Nathaniel," he said. "The world looks less harsh from on high."

Steadying himself on the balls of his feet, Will loped along the pitch of the roof. Progress was hazardous. The gusting air currents channelling through the wynds threatened to pluck him down the steep slope to the vertiginous drop at the end. Occasionally the wind direction changed and he was blinded by choking smoke from the rows of chimneys.

Whenever he came to one of the wynds that broke up the run of housing, he leapt the narrow gap, constantly aware of the black gulf beneath his feet. His landings were always a scramble for purchase, one wrong foot or twisted ankle a death warrant, but he kept up a relentless progress towards his destination.

As he neared the Fairy House, he leapt onto the roof of one of the lands and felt it shift beneath his feet. The highest story had been attached only recently, with nailed boards and beams but no proper joints as far as Will could tell. It felt as insubstantial as a pile of randomly heaped firewood, swaying whenever he shifted his weight, held up by luck and hope more than anything. Dropping to all fours, he edged along the top until he could move to the adjoining roof.

Finally he landed with barely a whisper of a footfall on the roof of the Fairy House, a five-story residence that had long since seen better days. Missing and broken tiles peppered the roof, and tufts of grass and elder sprouted from where birds had dropped seeds.

Flattening himself out, he moved down the pitch of the roof to the edge where he could peer over to the cobbles far below. A black carriage drawn by a sable stallion waited outside the front door of the house. There was no sign of any driver. All of the house windows were dark, and no sound issued from within.

Crawling back up the pitch to the roof's ridge, Will inspected the chimney stack, which was cold. As he'd guessed, the hole was wide enough to admit him, though a tight squeeze. The biggest danger was that he would climb down into the maze of flues and become trapped, especially in a chimney that had not been kept in good repair.

Steadying himself on top of the stack, he lowered himself into the hole, feeling for footholds in the crumbling brick. Amid the suffocating stink of soot, his clothes and skin were soon black. Unable to see anything in the dark, his senses focused on the tips of his fingers searching for cracks in the brick and the ache in his leg muscles as he braced himself against the sides of the chimney to stop him falling.

As he made his way down, intermittent noises floated up from the lower floors: garbled voices speaking no tongue he recognised, their emotions see-sawing in an extreme and disturbing manner, from barks of anger to frightened mewling to shrieks of insane laughter and mocking whispers; a sound like a blacksmith's hammers on an anvil, which came and went, echoing dimly then resounding near at hand; a dog growling that sounded disturbingly close, on the other side of the brick; and then music, pipes and a fiddle, eerie and haunting, fading in and out.

Feeling with his feet, Will came to a junction in the flue and decided to take the right-hand path. After a few feet, it turned so sharply he had to force himself around the bend a fraction of an inch at a time, leading with his sword which he had to flex and maneuver through the gap. His muscles were compressed so hard they ached, and his chest constricted so tightly that he could barely catch a breath.

Halfway around the turn, he became afraid he was jammed, unable to go forwards or backwards. He rested for a moment, fighting to breathe, and then relaxed his muscles just enough to edge on.

Finally, he rounded the turn, but he'd barely lowered himself another six feet when he realised the flue was blocked. Some of the stones had collapsed in on another turn—he could feel them grinding beneath his feet—but however hard he pressed, the obstruction would not shift.

There was no way to go but back. Steeling himself, he dug his fingers in the cracks between the stones and hauled himself up. Sweating, choking, every muscle burning, he came back to the turn. It was even harder going up, and it took him the better part of half an hour to maneuver himself around it in tiny increments, dragging with his fingertips and pushing with the tips of his boots. Again he got stuck halfway around, and this time it took so long to relax his muscles, he became concerned he would suffocate before he could move.

Once he'd pulled himself up to the junction and rested his head for a moment, breathing deeply, he realised there was a current of air rising through the other flue. It gave him heart, and once again he began his slow descent.

He'd passed the worst of it, and now there were regular junctions that led down to the large stone fireplaces in every room. But though the distant sounds continued to rise through the flues, there never appeared to be any noise coming from any room he passed.

When Will estimated he'd reached the second floor, he slid down towards a fireplace, bracing himself just above the hearth to listen. When he was sure the chamber was empty, he dropped into the hearth in a cloud of soot. The room was bare apart from a cracked mirror above the mantelpiece which revealed a white-eyed black figure. Moving swiftly across the dirty floorboards to stand by the door, he waited for any who might have heard his arrival.

The house was silent. What had happened to all the noises he had heard in the chimney? he wondered. Opening the door a crack, he peered out into the corridor where a candle flickered in a holder on a small table.

Not so empty, then, he thought.

He moved quickly along the corridor, checking the rooms on either side. All were bare. Outside the last room, the boards creaked loudly, and there was a corresponding growl from the first floor, followed by heavy paws padding onto the stairs. Lightly, Will bolted up to the next floor.

Flickering light on one wall brought him to a halt just near the turn. Peering round, he saw a figure—male, although the brown hair was long—moving away from him slowly, holding a candle aloft. Below, the sound of padding paws continued up to the second floor, accompanied by another deep, penetrating growl.

Caught between the two, Will weighed his choices. Just as he had decided to draw his sword, a door at the far end of the corridor opened and light flooded out. The figure paused and communicated in a low whisper with someone within before entering the room. The door closed behind him and the light winked out.

Instantly, Will darted to the nearest door, listening briefly before opening it slowly. The room was in darkness. He slipped inside.

Closing the door, he pressed his ear against it and waited. The padding reached the top of the flight of stairs and then moved towards him. It paused outside the door and growled again, disturbingly loud in the quiet. Will held his nerve. After a second, he heard the dog move on, and listened intently until silence returned.

Will wondered if it was the same dog that had accompanied the Hunter in Alsatia. That would mean the Hunter was probably there too, he thought coldly, and perhaps even the Silver Skull.

"Who are you?"

He started at the voice, soft and dreamy with the burr of a Scottish Lowlands accent. In the dark of the room, a man sat on a chair looking out of the window, his back to Will.

Drawing his sword in an instant, Will waited for the alarm to be raised, but the man did not move. After a second, Will cautiously approached. As the moonlight broke through the window, Will saw it *was* a man, not one of the Enemy. He was in his forties, grey streaks in his black hair, and grey eyes that had the faraway look of a sleepwalker.

"Who are you?" Will asked.

"John Kintour," he replied. "Advisor to my queen, Mary."

"Mary is dead."

"No . . . no . . . I saw her this morn. So beautiful. The sun made her hair glow like fire." His voice was as insubstantial as the moonbeam breaking through the window.

Will passed his hand in front of Kintour's face, but he did not blink. "How long have you been here?"

"A day? A week? A month? A year?" He paused thoughtfully, then said, "They gave me food and drink. The most wonderful food . . . The taste . . . I had never experienced anything like it."

Will realised what had happened. One of the first rules during his induction as one of Walsingham's men was that he should never eat or drink anything offered by the Enemy, for it would allow them to take complete control of you. Normally it was how they lured their prey for their sport, usually simple country folk drawn to hear the music on the hilltops or in the fields at night. Kintour was clearly not being kept a prisoner in the house for sport.

"You have had a busy time here," Will said gently.

"Yes. So many questions."

"And you answered them all?"

"As best I could. Some were beyond even me. The location of the Shield—"

"The Shield? What is that?" Thinking he heard a noise outside, Will glanced towards the door. After a moment he returned his attention to Kintour.

"The Shield protects against the foul diseases released by the Silver Skull, of course," Kintour said lazily. "It allows a man to move freely among the ranks of the infected and the dead, without any mark appearing upon him. That is what the Templar Knights said."

It was as Will had thought. Without the Shield, the Skull was a blunt instrument, laying waste to vast swathes of an enemy. With it, the attacker could loot the dead, or achieve more specific aims.

"What do the Templar Knights have to do with this?" he asked.

Kintour's head rolled from side to side and he smiled faintly. "I was keeper of the records at the palace. So much to read . . . so many secrets. Among the sheaves of crumbling parchment, I found many relating to the Knights Templar. At first they made little sense. It was only when I realised they were written with an obscure cipher that the truth began to emerge. The Knights encountered the Silver Skull in the Holy Lands, and knew the terrible threat it was to all Christendom. They had to act to protect all good Christian men."

"What did they do?"

"Separated the Skull from the Key and the Shield so it could not be used. They brought the latter two back here, to Scotland, and hid them well. The Skull . . . I do not know what happened to that."

"The Key and the Shield were hidden at the Palace of Holyroodhouse?" Will asked.

"Hidden well. The Knights had many strong connections with Edinburgh and the surrounding area, and they were involved in advising King David when he built Holyrood Abbey in 1126. There were rumours of secret chambers beneath the abbey, and extending under the palace west of the abbey cloister. It was one of the secret locations across Europe where the Knights stored items of vast importance."

Will recalled the stories of the Knights Templar he had heard told at court, and how the religious military order had brought back many secrets and riches from the Crusades. Dee had even suggested that the disbanding of the Order and the killing of many of the Knights was down to the machinations of the Enemy. *The Enemy's greatest victory*, Dee had called it.

"Mary charged me with finding the location of the Key and the Shield," Kintour continued. "I searched through the old papers and spent long days and nights breaking the ciphers the Knights used. I found the Key." His brow furrowed.

"Yes, the Key was found," Will responded. "But you could not locate the Shield?"

"Only that it was hidden somewhere beneath the abbey. But where . . . and how . . ." He shook his head sadly. "And so you still search?"

"Yes, we still search," Will said reassuringly. His mind raced as he tried to guess the Enemy's plan, which was clearly more subtle than he had anticipated. If the Silver Skull was simply a doomsday weapon, they would ensure it was triggered to wipe out the population, with no thought for the man who wore the Mask. But if the Enemy needed the Shield to protect themselves, it suggested they wished to move through the areas where the disease ran out of hand. Why would they want to do that?

"How close have you got to locating the Shield?" he asked.

Kintour bowed his head in shame. "I have the reference to the entrance, and the guide to the defences, but I cannot understand it." He pulled a piece of parchment from his pocket and handed it to Will with trembling hands. Will inspected it briefly before slipping it into his own pocket. "I know you requested an answer by this evening, and I am sorry . . . I am sorry . . ." He began to sob softly. "Please do not hurt me any more. Let me dream."

Will studied the wretched figure and wondered how long he had been a prisoner of the Enemy, without truly knowing where he was or what he did for them. "Why have they . . . we . . . not descended on the abbey and torn it apart to find the Shield?" Will enquired.

"Why . . . part of it is protected? You cannot walk there?" Kintour replied, baffled.

"So mortal agents are needed to search," Will mused. "You will not have to remain here for much longer. Firstly, I must find where they have hidden the Silver Skull here, but then I will return you to your life. Do you understand?"

Kintour nodded slowly until his chin drooped onto his chest and he fell into a deep stupor. Will crept back to the door and slipped out as soon as he had confirmed the corridor was clear.

The house pulsed with a strange atmosphere that reminded Will of a churchyard after a funeral, a hint of regret, a resonant note of grief, yet somehow the joy of a new day like the sun breaking through the branches of the yews. Behind it all, though, was an underlying tone of threat, rumbling so deep it was felt not heard.

He paused outside the door through which the Enemy had ventured, but there was no sound within. He hesitated, thought better of it, and moved on to the next floor; he could always return to that room if the rest of his search turned up nothing.

There was a different atmosphere in the next corridor, as though he had walked from one season into another. The air was rich with the perfume of a summer garden: he smelled lavender, rose, honeysuckle. The first door was locked, as was the second.

In the third room, it took a second for his eyes to adjust to the deep dark until he realised thick velvet drapes hung over the window. Pulling them back, he allowed the moonlight to illuminate the chamber. His initial shock at seeing glassy eyes upon him turned gradually to anger when he saw the pile of human heads in one corner, rising almost halfway up the wall. He guessed there were at least fifty, the features and bone structure heavy with the weight of poverty. Some of the heads were so badly decomposed only traces of flesh remained on the bone; others looked so fresh they may well have been placed there that night. The Enemy's sport, he knew, plucked from the dark, overcrowded wynds where the lowest stratum of society was all but ignored by the city authorities.

There, in one stark image, was the entire reason for his life's work, and why Walsingham and Dee, for all their flaws, were right. Damping down his anger, he moved swiftly back into the corridor and continued to search the house floor by floor.

More doors were locked, more rooms empty, although many held a tantalising sensation that they had only just been vacated, a wisp of scent in the air or a fading echo.

Finally, in a room at the end of the corridor, he found Don Alanzo, asleep, his sword by his side, on a four-poster bed with the curtains partly drawn. In a chair next to the bed, head on his chest in slumber, was the Silver Skull. The two of them together in the same room, in that position, was an odd sight, and Will couldn't tell if they were under the spell of the Enemy. But he knew that an arm around the throat of the Silver Skull for just a few moments with the pressure at the right point, and he would be able to transport him out of the room unconscious without waking his guard. The question then would be how to escape the house with both the Skull and Kintour.

The room was furnished with more warmth than the other chambers in the Fairy House, but there was an underlying stench of decomposition that drew Will's attention to one single rotting head on the mantelpiece.

Even here, Will thought. *A reminder to the occupants of their mortality.*

Searching for any creaking board, he edged across the room to within a foot of the Skull without any change in their breathing. But as he reached out a crooked arm to slide it around the Skull's neck, the head on the mantelpiece tore open its mouth and began to shriek.

The bloodcurdling alarm rang through the still house.

Shocked awake, the Silver Skull leapt to his feet, knocking over his chair. Grabbing his sword, Don Alanzo rolled off the bed and thrust himself between Will and the Skull.

"Intruder!" he yelled, unnecessarily, almost drowned out by the head's deafening shriek.

Deep in the house, doors slammed.

Will saw it was futile to attempt to escape with the Skull. "I will return to finish this at a later date," he said, backing towards the door. "Until then, enjoy your stay in Edinburgh."

Activity rumbled throughout the house, punctuated by the loud barks of the sentry dog. The sensible option would have been to enter one of the empty rooms and clamber back into the chimney, but Will couldn't bring himself to leave Kintour. The archivist had already suffered greatly at the hands of the Enemy, and Will felt instinctively that he would become superfluous to their needs very soon.

Racing for the stairs, he drew his knife. He took the steps three at a time, crashing onto the landing below where a shadow on the wall had already warned him of an impending assailant. Dropping and rolling, he brought the knife up sharply vertical into the groin of the waiting figure. The inhuman cry of pain made Will's head ring.

Without looking back, he ran for the next flight of stairs. Four more of the Enemy pounded up the steps to meet him.

On the top step, he threw himself forwards, crashing hard into the first attacker, who was propelled into the ones behind. They careered down the stairs with Will rolling across the top of them to land on his feet on the next landing. As he fought his way through to the corridor where Kintour's room lay, he found the Hunter waiting just before the door. Eyeing Will contemptuously, he put his fingers to his mouth and whistled. From below, his dog answered with a hunting howl.

Everything Will saw in the Hunter's face—arrogance, a dismissive regard for a lesser species, cruelty—made him desire revenge for Miller's death with a fierce determination, but he knew it would mean his own death; behind him, the other combatants had picked themselves up from the tangle at the foot of the stairs and were already advancing.

Will ran. The Hunter's eyes narrowed as he casually prepared to repel the attack. Instead of meeting him head-on, at the last Will leapt to the left-hand wall, propelled himself off it to the right-hand wall, and launched himself past the wrong-footed Hunter. In passing, Will's knife tore open the Hunter's cheek. The cry of anger-tinged agony brought a surge of black pleasure in Will.

"Something to remember me by," Will said.

He kicked out at the Hunter as he moved by him, knocking him off balance, and then he was in the room and sliding the bolt across the door.

"Come, we must leave this place," Will said, shaking Kintour from his stupor. Bodies were briefly thrown at the door before the bolt began to slide back of its own accord.

Staggering, Kintour allowed himself to be moved towards the fireplace. He was like a puppet, with no will of his own.

"We climb," Will urged. "You first. I will follow to hold off any pursuit."

Kintour was leaden, his fingers feebly feeling for handholds. Will put his shoulder to the man's behind and launched him up the chimney, climbing quickly behind him while bracing himself against the sooty stones with his legs. Black showers rained down all around.

In the room, the door crashed open and the heavy beat of boots crossed the boards. A wild barking followed in the wake.

"Where are we?" Kintour's dazed voice floated down to Will.

"On the road to freedom. Now: climb faster!" He gave Kintour a rough shove as the sound of canine scrabbling echoed from the fireplace below.

In the dark, Kintour began to panic. Will patiently explained what was occurring as they inched along the flue.

"What if we become trapped here?" The edge of fear in Kintour's dreamy voice was eerie.

"I came down. Ergo we can climb out," Will shouted up.

The snuffling and snarling began to rise up the chimney. Somehow the dog was climbing after them.

"No dog at all, then," Will muttered to himself before calling, "Climb faster, now."

As they drove up through the flue system, Will looked down between his boots and glimpsed the glint of the dog's teeth as it snapped only a few feet below him. Finding near-invisible footholds, it climbed with relatively little purchase on the blackened stone, so that it almost appeared to be gliding upwards.

"What is happening?" Kintour cried. The edge in his voice grew more intense as he surfaced from the spell.

Finally, they broke out into the chill night. Disoriented, Kintour almost pitched off the roof until Will burst from the chimney and caught hold of his shirt. The dog wriggled up the final few feet, snapping its jaws like a gamekeeper's trap.

"Along the roofs," Will urged. "We can be away from here before—"

"No!" Kintour clutched his head as though in pain, his legs buckling. Will held on to him tightly as his feet slipped on the tiles. "I . . . I remember now," Kintour stuttered.

Clambering fully from the chimney, Will attempted to guide Kintour along the roof's pitch. "Do not look down," Will said. "Keep your eyes on my face." The fingers of the gusting wind tugged at them. At their backs, the dog's snarling echoed from the chimney.

Kintour looked up at Will with an expression of devastation. "They told me . . . I could never . . ."

There was a faint *poof* and Kintour burst into silvery-grey dust. In shock, Will grasped for the glittering power, but it drained through his fingers, was caught on the night wind, and blew out across the city. Within a second, where a man had stood, there was nothing.

For a second, Will was rooted, aghast. His incomprehension at Kintour's sudden fate was eventually supplanted by the certain knowledge that the Enemy—the unholy, Unseelie Court—were capable of any atrocity. He was shocked back into the moment by the dog thrusting its head out of the chimney. Eyes glaring, it thrashed savagely as it attempted to extricate itself.

Will threw himself rapidly along the pitch of the roof as he heard the dog crash onto the tiles, slipping and scrabbling until it found purchase and balance. Caution was no longer an option—the dog's speed and strength would punish even the slightest hesitation—but at the speed he was travelling, one misstep meant certain death.

At a wynd, Will threw himself across the gap without slowing his pace. Tiles flew out into the void under his heels. He half slipped, caught himself on the brink of careering down the roof and over the edge to the cobbles far below, and almost fell the other way as his weight shifted. The dog thundered along the roof behind him.

When he landed on the roof of the haphazard construction he had passed through earlier that night, it swayed beneath his feet. A notion struck him. Casting an eye towards the dog bounding along the roofs and the Hunter loping with supernatural ease in its wake, he hammered a foot through the tiles and yelled at the two occupants he spied inside to vacate their rooms.

At the edge of the next roof, he braced his back against a chimney and pressed his feet into the shuddering roof he had vacated. After a second, it began to move.

The dog slammed onto the roof, only feet away from him. It was too late to escape now. Grunting, he drove all his strength into his feet. The roof shifted away from him, gathering speed as it moved, and with a lurch and a loud rending, it tore free from its slipshod moorings and slid off the top of the building. Frantically paddling to keep its balance, the dog continued to snap savagely, even as it fell away with the roof, over the edge and down. The cries that rose up from the ragged remnants of the tenements' lower floors were drowned out by the explosive boom of the entire floor smashing into the street.

Feet kicking, Will dragged himself up onto the next roof. As he caught his breath, he looked back to see the Hunter standing on the far side of the newly formed gulf, watching him with a cold, malicious eye, the gaping wound on his cheek visible in the moonlight. Will had no doubt that the dog had survived the fall, but it felt like a small victory and a marker for what he would do the next time he encountered the Hunter.

With a sardonic salute to his adversary, he continued along the roofs, filled with conflicting emotions, but sensing he had come a step closer to stopping the Enemy's plans.

CHAPTER 22

ill made it back to Reidheid's house on Cowgate within twenty minutes, taking care to scan every street and wynd he passed for the Enemy who would soon be flooding in pursuit.

"You have protection here?" Will asked as he bounded over the threshold when Reidheid opened the door.

Reidheid indicated the trail of salt and herbs across the doorway. "Every entrance to this house is defended. The Enemy will never enter. It is a safe haven."

"That is reassuring. I fear at this moment that the Enemy may well be consumed with a desire to see the inside of your house."

"Your mission was a success?" Reidheid guided Will into the drawing room, where Nathaniel and Meg sat in deep, quiet conversation. They left quickly at Reidheid's gesture.

"The Silver Skull is here in Edinburgh, as we presumed. Unfortunately, the time was not right to bring it back with me, but it is clear the Enemy is not ready to use the destructive force it carries with it. They need the Shield to complete their plan, and they have not yet located it."

"And do you know what this plan is?" Reidheid asked.

"Not yet. But now I have my own plan."

Reidheid smiled broadly. "Of course. I would expect no less from the great Will Swyfte! Could you enlighten me?"

"I am going to find the Shield myself."

Reidheid's eyes narrowed as he tried to ascertain if Will was serious. "But the Enemy have been searching for the Shield without any result."

Will shrugged. "But I am not the Enemy. And there are places I can go where they cannot. Do you know a man by the name of Kintour, a keeper of the records at the palace?"

Reidheid nodded. "He has been missing for a long time . . . since the days of Mary. Many felt he was loyal to the queen and fled when she fell from grace. That, or dead."

"He is dead now, another thing for which the Enemy must pay." From his pocket, Will withdrew the parchment Kintour had given him. He studied the scrawled writing. "He had found a guide to the whereabouts of the Shield, but had not yet broken the cipher."

"Oh? May I see?"

"Perhaps later. You have a library? With books pertaining to Edinburgh and the palace?"

"Of course," Reidheid said. "I have many books. Come."

Reidheid led Will through the house to a large library at the rear. The smell of great age lay across the shelves of leather-bound books. Reidheid indicated the volumes on local history and left Will to study them at a table by the light of a candle.

After several hours, when the bright morning light flooded the room, Will had become so engrossed in his work he didn't notice Nathaniel enter until a goblet of wine was placed before him.

"Thank you, Nat. You are thoughtful, as ever," Will said without looking up. "I see you have found a friend in the beautiful Meg."

"It is pleasant to speak with someone who is untarnished by this business of ours," Nathaniel replied. "She is entertaining and witty. A novelty," he added pointedly.

Will allowed himself a small, unseen smile. "Then enjoy yourself, Nat. God knows there are few entertaining distractions in this work."

His curiosity getting the better of him, Nathaniel leaned over Will's shoulder to examine the book he was reading. "It is also a novelty to see you with an open tome rather than a woman in your lap and a goblet in your hand. Which is why I brought you that drink, to right a world that has gone mad. What do you read?"

"The object of our search and the key to our success in defeating our Enemy is hidden at the Palace of Holyroodhouse. A ciphered text left by the Templar Knights points to its location."

"The Templar Knights? Their job was to protect good Christians in a dangerous world. What do they have to do with this?"

"There was more to the Knights than the world knows," Will mused while turning the pages. "As there is more to everything than the world knows."

Nathaniel picked up the parchment. "This is the cipher? *The protection lies where the heart of truth beats, beneath the Holy Rood where the martyr stands in black and white.*" He considered the words for a moment and then suggested, "Under a statue of a martyr in the palace?"

"A good attempt, Nat." Pushing his chair back, Will swung a boot onto the table and wiped a bleary eye. "Enlightenment might strike you if you had taken the time to read *The Matter of Olde English* by Williams, a dour fellow from Cambridge. I presume you have a copy on your bedside table?"

Sighing, Nathaniel motioned for Will to continue.

"If you had, then you would know of *heorot*, our ancestors' word for deer, which the rough-tongued people of England pronounced *hart*. H-a-r-t."

"Hart . . . heart," Nathaniel mused. "Ah, I see. We search for the deer of truth, who bounds through the glades of faith . . . or is it charity? . . . not far from the fields of hope. In the hunting grounds behind the palace, I presume."

"Why, Nat, in your sadly familiar mockery you come close to striking the nail upon the head."

"Is that a copy of *The Matter of Olde English* I spy before you?"

As Nathaniel leaned forwards, Will moved the book to the other side of the table. "Concentrate, Nat! I am here to add to your poor education. Another word for 'hart' is 'stag.' I read this morning of the early days of the palace, and more importantly of the abbey that stands beside it. It was built for the Augustinians by King David in 1128, guided, I was told earlier this night, by the Templar Knights. The location was precise, and chosen by King David following a vision he had of a white stag with the cross lodged between its antlers—the cross, or the Holy Rood, from which the palace gets its name."

"So the thing for which you search—"

"A Shield, or *the protection*."

"—it is at the abbey, not the palace."

"Correct. The Enemy presumed the reference to the Holy Rood meant the Shield was beneath the palace."

"And the martyr in black and white?"

"Still eludes me. But we have a start. And when we are entertained by the king this evening, we shall investigate further."

CHAPTER 23

As the sun set, the carriages rolled down the cobbles of the mile-long avenues that stretched from the castle to the Palace of Holyroodhouse, each one awash with peacock feathers, pearly beads, and gold banners. Inside were the Scottish aristocracy in their finest clothes, the ambassadors, and the senior clergy who had amassed great fortunes to match their indulgent lifestyles.

From the Cowgate house, Will, Nathaniel, Reidheid, and his daughter travelled together in a less extravagant carriage. Though it was protected, Will kept a close watch along the route for any sign of the Enemy.

"This will be a fine night," Meg said. Her eyes shone when they fell on Nathaniel. "The king's festivities are lavish. I think he likes to take the opportunity to rebel against the preachings of the church."

"Yet still no queen," Nathaniel noted. "And he is . . . twenty-two?"

Eyeing Nathaniel askance, Reidheid added with a strained note, "The king prefers the company of males. His advisors have struggled to find a suitable mate, but at least the damnable Earl of Lennox no longer exerts his influence over James."

"You know the court well," Will noted, "and you have some influence to gain an invite for a well-known English spy."

"Not influence enough. The king is suspicious of all beyond his immediate circle. The threats that preceded the forcible removal of Lennox from the king's company have made him wary of all. Indeed, he has moved to exert control over his lords. Yet I have been informed that the king was very keen to have you present."

Will raised an eyebrow. "Oh?"

"He has some concerns over mutual enemies. He is fearful of many things."

Will and Reidheid exchanged a glance while Meg and Nathaniel smiled at each other, oblivious. The carriage rattled past the last of Edinburgh's houses and the crowd of local people who had gathered to watch, to the wild, green land at the foot of the hills that surrounded the palace. The extensive gardens that James had remodelled when he took the throne overflowed with colourful blooms and the last strains of the day's bird-song filled the air. It was a far cry from the oppressive darkness of the city, and the filth and the crime. Yet the wilderness that stretched from the hunting grounds beyond the palace was disturbing in its own way, for it belonged to the Unseelie Court, and particularly after dark. To Will's eyes, the palace was an island extending into Enemy territory.

The building was much smaller than the Palace of Whitehall, though still imposing with its pale stone and red-tiled roof, towers and spires, and soaring diamond-paned windows that flooded the interior with light. Just behind it, to the south side, Will spied the solid bulk of the abbey, a brooding presence beside the bright palace.

There was already a queue of carriages passing through the gate in the wall to drop off the nobility under the protective arches of the large stone gatehouse on the west side of the palace. Once they had stepped down from their carriage to be greeted by a clutch of the king's busy but silent servants, Reidheid led Will, Nathaniel, and Meg through the gates to the quadrangle, a grassy area surrounded by the three-storey palace buildings, and from there to the State Rooms where the guests were gathered.

The court was big, almost six hundred people, swelled by the other guests, and the perfumed atmosphere was abuzz with conversation. Musicians played a masque specially composed for the occasion, with lutes, both bass and mean, a bandora, a double sackbut, a harpsichord, and several violins.

As Reidheid introduced Will around the room, the young wife of the Earl of Angus broke off from her conversation to be presented to Will. She looked him in the eye flirtatiously and smiled. "I have heard tell of your exploits, Master Swyfte, even here in Edinburgh, and I would know if they are true."

Will bowed and kissed her hand. "If all the stories about me were true, my Lady, I would be worn down upon my deathbed."

She laughed, her eyes twinkling. "How you evaded the Doge's men in Venice by disguising yourself as a Harlequin?"

"True, my Lady." Will hid his weariness at the familiar tranche of questions, smiled and nodded and answered several more.

"And how you have romanced all the women at the Court of Elizabeth?" She narrowed her eyes.

"I have not heard that story, my Lady," he replied.

As a ripple of excited conversation crossed the room when the king entered, she took the opportunity to lean in close and whisper in Will's ear. "I would hear more of your tales, Master Swyfte. Perhaps in a quieter place?"

Before Will could respond, the king swept towards Will under the guidance of an unsettled Reidheid, and the Earl's wife retreated with a knowing gleam in her eye.

"Master Swyfte, the king would speak with you in private," Reidheid said, clearly unused to such attention.

The king had inherited his mother Mary's red hair, but none of her good looks or sexual charisma. Slightly feminine in manner, he had a weak chin, a lazy eye, a prominent nose, and his lips pursed in a manner that suggested he was passing judgment, but as he spoke to his guests in passing, Will could see he had a ready intellect and a bright sense of humour.

Will bowed. "You honour me."

"Yes. I do." James gave a wry smile.

Will followed him to the edge of the room where Reidheid and James's aides kept a respectful distance so the conversation could be conducted privately.

"Master Swyfte, your reputation precedes you," James said.

"So I have just been told."

"I would say, firstly, that the execution of my mother at Fotheringhay last year was a harsh blow, 'a preposterous and strange procedure,' as I pronounced at the time." He chose his words carefully, hesitating for a long time at the end of the sentence. "How strange was it, Master Swyfte?"

"It was in accordance with the law of the land."

"That is not my meaning." After a moment's consideration, he continued, "My mother acted strangely for many years. She was not herself, do you understand?"

Will did not respond.

"The circumstances surrounding her execution led me to believe that there was more to her death than perhaps even I knew."

"These are matters of state, and I am a lowly—"

"I know what you are," James interrupted sharply. "I know the business of Walsingham's men." He leaned in and whispered forcefully, "Do you think me blind to the terrible ways of the world, when I am surrounded by vile things that seek to threaten everything we have built?"

"We have an understanding," Will replied.

"But you do not understand what it is like here in Scotland, Master Swyfte." Emotion rose in James's voice and for a moment it looked as if he might cry. "You do not understand the trials we face, the suffering inflicted upon my people in secret. They feel themselves the victims of a harsh fate, plucked from their homes, murdered as they cross the glens and hillsides. If only they knew the truth!"

"Which is why they should never know."

James calmed himself, nodding. "Scotland needs aid, Master Swyfte. We need the defences you have established in England."

"That is not a matter for me—"

James held up his hand. "I know. And I know you have the ear of some of the highest in the land. If you could take word back with you—"

"There are proper channels for that communication."

"And yet they are always closed to me! England does not want to know of our suffering!"

"England has suffering enough of its own. It faces enemies on every side, and from within. Many, I might add, that have crept in from north of the border, from your own Catholic sympathisers, and through the connections you have with France."

James's expression grew taut. "We need the aid of England. One day, if Elizabeth passes without issue, I will be king of England, and then there will come a change. I will save my nation, Master Swyfte."

"We all wish to see the Enemy defeated. This is not a matter of nations, or religion. Those are distractions . . . yes, that is tantamount to treason in some quarters, but it is the truth. We are a brotherhood of man, and we should stand together against the greater threat. Only by recognising our common values can we rise up from our knees."

James smiled with a touch of relief. "It pleases me that we share this common ground, Master Swyfte. Perhaps change will come in my lifetime. Perhaps—"

A commotion rose up near the entrance to the State Rooms, and a second later several of the king's advisors ran over, concern marring their features. Ashen-faced, they hovered near their king, until one said, "They insist on entering. They claim it is their right as nobility."

With Will close behind, James marched towards the door, the crowd opening before him. The music died away, and the conversation stilled.

As the doors to the State Rooms swung open, the light from the candles grew dimmer, although the flames burned as strong. Shadows fell at strange angles, and a suffocating atmosphere descended. Here and there across the room, blood began to drip from noses.

Ten members of the Unseelie Court stepped in, the terrible weight of their gazes ranging across everyone present. The king's guests recoiled as one. The strangers advanced with languid superiority, like wolves among sheep, their emotions, their thoughts, everything about them unreadable. No one could look them fully in the face, and if any caught an eye by accident, the blood drained from them, and they crossed themselves, muttering prayers. Will knew the unease went far beyond the physical appearance of the Unseelie Court; it was as if a grave had been opened in everyone's presence.

So potent was the sense of threat, it was as if the strangers were on the brink of falling upon those assembled and slaughtering them where they stood. Their clothes, while of the finest material, appeared to be on the brink of rot, stained here and there with silvery mildew, the style harking back to a distant age. A scent of loam accompanied them. Their cheekbones were high, their hair long, their eyes pale, but there was an odd quality to their features that meant they rarely registered on the mind; once they had passed from view it was almost impossible to recall the details of their appearance.

Instantly, Will went for his knife, but James stopped him with a cautionary hand. "Leave them," he said desolately. "If we dare to challenge them, my people will pay the price for months, perhaps years, to come. Now do you see what I mean? Now do you see?" His voice cracked with anger.

From his bearing, one was clearly the leader. His long hair, the colour of sun on corn, fell around his shoulders, but failed to soften his icy features.

Spying James and Will, he approached, while his advisors circled the room, pausing to stare into the faces of those nearby. Some of the guests sobbed or swooned under the attention. Others took on a fatalistic expression that was painful to see, as if they had accepted that the date of their death had been decided.

The leader studied James's and Will's faces for a moment as if examining a lesser species. His eyes were too black, his stare unblinking. "I am honoured to be in the presence of the great King James of the land of Scotland," he said, pronouncing each word as if he carried a pebble in his mouth. His voice was low, and quiet, and some quality to it made Will feel unaccountably cold. "I am Cavillex of . . ." He paused, and then added with a contemptuous nod ". . . the Unseelie Court."

"You are the king of your people?" James asked.

Cavillex's eyes narrowed. "My family guides the Court." His attention skittered on to Will. "You trespassed in one of my homes, hurt one of those close to me, took what is mine—"

"I freed a poor soul imprisoned against his will."

James flinched at Will's defiance.

"Took what is mine," Cavillex repeated. "The disrespect you have shown is unforgivable. I would know your name."

"You will learn it soon enough. It will be engraved in your heart."

Cavillex nodded thoughtfully as he searched Will's face. "You have been touched by us before."

"Many men have been touched by your kind. There will be an ending to that business."

Cavillex ignored Will's insolence and continued to peer deeply into his eyes. "What was her name?" he enquired thoughtfully.

Deep in his head, Will felt something shift. His thoughts unfolded, rolling away like the mist on an autumn morning, and in the sun-drenched landscape that was revealed, he saw Jenny again, coming towards him through the cornfield, her face ablaze with love. His heart pounded with joy. He wanted to feel the touch of her hand in his once more, the sweetness of her cheek against his lips, the perfume of her hair, the melody of her voice, her laughter; her love.

And then the image faded, and he knew it was an echo, fading with each passing day, slowly draining the happiness from his life. A wave of grief washed through him, but he held it back before it broke on his face.

"Would you like to know if she still lives?" Cavillex enquired.

"Why would I listen to your words? They are lies and obfuscations and swamp-lights that lead you on to disaster," Will replied.

"Because hope and yearning forces you to listen, even when you know it is painful or futile. That is the way of men. You follow the light to try to ease the pain of your existence. You need the promise because you cannot deal with the harshness of the truth."

"And you take advantage of our weakness."

"You carry your own destruction with you," Cavillex continued. "Love. Even as it leads you on, it ruins you."

"And yet we continue," Will replied. "And when you divine that mystery you will realise you can never win."

"I know where she is." Cavillex nodded as he saw the light rise up in Will's face. "Alive, yes."

"With your kind?"

Cavillex remained implacable.

Will privately cursed himself for responding; he had proved Cavillex right. He forced himself to dismiss Cavillex's admission as another manipulation designed to inflict pain, but something in his opponent's face, or tone, hinted at a deeper truth.

"We will meet again, when it is time to balance our accounts," Cavillex said to Will with a nod. He turned to James and added, "We enjoy our time among your people and the sport it gives us." James winced and once again Will thought he was on the brink of tears. "Now, you have a choir here?" Cavillex continued. "I would hear more of your music that celebrates the joys of your short lives. Let them sing the opening verses of the 137th Psalm, in the setting of Filippo de Monte, *Super flumina*. Please your honoured guests." He bowed, and moved away into the crowd.

James wrung his hands. "I am a king, yet I am a slave."

"None of us can be ourselves—our lives are not our own. We all make sacrifices for the good of the ones we serve, and that is how it should be."

"But I would not be a slave to him!"

"Nor shall you, for much longer. We will never be truly free of them, but there will be a time when we have driven them back to the edges of life, and for most people they will become a memory, nothing more."

"Your words give me confidence. Remember me to your Queen, and, if you find it in your heart, pass on what I have said." He gave a weary smile, a nod, and went in search of the choir.

His resolve reaffirmed, Will moved towards Nathaniel, Meg, and Reidheid, who had been watching from afar. All the joyous noise of the festivities faded into a dull background buzz as his thoughts coalesced around the image of Jenny in the cornfield. Was Cavillex telling him the truth, or was it a lie designed to cause emotional pain? New hope that would eventually be crushed so brutally it would be worse than not having hope at all? It showed the cold effectiveness of the Enemy: in only one moment they had identified and attacked his most vulnerable area. He tried to force the image back into the deep, dark place where he had learned to keep it so he could continue with his life, but it clawed its way back, refusing to be subdued. Raw once more, the old questions hit him with renewed force: alive or dead? Salvation or damnation?

Unsettled, Nathaniel wanted to know the identity of the new arrivals, and appeared only partly placated when Will told him they were Spanish agents, although Meg was convinced. "They are here because they know I have the cipher and they are afraid I will reach their prize before them," Will said. He watched the Unseelie Court select unsettled women and men for dancing partners, and added, "Though how they knew I would be here this evening, I have not yet concluded. But they must not be allowed to follow us, or prevent us reaching the object of our search. Nat, you must come with me."

"You can count on us," Meg said with a confident smile.

"Do not take any risks," Nathaniel said with concern.

"We shall not fail you," Reidheid added, "though our lives be forfeit."

"I said, do not take any risks!" Nathaniel stressed. He touched Meg's hand briefly before Will tugged him away.

"She has a brave heart, Nat. Trust her," Will whispered as they slipped across the room. Nathaniel cast one backwards glance as Meg drew attention to herself by causing a commotion with one of the attendants. At the door a guard barred their way, but James caught his eye and nodded. The king exchanged a brief, curious glance with Will before accepting that whatever was planned was in his best interests. He turned away as Will and Nathaniel darted through the door.

"I am in debt to the king," Will said as they moved through a chamber where servants bustled into a long corridor with views across the darkening hunting grounds at the rear of the palace. The sky was a deep blue, turning rapidly to black, the trees stark silhouettes, the moon and the stars gleaming. "He is a good man, burdened by the demands of his office." Will realised he felt a strong affinity for the young monarch.

All the activity in the palace was centred on the State Rooms, and the rest of the corridors and chambers through which they passed were still and silent. Returning to the quadrangle, they found a door on the south side that led to a short corridor with another door leading directly into the abbey.

Inside it was cool and dark, the glow from the candles flaring up the walls to the vast wooden beams supporting the roof and drawing sparkles of brilliant colours from the stained-glass windows. The empty abbey was filled with the pungent aroma of incense. Their footsteps echoed on the stone flags as they made their way into the nave and looked up to the transept and the choir where the shadows gathered.

"Where do we begin?" Even though Nathaniel whispered, his voice carried far amid the perfect acoustics of the interior. He shivered and glanced towards the door to see if he had drawn any attention.

"Search the interior for any sign of a martyr," Will said. "A statue. A painting. An icon. An image hidden in the stained glass. A carving in the wood. It is here somewhere."

Nathaniel moved off to begin his search at the west end near the tower. Will approached the transept. The original design of the abbey overseen by King David had been altered here. During an attack by the English army forty years earlier, the eastern part of the abbey church was destroyed where it enclosed the royal tombs of James V, Magdalen, his first queen, and his infant sons by his second marriage to Mary of Guise. Will studied the rebuilt section and wondered if his search was futile. Perhaps a statue of the martyr had not been replaced during the restructuring, or some other clue to the location was missing.

As he continued to scour the abbey, he began to fear he was correct for there was no sign of a martyr anywhere. Despondently, he returned to the nave where Nathaniel paced back and forth, scanning the interior.

"Anything?" he asked.

Nathaniel shook his head. "Perhaps we look in the wrong place."

"No, I am convinced the Templar Knights would have hidden the item here, beneath the protection of God, in the most reverent area of Edinburgh."

"Then perhaps there is some sign we are missing."

Will agreed. "Let us reconsider. We are dealing with a cipher after all. A martyr may not be a martyr." While Nathaniel looked up to the heavens for inspiration, Will sank into one of the wooden pews and rested his chin in his hand. Thinking aloud, he said, "David dedicated this foundation to the Holy Rood. His mother, St. Margaret, brought that precious relic, a fragment of the True Cross, back to Scotland from the land of the Magyars." He mused, "Margaret . . . martyr," then shook his head with frustration.

Craning his neck, Nathaniel continued to examine the shadowy ceiling of the abbey with curiosity.

"Nat! Concentrate on the matter at hand," Will insisted.

"There. Do you see that?" Nathaniel pointed at the main arching beam of the abbey roof.

"This is no time to search for bats."

"There! On the beam!" Nathaniel urged.

With irritation, Will followed his assistant's pointing finger. After a moment of squinting, he identified a badge above the centre of the aisle: a red cross on a square, half white, half black. "One of the Templar flags," he said thoughtfully.

"If you had spent more time on your studies of the Christian faith, and less in the stews of Bankside, you would know that the red cross is the mark of a martyr."

"Nathaniel, you are a constant source of inspiration to me. Disregard all I said about you."

Will dropped to his knees to examine the stone flags of the aisle. Hammering his fist on the one directly beneath the badge resulted in a hollow echo.

"*Where the martyr stands in black and white,*" he said with a pleased smile. "I think we have it." With his nail and then with his knife, he scraped the dirt of centuries out from around the edge of the flag. "If we had a tool, we could prise it up," he said.

"I will search." Nathaniel hurried off into the gloom of the abbey. Will heard him searching cupboards and opening doors, and after a while he returned and shook his head.

"What now?" Nathaniel asked.

Will looked towards the door to the palace. "We cannot afford to leave this to another day. The Enemy could arrive at any moment." He paused, and said to himself, "Though Kintour said they could not walk near the entrance to where the Shield was kept."

"Why could they not walk here?" Nathaniel asked suspiciously.

Will ignored him. "No, there is no choice. We must break through this flag. Fetch me that iron candleholder."

"I fear your constant desire for attention is getting the better of you," Nathaniel said. The candleholder was several inches higher than Nathaniel, and he had to brace himself to lift it with a grunt. He staggered over to Will and lowered it slowly to the flags with another grunt.

"You are growing soft, Nat. I must work you harder." Will braced himself and lifted the candleholder as high as he could. When he brought it down hard, the resounding crash boomed off the walls of the abbey. Nathaniel jumped and looked to the door. At Will's nod, he ran to it and peered out. Listening for a moment, he said, "Nothing yet. I can hear the music from the festivities. Perhaps it drowned out your attempts to bring disaster round our ears."

Once he had closed the door, Will brought the candleholder down again. A few flakes cracked off the centre of the flag, but it remained solid. With mounting anxiety, Nathaniel checked out of the door again.

The third time Will thundered the candleholder against the flags there was a loud crack, but no sign on the surface of the stone. The fourth time the flag shattered into pieces that plunged into a dark hole beneath. Cold, damp air and the smell of great age rushed out of the space.

Nathaniel checked out of the door one final time and then rushed back to Will with relief. But peering into the void by Will's shoulder, he grew hesitant. "There is something about that sight that fills me with dread," he said.

"Then let your heart beat slower, Nat, for I would have you wait here," Will told him.

Nathaniel bristled. "Are you saying I cannot match the courage and fortitude of the great Will Swyfte?"

"No, Nat, I am saying I need someone here to keep watch at my back," Will lied.

This placated Nathaniel, and his relief showed in his face, which pleased Will quietly. Crouching on the edge of the hole, Will prepared to lower himself in. "Wish me luck, Nat. Fortune favours fools!"

CHAPTER 24

ehind Will, a shaft of light plunged down into the hole from the abbey and he could hear Nathaniel moving around the edge, trying to follow his progress. With a single candlestick for light, he edged along walls lined with stone blocks, well aged and glistening with damp, the floor perfectly level. Despite the fine workmanship, he was aware that after four centuries collapses could lie ahead, perhaps even drops into the foundations.

The stale air told him that wherever the tunnel led, it was sealed. After a few paces, it sloped down until Will estimated he was at least twenty feet beneath the floor of the abbey.

Finally, he came to a raised step. The change in the timbre of the echoes suggested a large space lay beyond, but the candlelight barely penetrated a foot into the chamber.

A stone column topped by a plinth stood just inside the entrance. Carved into the top was the Templar cross and an image of two Knights on a horse, underneath which was engraved *Sigillum Militum Xpisti*—the Seal of the Soldiers of Christ.

Lowering the candle, Will saw a legend had also been engraved:

Under God's ever-watchful eye,
A Shield against Earthly decay shall lie.
But the fires of heaven and hell consume
The unworthy seeker who enters this tomb.

Studying the message of damnation, Will was puzzled by the reference to the "fires of heaven," but could see some greater meaning was coded into the legend. "There is a mystery here," he mused aloud.

Amid the disorienting echoes, Will edged past the plinth into the suffocating darkness of the chamber. It was impossible to tell how large the space was, or where the Shield was located. As he progressed, the candle revealed that plain flagstones were about to give way to ones engraved with the Templar cross, stretching as far as the candlelight penetrated.

The tone of the legend encouraged Will to advance with caution. Pausing at the line of Templar stones, he took one hesitant step. When the flag cracked and fell away beneath his boot, he threw himself back. From above, a stream of silvery powder fell towards a gleaming black liquid smelling of pitch that lay beneath the broken stone. As the powder landed, the liquid burst into a column of fire.

Kicking back several more steps as the heat scorched past his face, Will caught his breath and realised how close he had come to being incinerated. The flaming column died down a little, but still blazed intensely at its base. Its glare revealed a vast chamber bigger than the floor of the abbey, with the cross-marked flags reaching to the far wall where a niche held an object that he couldn't quite discern.

As Will rapidly processed what had happened, he realised some of the meaning of the legend on the plinth. *Fires of hell*, burning beneath his feet. He guessed what *fires of heaven* meant. Returning to the tunnel, he reclaimed a heavy chunk of the broken entrance flag and tossed it out onto the cross-marked stones. Two flags shattered. One ignited another hidden pool of the pitch-like liquid, while the other released a gush of the flaming liquid from above.

Somewhere, he guessed, there was a path across the flags to the niche that would not end in death, one the Templars had left should they, or their heirs, ever need to reclaim the Shield for their own use.

Will was acutely aware of the pressure of time. Sooner or later, the Unseelie Court would realise he was no longer at the festivities and would come searching for him, if they had not done so already. But the ferocity of the fire showed he could not take any risks. Even testing the flags with his boot could result in death, and the heat from too many blazing locations would destroy him, even if he did find a path among them.

For a few minutes, he walked up and down the boundary of the cross-marked flags, searching for any that were different, an angled cross, perhaps, or a completely bare flag, but even before he had completed one pass he knew that would be too easy. The Templars wanted to protect the Shield from anyone who wished to use it for malign purposes.

Yet they also recognised the Shield could be of benefit, perhaps in protecting against one of the Skull's attacks, and so they would have incorporated a way to it for someone who wished to use it for good. But how could they differentiate?

Leaning against the wall at the back of the chamber, he carefully turned over everything he had learned about the Templars. He knew of their public works, of course, and of their secret war against the Enemy that had been revealed to him by Dee. He had discovered that they used ciphers to disguise their true meaning, and that they enjoyed the use of symbolic representations.

Thoughtfully, he returned to the plinth. The key was there, he was sure. The warning to those who wished to use the Shield for evil, that was clear. But a clue to help the needy? He read the legend again, carefully.

The second half of the legend was specific in its warning. What if the first half was too? *Under God's ever-watchful eye.*

Walking back to the line of cross-marked stones, Will peered up to the ceiling high overhead. It would normally have been obscured by gloom, but a sacrifice in the *fires of heaven and hell* had revealed in blazing illumination what was hidden there. Will smiled, understanding the minds of the good Christian Templar Knights. The unworthy would focus on the perils of the fires. The worthy would look to the heavens for salvation.

The stones across the ceiling mirrored the ones on the floor, each marked with a Templar cross—*as above, so below*—except that a few were marked with an eye.

God's watchful eye.

If he followed the trail of the eyes, would he find his way through to the Shield? The reasoning appeared sound, but there was only one way to be certain. Placing his boot firmly on the flagstone beneath the first eye, Will shifted his weight onto it. The flag held.

Quickly, he followed the route, shying away from the roaring columns of flame. Occasionally, he had to wait for the thick smoke to clear so he could follow the safe path, and he realised that if he had cracked any more of the fire-stones, the smoke would have completely obscured the guiding eyes above. There was something symbolic in that, too.

The path turned left and right, weaving across the entire width of the chamber, but moving inexorably towards the niche. Finally, he stood before it. In the niche, resting on an angled plinth, was a silver amulet on a chain, inscribed in black filigree with symbols and words in a language Will did not recognise.

Snatching the amulet and turning to retrace his steps, he spied Reidheid waiting on the far side of the chamber, his sword drawn. Reidheid nodded slowly as he saw the thoughts play out on Will's face.

"Traitor," Will intoned gravely.

"I am not alone," Reidheid replied. "There are traitors everywhere among Walsingham's men. Sometimes I wonder if there are more traitors than loyal followers of the queen."

Holding the amulet behind him, Will strode back along the path. "How could you betray England?"

"England endures, whatever happens. The question is: how could you *not* betray the queen and her government? You have seen the Enemy's abilities. We can never win."

"What have they promised you, Reidheid? Riches? Congress with the most beautiful women in the land? A life eternal? They prey on human weakness, and find the spaces in our character that they can prise open from crack to chasm. You know that. They cannot be trusted."

"They promised me freedom from fear." A fleeting expression of desperation crossed Reidheid's face. "Imagine what that would be like. No longer glancing over your shoulder in search of death's looming, bony face. No longer waking with such bleak thoughts in the morning that you are unable to appreciate the new dawn, and no longer fighting to find sleep each night as the terrors race through your mind."

"We are mortals. There is no true freedom from fear. We live with it and learn to accommodate it. That makes us human. And that is where we gather our strength."

"Yes, we are mortals. We hate each other for being Catholic or Protestant, Jew or Moor, English, Spanish, or French. There is no hope for us. We must get what we can from this world, before heaven beckons."

"Or hell."

Steadying himself, Reidheid waved his sword towards Will. "Enough. Our philosophic discourse can be continued at another time. Give me the Shield."

"So you can in turn give it to the Enemy." Will held the amulet by the chain so that it turned slowly, reflecting the gold and scarlet of the flames.

"It matters not to you." Reidheid stepped to the edge of the cross-marked flags. "Another turn in a war that goes on forever."

Will smiled tightly. "I see the Enemy treats you like their dog, chained up in the kennel and thrown tidbits. Do you not know what is truly at stake here? You betray not only the queen and England, or your fellow man, but your own family, your daughter, Meg."

"And why should I believe you either?" Reidheid snapped. "Will Swyfte, who lives a lie as the greatest hero England knows, a fairy tale to soothe the nightmares of men and women so they think themselves protected by gods, and not, in truth, by an assassin . . . a torturer . . . a man of grey morals. You are no better than me. We have our ambitions and we pursue them vigorously."

Protecting the amulet in his fist, Will came to a halt a few flags short of Reidheid and drew his sword. "You speak like a child. Is this some revelation to you? That we all wear masks? Which is the true face? The truth is, there is none. We are all many things, and all of them insubstantial. Good and evil are elusive. But there is one thing that divides us. You do what you do for your own gain."

Reidheid's cheeks flushed and he held out his hand. "The Shield."

"It is here. You may take it, or try to." Will raised his sword.

Reidheid hesitated. "I am not afraid. The Unseelie Court will be here soon, and you will not escape their attentions."

"I think not. It is my belief that this place is protected. No Enemy foot can tread here without risking destruction. It is you and I, Master Reidheid. I hear you were a fine swordsman in your prime. Do your recall your skills?"

Reidheid stepped onto the closest of the cross-marked flags, and by chance it was one beneath an eye. Hesitating, he looked around at the blazing pools and realised Will was leading him into a trap.

He smiled and stepped back. "Clever, Master Swyfte. But you are at the disadvantage. The Unseelie Court even now prepare to close off your options for escape, and the Spaniard has been dispatched to collect your assistant. He will not last long."

"Then let us end this." Will raced along the true path across the flags, but at the last he stepped on the fake flag nearest to Reidheid. It crumbled under his boot, but his momentum carried him over it as he ducked the swing of Reidheid's sword and rolled across the solid stones of the chamber's entrance area.

As flames rushed up from the black pool, Reidheid reeled back, one arm raised before his face against the blast of heat.

On his feet in an instant, Will spun, planting one boot in Reidheid's gut. With a cry, he doubled-up and fell back, but a well-hidden agility came to the fore as he rolled across the chamber floor to avoid the thrust of Will's sword.

He was up quickly, blocking Will's driving thrusts and responding in kind. Their fight ranged along the edge of the cross-marked flags, evenly matched as Reidheid settled back into the duelling skills he had learned in his youth. Resounding off the chamber walls, the clash of their blades sang, thrust and parry, high and low.

But Reidheid was out of condition and after a few moments he began to tire. As his strength dwindled, Will saw his opening. He kicked one of the cross-marked flags next to Reidheid, withdrawing his boot sharply as the silvery dust fell. When the flames roared up, they engulfed the left side of Reidheid's body. Screaming, and ablaze, he dropped his sword and staggered away.

Instantly, Will knocked him to the floor and rolled him over continually until the flames were extinguished. The skin of Reidheid's face and most of the left side of his body was blackened, but he was alive. Will dragged him to his feet and propelled him towards the tunnel. "You are fortunate I am not the man you thought I was."

Near the entrance, the flames made their shadows dance along the tunnel walls, but soon they were in the dark again, with only the shaft of light from the abbey above to guide them on.

Whimpering in pain, Reidheid offered no resistance. Beyond his cries, Will listened for any sign of threat in the abbey above, but all was quiet.

"Nat," he whispered loudly, but received no response.

Beneath the shattered flag, he cupped his hands to propel Reidheid up, and then leapt to draw himself into the abbey. It was empty. Had Nathaniel gone to investigate the festivities, to ensure the Enemy was not closing on the abbey?

"Make no sound," Will said quietly to Reidheid as he held him by the arm, "or I will retract my previous decision and run you through."

At the door, Will listened. He could hear the distant music from the king's festivities, but there appeared to be no one nearby. Moving out into the short corridor that joined the abbey and the palace, he saw the quadrangle was now illuminated by the silvery light of the moon. Darkness hung heavily in the cloisters.

"Father!" Meg's cry rang out from the nearest cloister along the eastern edge, and a second later she separated from the darkness of a doorway accompanied by another figure. It was the Hunter, and he gripped her wrist tightly. Tearfully, she struggled to free herself so she could run to Reidheid, but the Hunter held her fast. As she fought, he moved a cruel, curved knife to her throat.

"See what you have done?" Will said coldly.

"Meg." The desolation in Reidheid's voice rose up above the pain of his injuries. "Leave her be."

In the moonlight in the quadrangle, several figures appeared, though there had been no sign of them before. Cavillex stood at the head of the other members of the Unseelie Court.

"There are places we cannot walk, but our influence never fades when we can always reach into human hearts," he said.

Drawing his sword again, Will thrust Reidheid away. Slowly he backed to the wall, his eyes darting along his branch of the cloister.

"Kill her," Cavillex ordered. "And then the rest of them."

Reidheid cried out, but before he could move, Nathaniel lurched from a doorway where he had been hiding. He manhandled a hefty iron candlestick and brought it down hard on the Hunter, who fell to the ground, his knife spinning across the flags.

"Run, Nat!" Will called. As he turned, he caught a glimpse of Nathaniel grabbing Meg by the hand and dragging her towards the abbey. Cavillex's orders echoed across the quadrangle, but Will was already racing along the cloister towards the tower in the far corner. He hoped to escape through the door to the gatehouse, but the Unseelie Court moved silently and stealthily past the entrance, revealed only by the moonlight throwing their fleeting shadows on the stone.

At the end of the cloister, Will plunged through a door that led to a spiral staircase passing windows with a view over the formal gardens. Only one pursuer appeared to be climbing the stairs behind him—the Hunter, Will guessed, seeking revenge for the wound Will had inflicted in the Fairy House.

At the top of the steps, he crashed into the outer chamber of a bedroom, dark with wood panelling. Each panel on the ceiling was marked with the royal seal, and as he ran into a chamber with decor that suggested it belonged to a woman, he realised he had arrived in the old quarters of Mary, Queen of Scots. Moonlight broke through the window across the boards. A wooden cabinet inlaid with red hearts and gold stood by a closed door to what he guessed was a dressing room, and a four-poster bed rested against one wall next to another door.

Will leapt onto the bed and drew the curtain. Steadying his breathing, he listened, and waited. The thunder of boots crossed the floorboards, and then his pursuer skidded into the room, coming to a halt as though he could sense Will was nearby. Will listened as he moved around the chamber. A soft tread, the brush of fingers on wood. The door to the dressing room thrown open. The cabinet knocked to one side. The other door torn open, a blast of chill air stirring the curtains around the bed.

The footsteps came to a halt, followed by a moment of searching silence, before they moved towards the bed and stopped on the other side of the curtain. Soft exhalations disturbed the quiet. Will pictured them only inches apart, looking directly into each other's eyes.

Will felt calm, his heartbeat steady. He was focused, staring directly at the thick, embroidered drape. A long moment of deathly quiet.

The curtains were torn back forcibly. For a second, Will's gaze locked on the Hunter's dark eyes, and he saw in their infinite depths a coruscating intelligence. Then, with a single fluid motion, he drove his sword through the Hunter's throat.

"For my friend," Will said quietly.

He continued to watch the eyes flicker in shock, and then roll towards white as the Hunter slid backwards, off the sword, his hands going to his throat. Will leapt from the bed and thrust his weapon through his adversary's heart, and held it firmly in place until the Hunter crashed to the boards, dead.

Standing over him, Will surveyed the body for a moment, seeing something less than the Enemy that had haunted the nightmares of Englishmen, thinking of Tom Miller, dead at the end of a rope long before he had begun to reach his potential. Thinking of Jenny.

"Not even a balance," Will said coldly. He withdrew his sword and wiped it on the body.

From outside came a keening sound that set his teeth on edge, and he realised it was the sound of grief from a world beyond the one he knew.

Somehow the other members of the Unseelie Court had sensed the death of one of their own.

As the sound of running feet echoed from the spiral staircase, Will bolted through the other door of the bedchamber into the Queen's Lobby, and then to a long gallery. Bounding down a flight of stairs, he encountered a mass of guards rushing towards him, led by the king himself. Fear burned in all their faces, and though they held swords and torches, there was little sign that they would be used.

"Master Swyfte," King James began, "I expected to find you at the heart of this disturbance."

"Apologies. I fear I have upset some of your guests."

A slight smile curved James's lips.

"They will not trouble you, but I believe they may want to introduce me to an unpleasant end," Will continued.

"Then I suggest you leave the palace forthwith, Master Swyfte, and we shall do all we can to ensure your pursuers are engaged in entertaining conversation! I hope you enjoyed the hospitality at the Palace of Holyroodhouse. You are welcome here any time."

With a grin and a bow, Will ran back out into the quadrangle, while James led his entourage towards the sound of the Unseelie Court in pursuit. Will knew the king would only be able to delay Cavillex and his group for a short while; time was of the essence.

He found an unsettled Nathaniel in the abbey, armed once again with the iron candlestick as he watched the door. Behind him, Meg tended to her father, who was sprawled on the flags.

"Come, Nat. We must take our leave," Will said.

Nathaniel's relief was palpable. "This is not the fun and games I was promised, Will. I will think twice the next time you invite me to a party." He turned to Meg and offered his hand, but she shook her head.

"I must tend to my father," she said, exchanging a long look of yearning with Nathaniel.

After a second, Nathaniel gave a restrained nod in parting and hurried to Will's side.

"There will be time to renew acquaintances another day," Will said.

"London is a world away." Nathaniel glanced back briefly as they passed through the door. With a wan smile, Meg waved goodbye. "And after this day, I understand why your time is spent in stews, and your heart your own."

"That is my world, Nat, not yours. I happen to like doxies. What they lack in romance, they make up for in vigorous entertainment."

The cloisters rang with the echoes of their running feet, and within seconds they were through the gatehouse to the forecourt where the carriages waited. Will informed Reidheid's driver that his master had instructed they be delivered to the house at Cowgate with speed.

Mere moments later, the carriage rattled through the gate in the west wall towards the sharply inclining cobbled street that led up to the castle. The city was dark, but candles burned in many of the windows in the tall stone houses on either side.

Will glanced back at the receding palace to ensure there was no sign of pursuit before settling back into the leather seat. He examined the amulet in the palm of his hand where it glowed dully in the half-light.

"This has been a good night, all told, Nat," he said. "We have escaped with the prize we sought, from under our Enemy's noses. We have shown them that England is a threat to be reckoned with—if they had not realised it yet, they know now they cannot abuse us with impunity. And—" He paused, allowing himself a moment to enjoy the memory. "—Tom Miller has been avenged. Our time in Edinburgh has been well spent. A victory on every front."

Lulled by the rocking of the carriage, Will put his feet up and considered the next stage. The Enemy would come looking for the Shield if they needed it to complete their mysterious plan, and that could possibly be used to England's advantage. A trap, perhaps. And then they could turn the tables and recover the Silver Skull, perhaps even strike a devastating blow at the Unseelie Court in the process.

He realised Nathaniel had slipped into morose silence, and was staring into the pitch black wynds that ran off the main street. "Thinking of Meg?" Will asked.

He shook his head. "Our enemies were not Spaniards, Will."

"Their allies—"

"Who were they?"

"Nat—"

"*What* were they, Will?"

A cold pit formed in the depths of Will's stomach. He would rather see Nathaniel dismissed and sent back to a more mundane life in the shires than be destroyed by the truth.

Before Will could put Nathaniel's mind at rest, a mournful howl echoed along the street from somewhere behind them. The cries of waking babies, the barks of chained dogs joining with it, the slams of shutters and doors, moved up the street like a drum roll.

Nathaniel started. "What was that? A hunting dog?" He paused uneasily. "I have heard no dog like that."

Will knew exactly what it was, and his frustration mounted and turned to anger. Pulling himself half out of the window, he peered back down the street, but there was only a sea of darkness. "Faster, driver!" he called. "As if the Devil was at your back!"

"Yes, sir!" At the driver's whip-crack, the horse picked up its pace so that Will and Nathaniel were thrown around in the back of the carriage.

"What is happening here?" Nathaniel said with an edge of desperation. "You urge the driver to speed because a dog howls? That makes no sense to me."

"The agents of the Spaniards do not give up easily, Nat," Will dissembled. "We need to reach the house in Cowgate where we will be safe, for now."

"Why safer there than here? Or at the palace?"

"Not now, Nat!" Will snapped.

Leaning out of the window once again, Will thought he could now see specks of red light swimming in that ocean of dark, and above the thunderous sound of the wheels on the cobbles, he wondered if he could truly hear the pounding of paws, like a blacksmith's hammers . . .

"Hold tight, Nat! If you thought the journey to Edinburgh was hard, there is a rougher one to come!"

Glancing over his shoulder, the driver saw something that Will couldn't, for his face grew white and fixed in horror.

"Keep your eyes on the road!" Will yelled. "Let me worry about what is at our backs!"

As the howling grew louder, the driver cracked the whip wildly, driving the horse into a panic. The carriage skewed across the street, and as the driver guided it to the left towards Cowgate, it lifted off two wheels and threatened to turn over. Will and Nathaniel hurled themselves over to the other side to use their weight to bring the carriage down with a jolt.

"Damn him!" Will cursed. "*He* will kill us!"

"What scares him so?" Nathaniel shouted.

As the carriage raced down the slope towards Cowgate, Will dragged himself to look out of the window once more. The dog was by the side of the door, keeping pace perfectly. It turned its red eyes upon him, and then it leapt, jaws torn wide.

Will threw himself back just in time. Saliva splashed across his face as the motion of its snapping jaws caressed his skin.

The beast slammed against the side of the carriage with such force that it felt like they had been struck by another carriage. As the wheels skewed across the road again, the wood of the side and roof cracked and splintered under the brutal assault. The dog crashed across the roof and a second later the driver released a sickening shriek, abruptly cut short.

The carriage spun across the road in the opposite direction, the sound of the protesting wheels lost beneath the terrified neighing of the horse, quickly swallowed by a horrifying snarling as the dog tore the creature to pieces.

In the frenzy of the attack, the carriage pitched at an acute angle, hovered for a scant second, and then finally went over. Will and Nathaniel were flung across the interior as it crashed on the cobbles and skidded to a sudden, bone-jarring halt.

Dazed, Will checked on Nathaniel, who was stunned, lying in a heap. From nearby came wet echoes of the dog tearing through the remains of the horse. As he watched his friend, conflicting urges tore through Will. Could he put Nathaniel at risk of greater contact with the nightmarish world Will had protected him from for so long? What was more important: his friend's sanity and life, or the secret war?

"Nat! Nat!" Will whispered insistently, coming to a reluctant decision. "No bones broken? Good. I have work for you."

"N . . . now?"

"Especially now." Will sat Nathaniel up and thrust the amulet into his hands with a pang of shattering regret and the feeling that he had damned him forever. "Take this back to the house. You will be safe there."

In the background, the rending and tearing died away.

"I am the one they want. I killed one of them. They believe I have the object they desire. You will have time to make good your escape before they realise their mistake."

"But they will kill you!"

A growl, circling the carriage.

"I made my peace with that outcome a long time ago. It is as inevitable as the snows of winter—if not now, then later." He pulled Nathaniel to his feet and helped him clamber out of the window above his head before flashing him a grin. "Know that I do not plan to go easily into the arms of the Reaper."

The dog was near the remnants of the horse. Coming to a halt, it raised its head towards Will, baring its teeth.

"Will—" Nathaniel began hesitantly.

"You know me, Nat!" Will insisted. "I will demand my due reckoning. Now go!"

Nathaniel hesitated for only the briefest moment longer, but in that time Will saw his depth of concern, and friendship. He nodded and was gone.

Will drew his sword as the great black dog prepared to leap. The last thing he saw was Nathaniel weaving into the intense darkness of a foul-smelling close.

And then, with a snarl, the dog attacked.

CHAPTER 25

As the dark of the close swallowed Nathaniel up, from behind came a chilling howl that ended in the sounds of a beast at slaughter. Will's voice rang out, as defiant as ever, the words lost beneath the bestial roars, and then there was only a distant silence against which Nathaniel's running feet sounded like whip-cracks.

His head still spun from the knock it had taken when the carriage crashed over, but he was resolute. Will had survived so many close encounters with death, Nathaniel had long since learned there was no point wasting time worrying about what might be. Instead, Will had trusted him with a matter of great import to England, and he would not let his friend down.

Slipping the amulet into his pocket, he sped on into the unfamiliar city. It was the easiest way to lose himself; the closes and wynds ran out from the king's High Street like the tiny spikes along the spine of a fish bone, numerous, narrow, dark, filthy, and rat-infested. If he reached out both arms he could touch the walls on either side, the buildings soaring up so high that only a tiny patch of star-sprinkled sky was visible. No moonlight reached the ground. Excrement and urine sloshed under his feet, thrown from the surrounding houses, and rotting domestic refuse was piled everywhere, seething with rats.

Pausing to catch his breath, Nathaniel leaned against the wall and looked back to see if the dog was pursuing him. Instead, he saw silhouetted figures searching near the entrance to the close.

As the figures darted into the dark close, an inexplicable fear overwhelmed Nathaniel, greater than he should have felt with Spanish agents at his back. Instinctively, he recognised there was something more here, and much that Will was not telling him.

Although he ran on in the gloom, his pursuers were remarkably fleet-footed. He could hear them searching the doorways and other potential hiding places as they passed, yet still they drew nearer; he was sure he would not be able to outrun them. What, then, when he broke out of the other end of the close and into the open?

"Quick! Tell me. They are coming?"

Nathaniel jumped at the voice, and was surprised to see a grey-haired old woman crouching in a doorway, peering back along the close.

"There are enemies at my back, yes," Nathaniel hissed.

"Enemies. That is a good word for them." The old woman peered at him with black eyes, her brow knotted, but whatever she saw appeared to convince her for she threw open the door to her hovel and urged him inside.

From the room, a rectangle of light flooded out into the close like a beacon. Behind, Nathaniel heard the voices of his pursuers rise up.

"They will know where I am!" Nathaniel said.

"Inside! Now!"

Torn, Nathaniel hesitated until the woman grabbed him with a strength that belied her age and dragged him inside. The door slammed shut behind them. Hastily, the woman poured a fragrant line of salt and chopped herbs along the doorstep, and then ducked down to floor level, urging Nathaniel to do the same. He saw a row of charms hanging above the door and along the length of the wall, animal bones, twisted pieces of metal, feathers, and painted jewellery.

"They will sense you are somewhere nearby, but they will not know where," the woman whispered. "And even if they come to the door they will not be able to enter."

"Have you lost your senses?" Nathaniel hissed. "They saw the light! They will be inside in an instant!"

The woman waved him silent as running footsteps slowed outside. Nathaniel's breath caught in his throat as he glimpsed movement along the gap beneath the door. He estimated there were three or four people outside, moving slowly along the close, pausing every now and then to listen. One hesitated outside the door, slow breaths clear in the silence. With widening eyes, Nathaniel focused on the door handle, waiting for it to turn. Silently, he mouthed a prayer.

After a moment when he thought his heart would burst, his pursuer moved on, and the running feet continued along the close until they faded from hearing. Bowing his head in relief, Nathaniel inhaled a gulp of air.

When he had recovered, he snapped at the woman, "We were fortunate. You could have doomed me. Believing in your magic!" He indicated the charms with contempt.

The woman narrowed her eyes at him with equal contempt. "I saved your life. You are a fool if you think otherwise. They prey on our people continually. Do you think we have not found ways to keep them at bay?"

Nathaniel snorted, although the woman's words caused unsettling ripples deep in his mind that he refused to contemplate. As he turned to examine the room, Nathaniel saw they were not alone. Twelve other adults crouched along the far wall, their faces pale and fearful. There was a baby, and children of all ages, too, all dressed in poor clothes, their hollow cheeks detailing their daily struggle for survival. But they, and their house, were clean, and the woman had offered Nathaniel the hand of friendship, even at risk to herself.

"I apologise for my poor manners," Nathaniel said to her with a bow. "You gave me refuge, and it is a truth, I think, that you saved my life. I am very grateful."

"Apology accepted." The woman hauled her old bones to a chair near the range.

"I will arrange for my master to send you a reward—"

She shook her head forcefully. A cold eye warned him not to continue.

"Then I will be on my way," he said.

"Are you in your cups?" One of the men bounded forwards and grabbed Nathaniel's arm forcefully. "They are still out there."

"I can slip back the way I came—"

"They can see a rabbit in a field ten miles distant. They can hear the breaking of an ear of corn from the same. They can smell the sweat of your fear on the wind."

Nathaniel tried to laugh off the man's concern, but there was no humour in his drawn face.

"You do not know what hunted you?" the man asked warily.

"Spanish agents."

He laughed contemptuously and spat on the floor. "They are—"

"Hush!" the old woman shouted. "We do not talk of them! Once they notice you, your time is done."

Hesitating, Nathaniel pieced together the woman's words. "You say they are—?"

"Hush," the woman said quietly, turning her attention to the pot bubbling on the range so she did not have to meet Nathaniel's eye.

"You are welcome to stay for a bowl and some bread." The man's voice had the unsettling sympathy of an adult talking to a child who had not grasped that a relative had died.

"Yes . . . thank you," Nathaniel replied, feeling a weight growing on his shoulders. "But I must reach a house in Cowgate."

"At dawn," the man said. "It will not be safe then, but it will be easier. For now, take your rest on our bed in the back room. We will call you when the food is ready."

His thoughts racing, Nathaniel allowed himself to be guided into the dark rear room. As he sat on the bed, listening to the dim, restrained talk through the door, his thoughts returned to the time in his life when everything changed. He was nineteen, and had been offered work as an apprentice in the nearest town, to start three weeks hence. His lodgings had been found, and his plans made, and then he had woken suddenly in the night to find his father missing.

CHAPTER 26

The harvest moon framed the silhouette of the church steeple and caught the wayward flit of bats from their roost in the bell tower. Across the churchyard, shadows cast by leaning tombstones and yews gently swaying in the breeze lay stark against the well-tended grass caught in the brilliant white moonlight. One yawning grave held the attention of the crowd of fearful villagers gathered around the lych-gate. None of them spoke, and it was as if they could not draw their eyes away from the black hole and piles of earth scattered all around.

Hurrying from the cottage, Nathaniel had found his father, the churchwarden, standing among the villagers with the air of someone wrestling with a harsh choice.

"Father," Nathaniel said, still half asleep. "What is this? The grave has been disturbed again?"

"Go back to bed, Nathaniel. This is not for you." His father was distracted, but his face looked grey under the moon's lantern, and much older, as if his features were attempting to catch up with his hair, which had turned white overnight after the death of Nathaniel's mother.

"Can this not wait till morning? I will help you fill in the grave—"

His father rounded on him, gripping his arm. "Anne Goodrick is missing. We fear she is within the church, taken there by . . . by . . ." The words died in his throat and he looked away quickly in the hope that Nathaniel would not see the horror in his features.

"Then this is not the work of grave robbers," Nathaniel said, "There is more to this. A plot." He considered for a moment, and then said, "Catholic sympathisers. They do this to disturb our faith. Is that it?"

After a moment, his father replied, "Yes, Nathaniel. You are correct. But now young Anne's life is at risk."

"Then we must storm the church to save her! All of us together can overcome any opponents, however well armed they might be—"

"No!" Nathaniel was shocked by the fury he saw in his father's face, who was always a gentle man. "You do not venture into the churchyard, do you hear me?" His father turned to the other villagers and said loudly, "Whatever might transpire, do not let my son follow me in there."

The villagers nodded, but in their shame at their inactivity they would not look his father in the eye.

"What? You cannot mean to go alone? If there is danger, it would be wise to enter the church together, and well armed."

"No arms will help us," his father muttered. In a surprising show of emotion, he hugged Nathaniel to him and whispered, "You must take care of yourself, Nat. This is a dark and dangerous world." The moment he had spoken, he darted under the lych-gate and into the churchyard.

Nathaniel made to go after him, but the strong hands of the blacksmith and his son gripped him tightly, and however much he fought he could not shake them off. They continued to restrain him after his father had slipped into the church, but gradually their grip eased, as they watched in anticipation. No sound came from within. The mood of the vigil gradually became darker as the minutes stretched on, and in the intense silence Nathaniel's anxiety spiralled and turned to fear when he realised his father was not coming back out; he was a prisoner, or worse.

Before his panic sent him into a frenzy, the crowd was disturbed by hoofbeats drawing near at a gentle pace.

Confusion at who could be riding into the village at that time of night took the sting out of Nathaniel's thoughts. A man not a great deal older than he rode up, dressed all in black, with black hair and black eyes and well-trimmed chin hair. Despite his appearance, there was no dourness to him. Nathaniel recognised a confidence, amplified by a touch of playfulness that in itself was dark, and a deep, reassuring strength.

"My name is Will Swyfte," the stranger said, "sent here from London to aid you with your difficulty."

"How did you hear of our problems?" the blacksmith asked suspiciously.

"Word of such matters travels quickly. The queen has good men everywhere who watch and listen for any threat to the nation."

As he dismounted, Nathaniel pressed forwards and said urgently, "My father has ventured into the church, and not come out. I fear . . . I fear . . ."

Will rested a hand on his shoulder and said, "We all do. Tell me what has transpired here."

"Three days ago, Nicholas Goodrick was buried." Nathaniel indicated the open grave. "He was . . . not a good man," he added hesitantly. "We thought some of his enemies had caused this desecration, but there was talk that Nicholas had been seen abroad, as if he were still alive."

"Your manner suggests you do not believe these stories."

Nathaniel shrugged. "Of course not. Dead is dead. We are not all superstitious fools. This is a time of knowledge and understanding." He cast an eye over his neighbours and saw the gulf between him and them.

"You have a strong will. I like that. What is your name?"

"Nathaniel Colt."

Will nodded. Nathaniel could see he was an educated man, storing away any information that might be of use to him. "And the corpse was gone?"

"We searched for it, but . . . These things happen, sometimes. Nicholas was—"

"Not a good man, yes. So you filled in the grave?"

"And the next day it was open again. There was a space beneath it, and tunnels leading under the churchyard and beyond. Animals . . ." He paused. "Though bigger tunnels than any animal could make."

"And more talk of Nicholas Goodrick at large."

Nathaniel explained the suggestion of a plot by Catholic sympathisers, or even foreign spies, and was rewarded with a reassuring nod and smile from Will. "And now they have taken Anne Goodrick," Nathaniel continued, "a cruel blow when she was finally free of her father." At Will's quizzical glance, Nathaniel added quietly, "It is common knowledge that he thrust an unnatural relationship upon Anne. Many times I found her crying, but she would never talk of it."

Will's expression darkened, and he looked back to the church. "And now she is in there, with her tormentor. Tormentors."

"Help my father," Nathaniel urged. "He is a good man, and only wished to aid Anne."

Nathaniel received a clap on the shoulder that he found oddly reassuring, and then Will drew his sword as he loped towards the church. Fearing another long silence and an uncertain outcome, the villagers were fixed on Will as he entered the church. At first the quiet confirmed their darkest thoughts, and then suddenly lights flashed inside as though lightning crackled across the nave. As one the crowd called out. Shortly after, bloodcurdling cries that were barely human echoed from inside the church, followed by the sound of fighting from within the bell tower.

As always, Nathaniel was torn between the religious teachings of his father and his own faith in reason, between a world that could be mapped and understood, and one filled with terror. Conflicting images of the battle taking place within the church fought in his mind.

The crowd pointed and called out as Will appeared in one of the small arched windows of the bell tower, fighting furiously. A collision made the bell toll loudly, followed by another inexplicable flash of light. All around him, people were cheering their support, and Nathaniel was caught up in the passion and the belief that here was a great man, a protector, fighting a harsh battle on which all their fates depended.

Finally, Nathaniel caught sight of a shadow vacating the bell tower and passing rapidly across the moon before whisking away across the fields. He told himself it was a trick of his eyes, nothing more.

Soon after, the church door was thrown open and Will emerged with Nathaniel's father and Anne. Overcome with relief, Nathaniel ran to his father and grabbed him, before turning to pump Will's hand. "You saved them," Nathaniel said with admiration.

"I did what I could," Will replied.

It was only then that Nathaniel noticed Anne's glassy stare and the expression of abject horror that appeared to run so deep it would never be expunged. Without uttering a word, she trailed away from them towards the lych-gate, pausing briefly to stare into her father's empty grave.

Nathaniel's own father was deeply troubled in a manner that surpassed the curt dismissal of some Catholic sympathisers, even if it was on hallowed ground. He pulled Will to one side and engaged him in intense conversation for several minutes. It appeared to Nathaniel that Will was attempting to reject what was being said, but eventually he relented.

When he had finished the conversation, he took Nathaniel by the elbow and led him away. "Your father has found you a new appointment."

"I have an appointment."

"And now you have a new one. You will accompany me to London, to the court, where you will be my assistant."

Nathaniel didn't know what to say. He looked to his father, who wore an expression of deep relief.

"Gather your things and say your goodbyes," Will said. "We leave tonight."

"He is scared," Nathaniel said. "I can see it in his face."

"It is a dangerous world, and your father wants you safe."

"And you are supposed to keep me safe?"

At first, Will didn't respond. Nathaniel saw deep thoughts and emotions play out across Will's face that convinced him that here was a good man, as his father was good.

Finally, Will said, "I can see, Nat, that you will probably be a terrible burden, with your worryingly quick mind and, I would wager, a quicker tongue. But it is too late to go back on my promise now. It seems we are stuck with each other for the foreseeable future."

Nathaniel saw through the words. "And I would wager the burden will be all mine," he responded in kind. "But if nothing else I suspect there will be interesting times ahead."

As Nathaniel headed to the cottage to collect his things, he glanced back and saw Will watching Anne with deep concern etched on his face. Nathaniel sensed dark currents that he didn't yet understand, but he was determined to learn all there was to know of the world; and of the world this brave, impressive figure inhabited.

 CHAPTER 27

Across a desolate moor where the standing stones raised high by ancient people stood against a lambent moon in a starry sky, Will ran. The muffled sound of fiddles and pipes drifted across the gorse and sedge behind him, and a sickly-sweet smell of honeysuckle tainted the warm breeze. Under his feet, vibrations ran through the soft ground accompanied by a dim clanging, like a blacksmith's hammers, never slowing, beating out the shape of his past and his future in dark caverns far below. Then, behind him somewhere, a hunting dog howled, familiar and blood-chilling, and within moments the howl was moving towards him at great speed, and he knew he would never escape his fate . . .

He woke in a cold sweat, tied to a chair in a shaft of moonlight breaking through a window. His hidden blade was useless to him, bound as tightly as he was. Beyond the dirty glass, he could see tall stone houses, the windows dark. The dusty boards under his feet were bare, the plaster on the wall crumbling. He could smell damp, and a hint of human decay, but also that familiar underlying scent of honeysuckle. He was in the Fairy House.

The last thing he recalled was standing on the upended side of the carriage, sword in hand, as the black dog attacked. He felt its hot breath, saw its teeth stained with the blood of the driver and horse it had slaughtered . . . and then nothing.

As his senses returned, he realised he was not alone. Presences waited, unmoving, in the dark at his back; he couldn't estimate the exact number, but instinctively he felt there were at least three.

"You have me, then," he said.

After a moment of hesitation, the measured tread of boots revealed Don Alanzo, dressed as though for court, in a ruff, a linen shirt, a crimson and gold beaded doublet, padded breeches, and stockings, topped off by a velvet hat at a carefully positioned angle. He rested one hand on the pommel of his sword and studied Will.

"You cut a fine figure, Don Alanzo," Will observed. "If I did not know better, I would think you dressed for royalty."

"I return to Cádiz tomorrow," he replied in his heavy accent. "And then to glory, to the beginning of the end of England. With my prizes in hand."

"Not all your prizes."

"No, one evades me."

"And it will continue to do so."

"I think not." Don Alanzo examined his polished nails with theatrical nonchalance. "Already our agents close upon it. It is only a matter of time before your assistant is located and the Shield returned to us. Edinburgh is not a large city, and the people have no love of an Englishman."

Will stifled a pang of regret that he had placed Nathaniel in danger, and hoped that it was some previously unseen Spanish agents pursuing him and not the Unseelie Court. As he had always feared, his vow to Nathaniel's father continued to haunt him. "Nathaniel has a surprising degree of animal cunning. You may well be disappointed," Will said blithely.

Don Alanzo's lips curved with a faint, mocking smile. "You have not disappointed us yet."

There was much unsaid in the smile. "What are you saying, Don Alanzo?" Gently, Will tested the strength of the bonds around his wrists. As he had expected, they held fast; Don Alanzo would not make any mistakes.

"You recovered the artefact for us, where we and our allies had failed."

Will quickly assimilated Don Alanzo's implication. "You let me escape with Kintour and the cipher."

"Of course. Your reputation is well known. If there is one man in this world who could break a cipher, and overcome the traps of those Templar Knights, it is the great Will Swyfte." His mocking smile grew wider and stated, quite plainly, that Will was not at all *great*. "Reidheid, who plays both sides in this game, fed you the information we required about the existence of this house, and then it was only a matter of waiting for your arrival."

"A good plan," Will said. "One that I would have been proud to put into effect myself. Except . . . one of your allies lies dead . . ."

Don Alanzo's features remained unreadable.

"And you do not have the prize you sought," Will continued.

"As I said, only a matter of time."

"Which is what all failures say." Will was pleased to see Don Alanzo flinch. "Your allies are a poor choice, Don Alanzo, and do you no credit. Do you think they would not slit your throat, and every throat in Spain, once you have served their purpose?"

Don Alanzo's eyes flickered towards the unseen presences behind Will. "Do you think we are not aware of that? Shared interests cross boundaries of suspicion."

"Men are judged by the friends they keep."

Don Alanzo laughed. "And we should only ally ourselves with people we like? How naive! Why, Master Swyfte, if that were the case, I think you would struggle to find allies even within your own court."

"We are not talking about the French here, Don Alanzo. Or Venice, or Florence, or the Hapsburgs, or even that weak and feeble Russian, Feodor. The Unseelie Court is a half-starved wolf waiting in your parlour."

"And you think Spain is not? England is a corruption upon the world. Your arrogance spins out of control, standing against God and Rome, over-throwing laws and truces and order whenever it serves your purpose. You are despised by all freethinking men, and soon you will see black sails on the horizon. The dark ship that reeks of rot approaches your land, and it is already too late to turn it back."

Don Alanzo summoned one of those who stood behind Will. The Silver Skull stepped into the shaft of moonlight, his mask glowing with white fire, and fixed his bloodshot eyes on Will.

"Who are you?" Will asked.

"His identity is not important," Don Alanzo said. "There are many people prepared to sacrifice all they have to ensure England is destroyed. It is the sacrifice itself that matters."

"Play the hero in your game. We all do the same," Will said. "In the end, there are only winners and losers."

"Sadly, your role is already defined. If you think the lack of the Shield will slow our plans, you are sorely mistaken. This grand weapon has many uses. While it remains in our hands, you will always be in danger."

"Then my best endeavours will go to returning it to the Tower."

"I think not." Don Alanzo caught the Silver Skull's arm and guided him towards the door. "I take no pleasure in the suffering you are about to endure," he continued. "This is war, and the stakes are high, but still . . . You will reveal the whereabouts of the Shield, and then it all ends."

Don Alanzo and the Silver Skull stepped out of the room, and for a while there was no response to Will's mocking questions. At his back, he felt the weight of the remaining people in the room, studying his strengths, mental state, resilience, turning over his flaws and weaknesses, like hunters circling their prey. He knew exactly what was to come.

Finally, Cavillex stepped before him. The superiority Will had witnessed at the palace had been replaced by a cold indifference, though Will thought he sensed an intense rage burning just beneath the surface.

"I have a question: how many of your kind have fallen by a mortal hand?" Will asked blithely.

Cavillex ignored Will's taunting. He was handed a small silver tray, but held it just above Will's line of vision.

"It was surprising. I found it just like killing a man," Will continued. "Or a dog."

"It is a while since you have eaten," Cavillax began. "Would you like a bite, to fill your belly?" From the tray he plucked a fragrant, golden biscuit and wafted it under Will's nose. The scent of honey, butter, and spices filled his senses, and despite himself, Will's hunger magnified unnaturally. "Or a drink of water?" Cavillex poured a goblet of crystal water from a silver jug. Suddenly, Will's throat was as dry as a summer street.

Overwhelmed by the urge to consume the biscuit and water, his head spun, but he forced himself to resist. He knew the consequences of accepting food and drink from the Enemy; he would not forget Kintour.

"Thank you," he said, "but my appetite has fled."

Cavillex leaned in and said quietly, "That would have been the easy road."

"I would give you the gift of a challenge," Will replied. "For life is nothing, if it is not tested."

"No challenge," Cavillex stated.

Behind him, Will could hear the sound of metal upon metal, the clink of objects being arranged upon another tray, the clack and whirr of items being tested. In his head, he began to picture their shape and purpose, and forced himself to stop.

"You will never defeat us," Will said.

"Us?" Cavillex said. "Ah. The brotherhood of man. You think yourself my equal. Of course. Yet in the New World, you treat your own kind like slaves, and slaughter them as if they have no value. As you did the Moors. As you have done, even your own countrymen, over the steady march of the centuries. We stood in our glades, and by our lakes, and on the hilltops, and watched, slack-jawed and silent, as you tore through your fellow creatures. When the Norman, William, invaded your nation, one hundred thousand fell before his will in the north. Thirty thousand dead of starvation in Ireland under your own queen's campaign. How many more have been sacrificed to your pathetic arguments about religion? You are animals falling on each other in the field. You do not deserve to exist."

Will could not deny the sting of truth in Cavillex's words. "That is not the sum of us," he replied.

"What makes a man, then?" Cavillex enquired. "Let us investigate."

Hands grabbed Will's shoulders roughly and flipped his chair backwards. Just at the point when he expected his head to slam against the boards, it came to a gradual rest. A member of the Unseelie Court supported the chair on either side, but he could not see the details of their faces.

Cavillex loomed over him with the water jug. "This gift is given freely, and without obligation," he stated.

He poured the water slowly from the spout, down Will's chest, allowing it to flood across his face and into his breathing passages. It was barely more than a trickle, but Will was forced to inhale it, and instantly he was overcome by a sudden sensation of drowning. His limbs thrashing involuntarily, he tried to draw himself up, but Cavillex's two helpers held him tightly in place. Choking, his attempts to breathe were crushed by an overwhelming feeling of water filling his lungs and of slow suffocation. Darkness closed around his vision and stars flashed across his mind.

When he thought he was about to die, the water flow stopped. Coughing and spluttering, he sucked in a huge gulp of air. His vision cleared to reveal Cavillex an inch away from his face.

"This is just the beginning," he said.

Retreating, Cavillex filled the jug from another source out of Will's sight with a meticulous, slow pouring. Will tried to respond angrily, but his throat was raw from his rasping breath, and the residue of the water in his lungs and nasal passages made him choke once more.

Hanging over Will again, Cavillex said, "Once more, before I begin my questions. To soften you." He poured again.

This time the flow was faster, the water gushing down Will's nose and filling his airways in an instant. He choked, thrashed, could not draw a breath of air as the sensation of the water flooding his lungs magnified.

I'm dying, he thought. It was the only conscious notion before the involuntary responses to drowning took over: a wild panic rising from the heart of him, lashing everything from his head beyond the darkness of death rushing in from all sides. Frantically, he fought, but his captors maintained their grip with ease. A fire consumed his chest. His throat was a solid block through which no air could pass. His brain fizzed and winked out.

When he came round, the chair had been set vertically once more. Uncontrollable convulsions gripped him briefly as his mind fought with the belief that it had died, and the acute sensation of water filling his lungs to capacity. Every time Will recalled it, panic surged through him; the experience had embedded it deep in his mind, beyond his control.

His heart thundered so hard the blood in his ears muffled every sound, and it took him a second or two to realise Cavillex was speaking. "I am told that is what it feels like to drown. You should thank me. I have given you knowledge that few men have: of the dark landscape beyond the edge of death."

"Free me and I will give you an experience beyond that," Will rasped through his raw throat.

"Where is the Shield?" Cavillex asked.

Will didn't respond. Shuddering, he filled his lungs with air and clung on to the memory of breathing.

The chair was upended roughly, and this time his head did slam on the boards. The water gushed onto his face a moment later.

After his ordeal, his consciousness returned in a flood and his furious reaction threw the chair to one side so that he slammed hard onto the floor. His captors left him there.

"What do you know of Dartmoor?" Cavillex asked.

Wrong-footed by the question, Will fought through the sensations of drowning that still washed through him. "Dartmoor?"

"What happened there?"

"I have heard tell of that wild place in the west, but I have never been there."

"What happened there!" Cavillex's voice cracked with emotion. For someone who had maintained his equilibrium from their first meeting, his loss of control was shocking.

"Hunting?" Will ventured. His mind raced to draw connections. Why was Cavillex interested in Dartmoor? What *had* happened there?

Before he could conclude his thoughts, the chair was flipped over again and the water flooded into his breathing passages with a force he had not experienced before. This time he blacked out quickly.

Cavillex roughly shook him awake. Will could see in his captor's drawn features that he had expected success much quicker.

"How do we break the defences that keep us from exerting our will over your land?" he asked.

"You will have to ask Doctor Dee that."

Taking a step back, Cavillex looked into the street below as he steadied himself. "You know you will not survive this hour. For the remainder of your brief life, there will only be a cascade of pain and suffering, tearing your mind into ribbons. Save yourself. Seek salvation. Tell me what I need to know and you will be spared that misery. I will end your life in an instant. You have my word."

"God gave us memories for when the world gets too harsh. I have much to remember," Will replied.

"Very well."

Will waited for the chair to be upturned again, but instead Cavillex nodded to one of his associates who ventured to the back of the room and returned with another silver tray. Cavillex placed it on the floor in the moonlight where Will could see it. Lined up across it was a row of cruel instruments, so strange that their use was barely imaginable. Will saw gleaming blades, tongs, bands, screws, needles, and clamps.

"The question remains: what makes a man?" Cavillex reflected. "We shall find out. Blood and gristle and meat and bone. This part fits that part. But where in that jumble of raw, bloody mass is the glimmer that thinks and feels? Or is it all just an illusion? Are men mere puppets made of meat that imagine themselves something more? Have you told yourself a lie for so long in your stories and mythologies that you have come to believe it?"

Turning his back to Will, he studied the tray of instruments, waving his slim fingers in the air over them until he decided on his selection.

"We have existed on the edge of your world for a long, long time," he continued. "Over the ages, we have probed the mysteries of this existence, plumbed the depths of life, climbed the peaks of experience. We have come to understand the minds of mortals with the eye of an artist. Like wizards, we can conjure miracles from the base stuff of your being. We can distil the finest evocation of pain from the mist of your lives. We have learned to draw out suffering in minute increments, each one blossoming like flowers into something beautiful and delicate." He turned back to Will and revealed what he held in his hand. "Once you have gained our attention, your time here is over."

"Get on with it," Will said. He focused his mind on the information about Jenny with which Cavillex had taunted him. In it, he found hope, and strength.

He woke to find his captors sluicing the blood from the floor with a bucket of water. His body was a symphony of pain, his thoughts floating in and out of the rhythm. He had lost track of how long Cavillex had been working on him, but he knew he had not answered a question, and he had not given up Nathaniel. He would stay true to his vow to the end. That could be a long time coming, he knew. True to his words, Cavillex was an expert in drawing out suffering, building then releasing the pressure only to build it again. Survival was no longer an option. It had come down to a battle of wills, as Will had always known it would.

"What makes a man?" he said to Cavillex. "Defiance in the face of brutality and oppression."

"The Spaniard was right, you know. You think you are the hero in this play? You are not."

Will spat a mouthful of blood. "There are no heroes."

"You will tell me what I need to know."

Will sighed. "Let us dispense with this chat. You already torture me with your words. Boredom is your greatest weapon."

Nonchalantly, Cavillex selected another tool from the tray. Gritting his teeth, Will steeled himself.

Through the window came the distant sound of voices. Briefly, Cavillex hesitated, then continued towards Will as he considered which new part of his body to assault. The noise continued to draw closer, a crowd, shouting angrily. Hazy from the pain, Will couldn't make out the words.

The crowd washed up against the building, their voices so loud Will couldn't hear Cavillex's quiet words. Somewhere below them a window shattered. Objects clattered against the side of the house. Puzzlement briefly crossed Cavillex's face, and he turned back to the window. Will watched his body stiffen as he studied the scene in the street below.

"It appears you have gained the attention of the good people of Edinburgh," Will said wryly.

A rain of missiles rattled against the wall, and a steady boom echoed from the front door as the crowd attempted to break it down. When Cavillex turned to Will, his expression was cold and murderous.

"Does it serve your purpose to stand and fight?" Will asked. "Or will you melt into the mist as you always do?"

Thoughts crossed Cavillex's face, all of them unreadable. He looked to his assistants and nodded.

"So, your pleasure has been cut short," Will croaked brightly. "It appears my life is to end much sooner than anticipated."

"No," Cavillex said.

"No?"

"I told you, our skill at drawing out suffering is unmatched. Your kind has woken an angry beast. And *you* have gained our attention. Your activities in the past were an irritation, easily forgotten, like all your kind. But this night you killed one of our own—"

"Who caused the death of one of *my* own."

"No matter. When you kill a rabbit in the field, do you give it a second thought? But you have slain something unique and wild and astonishing."

Will was surprised to see tears sting Cavillex's eyes.

"You have stolen from this world something wonderful. Yes, we have noticed you. And your crime against all there is must be punished."

"This is never going to end," Will replied. "You prey upon us, we shut you out. You attack us, we attack you. You kill one of ours, we kill one back. What is there to gain?"

"It will end, and soon," Cavillex said. "And your corruption upon the face of this world will be wiped away, and you will be forgotten."

The window burst inwards, showering glass all around Cavillex, but he didn't flinch. His attention was fixed solely on Will as if there was nothing else in the world that mattered.

"You have gained our attention," he repeated in a quiet voice that was filled with such emotion it carried above the roar of the crowd. "You have someone you love?" He let the final word roll around his mouth with contempt. "Not the one we spoke of earlier. Someone close to you now. A friend, perhaps, someone you hold in affection." His gaze was heavy upon Will.

Grace.

Cavillex nodded. "I see now. A woman. When we leave this place we will find her."

"No," Will said.

"We will take her. We will show her the heights of our skills. We will make the fibre of her being ring out with unimagined agonies. But she will live. Until we bring you back to us, and then we will slowly slaughter you in front of her, so that everything in her heart that she felt for you is corrupted by her final memory of your suffering. And then we will set her free to live with her misery. A life lived in that manner is usually short."

"No!" Will raged.

Cavillex's cold smile was the cruellest tool he had used that night.

"No!" Will roared until his throat burned, and tore at his bonds until his already bloody wrists were numb, and he threw himself against the chair in a futile attempt to break free. He thought of Grace, and he thought of Jenny, and his anger consumed him. If he could have freed himself, he would have torn Cavillex limb from limb. All the pain he had suffered in his life, and the agony that so many around him had suffered, was to be magnified.

It will never end.

When the fury finally cleared, Cavillex was gone.

Within minutes, the door to the street burst in and the mob raced through the building, smashing doors and windows, but they found no sign that the Unseelie Court had been there—just an old, deserted house left to its ghosts.

Calling for help above the tumult, Will was finally answered by Nathaniel and another man. When they paused briefly in front of him, concern lit their faces and he realised how he must look, covered in blood, with too many wounds to count.

"They are all small things," he croaked. "A physician will stitch them in no time. Help me." The biggest wound lay inside him.

The other man rejoined the mob, and as Nathaniel fumbled to untie Will's bonds, he said, "I returned to the carriage and when I did not find you there, I knew you must have been brought to this foul place."

"You disobeyed me, Nat. You put at risk everything for which we fight."

"You would never have left *me* behind, were I in need," Nathaniel responded defiantly. The bonds fell to the floor, and he helped Will to his feet. Though he struggled to stand unaided, he was too weak.

"Thank you," Will said. Though only two words, the depth of his gratitude was clear.

"I would be a poor assistant if I let my master die when it was in my power to prevent it."

"You have undreamed-of abilities, Nat. You raised a mob."

"Not an easy task. The people here lived in fear of . . . your enemy."

Will winced when he heard the beginnings of understanding in Nathaniel's words.

"But I convinced them that together they had a power they did not have alone," Nathaniel continued, before adding quietly, "That, and a promise of some small reward if they saved your life."

"Small reward?"

"Quite a large one, truth be told."

"You are giving away the queen's money, Nat. Walsingham will not be pleased that you have bought such a poor thing with her fortune. Help me out of here, quickly. There is much to do—"

"Not for you. If you lose more blood you will die, Will."

"I cannot rest. Grace is in danger." Will swayed, close to fainting.

"You must see a physician first."

Resting against the doorjamb, Will said weakly, "Then I must ask more of you. Leave Edinburgh now. Take whatever money you can from Reidheid's house, and a horse, and ride for London. Find Walsingham and tell him Grace is in danger from the Enemy. She must be protected at all costs."

"And the amulet?"

Will hesitated. "I would not wish this upon you if it were not an emergency, Nat."

"And if you did not call upon me in a time of crisis, I would not forgive you, Will."

"The amulet must be delivered to Walsingham. It is not safe here. You will be safer once you cross the border into England, but you will still be a target. Your life will be at risk. Keep to the highways. Avoid the moors and the hills and the lakes. If you can, find someone to travel with you at all times. Do you understand me?" Will caught Nathaniel's arm with a desperation that troubled his friend.

"You can count on me, Will."

As Nathaniel helped Will slowly out of the house, Will dwelt on the cold passion in Cavillex's words and wondered if it was already too late.

CHAPTER 28

In the cold, stone reception room at his sombre palace of El Escorial, Philip of Spain sat in silent contemplation of the heat of passion waiting for him in his private quarters. Increasingly, his daily life felt like a troubling distraction from the only thing he truly valued, at times almost an unpleasant dream. Yet every wave of desire was accompanied by an equal pang of self-loathing. Now Malantha had started to infect his prayers, looking down at him in the depths of his head where before there had only been God. He had so much to concern him, not least the invasion of England, but he didn't have the strength or the urge to resist. Only Malantha mattered.

A knock at the door was followed by the arrival of the seventh duke of Medina Sidonia, Don Alonso Pérez de Guzmán el Bueno, a quiet, unassuming man with a greying beard, whose obsession with money had led to repeated claims of poverty despite his great wealth. It was his very retiring nature that had encouraged Philip to place him in charge of the Armada; among the many competing arrogant and cunning personalities in the Spanish nobility, Medina Sidonia had made the least enemies. His appointment—at Malantha's request, he had to admit—had offended no one and had cleared all obstacles among his own people to a successful invasion.

"How goes it?" Philip asked.

"Well. Our preparations are almost complete and we will be ready to sail by the end of April."

"Parma's forces are not as great as we once hoped, but he still has a good seventeen thousand men," Philip said, "comprising eight thousand Germans and Walloons, four thousand of our own men, three thousand Italians, one thousand Burgundians, and even a thousand English exiles, ready to heap disaster upon their own land. Parma has made plans to protect our flanks in Flanders, and he will be ready to lead his men onto English soil as soon as you have done your work."

"I have made arrangements for the blessing of the standard in Lisbon on the twenty-fifth of April, the Feast of Saint Mark the Evangelist," Medina Sidonia said. "Will you come to oversee the launch of this magnificent enterprise?"

Philip felt a sudden pang of panic. He could not leave El Escorial, and the secret pleasures it held, not even for a night. "My viceroy, the cardinal archduke, will represent me on that day."

Medina Sidonia was unhappy with this response, but he bowed and said, "As you wish. My men would have taken some pleasure in seeing you, but they will understand there is much to do at this momentous time."

Philip gave a reassuring smile. "*La Invencible* is all you need. Once Elizabeth sees the mighty fleet you have amassed, she will surrender without a shot being fired."

Philip was eager to return to his private quarters and barely noticed the unease in Medina Sidonia's face. "There are many across Europe who question the wisdom of the coming battle," the duke began hesitantly. When Philip didn't respond unfavourably, he took strength and continued, "Our Catholic allies in the Vatican, and Venice, and Prague all fear an emboldened Spain. They believe we are too strong already."

"One can never be too strong."

"True, true," Medina Sidonia responded hastily. "However, I have heard word that Henri in France is afraid that he will be the next to be crushed. Once England is ours, we can starve the Dutch rebels into submission and then move on his country. And once Western Europe is ours, he says angrily to anyone who will listen, Spain will sweep away the Protestant rule in the German states, in Switzerland, and across Scandinavia."

"Henri is very wise." Philip smiled, but when he saw Medina Sidonia become more troubled he added, "We *are* strong, too strong for any of them to attempt to throw obstacles in our way, whatever their fears. Wherever we travel—here or in the New World   we see victory. We have a brilliant military commander in Parma with a great force, filled with fury. And the fleet you have amassed will tear through England's sad band of pirates and adventurers. There is no doubt here."

Medina Sidonia would not be deterred. Now the dam had broken, long-held anxieties were rushing out. "In thirty years, all our fortune and our might have not subdued the Netherlands. How, then, can we hold England? Even if we take London and remove Elizabeth's head from her shoulders in revenge for what she did to Mary, the rest of that damned country is near lawless. We could be fighting in the North, and the Fens, and Wales, and Cornwall forever." He caught himself, afraid he had overstepped the boundary. "And there is the prophecy of Cyprianus Leovitius," he added quietly.

Philip sighed. "A prophecy that is in our favour."

"Based on the numerology hidden in the Revelation of Saint John—"

"It speaks of the year of wonders. The beginning of the final cycle. Upheavals for all. The end of empires. The end of England."

Medina Sidonia was not convinced. "Some say—"

"*I* say!" Philip shouted. "The end of England! Do not question me!" Steadying himself, he studied the weakness in Medina Sidonia's face before trying to bolster his commander. "God is on our side. He will not allow us to be defeated. There is much you do not know, much that must be kept secret from you if our plans are to succeed. We have a secret ally, and a weapon of great power that will be at your disposal. England *will* fall, and such destruction will be wreaked on that country and its people that there will be no doubt to whom the prophecy refers."

Curtly, he waved his hand to dismiss Medina Sidonia, and then hurried from the reception room as quickly as his gout-ridden feet would carry him. By the time he reached his quarters he had already forgotten the duke, the Armada, and the invasion.

Malantha waited for him, naked, sprawled on the divan, so brazen in her sexuality that he could barely look at her, yet could not look away. As much as he desired her, he was unsettled by the way she watched him; and sometimes, when she fell into the corner of his vision, he was convinced he saw something white and cold and predatory, not Malantha at all.

"I have good news," she said, without warmth. "I have spoken with my brother Cavillex, and our plans proceed accordingly. Don Alanzo brings the Silver Skull to Spain." A brief narrowing of her eyes was replaced by a seductive smile. "As you acquiesced to his request."

"He deserves that at least for all his sacrifices."

"And after that brief respite," she continued, "the Skull will be readied to travel with the Armada."

"And the Shield?"

"Not yet under our control, but that is a trifling matter. It is unnecessary, in the end. England will still be devastated by disease."

"I worry about so many deaths upon my conscience." Trembling, he collapsed onto the divan and covered his face.

Sliding next to him, Malantha breathed into his ear, "God will forgive that, for the great works you do in His name." Gently, she pressed her breasts against his arm. The heat rose in Philip rapidly. "The High Family will ensure no other country stands in your way."

"You are sure?" He slipped a hand onto her thigh, his remorse already evaporated.

"My brothers have the ears of the greatest in Europe."

"You spin your web well."

"All for you, my love. All for Spain."

Another flash of chalky skin and red-rimmed eyes that held no compassion. He screwed his eyes shut and drove the image out, allowing himself to be pushed back as she climbed astride him. Within seconds he was lost in her lips and her perfume, like honeysuckle, and all his troubles and doubts and fears were washed away.

CHAPTER 29

Filthy from the road and exhausted after nearly two weeks' hard riding, Nathaniel guided his foaming, sweat-flecked horse through the dirty, crowded streets of London. It was not long after noon, the sun unseasonably hot for early April. He had found the city abuzz, as always, but for the first time there was a pervading uncertainty in the faces of the people he passed. In the time he had been away, the fear of the Spanish invasion had magnified, visiting merchants from the European ports spreading dark rumours and gossip as quickly as they distributed their wares.

At the gates of the Palace of Whitehall, Nathaniel could barely believe he had reached his destination. Since he had left Edinburgh as dawn broke all those long days and nights ago, he felt his life had hung by a thread many times. Within hours of his journey beginning, five hooded raiders had swept down from the hills to pursue him along the valley between the high summits that stretched south along Scotland's lowlands, and he was only saved by a small group of the king's men who had been sent to accompany him to the border. The fighting had been ferocious and many of James's men had died; Nathaniel had heard their death-screams echoing among the hillsides, and when he glanced back he had seen flashes of mysterious fire.

Once he had crossed the border into England, the attacks were not so overt, but he had been shadowed by riders near the moors as he passed Carlisle, and again as he made his way through the high peaks that formed the spine of the country. Someone had attempted to break into his room during a terrifying night in an inn, when every time he locked the door it would mysteriously open whenever he was distracted.

A pack of wolves appeared to track him across most of the country, and strangers waited at crossroads, threatening him as he rode by, or urging him to stop for food or drink. On the first occasion, he had brought his mount to a halt, thinking the stranger needed directions. Soon he had found himself listening to a long, involved story that quickly made him drowsy, and only when he realised the stranger was attempting to search his saddlebag did he ride on. Just as unnerving was that within a mile he couldn't recall the stranger's face.

He had always considered himself a man of reason, but as he passed Oxford the sticky weight of superstition had finally begun to lie upon him. However much he attempted to dismiss the chance occurrences, they piled around him to such a degree that he saw supernatural danger in every shadow, and felt the Devil was at his heels. To save his sanity, he knew he would have to question Will when he returned to London, however much he dreaded the answers.

Within the palace walls, activity was beginning to build towards lunch after another lazy morning of discourse, sewing, business with visitors from the shires, or walks among the perfumed gardens. Nathaniel guided his horse directly to the Black Gallery, and on weary, shaking legs sought out Walsingham who had been in conference with a man recently returned from France. Whatever he had heard in that meeting had left him in a dark mood.

Nathaniel quickly outlined the events in Edinburgh, as far as he had been told, and related Will's desperate plea for Grace to be protected.

"I do not know this woman, but I will send men to bring her here now," Walsingham said. "If she requires protection, we can offer her the best in the land." He paused. "If she is still here."

Nathaniel felt a pang of fear. He had ridden as hard as he was able, but could their enemies have beaten him to the palace and still found the opportunity to capture Grace?

"And the reason you travelled to Edinburgh?" Walsingham pressed.

From his pack, Nathaniel withdrew the folded cloth and revealed the amulet. "The enemy fought hard to retrieve this, and pursued me all the way from Scotland. It must be vital to their plans."

Walsingham's eyes gleamed, but he would not touch the amulet. He called loudly for Dee, who hurried in a few moments later as Walsingham paced the room.

"You must tell no one that the doctor is here in England," Walsingham cautioned Nathaniel. He left Nathaniel in no doubt that the punishment for disobedience would be severe. But then he and Dee huddled over the amulet with barely restrained triumph.

"Is this the object we sought?" Walsingham asked.

"See here? The filigree? This symbol here? It is the language of angels," Dee said. "This is a true object of power."

"Then you will study it? Unlock its secrets?"

Dee nodded excitedly. "The Enemy will be eager to reclaim this. It must be kept in a place of formidable protection. The Tower?"

"No. Its defences have already been breached," Walsingham said. "We keep it close. Here, at the palace." He fixed an eye on Dee. "The Lantern Tower."

Dee agreed this was the best option and hurried out with the amulet, but Nathaniel was left puzzled. He had heard much talk of the Lantern Tower, a unique, solitary tower constructed by Elizabeth at the heart of the palace complex, yet no one appeared to know its use, and few were ever seen entering it.

Eager to return to his business, Walsingham dismissed Nathaniel to the suite of rooms on the third floor of the western wing overlooking the tiltyard built by Henry for his jousting competitions.

As he stood at the window looking out over the smoky city, Nathaniel felt the tension of his long ride dissipate and a grey mood creep in its place. Though the view was drenched in sunlight, he could see only shadows. The world had changed, or he had, and where there had been joy there was now only incipient threat, and a sense of everything he knew careering off-kilter. Fear rumbled on the edge of his consciousness for no obvious reason.

The door closed quietly, and he started, but when he turned it was only Grace. With relief, he rushed to her and held her in his arms.

"Why, Nat," she said, surprised. "What is wrong?" She placed her hands on his cheeks to study his face, and became concerned by what she saw there. "What troubles you? Is it Will?"

"No, he is well. He recovers from a few injuries, but no worse than he has endured before."

She was relieved by his news, but her concern for him did not diminish. "There is a shadow over you. It is not good to keep such things locked away. Talk to me."

Shaking his head, he forced a smile. "Another time. For now, I am happy to see you well."

"And why would I not be?" She stepped away from him, before casting a suspicious glance back at him. "What business occupies Will?" she asked, as if making polite conversation.

"You must ask him that yourself, when he is back in London." He maintained a bright tone, not wanting her to realise she was in danger. But then the door opened and John Carpenter marched in. He nodded to Nat and waited.

"What is this?" Grace asked suspiciously.

"This is John Carpenter, an associate of Will's. You saw him in Alsatia?"

"Yes, I remember. Why is he here?"

"Lord Walsingham has sent him. He is to keep you from harm."

"Harm? I live and work in the Palace of Whitehall. Harm cannot reach me here. And who would ever seek to harm me?"

Nathaniel's laugh eased her concerns. "Why, no one, Grace! But Will—"

"Will! He would keep me locked away in a tower if he could," she said with bitterness.

"Indulge him," Nathaniel said quietly. "You would not wish him consumed with worry."

Knowing she had little choice, she glanced back at Carpenter and said acidly, "I never tire of witty conversation with one of Lord Walsingham's men."

"Do not tease him," Nathaniel whispered. "His humour is not good."

Quietly seething, Grace shook her head wearily and marched towards the door.

Once she had gone, Nathaniel felt relieved that she was in safe hands, but in the silence of the room, his uneasy mood descended once more. He returned to the window to study the booming city, the source of one of the greatest powers in the world, yet in the face of what he now feared existed beyond the walls, he wondered how secure it truly was.

CHAPTER 30

Despite her furious protests, John Carpenter bundled the cloaked and hooded Grace into the back of a servants' wagon beneath a heap of filthy sacks that had been used for transporting grain and still swarmed with beetles. Carpenter was not a gentle man, and treated Grace as he would any person who was not important to him, woman or not. Clearly, whatever mission had been imposed upon him, he felt it beneath his dignity. He told Grace to remain silent for the duration of their journey or he would stop the wagon and dump her out on the highway where she would have to fend for herself against whatever brigands and cutthroats waited.

His tone angered her; she had more value than he showed her, and from anyone else she would not have accepted such treatment, but there was an increasing urgency to the proceedings that had started to concern her. She remembered the strange expression on Nat's face, that sense that all was not well with the world, shocking in a man who always radiated a sunny optimism behind his sardonic exterior. What happened? she wondered. What could turn a personality on its axis to that degree? Something extreme, something terrible? And as she had told Nat, Will was always overprotective, but this was beyond even his usual concerns. Will feared for her life, and he knew things that no one else did. She felt strangely queasy at the thought, and the wagon bouncing wildly along the rutted road didn't help her disposition.

Was it something to do with all the spiralling rumours of a Spanish invasion that had blazed through the country since Mary's execution? There had been talk of a landing in Wales that had sent panic sweeping through the capital before it had proven false, and in August gone, word had circulated of two hundred Spanish ships in the Channel, driving the occupants of the coastal towns inland in fear, and bringing the rich to London for safety. Elizabeth had even been forced to issue a proclamation demanding they return to their homes in the country. But what if all those rumours were about to become true, and an invasion was imminent?

Obliquely, she realised she should have been more scared than she was, but ever since Jenny's disappearance—no, murder! she reminded herself—she had lived with the constant belief that tragedy was only a heartbeat away; ironically, that had made her take more risks in her life.

Reckless! she thought bitterly.

Her mind drifted back to that night when everything changed and her potential became a shadow of what it had been. She recalled the fragrance of the night-scented stock, and the moon on the wheat fields, the soft breeze that made them stir as if some animal moved along the rows. There was a full moon so bright that the sky could not be called black. *Silver*, she thought. *The world glowed silver.*

She was still a child, though by then she considered herself a lady, already well versed in the ways of the world. If only she'd known. The hounds still howled in the fields as the search for Jenny continued, and her mother and father were both still out.

She had found Will desperately rinsing his hands and face at the well. He looked like he had been crying, though she had dismissed it at the time as a trick of the moonlight. For some reason, he kept his hands from her view until he had finished his ablutions. He was barely a man himself, not long at Cambridge, but at that moment his face looked much older. It was funny she remembered that; she hadn't thought of it before. She had never seen that expression before, or that openly registered emotion since; after Jenny, she always had to decipher his true feelings.

When his hands were clean, he had stepped forwards and hugged her so tightly she could barely breathe. "This is a hard world," he had said to her with quiet passion, "but you will not walk through it alone. I will be here to keep you safe. I vow it."

Over the months and years that followed, she had turned those words over so many times, and felt her own emotions solidify around them. Of all the reasons why she loved him, that was the first and the most potent. In that hard, hard world, he would keep her safe. He cared for her in a way that the other boys and men she had met had never cared, could never care. They would love her, or promise her the world, but they would never vow to keep her safe.

She did love him, even though she would never give voice to her feelings; even though he could never keep her safe. The wanting was enough.

And so she had been quick to uproot herself from her family and the quiet Warwickshire way of life, and Will had arranged for her to work at the court, where he could keep an eye upon her, and guide her progress. And her father and mother too had been more than happy to see her under Will's care.

Shortly after her arrival at the Palace of Whitehall, when she was still learning the twisting rules of that place, both written and unspoken, Will had taken her to one side and repeated his vow that he would discover the truth of Jenny's disappearance. His work, which she later found out was as one of Walsingham's men, would, he was convinced, provide him with clues and insight. He was passionate in his belief, but however much she questioned the how and why of this, he would give her no answer.

"Just know that all my days are directed towards discovering what happened to Jenny, and every action I make in my work will, in some way, illuminate the path to knowledge," he told her.

Finding the truth about Jenny. It was the bond that united them both, on which her love for him had been built, and the thing that separated them both from the world. Her only fear, and it was one that nagged at her in the dark of the night, was that when the truth about Jenny was known, the truth that they both so desperately needed, it would destroy them. The bonds shattered. Hope for the future gone. Belief in life destroyed. Was that an overreaction? She always told herself it was, but in her heart she wondered.

With the afternoon sun beating down, it was hot and stifling under the stinking sacks. The wagon bounced along the road for an age, until every part of her ached. After a while the noise of the street traffic died away and she could hear only the sound of the birds. She was half tempted to peel away the coverings so she could look where she was going, but she was afraid of Carpenter's reaction.

After a while, the bark of deer echoed nearby, and she heard the splash of oars; somewhere near the river, to the west of London. The wagon eventually moved off the rutted road onto a more even surface—flagstones, she guessed—and a few minutes later, Carpenter brought the horse to a halt. The sacks were torn from her and she shielded her eyes against the blast of late-afternoon sun.

When her vision cleared, she saw a grand brick facade, two towers flanking an imposing gatehouse, rows of mullioned windows, and a hint of the great Italian style in the lines and symmetries. All around there was rolling green land, with hawks swooping in the blue sky.

"Oh," she said, surprised. It was Hampton Court Palace, the old king Henry's great joy and source of pride.

"Grand enough for you?" Carpenter said acidly, offering her a hand to help her down from the back of the wagon. Though his tone remained gruff, his features had softened a little, as though he had been considering her and her plight during the long journey.

Hampton Court Palace was one of the most modern palaces in the world, sophisticated in intent and magnificent in design with sumptuous decor that could still impress even the most jaded member of the court. Few could understand why Elizabeth preferred to live in smoky, foul-smelling London; few, Grace knew, understood her desire to be at the heart of government.

The palace had running water, transported from Coombe Hill three miles away via the lead pipes that Henry had interred when his vast reconstruction of the palace was finally realised in 1540. It had extensive kitchens that were the pride of the nation, an enormous dining hall, a chapel, pleasure gardens filled with perfumed flowers and herbs, tennis courts, bowling alleys, and a hunting park that sprawled for more than a thousand acres. Elizabeth still visited regularly, when she wanted to escape the pressures of the city, or to stage her fabulous court masques, or the great dramatic presentations that had become the talk of London. Grace had been allowed to visit with her mistress for some of the festivities, but much of the palace had been off-limits to her.

With her hood pulled over her face, they passed through the gatehouse into the courtyard where servants wandered lazily around with no monarch or aristocracy to keep them on their toes. As Carpenter had anticipated, they drew no attention.

"Nobody will know you are here. You are safe," he said.

"Why could I not stay at the Palace of Whitehall?" she enquired. "If I am in danger, it is filled with guards and spies and all manner of defences to protect the queen."

Carpenter smiled tightly. "If an enemy seeks you, why draw them to the home of our queen and the greatest in the land?"

Grace suddenly realised she was dispensable. They would keep her as safe as they could, but not at the expense of any of the other great men of the land.

It was something she knew instinctively, but which was shocking to have confirmed so harshly.

Grace paused briefly before the great clock tower bearing the seal of Cardinal Wolsey, from whom this fine palace had been stolen by Henry when he fell from favour. Everyone had their place, she recognised, and some people were worth more than others.

Carpenter studied the clock briefly with an odd expression of unease: it not only showed the time, but also the phases of the moon, the star sign, the month, the date, the sun, and the season.

"What is it?" she asked.

He shivered, didn't reply, and urged her on into the palace.

She attempted to make small talk as he guided her to the quarters Walsingham had arranged to be set aside for her use, but his mind was elsewhere, and all she got were short, dismissive replies. She wasn't surprised when he refused to discuss her questions about the threat she faced and the rumours of the Spanish invasion, but she didn't like the way his voice grew harder when he spoke of Will. Something lay between them; if Grace were Will she would not want Carpenter at her back.

He led her on a long walk through the palace to a small room overlooking the formal gardens, which was usually reserved for the servants of visiting dignitaries. It was plain but comfortable.

"I will be safe here?" She examined the wide-open spaces beyond the window.

"In our work, we have found it is sometimes better to hide something in the open if it is in a place where no one is looking," Carpenter replied. "Only a handful of people know you have been transported from Whitehall, and they can all be trusted. No one here knows who you are. Stay still, and calm, and let the background swallow you, and all will be well."

"And you?"

"I will be near at hand."

"How long do I stay here?"

"Until Lord Walsingham grows tired of wasting a man, or your *friend*—" The word rang with contempt. "—has decided the danger has passed."

"No one will give me a good answer why I would be in danger."

"There is no good answer." He shrugged, and left her alone.

The hours passed slowly. She watched the gardeners at work, drawing the weeds and deadheading the roses, and a man and woman from the kitchens grabbing time from the heat and the steam to court, walking together along the lavender path, hands behind their backs, heads down in quiet, intense conversation; it was a gentle love, slowly building upon pleasant foundations, that she didn't quite understand.

Food was delivered to her, and left outside the door. It made her feel like one of the prisoners in the Tower. She paced the room, sat on the bed and dreamed, tried to make sense of the shifting patterns of her life and the world in which she existed, and then as the shadows lengthened and merged into the encroaching grey, she returned to the window to watch the beauty of the silvery twilight drawing in.

At some point she fell asleep, only for a short while, for though the moon was bright in the sky, it was still not yet wholly dark. Long shadows reached across the grey, quiet gardens. Nothing moved. Grace was oddly out of sorts; she hadn't felt tired, or even felt the encroachment of sleep, yet there she was, head on her arms on the small table by the window.

Stretching, she rose and decided she could not bear to be in the room any longer. The palace was quiet, the servants returned to their quarters, the few highborn people drinking in the drawing room, as they always did after dinner.

Opening the door cautiously, she checked for any sign of Carpenter, and when there was none she stepped out with an odd tingle of excitement. She stifled a giggle; it felt like she was trespassing. Humming quietly to herself, she moved along the interconnecting corridors, secretly hoping she would encounter one of the servants so she could have even a passing conversation. She could pretend to be someone else! That excited her even more.

But as the time passed and she met no one, nor did she hear even the vaguest sound rising from the bowels of the vast building, she started to feel unsettled. It was as if everyone had vacated the palace during her short nap.

After a while, her wanderings brought her to the Long Gallery. She paused as she entered it, realising where she was and recalling the disturbing stories that had passed through the entire court. No one came to the Long Gallery after dark. It was only a year since William Grebe had been driven mad with terror. On that night, in high summer, he had seen the ghost of the old queen Catherine Howard running through the gallery, screaming, as she had done in life when she had begged Henry to save her before the guards had dragged her away towards her imminent death.

There were ghosts all over the palace. Jane Seymour haunting the staircase near the room where she gave birth to Edward. Even Anne Boleyn and Henry himself.

Drawing herself up proudly, she stepped into the gallery. Ghosts did not scare her; there was nothing on the other side of life that did not match what she had experienced during her years in the world. But as she reached the halfway mark along the room, she heard, or thought she did, faint words carried on the night breeze rustling under the doors. The insubstantial voice seemed to say: *"Death is not the end."*

She hurried on, relieved to leave the strange mood in the gallery behind her, but as she passed through a deserted room with windows overlooking the twilit countryside, something caught her eye. In the row of black trees along the river's edge, she was sure a shadow had swept along at ground level, like the smoke from a bonfire caught in a strong wind. It had gone now, but as she stood at the window to be sure, there was a burst of flames in the trees, and another, and another. Torches igniting? she wondered. Something in those dancing fires made her unaccountably afraid. Hugging her arms around her, she watched them moving slowly, wondering who held them, why it mattered, and then, just as quickly as they had burst into life, they winked out, one by one.

For a moment longer, she watched intently, wondering if anyone would emerge from the tree line, but there was nothing. Were they watching her watching them? she wondered briefly, before discounting the idea as ridiculous; no one could see her at that distance.

Yet for all her rationalising, she felt a sudden urge to find Carpenter. Worried now by the lack of activity, and the silence, in the palace, which was unnatural at that time of the evening, she picked up her pace. Her heels beat out an insistent rhythm on the floorboards. She desperately wanted to call out, but was afraid of attracting attention to herself.

In a large room, where the queen sometimes held a reception for foreign guests before one of the masques, she came to a halt before a long mirror. She didn't know why. For a while, she stared at herself, spectral in the half-light, and had the strangest impression she was looking at someone else, someone who had spent time shaping themselves to resemble her, but who couldn't disguise the malign thoughts that lurked in the features, in the set of the mouth, or the narrowing of the eyes. It felt as if the glass wasn't there, and that she could reach through the space. But then the other Grace would grab her wrist and drag her in. She half realised something about the mirror mesmerised her, was holding her fast, and she forced herself to move on, but not before she caught sight of a shadow on the edge of the mirror following her.

She turned suddenly, but the room was empty. The shadow had been in the mirror and not in the real world, though it was gone now. It must have been a trick of the moonlight, for there was no other explanation. She decided as she hurriedly left the room that she didn't like mirrors at all.

Her feet pounded louder on the floorboards as she raced through the silent rooms, no longer trying to keep her presence a secret. Doors slammed open and shut. Corridors rang with the echoes of her passing. After a while she called out, "Hello?" but there was only the sound of her voice returning to her after a journey around the palace.

Her uneasiness mounted, like the stem of a rose being drawn up the skin of her back. Where could they all have gone? Had the alarm for the invasion sounded and everyone had fled to the security of London's walls? Could she really have missed it? Would Carpenter have forgotten to rouse her?

In the room where the palace elders usually gathered to drink into the evening, there was no one. The guards' quarters: empty. No sound rising from the servants' quarters, where she would have expected singing and laughter, perhaps even a fiddle.

She found herself at a window with a view over Henry's great clock, the colours a dull grey in the gloom. Instinctively, she knew something was wrong, but in her anxious state her thoughts skittered too wildly across the details of what she saw. After a moment, it came to her: the clock was running backwards. She watched the gentle judder of the minute hand as it shifted counterclockwise and shivered, although she was not sure why.

Its workings are wrong, she thought. *That is all.*

The season now showed winter, the month December.

Overcome with the compulsion to search the darkening countryside around the palace, she ran to another window overlooking the approach. At first all was still, but then came another brief burst of fire, closer than the last one she had seen, and another way across to the right, gone almost in the blink of an eye.

The fires were hypnotic, and she waited for another while she considered what could possibly have caused them. Instead, she saw grey shadows bounding sinuously across the fields towards the palace, like foxes only larger. She tried to count them, but they moved too fast and were soon out of the moonlight and lost from view.

She stepped away from the window, her heart tap-tapping.

The kitchens! she thought suddenly. Everyone would be gathered there, telling stories, servants and gentlemen together, in the warmth of the ovens. It was the only explanation. Focusing on the hope rather than the nagging feeling that such a thing could never be true, she hurried for the stairs that led to the great kitchens underneath the palace.

Down the winding stairs she went, and down again, deep, deep down, leaving the stark regiment of the palace for the sumptuous underworld. She could hear the crackle of the fires under the ovens and the hiss of the pots boiling on the top, the clank of their lids as they were lifted by the steam, smell the aromatic after-scent of the evening's dinner, the capons boiled in a broth of oranges, sugar, mace, cloves, nutmeg, and cinnamon, rich and powerful, intermingling with the strong notes of the strawberries soaked in red wine and ginger.

Her senses were overwhelmed, so much so that she was not wholly aware that she heard no human voices. Only when she bounded excitedly from the stairs into the vast brick vault did she see it was empty. The light from the candles danced up the orange-red walls and sent shadows rippling along the roof.

The remnants of the dinner's preparation were still scattered across the great oak tables that ran along the centre of the kitchen, juices dribbling from the edges onto the flags. The cooking pots were piled high, still unwashed.

Grace's shoulders grew taut. The kitchens should not be empty at that time; indeed, they ought to be an industrious hive of activity. The kitchen master would have his staff working hard to clear everything away so that all would be left clean and ready for the breakfast.

She looked around. Jars were unstoppered. Pans almost bubbled dry. Cheese lay uncovered. It was as if everyone in the palace had disappeared in an instant, their tasks left half finished, the ghost of their presence still haunting the place.

Grace moved slowly through the kitchens, feeling the blood pound in her head. All the signals she received from the environment were conflicting. A disappearance of so many people without a hubbub? So quickly?

The black, brackish waters of fear she had managed to suppress for so long began to rise through her.

The fires off in the dark. The grey shadows loping across the fields. What was coming? She tried to laugh at her anxiety, couldn't. She should run, hide. But where would she go?

Instead, she crossed to the largest oven. The fire inside it was roaring out of control as if the flue had been jammed open. As she stood before it, she could feel the flames burning harder, faster, with each passing moment, a furnace, and the heat in the room rose accordingly. After a few seconds of fascination, she realised that the heat was increasing faster than the oven could account for, the air becoming dense and dry. Beads of sweat stood out on her forehead. It became hotter than the hottest summer day.

Although she had heard nothing, she realised she was no longer alone. She whirled, her breath catching in her throat. Several figures stood at the entrance to the kitchens, shimmering as if seen through a heat-haze. They were watching her, as still as statues.

"Who are you?" she gasped.

CHAPTER 31

ursting into the great banqueting hall at Hampton Court Palace, Will hurled Carpenter against a wall and punched him in the face three times before Carpenter had even realised he was there. Mayhew and Launceston threw themselves forward to restrain Will, but even the two of them combined struggled to contain him. His anger was like a storm, his face filled with lightning.

Blood flooded from Carpenter's nose and lips. Picking himself up, he wiped his face clean with the back of his hand and turned on Will angrily.

"Enough!" Walsingham strode into the room, and though his face remained as cold as ever, there was a crack of anger in his voice.

Will continued his furious attempts to throw off Launceston and Mayhew, but gradually calmed. As the fury drained from his face, he spat, "You were supposed to protect her!"

"I did all I could," Carpenter snarled.

"All you could? You ate and drank and idled your time with the women in the kitchens!" Launceston and Mayhew were forced to renew their efforts as Will strained at their grips.

"I did the work with which I was charged!" Carpenter raged. "I brought her here undercover, and secreted her in a room, and kept watch."

"Then how did Grace disappear under your nose?" Will snapped. He ignored Walsingham who waited at his side, as if he were incapable of understanding the degree of emotion being shown. "Or did you finally decide to act upon the grudge you hold against me?"

In a rage, Carpenter attacked. Launceston interjected himself, knife drawn.

Knowing Launceston would use his weapon without a second thought, Carpenter stepped back and contained himself. "You think I would sacrifice a woman to pay you back?" he snarled. "I am not like you."

"You were charged to watch her."

"And I did. Her dinner was brought to her room. She ate it. I remained in the room next to hers, with the door open at all times. No one came to her room. No one left. Yet when I knocked upon her door an hour later, there was no reply, and upon inspection the room was empty."

"You fell asleep!"

"No!" Carpenter's eyes blazed. Will tried to tell if he was lying, but as always Carpenter was impossible to read.

"How did the Enemy know she was here?" Containing a quiet power, Walsingham's steady voice cut through the angry atmosphere.

"I do not know," Carpenter replied, dabbing at his bloody nose. "No one here knew, nor anyone in Whitehall beyond our trusted circle, and his assistant."

Will brought his struggles to a slow halt as Carpenter's words settled on him. His head still pulsed with the beat of angry blood, but through it cut cold mistrust. Looking around the group, they all met his eye.

Never trust a spy, that was the joke when they were all in their cups. After Reidheid, Will was starting to wonder if he could trust anyone.

"That is enough for now," Walsingham said.

"No, it is not," Will replied, ignoring the flicker of wrath in Walsingham's eyes. "Grace is gone. The Enemy have her."

"I share your concern," Walsingham said insincerely, "and I understand she was important to you. But there are more pressing matters. For now." He fixed an eye on Will that was supposed to be reassuring. "Trust me, we will not let her languish in the hands of the Enemy. No Englishman or Englishwoman will suffer at the hands of our foes while I exert influence over this office."

Will understood the harsh reality. Grace was his personal priority, but she meant little against the great affairs of state. Deep inside him, the feelings he had kept locked down for so long threatened to tear him apart. He thought of Grace, saw Jenny, couldn't help but imagine what terrible things were happening to her now, what would happen in the days, months, years to come, unless he saved her.

Walsingham was speaking, but Will heard none of the words. His head buzzed with the pulse of his blood, and thundered with his anger and self-loathing at his failure to protect Grace when she needed him most. But he would not give in to despair. His task now was to balance the demands placed upon him by his work with his need to find Grace before something monstrous took place. Yet he recalled clearly the plain cruelty in Cavillex's words in the Fairy House in Edinburgh. The Unseelie Court had embarked upon a path of torture. Their aim was to cause him pain, and to twist it and magnify it. The theft of Grace was only the beginning.

"Will?" Walsingham questioned. "You are with us?"

"Of course."

Carpenter eyed Will murderously, still dabbing at his nose and mouth. Launceston's ghostly face remained a frozen mask, but Mayhew held his head as if the world was spinning out from under his feet.

"The Spanish are preparing to invade?" he said. "We have heard that so many times. It is now true?"

"Their Armada will sail upon England shortly." As Walsingham clutched his hands behind his back, Will thought he could see a faint tremor in them.

Steadying himself, Will said, "Philip has attempted an invasion with his Armada before, and failed. Badly."

"We all know what happened," Walsingham said dismissively. "Two hundred ships amassed at Santander in 1575. After disease and incompetence, only thirty-eight finally sailed for Dunkirk. Five ran aground on shoals, three were driven back by storms, and the remainder were forced to shelter in the Solent before fleeing home."

"After such a folly, then, why should we give his current plans any credence?" Will asked.

"And what of our ambassador in Paris," Mayhew continued, "Stafford—his dispatches state very firmly that Spain is in no position to invade, and this Armada is a flight of Philip's fancy."

"Stafford is wrong—or worse," Walsingham replied.

"You suspect him?" Launceston enquired.

"Sir Edward likes his money a great deal and he never has enough of it, by his accounts."

"What other information do you have?" Will asked.

"The Dutch captured and interrogated the nephew of one of the cardinals who has had close dealings with Philip," Walsingham said. "He revealed that a year ago, the Vatican transferred a million ducats to a Spanish bank where it is held in trust until the pope receives notification that the invasion of England has begun."

"So Philip has the funds he needs," Will mused.

"The nephew also spoke of the Armada's destination and timetable." Walsingham paused as he considered his choice of words. "Unfortunately, the queen has chosen to believe Sir Edward's missives—he has always been one of her favourites—and so the necessary preparation work to ensure our defences are robust is not yet under way."

"And the Armada will sail soon?" Will asked.

"Soon." Walsingham was clearly not prepared to reveal all that he knew.

"We cannot conjure defences overnight," Carpenter said. "If Philip truly has a great fleet, we would be stretched too thinly once he reaches our coast."

Walsingham slowly paced the Great Hall, looking like a raven searching for carrion. "Your analysis is correct. Time is fast running out."

"And the Silver Skull must be part of this invasion plot," Will said. "The Enemy and the Spanish walk hand-in-hand. Each feels they use the other to gain their stated aim—the destruction of England, and the conquest of England."

"There will be little left for the Spanish empire if the Enemy gets its way," Carpenter noted bitterly. "Can Philip not see that?"

"Philip sees what he wants to see," Walsingham replied. "He believes God is on his side, and so all things will turn out well."

"When God is clearly on our side," Will said acidly.

Walsingham eyed him coldly, but did not respond to the barb.

"In Edinburgh, Don Alanzo de las Posadas said he was transporting the Silver Skull back to Cádiz," Will continued, "to keep the weapon safe until they are ready to use it, one would think. The Skull's powers could be unleashed anywhere from Norfolk to the south coast to Wales, and disease would spread across the land in no time. When the Armada has defeated our feeble fleet, and the disease has run its course, the Spanish will march into London with no opposition. They do not need the subtleties of the Shield for that. Let the Skull kill all."

"And rule a land of the dead?" Carpenter said.

"They have no need of Englishmen," Will said. "They know that for the rest of their days, they would be attempting to stifle revolt after revolt. Best to be rid of us for good."

"Philip is not an evil man," Walsingham said. "Merely misguided. He does what he does for his country and his religion, as do we. He would not want to see innocents suffer on a grand scale, Englishmen or not. No, I feel the Spanish will direct their attack along narrower lines."

Will considered this for a moment. "In London. If the Silver Skull is smuggled in, the queen, the government, the entire court could be wiped out. Our resistance would crumble."

Launceston nodded. "That makes sense. But other things do not: why travel from Edinburgh to Spain, when the Skull could have been brought directly to London and hidden away in the depths of the city until it is needed?"

"Because they know what we would do," Carpenter said firmly. "Trawl every part of London until we found it. No, Spain is the safest place for the Skull until the time comes to unleash it."

Will understood that a Spanish invasion weighed heavily on Walsingham's mind, but his own thoughts turned towards the Unseelie Court. Their aims were elusive, constantly shifting. Their manipulations often appeared to point in one direction, while the results lay in another, and they continually circled the great events that were unfolding so it was hard to mark their place in them. They clearly needed the Silver Skull to strike a blow that would bypass Dee's defences that kept them from crushing England in their fist. But why did they require the Shield to protect them so they could move through the disease-ravaged land?

"The Shield is well protected in the Lantern Tower," Walsingham replied to his query. "It is now beyond the Enemy's reach. Whatever they planned is no more."

Will was not convinced, but he did not pursue the matter. His immediate concern was where the Unseelie Court was holding Grace, and he thought he knew.

"You want us to go to Spain, to kill or capture the Silver Skull," Will said, "and to do whatever we can to undermine the plans for the invasion."

A faint smile flickered across Walsingham's lips, quickly stifled, acknowledging that Will had clearly predicted his intentions.

"You want us to travel into the heart of our enemy's land?" Mayhew said incredulously. "The Skull will be the most closely guarded object in the whole of Spain, as closely guarded as Philip himself. How can we be expected to survive such an assault?"

"We aren't," Will responded, "but if we can destroy the Silver Skull in the process, our work will be done."

Though he blanched a little, Mayhew nodded; he understood their responsibilities.

"You have only returned from Edinburgh this morn," Walsingham said. "The report I received from your assistant suggested the injuries inflicted on you by the Enemy were extreme."

"Nat is prone to exaggeration," Will replied. "I am in good health, and fit to lead the mission into Spain."

Walsingham studied Will for a moment, not wholly convinced. He had every right to be doubtful; Will's wounds were still knitting, but the sea journey would give him plenty of time for recovery, Will anticipated. Walsingham clearly agreed, for he nodded and said, "Then these fine men will accompany you. Arrangements have already been made—your ship leaves today. But first you must visit Dee in Whitehall, for he has some new surprises for you. May God go with you."

Walsingham gave a curt bow and strode out of the room to the carriage waiting to take him back to the Palace of Whitehall. Will admired the spymaster's cold focus upon his business; he had essentially sent them all to their deaths, and dismissed them with nothing more than a nod.

"Well, then," Will said. "There is time for drink and a visit to the doxie of your choice. Make the most of this time, men, for there will be few comforts in the days ahead."

As his eyes briefly met Carpenter's baleful gaze as he walked from the room, he wondered how much he could trust the man. Carpenter's grudge had festered for a year, and he was not someone who easily let go of his desire for revenge. The Enemy was expert at driving a wedge into men's hearts through the flaws in their character. Had Carpenter betrayed Grace to them? Would he betray them all further? Will decided he needed to keep a close eye on his rival.

As he strode through the sunlit rooms of the palace, his thoughts turned back to Grace. In Edinburgh, Cavillex had stated clearly his intention to torture and kill Will in front of Grace. He knew Will would travel to Spain in search of the Skull, and so logic dictated Grace would also be held there ready for Will's capture. The Enemy would be waiting for him; Grace too would be waiting. Nat would say he was ready for a trip to Bedlam to so knowingly walk into the Unseelie Court's machinations, but Will hoped that knowledge would be enough to protect him.

He caught up with Walsingham briefly as he paused in deep contemplation, looking out of an open window across the peaceful grass running down to the slow-moving river. Whatever was on Walsingham's mind, it caused a troubled cast to his expression. He started when Will appeared at his side, and was inexplicably angry at being disturbed. Will knew from experience he had only a moment to ask his question.

"In Edinburgh, I was questioned at length by the Enemy. I gave nothing away—"

"As I would expect."

"—but my interrogator was under the mistaken belief that I was kept informed of all that happens in England. He asked me what I knew of Dartmoor."

"What did he mean?"

Will watched Walsingham's face for any sign that he knew more about the subject than he was saying, but his face remained a clean slate, with only a faint knot of puzzlement in his brow.

"All I know of Dartmoor is that it is a bleak, inhospitable place."

"I will discuss this matter with Doctor Dee. He may bring some sense to it, though I doubt it. Dartmoor?" He shook his head slowly, and then continued on his way. Despite Walsingham's seeming ignorance, Will knew from Cavillex's tone and manner that Dartmoor was important to the Enemy. He resolved to make further enquiries.

Nathaniel and Christopher Marlowe waited lazily in the sun by the carriage, where Will had left them on his arrival, once he had received news of Grace's disappearance. Nathaniel appeared close to tears.

"Is it true?" he asked.

Will nodded. "Grace is gone."

"How could the Spaniards have stolen her from within the palace?" he cried.

"They have their ways," Will replied flatly, "and nowhere is truly safe." Marlowe caught his eye, understanding the truth.

"It seems the Enemy wishes to cause you pain, for the suffering you have inflicted upon them," Marlowe said. "I have not heard of the struggle being made so personal before."

"It shows that what I do is working, then, Kit." Will held open the carriage door for them to climb inside.

"That does not help poor Grace." Nathaniel wrung his hands.

"Then it is a good job I have a plan to rescue her. Do you think I would leave her to the torments of the Enemy? I would go to the very gates of hell to bring her back."

"I understand your affection for Grace," Marlowe began hesitantly, "but would this plan be a wise one?"

"I have decided to sail rapidly away from the shores of wisdom into the vast, heaving oceans of foolhardiness. Do not worry about me, Kit. Save your condolences for the Enemy." Will kept the mood light, but he could not prevent an edge creeping into his voice, and he saw they both recognised it. "Bankside," he called to the driver as he climbed in behind the others.

"How can you even think of dallying with doxies and drunkenness when Grace is gone?" Nathaniel asked, his voice breaking. He gave Will a brief, fractured look of betrayal.

What could Will tell him? That it was the only way he could numb the pain he felt, and the fears of what might be happening to Grace at that very moment? Nathaniel deserved better.

"There is always time for drink and women, Nat," he replied. Nathaniel wouldn't look at him for the rest of the journey.

Will was aware Marlowe was filled with questions about the Enemy, but could not raise any of them while Nathaniel was there. But what concerned Will the most was the odd cast to Nathaniel's face. He had seen it many times before, the ghost of doubt, the spectre of fear, the dawning recognition that the world was not the way it appeared. Soon he would be faced with a dilemma: to break his vow and send Nathaniel away, into the dangers that his father always feared, or to risk a fate that mirrored Miller's, once the infection of the Unseelie Court finally struck him hard.

Will knew he was responsible for the change that had come over Nathaniel, but even now he could not leave him alone. "I must go away for a while on Lord Walsingham's business," he said, trying to make light of what lay ahead. "While I am gone, there is still much to do here." As the carriage came to a halt at Bankside, he paused and searched Nathaniel's face, unsure if he should continue. Finally, he said, "I have work for you both."

CHAPTER 32

The sun was low on the horizon and a scarlet path flowed across the white-plumed waves. As the dark began to press in, the lights of Cádiz blazed along the harbour, outside the taverns and in the squares, in the convent windows and the castle.

With sails billowing, the *Tempest* ploughed across the swell towards the town. A legend among seafaring men, some considered the vessel a harbinger of doom.

Captain John Courtenay stood on the forecastle, unfeasibly tall and powerfully built, tanned from the sun and the salt, his brown hair and beard wild in denial of the urbane, sophisticated style of the day. His untamed appearance was magnified by two ragged scars that marked his face in an X from temple to jaw, the result of torture at the hands of the Spanish in the New World. Beside him, Will watched the nearing lights.

"You have recovered well, Master Swyfte. You have a powerful constitution." Courtenay understood exactly what Will had endured in Edinburgh.

"A few scratches. We put these things behind us."

Courtenay nodded thoughtfully. "Aye. We would be poor men if we shed tears over every pinprick."

Although the wounds of Will's torture had healed, the memory had not. Every time he stared down into the green waves, he recalled the horrific sensations of drowning burned deeply into his mind. He kept it close to him, a stoked furnace providing the heat that drove him on. With every new blow struck, the Unseelie Court raised the price they would have to pay sooner or later.

Courtenay trawled the deck, inspecting his crew at work with a sharp eye and a salty tongue, readying them for what was to come. He had been inducted into Walsingham's band of spies only a few months ago when he had been given the captaincy of the *Tempest*, the private galleon set aside for the affairs of England's secret service. Kept off all official records and secure within its own well-shielded mooring at Tilbury, the stories of supernatural prowess were only encouraged by Walsingham, who knew that fear was a powerful weapon.

In truth, the *Tempest* was England's most advanced warship, a race-built galleon of the new design developed by John Hawkins, longer and with a reduced forecastle and poop deck that made them faster and more stable than any other at sea. Three-masted, with an advanced rigging system, it could easily be navigated by only a skeleton sailing crew.

And Courtenay was the perfect captain for such an advanced vessel. He had been at Francis Drake's side during his expedition against the Spanish in the New World, and had helped claim Nova Albion for the Crown. When war broke out between Spain and England in 1585, Courtenay had once again accompanied Drake to the New World, to sack the ports of Cartagena and Santo Domingo, and then to capture the fort of San Agustín in Spanish Florida. *Bloody John* earned his name there, tearing out the throat of a Spanish soldier with his own teeth; his wild beard was stained red with blood for days after, Will had heard, and he now dyed it red as an affectation whenever he sailed into battle.

Will watched him prowl the deck barking at his men. Though everyone on board presented an air of calm detachment, beneath the surface tension grew.

It was April 17. A fierce storm sweeping out of the Bay of Biscay had delayed their progress, but they had still reached their destination in just over two weeks out of Gravesend, at a good speed of seven knots an hour once the high winds had passed. In the billowing black clouds, Will had seen a premonition of what was to come. It didn't deter him. Somewhere ahead, across the sun-baked Spanish countryside, Grace was being held, he was sure of it, a lure designed to draw him in. Against his own desires, this part of the war had become personal.

At his back, the people of England were relying upon him. Since Mary's execution, it had felt as if the clock at Hampton Court Palace was ticking inexorably towards midnight, an apocalypse of invasion and disease and mass death drawing steadily in, and there was nothing any of them could do about it. The forces shifting just beyond their perception were too big for one man to confront, perhaps even too big for a nation. In the midst of that, his own troubles appeared minor, but that did not diminish the pain.

As he watched the fading light on the waves, one fear stayed hard with him: that he would be forced to sacrifice Grace to save England; and then he would truly be as damned as he always imagined.

When they had rounded Cape St. Vincent, a southwesterly had propelled them past the salt marshes along the Spanish coast towards the rocky spit that protected the harbour of Cádiz, the second most important port in all of Spain.

Courtenay strode back to Will with a broad grin. "Get your mates ready, Master Swyfte," he boomed. "Time is growing short."

"A direct assault on Cádiz is a brave strategy, Captain. Are you sure this is the wisest course?"

"You stick to your devilish games on dry land. I know my business on the waves." His rolling laughter gave Will doubts that his sanity was entirely intact. "Any opportunity to lay some fire across the Spanish is a good one."

"The port is not protected by shore batteries?"

"It is," Courtenay replied, "but we can be in and out before those devils find their bearings. There is much in our favour, Master Swyfte. With the Armada gathering, the Spanish will expect the English to be occupied with thoughts of invasion. No captain in his right mind would consider such a daring assault at this time." He laughed again, too loud, too long. "Even when they sighted us passing the Pillars of Hercules, we were but a lone ship. One solitary vessel sailing into Spain's great port! Why, all the nobles and the filthy commoners will sit up in the town square where they take their drink and gamble and watch the strolling players, and they will give us not a second thought, if indeed a first."

"Then I will be guided by your wisdom, Captain. You are a veteran of these matters, after all."

"Ha, ha! We tore those Spaniards in two that day!" he roared. "Drake said we singed the beard of the king of Spain and he was right. April, it was, but still hot. We sailed our fleet straight into the harbours, here and at La Coruña, occupied both, and laid waste to thirty-seven naval and merchant vessels. Set the invasion back by a year! Then they had their ships and men here to fight, if they had found the wherewithal. Now they are all with the Armada. So, by my calculation, one good English ship will suffice for a little mischief."

"That sounds finer sport than my men landing silently under cover of darkness. We will sign our names in fire and iron."

"I like your spirit, Master Swyfte. Now, I must be off to dye me beard."

He marched away, singing a shanty noisily while directing his men with points and gestures.

After the tedium of the journey, Will was ready to act. Below deck, he found Launceston, Mayhew, and Carpenter playing cards in sullen, silent boredom. They abandoned their game quickly at his nod, and gathered their weapons without a word.

Carpenter exchanged a brief glance with him, making no effort to hide his contempt. Will suspected there would be a problem with Carpenter at some point; his resentment and bitterness seethed, and were clearly growing stronger with each imagined slight Will inflicted on him. Too much was at stake for Will to allow any personal abrasiveness to compromise their mission, and he was afraid he would soon have to make a difficult choice.

On deck, the crew directed the ship towards the harbour, singing loudly of skulls piling high and the women who waited for them at home when their death-dealing ways were done. Salty spray misted the air.

The city was in an unusual position on a narrow spit of land surrounded by the sea, and had seen the ocean shape its history. Christopher Columbus had sailed from Cádiz to the New World, linking Spain forever with its source of riches, Will knew. When Cádiz later became the home of the Spanish treasure fleet, the city became a target for all of the nation's enemies. Barely a year passed without the Barbary Corsairs launching a raid that was usually repelled. And once again England was testing its defences.

His beard now a flaming red, Courtenay strode across the heaving deck as if he was on dry land, his eyes on fire too with a mad passion for what was to come. "Spain embarks on an invasion of England, and so England invades Spain—with four men!" He laughed loudly at the insanity of a mission that dwarfed his own madness.

"But what men," Will responded wryly.

Courtenay looked at each of them and nodded with approval. "I think you will provide a robust test for those Spanish dogs." He peered across the water towards the city. "We are worse than any pirate. What has the world become?" Despite the words, there was a note of pleasure in his voice. Taking a deep breath of the sea air, he closed his eyes for a moment and then roared, "Break out the colours!"

As the English flag ran up the mast, he signalled to the quarterdeck, and the trumpet blared out the call to arms, followed by the three sharp bursts

Will had specified. In the harbour, Will knew what few men had remained behind to defend Cádiz would now be racing for the galleys, but Courtenay didn't give them a chance. At his command, a hail of cannon fire thundered against the city.

Shrieks echoed across the waves at the sound of gunfire, and as the alarms rang out, the townsfolk fled in terror along the snaking path above the sea to seek refuge in the castle of Matagorda, where the commandant and his men waited to close the gates.

"One English ship!" Courtenay raged at the lights in the gathering gloom.

A galley began to make its way from the harbour, but a direct strike from the *Tempest*'s guns sank it before it got close enough to use its own lesser weapons. Courtenay ordered his trumpeter to play a mocking blast as those on board swam to shore.

Chaos erupted among the merchant ships anchored beyond the promontory of Puntales. Some were waiting for a change in wind, others en route to Northern Europe or the Indies, yet more loaded with wine from Jerez, wood, wool, and cochineal for trade across the Mediterranean. Several clearly feared the *Tempest* was a precursor to a wider English attack and tried to escape, narrowly avoiding collisions as they fled to shallower water where the galleon would not venture.

One of the smallest vessels was not so fortunate. Courtenay sent a small party to seize it, and once the crew had abandoned ship, set it alight. The furiously burning ship was then set adrift. The currents carried it towards the harbour, where it ignited small boats and another galley. The panic across the harbour among the merchants watching the carnage added to the tumult ringing out through the night.

One final volley of galleon fire hit a gunpowder store on the harbour, and it went up in a burst of gold and crimson that set alight adjoining buildings. The thick, black smoke drifted across Cádiz, obscuring the twinkling lights. On board the *Tempest*, the crew cheered loudly, and Courtenay nodded proudly. He signalled the dropping of the anchor and then turned to Will and said, "I think that will end any resistance. They will be distracted by the fire and will try to stop it spreading across the city, or they will be cowering in their homes or the castle, afraid we are going to ransack their riches. No one will notice four drowned rats slipping into the alleys."

Forcefully, he shook their hands in turn, and wished them good fortune, before returning to his men.

"Whatever lies ahead, know this: I have been proud to serve beside you," Will said to the others. He held out his hand and three others took it, held for a second, then shook free.

"Now," he said, "let us take this war to Spain . . . and the Unseelie Court." Bounding onto the rail, he dived into the ocean. The others followed without a second thought.

The water was cold after the hot day. The night cloaked the waves and they struck out towards the city, confident they would not be seen. Courtenay's plan was perfect: all eyes would be on the *Tempest* to see what it did next, or the townsfolk would be manning the defences or putting out the fires which now burned fiercely along the waterfront.

From the old fort and the battery on the harbour, the cannon continued to pump out an intermittent barrage, but the *Tempest* was out of range, and it was little trouble for Will and the others to swim out of the line of fire. They also kept far away from Puental, the small, rocky landing area outside the city walls, which was under heavy guard as the only likely place for the English to set down their landing parties.

The harbour was a hellish scene. Boats blazed, the flames dancing across the black water and clouds of inky smoke billowing into the city. Along the harbour's edge, tubs of pitch for repairs had been set alight, and the buildings near the gunpowder store were now ablaze. The white walls of the town glowed red in the firelight.

Will led the way through the choking smoke and burning refuse to the edge of the harbour wall where a rope dangled down into the water, unseen in the confusion. Hauling himself up, he crouched behind a pile of sacks waiting to be loaded onto a merchant ship. Once the others were with him, they peered over the top at the abject confusion along the entire length of the harbour.

Men ran with buckets of water as they feebly attempted to put out the conflagration at the far end of the row of buildings lining the edge of the harbour nearest to the town. Foot soldiers raced to oversee the Puental and to keep guard at the end of the harbour in case the *Tempest* sent landing parties. Lining the shore, watchmen peered into the dark in case more galleons were on their way. Across the length of the harbour, merchants bellowed their concern in a babble of conflicting tongues—French, Dutch, Spanish, and a variety of dialects from the North African coast just across the straits.

"Look at it—it is madness," Mayhew said approvingly.

"We asked Captain Courtenay for cover to mask our arrival in Cádiz. I think he served us proud," Will agreed. He scanned the hectic mass of bodies. "Now, where is our man?"

In the shadows of one of the many alleys linking the town's large plazas stood a man wearing a wide-brimmed hat pulled low over his face. The glare of the fire revealed the lower half to be clean-shaven, and that he carried a walking stick with a handle carved into the shape of a swan.

"There," Will said. "Stay here. I will make the introductions in case there is a problem." Edging around the sacks, he waited for the fast flow of towns-folk to pass before darting into the alleyway.

"De Groot?" Will asked.

Eyeing Will's sodden clothes, the man nodded. "You found the rope easily?" He spoke English with a strong Dutch inflection.

"You did well."

"I ran here as soon as I heard the trumpet signal." He glanced back up the alley. "This way, I think. We must move away from the harbour. There are men of many nations here, but wet Englishmen will soon draw attention."

More gunfire from the *Tempest* crashed against the far end of the harbour followed by a futile return of fire from the battery. In the confusion that followed, Will summoned his men. But as they sprinted towards the alley, a cry rang out from one of the watchmen, who had by chance been looking back towards the fort.

"Quickly," de Groot urged from the depths of the alley. "I cannot be seen or my use here will be over." He ran off into the dark.

Cursing, Will saw four foot soldiers give pursuit as Carpenter, Mayhew, and Launceston darted into the alley. The route was steep and wound round so tightly it was impossible to see more than ten feet ahead or behind. As they moved away from the harbour, the sound of gunfire became muffled, replaced by the crack of their boots on the cobbles and the intermittent tolling of the fort bell signalling the alarm.

As they ran, Will made a chopping motion with his hand, and the others melted quickly into doorways on either side. Will ducked behind a water barrel and waited until the foot soldiers neared. As the first passed him, he lunged up with his knife and thrust it straight into the soldier's throat. A gout of blood gushed onto the cobbles.

The other soldiers cried out in alarm as the first pitched forwards, gurgling and clutching at his throat. Will instantly engaged the second with his sword, while Mayhew and Carpenter took on the third soldier and Launceston slit the throat of the final one with a silent, fluid movement. The soldiers were poorly trained and overweight. Will ran his opponent through in an instant. By the time he had cleaned his blade, all the soldiers were dead.

De Groot emerged from the dark further up the alley and beckoned them on. Within five minutes they were in de Groot's rented house on the Plaza de San Francisco overlooking the San Francisco Church and Convent, the white walls glowing in the light of lanterns strung along the eaves of the red-tiled roof, and in the branches of the sprawling orchard beside it.

De Groot, a merchant who plied his trade between Flanders and Spain, was a dour man who had been recruited by Walsingham three years before. His heavy-lidded eyes and hollow cheeks gave him a cadaverous air, but he was friendly enough. He provided Will and the others with clean clothes that would allow them to blend in, and then brought them hot food and drink.

"There is jubilation across all Spain at the moment," he told them. "Word has spread far and wide of the size of the Armada and the martial power it wields. The common man believes England already defeated."

"They may be correct," Mayhew muttered before Carpenter fixed him with a contemptuous glare.

"Our job here is to make sure the Spanish are thwarted," Will said. "We can do nothing about the Armada, but we may still upset their wider plans."

"And what are those wider plans?" de Groot asked, as he rapidly refilled Mayhew's goblet. He caught Will's eye and nodded. "Questions for another time."

After Reidheid's betrayal in Edinburgh, Will was not about to trust any other spy quickly. Shifting allegiances were, it seemed, as common to the fraternity as an early death.

"We seek information on a ship that would have dropped anchor within the last few days," Will said. "Among its passengers would be a Spanish nobleman, Don Alanzo de las Posadas."

"Yes, yes, I know the ship." De Groot nodded enthusiastically. "There was talk of it in the taverns along the harbour. It dropped anchor in the morning, but a boat containing several passengers was not sent ashore until the dark had fallen. One of them was indeed Don Alanzo. He spent a while trying to procure several carriages to take him to Seville."

"Then that is our destination," Will said.

"One other thing that may or may not be of importance," de Groot continued. "He was insistent that before he left he should call at both the San Francisco Convent and at the cathedral."

Carpenter snorted. "Saying his prayers to clear the stain upon his soul."

"The cathedral perhaps, but at a convent?" At the window, Will peered through the jumble of buildings falling down the slope towards the harbour, where he could make out the *Tempest* in the light of the burning debris in the water. Now they were safely ashore, Captain Courtenay had ended his barrage and was sailing back out to open water. He tried not to think of Grace and what she might be enduring, but the unbidden thoughts fell across him like a shadow.

"We do not let small things pass us by, for greater things may lie behind them," he said. "But even if there is nothing more to it, a man's religion in this world may well be a weakness we can exploit to our own use."

CHAPTER 33

Will crept along the top of the whitewashed wall like a cat, stalking the woman who hummed a lilting melody as she took her constitutional in the orchard. Dappled by the sunlight through the leaves, her head was bowed in reflection, her white cloak caught by the cooling breeze. A glance back to the convent revealed they were alone.

Dropping silently to the grass, Will darted through the trees, keeping enough cover between him and the nun in case she looked back. It was a bright, glassy morning, shortly after dawn, already warm, and likely to get a great deal hotter.

De Groot had worked wonders in the hours of darkness. The spy admitted openly that he worked for gold and nothing more, not love of England, nor hatred of Spain. Walsingham paid him an annual stipend to pass on all the information he gained along the trade routes, and every year he threatened to go over to the Spanish, only to be bought back to the cause. It was a game that all sides understood. Will promised him a significant one-off payment, and in the early hours he had sent the local girl who cleaned his house to the convent under the pretence of arranging a donation from de Groot. After the nuns had finished their morning prayers just before first light, the girl spent an hour casually chatting until she had gathered the information Will required.

The nun never heard him until his hand was clamped across her mouth and another pinned her arms to her sides as he bundled her to the rear wall of the orchard. She struggled and tried to cry out, but he was too strong.

"Sister Adelita, I have no wish to harm you. I require your help," he whispered in fluent Spanish.

On hearing her name, she calmed a little and allowed herself to be pressed against the wall. Her eyes were large and dark as they searched his face, but steely defiance lay within them. She was beautiful, with the delicate bone structure of a noblewoman, dusky skin, and black hair pulled back beneath her head covering.

"I am about to remove my hand," he continued. "Please do not call out. I have no desire to overpower you." He allowed the hint of a threat to lace his words.

Once he had taken his hand away, she narrowed her eyes. "How dare you trespass on this sacred land? We allow no men in this convent."

"My apologies, Sister Adelita. If I could have approached you in any other way, I would have done so. But time is short, and matters urgent."

"You are English," she spat, identifying the hints in his pronunciation. "Your people were responsible for the attack on my home yesterday?"

Ignoring her, he said, "I must talk to you about Don Alanzo de las Posadas."

"My brother?"

The connection surprised Will, but he didn't show it. "He visited you here at the convent the other day."

Sister Adelita nodded, her thoughts racing. "Why do you want my brother?"

"I would know of what you spoke."

"No!" she replied indignantly. "Those are private matters between brother and sister. Who are you to ask?" She grew suspicious. "I will tell you nothing. You wish to harm him."

"Untrue. I saved your brother's life, and he mine. We are divided by our homelands, but I have only respect for him."

"Then what is your business with him?"

"A friend of mine is in great danger, a woman I have sworn to protect. She was taken by evil men who claim to be allies of Don Alanzo, but may be just as much of a threat to him. I want to save her, and take her home. If Don Alanzo said anything of her to you, please tell me." Will wondered how far he would go to get the answers he needed if she did not answer of her own accord.

Sister Adelita searched Will's face for any lies and what she saw appeared to satisfy her a little. "She is the woman you love?" A half smile ghosted her lips.

"No. She is the sister of the woman I loved," he said with such honesty she was taken aback. "There is little enough room for love in this world, Sister. It is a hard place, filled with duplicity, and violence, and loss, and we must seize our moments for comfort when we can, for they are stolen from us when our guard is down. The man I am now was forged by the loss of my love, and I will not see others go easily down that path. This woman I speak of . . . she is young and filled with hope and all the opportunities for joy that life lays before her at that age. She deserves her chance to achieve them, and I will do all I can to ensure she gets it."

"Even though it might harm you in the process?" Sister Adelita pressed.

"My moment for love is gone. I am, to all intents and purposes, dead to the world. I have nothing left to lose."

"I do not believe that," she said.

"'Tis true."

He could see his words had touched her, but she still continued to probe. "And you believe this is the path God has chosen for you? A selfless duty to protect others on the hard, dark road?"

"I wish I had your faith, Sister. I do what I do."

She smiled tightly. "And there is no benefit in this for England?"

"I have spoken truly."

"I am sure that is correct . . . of the words you have spoken. But there are many more unspoken, are there not? I know the ways of spies. Yes, I see that is what you are. I lived with my brother long enough to understand that the spaces between words are more important than the things that are said." Her voice hardened and her eyes flashed. "I understand the deceit that is set in the very fibre of your nature, and the lies you tell yourselves to do your job. I could not trust my brother. I will not trust you, even with your gentle talk of love and yearning hearts." She stared deep into his face and added, "However true that may be."

"Sister—"

"No, leave here now and this matter will be forgotten. But if you persist I will raise the authorities on you, and you will pay the price faced by all English spies found on Spanish soil." Turning without waiting for an answer, she walked back through the trees towards the convent.

For one moment, Will wondered if he should force her to speak. A part of him would do anything to get the answers he needed to save Grace; another part knew that he killed himself a little more with every step he took down that road. Finally, he relented. "Sister, I go now to the cathedral," he called after her. "If you change your mind, you will find me there."

She didn't look back.

Had he given up his best chance to understand the plans of Don Alanzo and the Enemy? Conflicted, he climbed back over the wall.

Most of Cádiz was infused with the bitter smell of burned debris. In every face, Will could only see the ravages of the plague; every woman reminded him of Grace and what she might be suffering. He was consumed by a desperate sense of time running through his fingers like sand.

Launceston, Mayhew, and Carpenter waited in the shade of a large, old tree in the centre of the plaza. In the smart but hard-wearing clothes de Groot had given them, they looked like merchants debating a deal before the start of the day's business.

"There is nothing for us here," Will said.

Launceston read Will's expression. "She did not talk. Then we should take her and offer her some encouragement."

"Torture a nun. Very good," Will replied. "Shall we then burn down the convent? Just to teach them a lesson?"

Launceston was unmoved. With a slight shrug, he replied, "She is Spanish."

"You inhabit a simple and soothing world. I am faintly jealous." Will surreptitiously eyed the first few townsfolk of the day to wander across the plaza, a couple of merchants, he guessed, a woman off to the market to buy food for one of the large houses. "We should not stay in the open too long. The cathedral and then to Seville."

"Why waste time at the cathedral?" Mayhew sounded drunk. Will had noticed he increasingly appeared inebriated and wondered if the corrosive despair of the Unseelie Court was finally seeping into him. That could make him a liability in the middle of Enemy territory.

"A man like Don Alanzo would not break his mission to visit the cathedral unless it was on an important matter. I do not see him as someone who is ruled by his religion."

"Show me a devout spy and I will show you a man about to slit a priest's throat." Carpenter's laugh had no humour.

"Where does that damned Spaniard plan to take the Silver Skull?" Mayhew continued morosely. "What does the Enemy have planned? And why are the Spanish—?" Catching himself, he flailed erratically.

Carpenter clutched his arm roughly and hissed, "Contain yourself."

"We should turn back," Mayhew said. "What can we accomplish here, apart from our own deaths? Even if we find the answer to those questions, we will never get near to the Silver Skull. All is lost here. We must find other tactics—"

Carpenter drew his knife and kept it hidden in the folds of his shirt, but he pressed the tip against Mayhew's chest. "Your weakness endangers us all. Any more and I will be done with you."

"Leave him," Will interjected. "He needs some time to recover from the strain of travelling. Take him back to de Groot's house. I will go to the cathedral alone, and meet you back there. But keep him away from the wine."

Mayhew appeared devastated by Will's intervention, but he left between Launceston and Carpenter without another word, shoulders slumped in a pale reflection of the arrogant man who had survived the Unseelie Court's assault on the Tower. Will was frustrated that he had not noticed the decline earlier.

As he passed through the town, his unease at being alone in enemy territory was emphasised by the unfamiliar surroundings, the North African influence in the architecture from the days of the Moorish occupiers, the scents of exotic spices and unfamiliar blooms. The town had prospered from the riches brought back from the New World. After the panic of the *Tempest*'s attack, the now-bustling market was filled with loud haggling over fish and vegetables. Beautiful women enjoyed the appreciative gazes of the traders while pretending not to notice the stir they created in their wake. Aromatic smoke drifted from the street-side food-sellers heating their charcoal to cook the seafood brought up fresh from the harbour.

Skirting the edge of the market, Will kept to quiet, shaded streets until he found the Plaza de la Catedral where the medieval cathedral looked over both the town and the sea. Painted white, it shone so brightly in the early morning sun that Will had to shield his eyes. At that hour, the large wooden doors were bolted and the cathedral was still, the plaza before it deserted.

Conscious of drawing attention to himself, Will retreated to the winding alleys that made the town feel like a mass of rat-runs. They were much cleaner than the streets of his home, and sweeter smelling. He had not gone far into the maze when footsteps echoed behind him, soon joined by two or three other pairs of feet. In the quiet around the cathedral, the sudden activity jarred.

Will ducked into a branching alley. One pair of footsteps followed. Now he could hear more feet drawing nearer ahead of him too. At the junction with the next alley, he peered around the corner. Two soldiers, swords drawn, searched every doorway and open window.

Doubling back, Will darted up another alley, only to find more foot soldiers coming towards him. A net had been cast and was drawing tighter.

He had been betrayed. Sister Adelita must have gone straight to the authorities and informed them he was on his way to the cathedral. He had looked in her eyes and convinced himself he could trust her, but it had been a stupid, naive mistake that might well cost him his life, and England its survival. Nathaniel had always told him he allowed women to make a fool of him.

The search party drew closer on every side, methodically closing off his escape routes. Will tested the handles of the nearest doors, but they were all locked.

He drew his sword, but knew that in a fight he would be overpowered within moments. As he searched for some route he may have missed, a figure stepped out before him.

He thrust his sword instinctively. When he saw it was Sister Adelita, he halted the blade a fraction of an inch from her throat. She swallowed when she realised how close to death she was. "If you wish to keep your freedom, you must follow me," she said.

"So you can betray me again?"

"If I had betrayed you once, I would not be here." Her eyes flashed.

Accepting the logic of her statement, he nodded and sheathed his sword. "Lead on."

Sister Adelita led him back down the alley towards the sound of approaching feet. Will briefly wondered once more if he was mistaken to trust her, but then she opened a rickety wooden door that led into a small, well-kept courtyard where herbs grew in stone troughs surrounded by alabaster statues. On the steps to the kitchen, a suntanned old man flashed Sister Adelita a toothless smile as she passed.

"The almshouses," she whispered, "provided by our convent for the sick and the needy."

Still wary that he was being led into some kind of trap, Will kept a close watch on the surrounding rooms as they moved through the cool house. At the front, Sister Adelita waited until all the foot soldiers had passed and then hurried Will out beyond the edge of the closing net.

"I should not be seen talking to you—" she began.

"I agree. Come with me—I have a safe haven, a house we have seized. The owner is unaware of our presence," Will lied.

Back at de Groot's, Will entered first and waved the Dutchman out of the back of the house so he would not be identified. Sister Adelita was so troubled she probably would not have noticed him. Clearly unsure whether she was doing the right thing, she clutched her rosary so hard her knuckles were white.

Launceston waited alone in the front room, keeping watch through the window.

"Where are the others?" Will asked.

"Mayhew has lost his mind. He began to curse and cry, and then ran off into the alleys. Carpenter has given pursuit."

Carpenter could have alerted the Spanish authorities—he knew of Will's destination, Will thought, but then he eyed Launceston, as unreadable as ever, who had also been left alone and had the opportunity for betrayal. Who could he trust?

"I must have words with Sister Adelita, who has proven a friend in our time of need," Will said. "If there is any sign of the soldiers drawing near, inform me immediately."

Will took Sister Adelita to a bedroom where they could have some privacy. She initially appeared uncomfortable at being in such a place with a man, but it quickly passed.

"I would thank you for coming to my aid," he said. "What made you change your mind?"

She gave him an honest look filled with such pain that he was taken aback. "I see you are a good man, if misguided." She swallowed to damp down the emotion that was close to the surface. "We are all misguided at some time."

"I wish no harm personally to your brother, or to you," he said gently, "but there are bigger things at play that dwarf us all."

She nodded slowly. "This is not the life I would have chosen for myself. But someone had to make amends." She searched his face for a moment as she weighed her next words, and then grabbed his shirt with an edge of desperation. "You know of the night-visitors. I see it."

"Night-visitors?"

"Do not play with me! I am no girl!" Her eyes flashed with passion once more, and she pulled herself closer to him with the hand entangled in his shirt. "The ones who watch from the dark fields. The meddlers, the invisible hand that continually steers us onto the rocks, the tempters and the tormenters. The Fair Folk," she added with bitter irony.

"The Unseelie Court." He placed his hand on the back of hers; it was trembling. "They are our Enemy. It is my life's work to oppose them. A secret war has been fought between England and these damnable predators for a great many years, and now it is on the brink of becoming an open battle."

"You fight them!" Her large eyes glistening, she pressed herself against him so he could feel the shape of her body through her thin dress. "My brother forged an unholy alliance with them. Or rather Spain has, sanctioned by the king. We have grown fat on the riches from the New World, and cannot bear to lose them to England, and so we will do anything to protect our status. But the ends do not justify the means!"

He put his arms around her to comfort her, and she allowed her head to rest on his shoulder. He imagined it had been a long time since she had felt the comforting warmth of another's embrace.

"I fear for my brother," she said softly. "He is a loyal subject of the king, and will do whatever he is told in the pursuit of his business of spying. All must be sacrificed for the future of Spain! But God is greater than our country, and the king, and men, and God would not wish us to do deals with these devils to keep us in gold and silver, or even to bring the one true religion back to England."

"You discussed this with your brother?"

Nodding, she gripped him tighter. "We argued, and fought, but he would never see reason. Our father disappeared when we were young, and since then he has grown hard, and driven."

Will understood Don Alanzo a little more in that moment. Had the Unseelie Court taken their father? Was Don Alanzo now allying himself with the Enemy to get his father back?

"I was set to be wed," Sister Adelita continued, "and on the day before my marriage I told my brother he must break off all dealings with those vile things or I would be forced to do penance for the sake of my family. He refused, and so I left behind my love and my heart and came here to the convent. And still my brother continued along his path to damnation." She stifled a sob. "Does he think so little of me?"

"Men like us are pulled by greater currents. Our lives, and our desires, our hopes and dreams, become as nothing next to the demands and responsibilities placed upon us. I am sure your brother cares for you deeply. I am equally sure he feels he has no choice in the course that he follows."

She softened against him. "When my brother came to me the other day, he seemed changed . . . hopeful. He told me he may soon have good news for me."

The destruction of England, Will thought.

"And he said he hoped my penance at the convent would soon come to an end."

"You would break your vows?"

"I . . . I do not know. I believe . . . I have given my life to God. I never expected, or hoped for, anything to change." She looked briefly into his face, and then kissed him, softly at first, but then with increasing passion.

After a moment, he pulled away, though she fought to keep him in an embrace. Gently, he prised her from him. "I am a man of easy morals, but you will regret this if we continue," he said. "I would not wish that upon you."

She bowed her head in shame, but he raised her chin and added, "There is no shame in honest emotion. This business makes us into people we are not. It ruins lives, and forces us to battle with ourselves along the road to misery. We deserve better, all of us. Do not think badly of yourself, Sister Adelita."

She allowed herself a slight smile, but her breath was still short with passion. "One day we can all be who we are."

He nodded in agreement without really believing it. The war would never end, he was sure of that. There would be battles and bloodshed and death, but it would continue as long as men were men and the Unseelie Court were whatever they were, both sides led on by their own weaknesses. To fight without hope of victory, to fight without truly knowing the reason for that fight, was the very definition of madness, but as long as it was a shared madness there would be no end to it.

"Did your brother give you any reason for his hope? Any information that might help me?" he asked.

"He sought my aid. There is a priest in Cádiz who is known for his struggles with the Devil. He undertook the rite of exorcism for the soul of a young girl in Arcos de la Frontera and cast out several demons, and he is knowledgeable in matters of the occult and those who practice such things. Father

Celino is often petitioned by the local people, but many of their requests are frivolous and so he will only consider matters on recommendation."

"And your brother asked you to recommend him to this priest?"

She nodded. "He met him at the cathedral. I do not know what they discussed, but later that night my brother left for Seville in a great hurry."

"Then I would wish to meet with this Father Celino."

Her face fell, and Will knew that if she recommended him to the priest she would be accused of aiding a foreign spy, and that would likely mean her death.

He held her for a moment longer and then guided her back to the front room where Launceston still watched the street. The door crashed open as they entered, and Carpenter burst in dragging Mayhew, who threw himself free and stalked to the corner of the room, shifting sheepishly.

"Do not accuse me!" Mayhew jabbed his finger at each of them in turn. "I needed air and some time to gather my thoughts!"

Carpenter toyed with his knife, his eyes flickering between Will and Launceston, who also had his hand on his hidden dagger.

Will stepped before Mayhew to calm the situation. "We need to know you will not drag us down to hell, Master Mayhew," Will said calmly. "Your absolute support is required in this work. We cannot afford your personal weaknesses to lead us to disaster."

"Or what? What will you do?" Mayhew raged. "Kill me? Do it! Nothing can be worse than this life!"

Without hesitation, Sister Adelita stepped by Will and took Mayhew's hand. He was surprised and unbalanced by her touch, his anger dying in his throat. "You have troubles," she said. "I have spoken to your friend here, and I understand what you do. It is God's work, and that is never easy, but the rewards are shared by all."

Tears sprang to Mayhew's eyes, and he blinked them away quickly before the others saw it as a sign of weakness. "I do not do God's work," he replied quietly. "I am weak, and I am not up to this."

Sister Adelita looked to Will and said, "Let me speak with him in private while you make your arrangements. If you wish me to make recommendations to Father Celino, I will."

Will agreed, but he had already started to formulate a plan. Once Mayhew had been led away, Carpenter said vehemently, "He will be the death of us, I tell you now."

"Then let him stand in line. There are more pressing matters that could lead us to the grave," Will said.

"How long are you going to keep protecting him?" Carpenter snapped.

"Till I am certain he is a danger to us. I am not so quick in taking the life of a fellow as you, Master Carpenter."

"No, but you are quick to abandon them."

"You know I thought you dead."

Bristling, Carpenter made to confront Will until Launceston stepped between them. "Is this how it will be? We do the work of the Enemy and the Spaniards ourselves?"

"Listen to the voice of reason, Master Carpenter," Will said.

"Besides, I can slit Mayhew's throat in an instant if he truly becomes a problem," Launceston continued.

Will sighed. "Enough talk of slitting and cutting and stabbing the people we know. Let us direct our attention to the matter at hand."

Sister Adelita emerged with Mayhew shortly after. Whatever she had said to him, he had calmed considerably and was contrite. Offering his apologies, he promised not to give in to his weaknesses. "It was a momentary lapse," he said.

After Will had ordered de Groot to make arrangements for their urgent departure from Cádiz, Sister Adelita guided them along a circuitous route to the cathedral that avoided all the busy areas and the plaza in front where they guessed the foot soldiers would still be watching. A side door used by the cathedral staff was open. Sister Adelita ushered them inside.

The cathedral was cool after the heat of the day, and at that time was still and quiet. Soon, Will knew, it would be bustling with merchants arranging business and the local people at their devotions or lighting candles for loved ones at sea. The stained-glass windows cast jewels across the flagstones, and the great vaulted roof high overhead caught and magnified every sound with the perfect acoustics of the medieval builders. Will silently cautioned the others to move with extreme quiet.

Like all the Catholic cathedrals Will had seen, the chapels were filled with paintings and relics, gold chalices, crosses, and other iconography that showed the great wealth of the Church.

Mayhew, Carpenter, and Launceston slipped into hiding places along the nave, while Will waited in a small chapel close to the high altar. Nodding to

Will, Sister Adelita stood in the nave and called loudly for Father Celino. He emerged with a lazy gait, a tall man with a Roman nose, heavily tanned, and with jet black hair despite being in his fifties.

"Sister Adelita, is there a problem?" he asked with a note of concern. "I did not expect to see you here."

"Yes, Father. It is about my brother," she replied, her head bowed.

"Don Alanzo? Is he well?"

"I am worried about him, Father. I have not heard from him and I would know where he is so I can seek him out."

"Your brother is in Seville, Sister," Celino said with an aloof manner. "As always, he is engaged in important matters. He would not wish to have his affairs intruded upon by one such as you."

"Then you cannot tell me who he sees?"

"Of course not!" Celino snapped.

Will caught Launceston's eye, who waited like a spectre in the shadows behind a stone column, and he passed on the sign. Instantly, Carpenter, Mayhew, and Launceston darted from their hiding places and grabbed Sister Adelita, who screamed as she attempted to fight them off.

"What is this?" Celino raged. "Leave her alone! Help! Help us now!"

Drawing his knife, Will glided silently to Celino's side and whispered, "Silence, Father, or it will not only be her blood that stains the flags."

Celino fell silent. "Who are you?" he asked gravely.

"English cutthroats who think nothing of spilling Spanish blood."

Celino blanched.

"Kill her," Will said.

"No!" Celino cried, but Launceston and Carpenter were already dragging Sister Adelita into one of the chapels. Her screams rang off the walls, until a moment later there was only silence.

"Lock the doors," Will instructed Mayhew, "so we are not disturbed."

Grabbing the priest roughly by his cassock, Will threw him across the altar. His head bounced off the table and his eyes grew wide with fear as he began to intone a prayer.

"Do not waste your breath, Father," Will said. "No higher power will save you, and none on Earth either."

Blood pumped through Will's head as he stared into Celino's face. All his repressed fears about Grace rushed up, and his rage at the suffering heaped on an innocent person, and his frustration that he could not move faster and harder to find her.

"You would dare harm a servant of God in His very house?" Celino uttered.

"There is a woman under my protection whose life is at risk. I would dare anything, Father."

"What about your eternal soul?"

"My soul was lost long ago."

"But God—"

"I care not for God!" Will snapped. "The things I have seen . . . the pain that has been heaped on the people I know . . . If there was a God, would he allow such things to exist? This religion tears us apart when we should be joining together to fight greater threats."

"The word of the Lord brings comfort—"

"And pain and suffering to many who have suffered the whip of the Catholics, or the persecution of King Henry's church. This world will be consumed by the flames of hell and you will still be arguing over whose Bible is stronger."

Celino saw something in Will's face that made him even more terrified. He began to intone another prayer until Will cuffed him forcefully across the face.

"I have questions, Father, and I am not in the mood to be resisted." Will moved the tip of his knife slowly across Celino's cheek to touch his lower eyelid. The priest's breath caught in his throat. "If the answers I receive are not to my liking, I will cut out this eye," Will continued. "And if you continue to live out your fantasy of being a martyr, I will cut out your other eye. And then I will whittle you down little by little until there is nothing left. We shall see whose will is stronger."

Celino began to whimper and struggle in the panic that consumed him. Slipping the tip of his knife into the priest's nostril, Will ripped up through the flesh. Celino howled as blood spurted across his cassock and onto the altar.

"Pay heed to that pain," Will said. "It is nothing compared to what is to come. Are you ready to answer my questions?"

Trembling, the priest nodded.

"Don Alanzo de las Posadas visited you here at the cathedral this very week. What did he want?"

Celino swallowed, his eyes darting towards the chapel where Sister Adelita had been killed.

"Yes, we forced her to ask you these questions. You could have saved her life if you had answered them then," Will said. "Her death is on your conscience. Now . . . what did Don Alanzo want?"

Blinking away tears, Celino replied, "To find the most knowledgeable man in all of Spain on matters of the occult, and ancient mysteries, and the secrets of the past."

"And you helped him?"

"Yes—there is such a man in Seville, a great philosopher and alchemist who knows the languages of the ancient Greeks and the Moors and the Arabs, and who owns the most extensive library of occult volumes in existence. His reputation is known only to a few, but I have consulted with him on more than one occasion."

Why would Don Alanzo want to contact such a man so urgently? Will wondered. The Spanish had all the knowledge they needed to use the Silver Skull in the invasion, if not the Shield that allowed protection from it. "Who is he and where do I find him?" Will drew a bubble of blood from Celino's eyelid with the tip of his knife.

"He is of mixed Moorish descent and he has taken the name Abd al-Rahman after the emir and caliph of Córdoba, a prince of the Umayyad dynasty in the Moorish occupation of our land. His true name is not known." Celino tried to swallow, but his throat was too dry. "You will find his shop in the Barrio de Santa Cruz, the Jewish quarter, on Susona Street, just north of Real Alcázar, the royal palace," he croaked.

As Will withdrew the knife, Celino was convulsed by a shudder of relief. "Very good, Father. You live to pray another day."

At his command, Launceston and Carpenter emerged from the chapel dragging a still-living Sister Adelita. They threw her onto the flags before the altar. Gaping in shock, Celino stumbled down to put his arms around her.

"They held a hand over my mouth so I would not call out," she gasped. "I wanted to, Father. Oh, I did . . ."

She was a good actress, Will noted.

"You are the Devil himself," Celino growled.

Shrugging, Will returned his knife to its sheath and indicated to Mayhew to begin scouring the rooms along the nave as they had agreed earlier.

"Do you think four Englishman can attack the heart of Spain with impunity?" Celino continued angrily. "We are the most powerful nation in this world and you . . . you are nothing but dogs. Your deaths will be upon you before you know it."

"*My* invasion of Spain is built on more solid foundations than your attack upon England," Will replied, "and I will not be turned away by prayers or curses or all the swords you can muster."

When Mayhew returned, Will gave the signal and Launceston and Carpenter roughly dragged Celino to a small, dark room near the altar that contained the tabernacle. Will and Mayhew accompanied Sister Adelita. As they walked, she kept her eyes ahead and her chin raised defiantly, but she secretly felt for Will's hand and gave it a brief squeeze of support. He returned her touch.

Once Celino and Sister Adelita were in the room, and Will had the large iron key to lock it, he said, "Take heed, Father. No lives have been lost here this day. But if you raise the alarm before we leave Cádiz, I will make it my last act on this Earth to return here and slay you both."

As he closed the door, the last thing he saw was Sister Adelita's face, pale in the growing gloom, and filled with a look of such yearning, it caught him by surprise. He held her gaze for a moment before locking the door.

Slipping the key into his pocket, he led the way to the side door through which they had entered. "We must move fast," Will said. "Celino will be discovered in no time, and he will have the authorities on our heels before the sun has started to move down to the horizon. We must be into Seville and out in a flash. Are you ready for the flight, and the fight, of your lives? Then let us depart!"

CHAPTER 34

lizabeth's incandescent fury terrified the greying men gathered around the meeting room. "One man!" the queen raged. "All our futures are dependent upon one man!"

All eyes looked down. The queen turned her powdered white face from one to another of her circle of closest advisors, waiting for a response.

Walsingham understood their reluctance. Elizabeth was like a storm at sea, as quick to turn from coquettish flirtation to volcanic anger without the slightest warning. But who would tell her that her own indecisiveness had led the country into the desperate strait in which it now found itself?

"Will Swyfe is—" he began.

"Yes, yes! I know all about Master Swyfte's abilities!" she roared. "Now where are the bearers of good news?" The whip-crack in Elizabeth's voice kept all heads bowed. "Lord Walsingham," she pressed. "You still say the Armada will sail shortly?"

"That is the information I have, Your Majesty. There are conflicting reports—some say five hundred ships, some fewer, manned by a good eighty thousand men, perhaps fewer—but ships and men there are, in Lisbon, ready for the off."

Walsingham saw the blood drain from faces at the numbers he had presented. A fleet that large would destroy the English navy in no time.

"Why can you not get good intelligence?" snapped Lord Burghley, the queen's principal advisor. Though a master of statecraft, he was a grey man in both appearance and manner. Too weak by far, Walsingham felt.

"Good intelligence costs money," Walsingham replied sharply. He didn't need to mention that the Treasury was drained after years of slow-bubbling war with Spain. "How go the peace negotiations?"

"Your sarcasm is unwarranted," Burghley responded.

Lord Howard, a fierce but thoughtful man, commanded the English navy. His eyes flickered briefly towards Walsingham before he spoke. "When we received reports last month of Santa Cruz's death, you made the wise decision not to put our fleet to sea," he began.

Liar, Walsingham thought.

"But now Philip will have filled his vacancy and the Armada will have direction again," Howard continued. "More urgency is required in the defence of the realm, I feel."

Walsingham could see Elizabeth evaluating the potential cost.

"Drake calls for the fleet to be based at Plymouth," Howard continued. "From there, it will be better able to guard the full length of the south coast and to prevent any Spanish landing. And he argues most strongly for us to attack the Spanish first. He is a great strategist, as you know, Your Majesty, and he feels this is the best defence."

After a moment's thought, Elizabeth said, "Let us wait for more intelligence."

"If the prince of Parma lands his fierce troops upon England's shores, the battle is lost," Walsingham began cautiously. "We have no army save for the garrison at Berwick and the Yeoman of the Guard. Our fighting men are mainly raw and will be crushed by Parma's warriors. And those of ours who have been hardened by battle can scarcely be trusted. Many are Catholics, many Irish."

Elizabeth's anger drained away at his words. She knew the truth when she heard it.

"We are short of weapons and gunpowder supplies are dangerously low," Walsingham continued, gathering force. "The coastal defences are rudimentary, and in some places construction has not even begun. Once the invasion begins, there is a danger the Catholics within will rise up in force. That James, who lives in mortal fear of the Enemy, will invade from Scotland to gain control of Dee's defences. These are our most desperate times."

"And you work to rally good Englishmen behind us?" Elizabeth demanded.

"Of course. The pamphleteers publish the stories we require—that the Spanish ships are filled with instruments of torture to inflict torment upon all good people, and pox-ridden doxies to be loosed upon our men and kill them with disease. That Philip has ordered his men to put children to the pike and bash in the brains of babies. Others will be branded on the face so they know they have been conquered. They will have the fear of God in them if the Spanish land, but that will not be enough."

"So we must rely upon our warships," Elizabeth said quietly, "and they may not be enough either. And the part the Enemy will play with this Silver Skull?"

"Their plans are still lost in the fog that they draw around them so well." Walsingham was careful not to leave Elizabeth despairing; it would not help the cause. Bad enough the Spanish had an overwhelming force, but that they also had a weapon that could unleash plague across the land? That was too crushing to consider. "Will Swyfte leads three of my best men. They will not shirk the task ahead of them."

"And if they are caught?" Burghley enquired. "They will give Philip the reason he needs to invade."

He needs no reason! Walsingham kept his face calm. "If William Swyfte is captured, we will deny all knowledge of his mission. He has been driven half mad by grief over the loss of his close friend, Grace Seldon, and holds a personal grudge against Spain."

"You will abandon him?" Burghley said. "He will be tortured and executed."

"That is the price we must pay."

"If Swyfte does not reclaim the Skull, all is truly lost!" Elizabeth raged. Even with his caution, Walsingham could see that Elizabeth understood the true situation. "He cannot fail. He cannot!"

Without another word, she flounced from the chamber so her senior advisors could not see her tears of fear. Burghley made to take up the queen's words, but Walsingham cut him short. "William Swyfte will do whatever is necessary to retrieve the Skull, even at the cost of his own life," he said. He left the room before Burghley could question him further. The less he knew, the less he could bend information to underpin his own feeble prevarication when advising the queen.

Dee waited outside, his hood pulled up to hide his identity from unwelcome eyes.

"Any news?" Walsingham asked.

Dee shook his head. "The Enemy's true plans remain hidden. They move pieces here and there to distract us, but I can find no guiding principle."

"Except our destruction."

"Except that."

"You have heard all the prophecies circulating in Europe?"

"Of course. Things do not look well for any of us." Dee took a deep breath. Walsingham could see the strain in his features. "I have cast Elizabeth's horoscope," he continued. "The second eclipse of the moon this year arrives when her ruling sign is in the ascendant, twelve days before her birthday. That is a powerful portent. Momentous events lie ahead, and all that stands is at risk. The Enemy may finally destroy our defences and achieve their goal."

"Do not tell Elizabeth this."

"Why, I planned to tell her this very moment," Dee said tartly. "I cannot wait to have my head on a pole above the gates of London Bridge for such high treason. So we put our faith in Swyfte?"

"We do. Unless you have another plan?"

Dee said nothing.

Walsingham left him studying his astrological charts, and Walsingham made his way to the gardens to be alone with his thoughts. Deep in conversation on the bench beside the lavender were Marlowe and Nathaniel. Walsingham read the concern etched in the face of Will's assistant and recognised the cause immediately. It brought back a rush of memories and feelings still raw after all the years.

His mother telling him the circumstances of his father's death. "They haunted him until his heart failed him. They had noticed him, you see."

His dreams of following his father into the legal profession when he enrolled as a student at Gray's Inn, dashed by the thing that sat in the corner of his room and told him cruelly that his mother would be next.

At her graveside near thirty years ago, watching the figures hiding among the yews, sensing their jubilation at his mother's final suffering, at his own suffering.

"We have long memories, and our punishment reaches down the years, down the generations."

His mounting sense of injustice, tempered always by the hope that soon the misery would stop. His wedding to Anne. Her funeral just two years later. The coils of the Enemy drawing tighter and tighter around him.

His two stepsons, dying in a conflagration when a barrel of gunpowder blew up in the gatehouse where he had sent them to be safe.

So many deaths, so many tears, and all because of an act committed before he was even born. His father's crime? To help a young boy the Enemy were tormenting.

Over the years, through all the pain, they had driven him to be the man he was. And they would pay the price.

At Walsingham's curt summons, Marlowe came over, trying to hide his sheepish expression. Walsingham would have preferred him to stay out of sight—he had too many weaknesses, too many cracks for the Enemy to prise open—but more important matters pressed.

"He has been touched by the Enemy?" Walsingham said, nodding towards Nathaniel.

"Lightly." Marlowe was pleased Walsingham did not have stern words for him. "He still has many doubts, and searches for ways to dismiss what his heart knows to be true."

"Then help him in that task. Do not let him onto the path we walk. He deserves a better life."

"I will lead him down a garden path filled with sunshine and flowers."

"Good. We must never forget why we fight." He fixed an eye on Marlowe. "And why are you here?"

"Will has charged us both with keeping watch upon the Lantern Tower. The Enemy have shown how badly they require the Shield, and he fears they will attempt to steal it."

"The Lantern Tower has many, many defences. But still . . . you do good work."

Marlowe beamed. It was a small act of kindness, but Walsingham felt pleased that he had done it; he was allowed little opportunity to be kind these days.

But as he moved away, the shadow fell over him quickly once again. He could see the Enemy's hand everywhere. No one was wholly trustworthy, not even those closest to him. He had made so many sacrifices, and it was all on the brink of being for naught. On any given day, Swyfte was the best man he had, but he was afraid the Enemy had found Will's weakness—the girl, Grace—and would use that to destroy him.

CHAPTER 35

"How long do we have?" Mayhew asked.

"An hour. Perhaps two," Will replied. In the garb of Levantine sailors, he led the others away from the crack of rope and the slap of billowing sails at Seville's harbour. De Groot's carriage had dropped them off at the waterside after the two-day journey across the dusty tracks of Andalusia, in the shade of undulating hills awash with olive trees and vines. With the loop of cloth from their headdress pulled over their lower faces to disguise their identities, they quickly merged into the thick flow of people milling along the dock-side, merchants barking orders or haggling over prices, swarthy workers unloading bales and urns, sailors lounging in the shade, drinking and playing cards as they waited for their ships to sail.

"That does not give us much time," Carpenter growled.

"Time enough to cut off the Spaniard's ears if he is still here, and to encourage him to tell us the whereabouts of the Silver Skull and the girl," Launceston mused.

"Any more talk of the removal of body parts and I will start to think you consider it more entertainment than encouragement," Will murmured.

"One cannot escape the fact that it is entertaining," Launceston replied, "and has been since I was a child, cutting up cats and dogs to see how they work."

No one spoke for several minutes.

Beneath an azure sky, Seville carried its age with great dignity and sophistication. Gleaming white walls and spicy Moorish domes of orange and brown and gold, straight lines from the Romans and horseshoe arches from the Visigoths, faded Phoenician carvings on the old stones torn out during the rebuilding of the busy port along the slow-moving Rio Guadalquivir, where the ships backed up for miles laden with produce bought with New World riches. On the streets, under the swaying palms, people moved at a lazy pace, their faces betraying the heritage of two thousand years of invaders. Though the Christian rulers had tried to drive out the Moors and the Jews, they could not eradicate the subtle influences of North Africa and the Holy Land that had burrowed into the features of the residents over the centuries.

It was a city where anything could be found: silver and gold from the Spanish Main, silk and spices from the distant East, rare books and telescopes from Constantinople, secrets from the four corners and the answers to age-old mysteries.

They headed east through the sweltering stores and clattering shipyards of El Arenal towards their destination. Mayhew appeared to have regained much of his equilibrium since they had left Cádiz, although his face still showed the stress of surviving in the heart of enemy territory.

Continuing east, they soon spied the soaring bulk of the Gothic cathedral. It was dominated by La Giralda, the Moorish bell tower, its geometric stone patterns lining the tier of arched windows that revealed its origins as a minaret where the muezzin called the faithful to prayer during the long occupation. The cathedral stood just beyond the solid walls of the Barrio de Santa Cruz, erected, according to the city fathers, to protect the Jewish inhabitants, but which made the quarter seem more like a sprawling prison.

Passing through the arched gates into the warren of whitewashed alleys and patios, they saw that New World wealth had already flowed into the redevelopment of the ghettos. The architecture here had a different flavour, with tiny grilled windows on tall, plain-fronted buildings, simple next to the ornate designs of the Moorish structures that dominated the rest of the city.

In the Barrio the streets were quieter, and they could move faster towards the Real Alcázar. Its spacious gardens soon came into view, lush rows of palms, terraces, fountains, and pavilions. The sprawling, ornate complex of buildings with the Palacio Pedro I at its heart was like a jewel box with its blend of Islamic and Christian styles on a soothing geometric design of patios and halls. It had a grandeur that dwarfed the more stoic and shadowy Palace of Whitehall.

They avoided the guards at the gates and headed north until they found Susona Street, a narrow route between larger thoroughfares with tiny, dark shops like caves, goods and produce piled high on tables beneath awnings—

gleaming brassware, pots and pans, fruit and spices—and an inn where old men with long, white moustaches and snowy beards drank wine and talked quietly about the old days.

Their destination stood out from the other stores with a simple painted sign of yellow stars and a crescent moon on a deep blue background. The window was filled with chalices, swords, and other items of dubious use but clear ritual intent. The door stood open and the heavy, spicy scent of incense drifted out. It was too dark inside to see much, but Will could make out strange objects hanging from the rafters and piles of large books.

He ordered Launceston to keep watch and slipped inside. Carpenter and Mayhew pretended to browse the books near the door while he pushed his way into the gloomy depths through a series of heavy drapes, where the only light came from intermittent candles. Here were stored items of a more obvious occult nature—balls of crystal, scrying mirrors, human skulls, knives with obsidian handles, jewels, wall coverings marked with arcane symbols, and books so big they looked impossible to lift. Shadows swooped with every flicker of the flames so that the jumble of treasures appeared to move of their own accord. The breeze from the open door shifted hanging columns of colourful beads glistening in the faint illumination and stirred wind chimes, so the senses were continually stimulated and the thoughts distracted.

A whiff of sweat beneath the disguising incense. Whirling, Will saw white eyes in the corner next to the drapes through which he had entered; he had passed within a foot of the watcher without even knowing he was there.

"You are Abd al-Rahman?" Will asked, in Spanish.

A North African man stepped into the candlelight. His shaven head was covered with swirling tattoos made by a needle with ashes rubbed into the wounds. One tooth was missing. Will noticed his fingernails were excessively long and filed like an animal's claws.

"I am Abd al-Rahman," he replied in English, noting Will's slight accent, and added with a faint sibilance, "You search for something in particular?" He was a big man, strong and muscular. One hand rested on the hilt of a curved knife at his belt.

"I hear you are a wise man, and knowledgeable in the ways of the ancients."

Al-Rahman brought his hands together slowly and gave a faint bow, although he showed no pleasure. "You honour me."

"I am surprised the Christian leaders of Seville allow a practitioner of the Devil's arts in their midst."

"They drive out only those who are not useful to them."

"You help them?"

"I help all, for the right fee."

"Then you may come to my aid, for I am a weary traveller in search of information. And I can provide all the gold you need."

Al-Rahman wryly indicated a table for Will to make his payment, but it was clear he knew Will had no gold.

Will shrugged. "Perhaps I can find another inducement."

Faintly smiling, al-Rahman partially drew the knife at his belt.

With a weary shake of his head, Will said, "One day things will go as smoothly as I imagined them before I opened my mouth." He snapped his fingers.

Bursting through the drapes, Carpenter and Mayhew each caught an arm, and with his free hand Carpenter brought his knife to al-Rahman's throat.

Will propped himself against a table and folded his arms. "Sadly, we are desperate men. Who knows to what depths we will stoop?"

"Do not threaten me," al-Rahman replied. "I make a dangerous enemy."

"Then we are evenly matched. I seek a Spanish nobleman—Don Alanzo de las Posadas. You know him?"

His eyes heavy-lidded, his features impassive, al-Rahman shook his head.

"He has not been here?"

Al-Rahman shook his head again.

"My assistant Nathaniel always says I am too trusting, but in this instance I believe you are not wholly at ease with the truth. Don Alanzo left Cádiz in search of you several days ago. It is inconceivable that he has not yet called at these premises."

Al-Rahman's eyes darted from side to side. Before Will could alert the others, al-Rahman tore himself free, plucked a handful of powder from a pouch at his belt, and threw it into the air. As the white powder swirled into Carpenter and Mayhew's faces, they couldn't help but inhale, and a second later they jacked forwards at the waist and began to vomit uncontrollably.

Will pressed the cloth from his headdress tighter across his face, but some of the powder had already worked past the protection. His vision swam and his gorge rose. Through watering eyes, he saw al-Rahman lunge forwards with his knife drawn.

Will threw himself to one side, upending a table piled high with bones and crystals. They clattered across the floor noisily and brought more artefacts crashing down. Flinging himself upon Will, al-Rahman stabbed viciously and it was all Will could do to hold him off. He tried to reach his own knife, but al-Rahman wielded his blade back and forth in a blur of slashes, drawing closer to Will's throat with each arc.

Glass exploded at the back of al-Rahman's head with a loud crash and he pitched forwards across Will, unconscious. Launceston had entered silently during the fight and now stood over them holding a broken bottle.

"Quickly," the ghost-faced earl urged. "A carriage approaches. It is Don Alanzo."

"Go," Will gasped, throwing al-Rahman off him. "Take the others."

"You?"

Looking around quickly, Will replied, "I will find somewhere to hide so I can observe events. I will meet you later at the arranged place. And if I do not join you, you know what to do next."

Will and Launceston exchanged a brief look of understanding before the earl fled the room, followed by Carpenter and Mayhew, still retching. Will stumbled to the back of the shop where a purple drape covered a door to a flight of stone steps. Behind him, al-Rahman stirred. Will staggered up the steps to a large room that covered the entire floor of the house, with brick pillars supporting the ceiling where the walls had been removed. Occult symbols were painted on the floor inside a ritual circle, and all across the walls, which were the dark blue of the night sky. In one corner stood a seven-foot-high, three-faced hinged mirror with a gilt-covered iron frame.

Silently, Will slipped back down the steps and listened at the drapes. Peeking through the gap, he saw Don Alanzo burst in, accompanied by a man in a thick cloak and cowl that plunged his entire face into darkness. The Silver Skull, Will suspected.

Don Alanzo helped al-Rahman to his feet. "I saw men running from this place."

"Englishmen. They were looking for you." Shaking his head, al-Rahman recovered quickly. "I told them nothing."

"They are gone now. I will alert my men to begin a search, but the other matter is more pressing. Have you all you need?"

"I have both items. But I warn you: the red dust is in short supply. It is fresh off the ship today, from the high land near my home. If we fail, there will be no other opportunity."

"Then we do not fail!" Don Alanzo said vehemently. "Make sure you succeed, or as God is my witness . . ." Don Alanzo caught himself. Will was puzzled to see his edgy mood; even in the danger of the bear pit, he had retained his composure. "What time?" Don Alanzo pressed.

"This business can only be conducted under cover of the night."

"Thank God, there will finally be an end to it." The note of desperation in Don Alanzo's voice was palpable. He turned to the Silver Skull and said in a more measured tone, "Do you hear—an end to it?"

The dark cave of the cowl was turned to Don Alanzo, but the Silver Skull's posture gave no sign that he had heard, or even cared. Will thought of him, a prisoner inside his mask, and then a prisoner in the Tower, and now a prisoner of the Spanish, for all those years, and wondered if the Skull could bring himself to care about anything anymore.

They were interrupted by one of Don Alanzo's men: word had arrived from Cádiz that an English spy was en route to see al-Rahman. Don Alanzo sent an order to mount a guard at both ends of Susona Street until his business was done, and that a messenger should be sent to the Real Alcázar so that a citywide search could be mounted for the English spies.

Once he had departed, al-Rahman intoned, "The preparations will take some time and you must both be involved."

"In the room upstairs?" Don Alanzo asked.

"The space has been prepared," al-Rahman replied.

Will quickly mounted the stairs and squeezed behind the mirror in the dark room with its unsettling atmosphere. It was too late to wonder if it was the wrong decision; there was no way out for him.

On the dusty floor, he made himself comfortable as he listened to the sound of al-Rahman and Don Alanzo beginning their preparations. The sound of scraping across the floor as objects were dragged into position. Flints being struck, and candles lit. The smell of tallow smoke and sickly-sweet incense. A brazier ignited, bitterly sulphurous, and the loud exhalation of bellows.

Don Alanzo and al-Rahman barely spoke, and when they did it was only to proffer or request instructions; it was clear no love was lost between them, their relationship based on need and gold.

Enclosed in his constricting hiding space, cut off from the world, the background noise became a hypnotic susurration, lulling him into a state where his thoughts roamed free. Time passed without him knowing it, interrupted only by the presence of new aromas, subtly different sounds, the murmur of voices rising and falling. From his restricted vantage point, he watched the shadows grow along the walls and the gloom fold around him.

From the open window, the sounds of the working city slowly died away, the shouts of workers, the dense conversations passing beneath, the bang and rattle from the shipyards, the back and forth prattle of merchant and buyer. For a brief while it grew still. Then came the music drifting from different windows, fiddles and voice and harpsichord, rhythmic songs from Africa and the Orient colliding with the passionate whirl of Spain, and the noise swelling from the inns, voices raised in celebration of another hard day passed, in song and in love. It was hot and muggy, the cooling breeze long gone. It felt like a storm was coming.

In the room, the mood had grown tense. Don Alanzo and al-Rahman's exchanges were clipped. Objects clattered on the floor with barely restrained vehemence.

Just as Will's thoughts once again turned to Grace, a low chant broke out from the centre of the room. Although he didn't recognise the language, there was something in the cadence or the rhythm of the words that made him uneasy.

In the distance, thunder rumbled.

Al-Rahman's voice grew louder. He held on to certain syllables in unnatural ways, punctuating each volley of noise with a click at the back of his throat. Will felt the pressure of ancient days begin to build in the room. He was sick of it all—the Unseelie Court, the dark arts al-Rahman practised, the world they represented. The comfort and stability of his childhood seemed like a light on the horizon.

What are they planning? he wondered. *Thank God, there will finally be an end to it*, Don Alanzo had said. *An end to what?*

The chant reached a crescendo. In its odd intonation, Will had the feeling it was a petition; or, perhaps, a summoning. Confident he would not be seen in the dark, he pushed his head close to the space between the mirror and the wall, but all he could see were the shadows of three people swaying in the candlelight.

One of the shadows ducked down to plunge a hand into an object on the floor, and emerged with a writhing object. The cries of a cat echoed around the room. A shadow-knife darted, and was greeted by a gush of liquid before the cries stopped abruptly. Once the cat had been drained, al-Rahman tossed it away. It hit the wall and came to rest on the floor, glassy eyes staring directly at Will.

"Can this work?" Don Alanzo whispered.

Al-Rahman did not reply at first, and then said, "You must be prepared for what is to come, both of you. These matters are not easy for the untutored."

"I am ready." Don Alanzo attempted to deliver the words forcefully, but a waver revealed his true feelings.

The shadow-al-Rahman picked up a small pot and balanced it on the palm of his hand.

"The red dust?" Don Alanzo asked.

"So rare," al-Rahman replied. "You have paid a great deal for it."

"It will be worth it."

"Again I stress, the ritual must be completed or there will not be another opportunity. The Silver Skull will remain fastened to his head for all time."

Will flinched with sudden awareness: Don Alanzo sought to remove the Skull from the man who wore it. What purpose would that serve?

The thunder rolled quickly towards Seville. The wind blew heavily now, rattling the window shutters where they lay opened on the wall. Lightning flashed. Will couldn't shake the uneasy feeling that the approaching storm was a by-product of al-Rahman's ritual.

"The moment approaches," al-Rahman stated. "One more time: are you ready? Once this act is done, there is no going back."

Don Alanzo hesitated. "There is no other way?"

"This is the only way to break that which binds the mask."

Silence for a long moment, and then Will saw the shadow–Don Alanzo nod reluctantly.

The storm boomed overhead. Rain lashed against the building in gusts, and lightning crashed across the city.

Al-Rahman began his chanting again, his voice ringing off the walls as he attempted to be heard above the thunder. The tone of the words inexplicably set Will's teeth on edge and made the pit of his stomach roil. The mirror rattled in the blustering wind tearing through the window, so much that Will was afraid it would tip over.

"Now!" al-Rahman cried. "Raise him now!"

The candles began to extinguish one by one in a steady progression that did not appear natural. The shadows on the wall became more distorted, but Will made out a shape being lifted by Don Alanzo, larger than the cat but one he could easily hold in two hands.

Raise him now.

Will grew cold. His fears were confirmed when a faint, dreamy whimper rolled out in a lull between the thunderclaps and the gusting wind.

If Will intervened, he risked losing the Skull, the chance of finding the path to Grace and his own life. His wavering only lasted a fleeting moment, and as another whimper echoed, he pushed his way out from behind the mirror and drew his sword.

The final candle winked out.

A moment of darkness was blasted away by a flash of lightning. In its brief glare a horrific tableau was frozen: al-Rahman, hands raised high, holding a ritual knife with a curved blade, the cat's blood streaming down his face and bare chest; Don Alanzo, his face a rictus of self-loathing that revealed his despair, the bundle in his arms his passport to hell; the Silver Skull, cowl thrown back, head aglow, standing rigid behind them. Every eye was fixed on Will.

The dark swept into the room.

Al-Rahman barked an angry warning, and Don Alanzo shouted something behind it that Will couldn't translate. He moved quickly from his position before they could attack.

A flare of red light painted the room with a hellish glow. Al-Rahman had thrown his mysterious red dust onto the brazier; Will wrinkled his nose at the foul odour, like the burning flesh that permeated the torture room beneath the Tower.

"Stay back!" Don Alanzo raged, his sword drawn. The bundle was now held by al-Rahman. "Disrupt the ritual and I will kill you!"

"Harsh words for an old friend," Will replied.

The flare from the hissing brazier began to die down. As he circled, Will glimpsed something in the mirror in the dying light: the glass did not reflect the scene within the room, but appeared to show another place, and in it a woman, beautiful and terrible, looked out at him with a fierce expression. He dismissed it as a hallucination caused by a brief glance in the half-light, but once the gloom had descended he could still feel the weight of her chilling gaze upon him.

Al-Rahman continued to chant loudly. An odd pressure began to build in the room. One shutter tore free from its hook and crashed back and forth in the ferocious wind.

Another flash of lightning.

The white glare caught al-Rahman poised with his knife held high once more, the soft, small bundle crooked in his other arm. Sword raised to parry, Don Alanzo stood between the Moor and Will, tears streaming down his face, his eyes flickering towards the bundle. Will would not be able to prevent al-Rahman from bringing the knife down.

Another option reached him as the dark returned. Darting to the right of Don Alanzo, he was ready when the lightning flashed again. Before al-Rahman could complete his sacrifice, Will drove his sword towards the Silver Skull.

"No!" Don Alanzo cried.

Will thrust straight into the Silver Skull's heart. As the Skull crumpled to his knees, Will had the odd impression that he had moved his arms wider as if opening himself to the strike; as if he wanted to die. Blood ran from beneath the mask before Will withdrew his sword and the Skull pitched forwards, dead.

Shock fixed a terrible, broken expression on Don Alanzo's face. "Father!" His devastated cry tore his throat.

One word, and Will understood everything. Sister Adelita had told how their father had disappeared when they were young. Away in the New World, he had come across the Silver Skull and had chosen to wear it, or had it thrust upon him, and then he had been spirited away to England and locked in the Tower. Don Alanzo must have negotiated for one chance to free him from the mask before the Skull was used in the invasion, knowing it could just as easily be utilised by another victim.

Will knew how the mysterious disappearance of a loved one could turn a life on its axis and keep it locked in a frozen world of not-knowing and wishing. And then Don Alanzo had been given hope, as Will had too, in Edinburgh, only to see it snatched away; only to see everything he had hoped for since childhood destroyed. By Will.

In the sheer, bloody hatred in Don Alanzo's face, Will recognised he had made an enemy driven by a passion that went beyond the cold mistrust of national rivals. Don Alanzo would never stop until he had achieved his revenge.

His face contorted by an animalistic fury, the Spaniard threw himself at Will, slashing with his sword in such an uncontrolled manner it was easy to sidestep the attack. "I am sorry," Will said plainly, before bringing the hilt of his sword sharply against Don Alanzo's temple. The Don fell, unconscious.

Seeing there was no longer any need for him, al-Rahman threw his burden and darted from the room. Will dropped his sword and dived to catch the bundle. Peeling back the swaddling cloth, he found a boy of around two, hair black and eyes wide but drugged and dreamy, stolen, he guessed, from the ghetto that morning.

"You will be back with your mother and father soon, little one," he whispered. He laid the boy gently on the floor and turned to the body of the Silver Skull. The alarm would soon be raised, and he had little hope of making an escape with the corpse on his back.

After a futile attempt to prise the mask free, he accepted his only course of action. With al-Rahman's ritual knife, he took a moment to saw the head off the corpse. The knife was sharp and he met only brief resistance at the joint with the spine. Don Alanzo's father had given no sign of being a true enemy—indeed his final act had suggested he had been as much a victim of the war as anyone—and Will wished he could treat his remains with more respect, but he had no choice.

Once the head was free, he put it to one side and dragged Don Alanzo down to the front of the shop where he would be found. Once he'd reclaimed the swaddled child and head, he dropped a hot coal from the brazier onto a heap of drapes in the centre of the room. It would be easy to extinguish the fire before it spread. As the smoke rose, he tucked the head under one arm and the child under the other and slipped out into the raging storm.

In a doorway opposite, he waited until the smoke billowed out and then shouted the Spanish for fire. The alarm soon rang from newly opened windows and doorways along the street. Pressing himself back into the shadows, he watched the guards run up to the shop and find the unconscious Don Alanzo. Unseen, he ghosted away while the men dragged Don Alanzo free and attempted to put out the blaze.

With the Skull in his hands, he had done his duty to England. Now he could turn his attention to Grace.

But as he moved quickly through the deserted, rain-lashed streets, he noticed grey shapes flitting behind him, caught from time to time in the brilliant glare of the lightning flashes. They appeared insubstantial, but he knew what they were, as he now knew what he had seen in the mirror in the room above the shop.

Nothing good lay ahead, and he feared for the safety of the child in his care. His instinct was to escape the deserted streets for an area of night entertainment where he could lose himself in the crowds and where the Unseelie Court would be less effective. But if they caught him before he reached his destination their attack would show no mercy for an innocent child. His frustration turned quickly to anger.

At a crossroads, a lightning flash revealed more grey figures racing from both sides. They were herding him away from the city's busier areas towards the lonely streets behind the Real Alcázar.

Blinking away the rain, he saw the best hope for his charge silhouetted against the roiling black clouds. "Not much farther, little one, and you will be warm and dry," he whispered. He allowed his defiance to muffle the certain knowledge that by saving the boy he would leave himself trapped.

He was ready.

The reassuring glow of candlelight glimmered through the stained-glass windows of Seville Cathedral. The largest cathedral in Europe, it had only been completed a few decades earlier after more than a century of construction on the site of the great mosque, and the walls still had the creamy complexion of new stone.

At the main entrance, he shouldered open the great oak doors and briefly placed his burdens down before drawing the iron bolts behind him. The nave was awash with golden light from row upon row of candles. Away from the booming storm, the cathedral felt safe and secure. Will knew it was a lie.

As he raced along the nave past the lavishly carved wooden screens around the choir, his footsteps echoed up to the vaulted roof high overhead. At the cascade of gold over the high altar, the Retablo Mayor, he called for help. The figures on the gilded relief panels around the stately figure of the cathedral's patron saint, Santa María de la Sede, appeared to mock him.

"Sanctuary!" he called loudly in Spanish.

From the passage to the right of the altar ran a priest, balding, bushy grey beard, eyes dark pools. Hesitating, he took in Will's appearance, his sword, the Silver Skull.

"Take this boy—he was stolen from his parents." Will thrust the bundle towards the priest.

From the far end of the nave came the low, grating sound of the first door bolt drawing back. No one was near it.

When the priest gaped, unmoving, Will shouted, "Take him!"

The priest grabbed the bundle and examined the child's face with a nod. "You want sanctuary?"

"For the child—nothing can be done to save me."

The priest shook his head forcefully. "The Church will protect you."

The second door bolt ground slowly back.

"No, I am done. Protect the child and return him to his parents in the morning."

Quickly, he looked around for a place to make his stand. The nave was too open. The priest recognised what he was doing.

"I will hold them off while you make good your escape," he said.

"No!" Will said firmly. "The child is your only responsibility now. Go. I will lead them on a merry chase before I arrive at my destination." *And in that way they will believe me*, he thought.

The great oak doors blew open with a resounding crash. Rain gusted up the nave. In the dark mouth, Will could see no movement, but he knew they could see him.

"Go!" he shouted to the priest before running towards the north door. He felt a passing twinge of irony at his predicament after he had so abused the priest on the altar at Cádiz, and then he was out in the storm again, surrounded by the overpowering aroma of oranges. In the white glare of lightning, he saw rows of orange trees in a large, rectangular orchard with the Patio de los Naranjos at the centre, a fountain where worshippers would wash their hands and feet before praying.

Will hoped the trees might obscure his progress, but he'd barely crossed the edge of the fountain square when another lightning flash revealed movement along the roofs of the low buildings that enclosed the orchard. Members of the Unseelie Court loped along the orange tiles oblivious to the violent winds and the rain, converging on him from all directions. Behind him, the door from the cathedral crashed open.

He turned east and dashed to the cloistered walkway, his ultimate destination now within reach. Over his head, tiles rattled and shattered, fragments raining down in his wake. Across the orchard, the grey ghosts moved relentlessly towards him.

Crashing back into the cathedral, Will followed the short corridor to the foot of La Giralda. He bolted the door to the bell tower behind him and bounded up the steps two at a time; the stairway was wide enough for the muezzin to ride on a horse to deliver the call to prayer.

As he spiralled breathlessly upwards, it felt as if he was rising into the very heart of the storm. The wind and rain blasted through the open windows, and the lightning flashes allowed him views over the whole of Seville and the Andalusian countryside beyond. As the thunder boomed again, he only faintly heard the door at the foot of the bell tower crash open.

No way back.

The minaret accounted for the first two-thirds of the tower and then the stairs took him up to the belfry, added by the Christian rulers only twenty years before to replace the Moorish iconography that had originally topped the minaret. He locked the door into the belfry and ran up the final set of steps.

At the very summit, he gripped the walls for support as the wind and rain tore through so forcefully they threatened to drive him through the large arched windows onto the ground far below.

Drawing his sword, he prepared to fight to the last. It was a good, defensible position for the Enemy could only approach him up the short flight of steps from the belfry door, and he was determined to take as many with him as he possibly could.

But as he stood poised, he became aware of sounds rising up the outside of the bell tower in the brief lulls when the thunder rolled away and the wind gusted in a different direction. Cautiously, he hung out of the window.

As his eyes adjusted to the world of white flashes and all-consuming dark, he saw grey figures steadily climbing the outside of the bell tower like insects, clinging onto the carvings and ridges as they made their progress oblivious to the storm. Quickly, he checked all four windows and saw the same from each one. Drops of blood began to fall from his nose to the wet flags, and a disorienting buzz echoed through his head.

The door to the belfry flew open.

CHAPTER 36

*T*he cries of the hunting party echoed through the frozen forest, accompanied by the occasional crack of an arquebus that sent the birds shrieking through the black trees.

"They waste their ammunition when they cannot see us," Carpenter gasped, his breath clouding in the subzero temperatures. Shivering uncontrollably, he pulled his thick woollen cloak around him, but could find no warmth.

"If fortune is with them, they can still hit us," Will replied. In the pack under his arm, he clutched the object Dee had treasured for so long, the thing that could only add to England's mounting power.

They struggled through the calf-deep snow in the face of the bitter wind, scrambling over fallen branches and plunging into hidden hollows where the brambles lost beneath the white blanket tore through their skin and left splashes of red in their wake. The wind was laced with snow and the grey clouds banking up overhead suggested another blizzard like the one that had disrupted their escape from Moscow.

"If we do not find our man soon we will freeze to death out here," Carpenter said. He no longer attempted to hide his fear. The bravado he had exhibited shortly after Walsingham had brought him into the fold had dissipated in the harsh reality of his very first undertaking. What he had seen in the snow-covered courtyards of the Kremlin fortress had changed his life forever. There would be no peace for him again. It was a feeling Will knew only too well, and he regretted it being inflicted upon Carpenter, however inevitable it had been.

"We must first lose our pursuers." Will glanced back, but there was no sign of the tsar's men in the half-light. "We cannot lead them directly to our man or all will be lost."

A ferocious roar rolled out through the forest from somewhere at their backs.

What little blood remained in Carpenter's face drained away and he gripped Will's arm. "What was that? A bear?"

"Nothing to concern us." Will tried to urge him on, but he was rooted.

"It was with the tsar's men. With them!"

"The Enemy have many weapons at their disposal, and employ many beasts to do their work. You know that," Will said, trying to calm him. He watched the spiralling panic in Carpenter's eyes with concern. At the outset, he had been afraid Carpenter had been sent on such an important mission too early, but as ever they were short of men.

"Is that what killed Jack and Scarcliffe and Gedding?" The scene of slaughter in Kitai-gorod, the walled merchant town beside the fortress, still lay heavily on both of them, but it had taken all Will's abilities to talk Carpenter through his devastation at the time.

Will grasped Carpenter's shoulders. The barks of the hunting party's dogs drew closer by the minute. "John, our lives mean nothing here. We do this not for personal reward, or acclaim, or the queen's favour, but for the people of England."

Carpenter stared at him, seeing only the pictures in his head.

"John." Will shook him, too hard. "Though we both give up our lives here, we must see our burden delivered to London and to Dee. The safety of our country depends on us. We do not matter. Our lives are not important. Once you accept that fact, you are free. Do you understand?"

He nodded slowly, but Will was not sure he was convinced.

"If one of us falls, the other must make sure the package reaches our man so he can deliver it to the ship. That is the only thing that should concern us. You know the laws of our business: do not risk all we seek to achieve for the sake of one man. We are already dead. Repeat that."

"We are already dead," Carpenter said flatly. He blinked away a tear.

Another roar, so loud it felt like whatever had made the noise was only feet away. The hairs sprang erect on Will's neck.

It jolted Carpenter out of his stupor and together they drove on into the forest, increasingly thankful for the white snow as the light began to fade. Branches tore at their faces and objects hidden underfoot threatened to trip them, but they continued as fast as they could.

Another roar, close behind. The sounds of the hunting party had faded away as if they had decided to leave the pursuit to a more effective hunter.

"If it has our scent, we will never lose it," Carpenter gasped.

"There is a storm coming and that may provide cover for us and our tracks," Will replied.

For ten more minutes, they scrambled through the bitter Russian winter, no longer feeling their feet. The heat drained from their limbs until they felt leaden and only the threat of what lay behind drove them on.

Finally, as the gloom descended among the branches, a light appeared ahead: a lantern, gently swinging to draw them in.

"There!" Carpenter said with exultation.

Will was distracted by fleeting movement in the trees to his left. Afraid their pursuer had pulled ahead and was circling, he came to a halt and peered into the gloom. "We may need to take a different path," he said.

"What is it?"

"Whatever was at our backs could be lying in wait to attack us unawares." He searched the trees, listening intently, but the snow muffled all sound. Another movement shimmered on the edge of his vision, closer to hand, a figure that was nowhere near as large as the roars of their pursuer had suggested.

"You see it?" Carpenter hissed.

And then Will did, and the cold that crushed the forest in its grip swept into every part of him. Standing among the trees, almost swallowed by the encroaching dark, was a woman, her leaf green dress floating around her in the wind.

Jenny.

His Jenny.

The cold did not appear to touch her. Her arms and head were bare, her skin so pale. She looked exactly as she had done that last time he had seen her, stepping through the cornfield to meet him, her eyes like the sun, her smile filled with love. Was she a ghost? A dream caused by the cold? Had she come to haunt him at the moment of his own death, as she had haunted him in the time since she had disappeared?

His heart went out, and then he was running towards her, oblivious to all else but the dim sound of Carpenter calling his name anxiously.

The roaring was so loud it felt like he was in the middle of a tempest. Whirling, he saw a huge, dark shape erupt from the trees and drive into Carpenter with such force he was thrown several feet against a tree. The beast descended on Carpenter in a storm of fangs and rending claws. Will was fixed to the spot in the shock and horror of the moment as the creature ripped through the clothes on Carpenter's back and sent a mist of blood into the air. Carpenter's screams were too painful to hear. Somehow he scrambled free and managed to draw his knife, but then the beast fell on him again.

It looked like a bear, but somehow more than a bear.

Will ran several steps towards the bloody scene and came to a slow halt. There was nothing he could do to save Carpenter.

Whirling, he searched the trees for Jenny, but only the wind whistled through the *area where she had stood. He ran, calling her name, but there was no response, nothing to show she had ever been there.*

Had she saved him from the beast's attack?

The ache in his heart was agonising, but he drove it down inside him, as he always had, and ran for the light, trying not to think about Carpenter and the awful sounds rising up behind him.

Within minutes, he was packed under heavy blankets in the back of a sleigh, hurtling down a steep track through the trees, with the crack of a whip echoing around him, and promises from his saviour that he would not rest until Will was at Arkhangelsk on a ship chartered by the Muscovy Company. England beckoned.

Lulled by the motion, his despair came and went on the edge of sleep. Wherever he was, he hoped Carpenter would forgive him, but the success of their task was paramount.

Obliquely, he recalled Walsingham telling him, "There is no room for any emotion," and at the time he thought he understood.

And he thought of Jenny, and however much he told himself it was a vision, he was sure something substantial was there, a hint, a hope, although he couldn't understand the whys of it.

Jenny was alive, he was sure. And he would not rest until he had discovered the truth.

CHAPTER 37

Will came round, not knowing how long he had been unconscious. Sensations flooded in: the fragrance of pine and the sweet scent of Spanish broom. Heat leavened by the occasional breeze of chill air. Dust on the back of his throat, and the rough rocking of a carriage.

The bitterness of the Moscow winter lay heavily on his mind, and Jenny, always Jenny, her face fading as the world around him rose up. His wrists were manacled behind his back and his feet were shackled, and his body ached from too long in one position. Underneath that was the dull throb of new bruises.

Fragmentary memories returned from his stand at the top of the bell tower in Seville, the lashing rain, figures climbing through the arched windows while others came up the steps from the belfry door, too many for him to fight. A flash of light like a glint from a mirror, a sudden pain at the base of his skull, and then nothing.

As he had expected, they hadn't hurt him too badly. They were saving him for the horrors to come, as Cavillex had promised.

He wasn't alone. A glowering Spanish guard sat on the opposite seat next to the other door, but however much Will tried to engage him in conversation, he gave no indication that Will was even there.

Through the window, he could see a mountain peak, the source of the chill air occasionally blowing through the carriage. It was a blazing hot day with no sign of the storm that had swept Seville. The landscape around the road was dusty, and beyond that it drifted into a bleak, depressing vista of rock piles and detritus from old mine-workings scattered far and wide. Beyond that a pine forest rose up the windswept slopes to the foot of the mountain.

"Why, if I did not know better I would say that was Mount Abantos," Will said. The guard's eyes flickered towards him.

The carriage continued ahead for another mile until a grand grey-pink-granite complex rose up from the desolate landscape. El Escorial shimmered in the hot sun.

"I hear the king is more a monk than a man of the world," Will noted. "He likes his prayers where others enjoy their tupping, and they bring him to a similar climax."

Flinching, the guard went for his knife until he realised Will was trying to goad him. He grunted and looked out of the other window.

Will watched the village of San Lorenzo de El Escorial pass by in the shadow of Philip's gleaming new monument to his ego, twenty-one years in the building and the centre of the Spanish empire. As they drew nearer, he could see the grand achievement of the construction, its magnificence amplified by the scale reflected in the pools of the formal gardens. Nine towers reached for the sky above the vertiginous, plain walls that resembled an unassailable cliff-face. Its appearance was as austere as the king was rumoured to be, yet in its proliferation of fountains and its rows of exquisite statues, its glorious basilica and its spires, and the sheer size of the construction, it appeared as much an illustration of the monolithic power of Philip and Spain as it did a monument to the glory of God.

The carriage rolled up the sweeping driveway where several guards ran out to greet it. Will was dragged roughly from the carriage and thrown onto the stones before he was forced to his feet at sword point and accompanied by six men into the forbidding palace's interior. The Spanish were taking no chances.

The palace was laid out on a huge quadrangle with a series of intersecting corridors, courtyards, and chambers. He was hauled along at a fast clip, cuffed every time he fell, and cuffed again for every sardonic response. Finally, he was thrust into a large hall lined with dark portraits of severe faces and accusing eyes.

At the far end of the hall, dressed in black, Don Alanzo kneeled in prayer. The guards threw Will to the floor before him, and surrounded Will with levelled pikes.

"You think highly of me to believe so many fine men are necessary to keep me contained," Will said.

"You are no threat," Don Alanzo replied. "You never were."

It was only then that Will saw the black coffin resting on a trestle near the window, with a smaller black box on top, which Will guessed contained the head of Don Alanzo's father.

"I would give my condolences," Will began honestly. "Your father was a casualty of our war, but I had no ill feeling towards him personally."

"Shut up!" Don Alanzo raged. "You cut off his head!" He struck Will across the face with the back of his hand.

Turning so the guards would not see his emotion, Don Alanzo rested one hand upon the coffin. "He was a great man, and an honourable one. He gave his life for Spain. That will not be forgotten. An English city will be renamed after him once we crush your country underfoot."

Will had a sudden flash of Sister Adelita inadvertently setting in motion the events that led to her father's death, and he felt a deep regret at the guilt he knew would consume her. The corrupting touch of the Unseelie Court affected everyone, except themselves.

"Your father was an honourable man," Will admitted, "and I am sure he had no knowledge of the destructive power of the Silver Skull when he first affixed it to his head."

"You know nothing of those circumstances," Don Alanzo spat.

"And for all our bitter disputes, I know you are an honourable man too," Will continued. "Would you see such terrible disease inflicted on my people? Is victory for Spain worth the deaths of innocents on so grand a scale? Where is your God in all of this?"

"Quiet," Don Alanzo said in a low voice trembling with passion.

"Spain is our enemy, but never did I think Philip would sanction such devastation. Victory at any cost? Where is just rule in that? It was not too long ago when my people fell under Philip's aegis during his marriage to Mary Tudor—"

"Quiet!" Don Alanzo whirled, spittle flying from his mouth. Will could see those very doubts tormented him. "I would see all of your countrymen slaughtered for what you have done," he hissed.

"I do not believe it. I see the hands of others in this impending atrocity. The whispers in Philip's ears lead him down a dangerous path from which there is no return."

Don Alanzo steadied himself before uttering cruelly, "From the outside, El Escorial is a palace, and a monastery, and an impregnable fortress. From the inside, it is a prison from which you can never escape. More secure than your Tower in London, it is the most heavily guarded building in the whole of the empire. Do not harbour thoughts of escape. No one can get in. No one can get out. This will be your home in your final days. Take him away."

The guards grabbed Will's arms and dragged him to his feet. The pikes were kept within an inch of his throat at all times. As he left the room, he glanced back at Don Alanzo, a forlorn figure, head bowed in front of the coffin.

Outside, Will was beaten severely until he lost consciousness.

He came round tied to a chair in a great hall whose walls were covered with frescoes depicting scenes from Spanish military victories: the defeat of the Moors, and images from several of Philip's campaigns against the French.

"The Hall of Battles." The voice was like the wind across snow. In the corner of the hall, a woman stood, motionless, shoulders slightly hunched like an animal on the brink of attacking. Her hair hung lank around a bloodless face, her eyes red-rimmed, unblinking. There was something of the grave about her. With excruciating slowness, she stalked towards him.

"One of the Unseelie Court," he said.

Her dark, hungry eyes never left his face. "My brother told me that is what you call us. *Unholy.*"

As she inched forwards, a suffocating dread closed about him, a visceral reaction to something beyond his five senses. With each step, the tension increased a notch until his breath burned in his chest as he waited for her to lunge at him.

"I know you," she intoned. That simple statement carried with it the weight of something terrifying.

Before Will could consider its implications, his vision swam. When it cleared, her unsettling appearance had shifted to take on an unearthly beauty. She was undoubtedly the same person, with that same hungry gaze, but now she radiated a deep, powerful sexuality that affected him despite himself.

She came to a halt before him. *Presenting herself*, he thought. Her posture accentuated every curve of her body, the swell of her breasts, her hard nipples protruding through the thin silk, her hips at an angle, crotch slightly pushed forwards. She challenged him to admire what he saw.

Knowing what lay beneath sickened him. As he looked away defiantly, he realised her sexuality was more than just physical. Slowly, she drew his gaze back to her, and however much he fought he could not resist. Sweat beaded his brow, and he shook from the strain of fighting her. The heat rose in his groin.

She leaned forwards until her luminous face was only inches from his, and he could smell the perfume of her skin, and her hair, and a muskier scent beneath it. "You are mine now," she whispered. Reaching down, she ran the tips of her fingers along his thigh.

"Your brother," he said, pointedly ignoring her teasing, "is Cavillex?"

She nodded slowly. "My name is Malantha."

He looked around for the guards, but they were alone.

Malantha appeared to sense what he was thinking, for she said, "I do not need protection."

"If I were free—"

"Not even then. Cavillex presents a fearsome face to the world, but I am worse. Much worse."

"I imagine Philip finds your wiles invigorating," he said.

"Personal weaknesses exist in all humans. You can hide them away, pretend they do not exist or that God and prayer have expunged them, but they remain."

"Until you work them loose."

Her gaze held him fast.

"I have many weaknesses," he continued. "I must be easy game for one such as you."

"You pretend to many weaknesses," she replied, "but only one truly matters."

"You see the weaknesses that clearly?"

"All people can see weaknesses if they open their eyes. But most of the time, you choose to ignore them, or you pretend, or you lie to yourself. But they are there. What is writ clearly in the heart is clear in the face."

"You see them as weaknesses. But they can also be strengths, driving us on to achieve great things, to strive, to overcome pain and hardship."

"Believe that if you wish," she replied.

"Is your brother coming to oversee my torture again?" he asked.

"My *brothers* are engaged in important affairs that demand their attention. Not just in Edinburgh, but in France, and Venice, Moscow, and the New World. We have been playing this game for a long time, by the way you measure it, and we move with the slow turn of the seasons, a slight push here, barely noticed, another shove there, unseen, guiding, steering, drawing strands across your entire world until everything is in place. And then you will see the true design of the plan we have wrought.

"Cavillex trusts me to ensure you pay the price for what you did. We have only contempt for England and we will destroy it piece by piece without emotion. But you have gained our attention. You slew one of us." In the blaze of her eyes, he saw clearly the monster that lurked beneath the flirtatious surface. "This is now a personal matter. Quid pro quo. And," she added, "by the end, you will wish it was my brother here."

"True. His own brand of torture already failed."

"Torture is not a fair word for what I do. There is something of creation about it, a skill that makes the heavens sing, a drawing together of subtle themes, of resonances, a slow build of contrasting emotions, desires, and agonies, until they fall into a glorious harmony, and then you will be crushed by the artfulness of it." Her voice lost its honeyed tone and became gravelly. "Your mind and soul will be destroyed long before your body falls apart."

"And Philip sanctions that?"

"Philip will do whatever I tell him to. His only concern is that the Armada succeeds and England falls. Failure could wreak untold damage on the Spanish empire and his own reputation. And if I tell him a dangerous English spy is a threat to his Enterprise of England—however ridiculous that might seem—he will do whatever he deems necessary."

"With a little push and shove from yourself, perhaps, when he is entranced by the comfort of your thighs."

"Men are men. It is their nature, and easily manipulated by any woman who knows."

"But Philip knows nothing of your true plans. How you will use the Silver Skull to achieve your sly aims."

"*You* know nothing of our true plans. You think you know, but you have been wrong at every turn. We are too subtle . . . too sly . . . that is why we win. We are the wind that moves the oceans when all your power could not achieve more than a few ripples."

"My ripples ended the life of the last Silver Skull. You will now be looking for another candidate, I assume?" She leaned close until he was lost in the dark, echoing depths of her eyes. His thoughts squirmed at the contact.

"A small victory, if such it was. Now we will find one we can truly control." She made a dismissive gesture. "But that was always our plan."

"And so you will destroy all of England's peoples."

"In part. But if that were all, 'twould be a sorry response to your crimes."

"Our only crime is to defend ourselves. In your arrogance, you may think that is crime enough." He tried to uncover hints of what she was scheming in her face, but it was a mask; she was too clever to reveal anything she did not want him to know. "Then what else do you plan?" he pressed.

"A message, delivered with accuracy, that shows we will never be opposed again."

"Something beyond the death of all Englishmen and Englishwomen?"

"That is a cudgel-blow. Our true message will be delivered with precision to amplify the pain and to underline that for every slight against us we will respond a hundredfold . . . a thousandfold." Her eyes narrowed hatefully. Will was left in no doubt as to the intensity of the threat.

"And how soon do you plan to ship the Silver Skull to my home?" he enquired blithely.

"Soon."

"And where—?"

"Enough questions!" Her bony fingers scraped up his neck to his cheeks. "It is time to prepare the way for your torment. You recall what my brother told you lay ahead?"

Will did not respond.

The doors at his back opened and someone walked slowly towards him. He strained to see, but the new arrival remained out of his frame of vision.

Malantha drank in every expression, every flicker of emotion, and when she was satisfied, she summoned the person to stand in front of Will.

It was Grace. She was unharmed, though pale.

Will struggled to disguise his relief. Over the days, terrible thoughts had forced their way into his mind of the suffering she was enduring at the hands of the Unscelie Court. It was more than he could have hoped to see her in such good health.

"You are well?" he said. His face revealed nothing that would give Malantha joy.

Grace responded with a pale smile. "Yes. It is good to see you."

"They will pay for what they have done to you," he said emotionlessly, adding so quietly that Malantha could not hear, "We will have you away from here in no time."

Grace's brow furrowed. "But . . . I do not want to leave."

Her words were like a slap across his face. "What do you mean?"

"This is our great chance. These people . . . your Enemies . . . they know what happened to Jenny. I see now why you do what you do. You knew they had knowledge of her disappearance."

"No—"

"You know. Do not lie to me. And they have promised me they will tell all about Jenny, and then I . . . we . . . will know the truth, and we can finally find peace."

"You cannot trust them. She is lying," Will said forcefully. "She knows nothing. Jenny . . . Jenny is dead." He couldn't bring himself to believe it even as the words left his mouth.

"Is she?" Malantha said. "Would you not like to know the truth once and for all, like your friend here?"

"Not in this manner. Your manipulation will not work."

Standing behind Grace, a touch of the true Malantha showed in her features; she did not believe him.

Grace kneaded her hands uneasily. "I cannot bear not knowing any more. I will do anything they ask of me to discover the truth. Anything. And the only way to stop me is to kill me."

CHAPTER 38

here was no escape. Will hung out of his cell window at the top of the tower, but the walls were sheer. Even if he found a rope of sufficient length, the tower was in clear view of the army of guards swarming around the palace far below. Don Alanzo had been correct: El Escorial was the most secure building in all of the Spanish empire, a true fortress, the perfect prison.

From his window, he had a vista that at any other time would have been reserved for visiting dignitaries or European royals, across the desolate waste surrounding El Escorial towards the lush green near Madrid. His cell was filled with the finest furniture and works of art from across the empire. The irony was not lost on him.

Grace's appearance had deeply disturbed him, but his concerns were interrupted by the key in the lock. The door swung open to reveal several guards—he was never left alone with any less than five—the captain stepping in to bark, "Kneel, English dog, in the presence of the king."

"I kneel only before those who are worthy of my respect," Will stated. The guards threw him to the floor, pikes pressed against the back of his neck so that he could not raise his head.

From his reduced perspective, he watched a pair of black velvet slippers walk slowly into the chamber and stand before him, and only then was he allowed to look up. Dressed all in black with his hands clasped tightly behind his back, Philip was an ascetic figure, but Will saw in his eyes a gentleness not normally evident in monarchs.

"An English spy." He looked Will up and down with disdain. "And not just any spy. They tell me you are England's greatest spy, William Swyfte. Is that correct?"

"We are all burdened by our reputations," Will replied, "but mine provides me with a parade of entertainment while yours, I am sure, does not."

Philip ignored the gibe. "Tell me, what is the point of a spy when everyone knows his name?"

"You are not the first to ask that question."

"Does not your whole business involve secrets, duplicity, deceit, and shadows?"

"And you think I am not involved in such things?"

Philip nodded condescendingly. "I understand. What you see is not always what is. You are not England's greatest spy, for if you were you would not be here."

"I would rather be perceived as victorious than great."

"You shall be neither. Your execution is forthcoming—"

"After my torture."

Philip winced and looked away as if he had glimpsed something distasteful. "And your country's days are numbered," he continued regardless. "The Armada is to sail soon."

"Your Armada has floundered before."

"Not this time," Philip said sharply. In that instant, Will could see the strain the king was under: victory would cement Spain's reputation and empire for all time; defeat would deal a blow from which he might not recover. Realising he had revealed too much, Philip sniffed and said, "I wished to see what kind of man England thought was the best it could offer in opposition to my plans. I am not impressed. If you are the best, this business is already concluded."

Philip spun on his heel and marched to the door, coming to a slow halt when Will said, "You pray to God, but a devil whispers in your ear."

Uneasily, the king turned and fixed a warning eye on Will.

"Do her kisses ease your conscience?" Will pressed. "Do her honeyed words cause blindness to the choices you make?"

"Beat him," Philip said to the guards. "Severely."

"You fail to understand," Will continued. "You think you have taken me prisoner. But I am exactly where I wish to be."

A shadow crossed Philip's face when he saw Will's expression and he hurried from the room.

CHAPTER 39

In the lee of a heap of ancient mine-workings on the edge of the spoiled land around El Escorial, Launceston, Carpenter, and Mayhew waited. Every now and then they scrambled over the blackened rocks to peer at the stone fortress through the yellowing grass and weeds. The sky was aflame with the end of the day, scarlet and gold and orange.

"Do you think Will still lives?" Mayhew had a feverish air that had only grown worse as they made their way to the plateau from the Madrid road. His knuckles were red and raw from where he had worried at them.

Balancing his throwing knife on the tip of his finger, Carpenter did all he could to show he really didn't care what the answer was. "Perhaps," he said.

"Then why should we risk our own lives on a maybe?" Mayhew added desperately.

"Because it is what we do." Launceston studied the guards at the gates, and those patrolling around the walls. More came and went on the road winding around the small village that was now dwarfed by the sprawling complex. There was no visible way through the defences.

Mayhew rested his head on his knees with a resigned sigh. They were all exhausted after tracking the carriage that had brought Will from Seville to El Escorial. But his plan had worked so far. As they had agreed on the journey from Cádiz, sooner or later Will would allow the Enemy to take him so they would deliver him to Grace for his punishment, and they were to follow at a distance. Hidden by the storm, Launceston had kept watch on al-Rahman's shop, and had followed Will and his pursuers to the cathedral. He and the others were waiting when Will was brought out unconscious.

"He took a great risk. They could have killed him the moment they captured him," Mayhew said.

"Will knows the Enemy well," Launceston replied without taking his gaze off the palace. "Simple death does not provide enough revenge for them.

Pain in the heart and mind is their preferred response to an act against them, and they had already told him he would be brought to his friend, Grace, to watch her suffer at his own slow torture and death. They would not walk away from such an exquisite response."

"Exquisite?" Mayhew repeated, unsettled.

"Swyfte is a gambler. Risks filled his plan, as they always have, and it is others who pay the price," Carpenter said bitterly. "We could have lost the Silver Skull if it had gone west to a port. While gaining his friend, we may have lost the battle and the war."

"He knew what he was doing," Launceston said distractedly. "The girl would have been held at the centre of the Enemy's plans. And where else would the Skull have gone before it was used?"

"They could already have tortured him," Mayhew continued. "Cut bits off him. He might be useless to us. He may not even be able to walk."

"Then we leave him and finish the important business—the girl and the Skull," Carpenter said.

"Do you hate him so much?" Mayhew asked.

"He left me for dead." The edge in Carpenter's voice revealed his raw emotions, even after so much time had passed. "The tsar's soldiers found me, and their allies . . ." He spat. ". . . and they called off the beast that was tearing me apart. If Swyfte had waited, he could have rescued me and I would not have had to suffer all those months of . . . of . . ." He swallowed, waved the remainder of the sentence away with the back of his hand.

"You are a child," Launceston said baldly.

Carpenter was so taken aback by the insult, he could only gape.

"Or a dog," Launceston continued, not caring what Carpenter's response might be. "You whine and whine. 'Poor me, I have been so mistreated.' But you live, do you not? You survive. You are stronger."

"You do not know what deprivations I suffered at the hands of the tsar's torturers," Carpenter snapped.

"Whine and whine," Launceston continued. "You think you are the only one to suffer? To experience pain in the line of our work?"

Carpenter thrust his knife towards Launceston, but the earl only gave it the merest attention before returning his attention to the guards swarming around the palace. "Master Swyfte remained true to his work. He completed his business, as directed, and England is better for it."

"Is it?" Carpenter growled. "I have seen no sign of the object we retrieved since the day Swyfte brought it back. And I paid for it with my agonies!"

Launceston shrugged. "He was not distracted by emotions. There are bigger things here than your petty feelings. Child."

Trembling with emotion, Carpenter could barely hold the knife still, but Launceston no longer gave it, or Carpenter, even a cursory glance. Carpenter slumped back against the rocks and ran his still shaking hands through his hair, casting brief murderous glances towards Launceston.

"You trouble me, Carpenter," Launceston continued. "If you give in to your emotions so, it makes me wonder how far you will go to gain revenge to soothe your poor, hurt feelings."

"What are you saying?" Carpenter snapped.

"Perhaps you would even go so far as to ally with the Enemy to see Master Swyfte paid back in full."

Barely had Carpenter begun the lunge with his knife when Launceston's own knife was at his throat.

"Stop now!" Mayhew interjected. "If we cannot trust each other, we will forfeit our own lives when we are in the thick of it. We must protect each other's backs."

Slowly, Carpenter relented, although his emotions barely subsided.

"You have never given in to your emotions?" Mayhew said to Launceston.

"No." The earl's face became more ghastly as the shadows lengthened.

Mayhew eyed him curiously. "You speak little about your past. We have all been touched by misery, or by the hand of the Enemy. Why have you given yourself to this business?"

"Sport," Launceston replied.

"Sport?"

"Yes, I like to kill our Enemies."

They sat in silence until night had fallen.

Finally Launceston prised himself from the top of the spoil-heap and said simply, "It is time."

Across the desolate landscape they moved, hoods pulled down to hide their faces. As they neared El Escorial, Launceston motioned for them to use more caution. The guards watched the approach to the palace and continued to patrol the perimeter. Others were stationed in the vast formal gardens.

"Impregnable, they say," Launceston mused.

"I do not know who I fear for the most," Mayhew said. "Us trying to get in, or Swyfte trying to get out."

Launceston levelled his knife at the guards. "I fear for them."

CHAPTER 40

Still raw from his beating earlier, Will was dragged through the palace by the guards. From a courtyard open to the moonless sky, and under one of several porticos, he eventually arrived at statues of David and Solomon flanking the entrance to the basilica, the central point of the whole complex. Philip waited for him there, and motioned for the guards to take him in.

"A fine place for torture." Will admired the huge dome overhead and the granite simplicity of the basilica's interior, which perfectly reflected Philip's character.

Still dressed in mourning black, Don Alanzo waited by one of the Doric columns with Grace beside him. She met Will's eyes once, then looked away.

"There will be no torture here," Philip said.

"No physical torture," Don Alanzo added, bowing apologetically when the king glared at him.

Philip motioned for the guards to wait outside. They were reluctant to leave their monarch alone with a potential assassin, but they checked Will's bonds one more time and whispered threats in his ear before departing.

Once the door to the basilica was closed, Malantha appeared from behind one of the columns. Will had the briefest flash of chalky skin and her implacable gaze before she unveiled her potent sexuality, at odds with the sanctified surroundings.

"I am starting to believe you are a guilty secret," Will said. As she levelled her icy, unblinking stare at him, Will had the impression she was imagining slowly opening up his body.

Shifting uncomfortably, the king quickly changed the subject. "Today saw the funeral of Don Alanzo's father. A great man, brought low by a dog."

Will glanced over at Don Alanzo, whose hateful glare never left Will's face. "You will not believe me, but I offer my condolences again, in good faith," Will said.

"My sister refused to come to the funeral," Don Alanzo said. "She blames me for our father's death. She will have nothing more to do with me, she says, and has ensured I will be refused entry to her convent. Now you have taken two people from me. You will pay for both of them." He bowed curtly to Malantha, who gave a brief, dismissive nod in return. "Our allies . . . your Enemies . . . are correct. Sometimes death is not enough to right a wrong. Pain must be inflicted in the heart, and the mind, and on the soul."

Will looked to Grace. "Do you see now what you stand with? Do not trust them, Grace."

Striding forwards, Don Alanzo struck Will forcefully across the face with his leather gauntlet. Blood bloomed on his lip.

"Please do not hurt him," Grace begged. "I will do anything."

"Of course you will," Malantha said.

"I have brought you here," Philip said to Grace, "under the eyes of God, so you will know there is no treachery in my words when I make this offer: help us and we will spare your friend's life."

"No!" Will shouted. "Do not believe them!"

Don Alanzo struck him again.

"You vow, before God?" Grace said.

"I so vow."

"The Unseelie Court will not allow it," Will spat. "He is so under their spell that even the threat of damnation will not deter him."

This time Don Alanzo knocked Will to the floor.

"Please," Grace sobbed, wringing her hands.

"I so vow!" Philip said firmly.

"I will do anything you ask. But please . . . please . . . do not hurt him anymore."

Philip nodded to Don Alanzo, who guided Grace to the door as Will struggled to his feet. By the time he had shaken off the effect of the blow, Grace had gone.

"And so the torture begins," Malantha said.

"And you save my life?" Will sneered, spitting a mouthful of blood.

"Once she has done her duty, we will allow you to live," Malantha replied, "although you will be in no state to enjoy it. We will ensure your friend gets to see how you work. Inside. In your mind, when you scream and cry and beg for us to take her life instead. And then you will know she must live on with the knowledge of what she saw, and it will never leave her." She raised her arms in a flamboyant request for applause. "My brother proposed your death, I know, but he lacks my assured touch in these matters."

"An honourable man," Will accused Philip, who made to leave. "Wait. You have an aspiration to higher wisdom," Will continued.

"What do you mean?" Philip asked suspiciously.

"The design of this building, your great monument, is based upon the Temple of Solomon, as described by Flavius Josephus."

"You are an educated man? And a spy who deals in death and deceit?"

"I am a man of contradictions, like all men," Will replied. "My point being that you would not have chosen this design, nor selected the statue outside that door, if you did not aspire to the Jewish king's great wisdom. Then rise to it. There is still time to walk away from the path you have chosen."

"The war I fight is a just one. I have the support of the pope himself. God, Master Swyfte, is on my side."

"If God is on any side, it is certainly not the Devil's."

A tremor crossed Philip's face, but before it could spread, Malantha stepped behind him, her hand rising to caress his neck out of sight of Don Alanzo. But she kept her icy eyes on Will the whole time, flaunting her power.

Philip's face hardened. "This world will be a better place when England is crushed."

"Our differences are clear, but what we share is much stronger," Will pressed. "I ask one final time, not as Protestant to Catholic, nor as Englishman to Spaniard, but as a man to another man, as members of the great brotherhood of men, I ask you again, turn away from the path you have chosen. Or else you must suffer the consequences."

Philip gave a weak, boyish laugh. "You stand before me in chains . . . on the brink of humiliation, and pain, and death . . . and you give *me* an ultimatum?"

"You should kill me now. It is the only way you will be safe," Will replied calmly, seeing in Philip's eyes that he would not be swayed.

Philip laughed again, but with an unsettled note, before stepping to the door near the altar that led to his private quarters. Before he left, he turned to Malantha and said, "You will come to me tonight?"

"Of course," she said.

A simple smile leapt to the king's lips and he hurried out, closing the door behind him.

"Now the children have left, you can be about your adult business," Will said.

"We have no need to sully our hands with your blood at this point," Malantha replied archly. "For now, only one thing remains to be done."

Barely able to stop himself shaking with emotion, Don Alanzo loomed over Will. "The time for talk has passed. The end of Philip's Enterprise of England and the end of this business begins this night. And your end too. I leave with your friend, Grace, within the hour, to join our Armada and to continue to England."

"What do you plan?" he demanded.

"We will affix the Silver Skull to your friend's head and when she is delivered to England she must choose, between her country and the man she loves," Malantha intoned. "Release the power of the Skull, or see you torn apart as we discussed."

"You will do that anyway."

"We will," Malantha said.

"Grace will choose England," Will stated.

"You truly believe that?" Malantha nodded when she saw the response in Will's eyes. "And in this way we will destroy everything."

CHAPTER 41

Rising up like a spectre, Launceston slit the guard's throat, holding his head back by the hair so the gush of arterial blood avoided his uniform. Once the guard's convulsions had ended, Launceston stripped him naked and wrapped the uniform tightly in his cloak.

As they emerged from the dark of the rough land still scattered with the detritus from El Escorial's construction, Carpenter and Mayhew discarded the rattling stones they had used to attract the lone sentry from the approach to the palace. In the shadow of the monolithic building, they studied the clockwork maneuvers of the guards once again.

Carpenter's throwing knife drove deep into the temple of the second sentry. Catching the guard before he fell, Carpenter dragged him back into the shadows, away from the torch under which he had stood.

When the sentry's uniform was secured, Mayhew selected a young guard who had broken off from the patrol to urinate on the edge of the wasteland. But Mayhew's clumsy approach dislodged a shower of rocks down a slope to splash in a muddy pool. Whirling, the guard saw Mayhew as he stumbled towards him, and struggled to lower his pike at the same time as he forced his manhood back in his clothes.

As Mayhew desperately threw himself forwards, the pike head ripped a gash across his cheek. His pained cry shocked the guard so much he dropped both his weapons. Wild with fear that the noise would bring other guards, Mayhew flailed into the sentry. Thrashing together on the ground, Mayhew eventually managed to clamp his hands around his opponent's throat. Spitting and gasping and clawing at Mayhew's face, the guard continued to fight while Mayhew increased the pressure.

Consumed by his desperation, he continued to choke the guard long after any motion had ceased. Carpenter and Launceston finally dragged him off and shook him roughly.

"Steady yourself!" Carpenter hissed vehemently. "You are going to be the death of all of us!"

Once Mayhew had calmed, Launceston rested his hands on his associate's shoulders and said, as if offering friendly advice, "At even the first sign that you are allowing your emotions to run free, I will slit your throat and leave you for dead. Do you understand?"

Mayhew nodded.

Carpenter continued to flash murderous glares at Mayhew as they took the final guard's clothes and wrapped them securely in Mayhew's cloak before dumping all three bodies in the bog.

"What if he does not come?" Mayhew asked.

"This is the hour, this is the night. If he is able, he will be ready for us," Launceston replied. "And if he is already dead or disabled, then we look for the Silver Skull, and then the girl."

"And leave him here?" Carpenter pressed.

Launceston nodded. "We are ready?"

Crossing the wasteland, they were all acutely aware they only had a little time before the sentries were missed and the alarm raised. Further down the slope towards the village, they found their location by nose alone. Like Hampton Court Palace, El Escorial utilised advanced construction techniques: water piped in, waste taken out.

The sewer tunnel emptied onto the slope and flowed away from the palace so the stench never reached the walls. Lined with granite, the sewer was big enough for a grown man to crawl along, as black as pitch with a choking stink that left them all gagging as they stood at the opening. Tying kerchiefs across their mouths and noses, they fixed their cloak bundles on their backs, and then exchanged a brief glance as they decided who would go first.

With a shake of his head, Launceston dropped to his knees and splashed into the sewer. Carpenter roughly thrust Mayhew next, before taking up the rear. Within seconds, they were all coughing and spluttering, swearing profusely, yet obliquely thankful that the vile smell distracted them from the oppressive claustrophobia of the dark, stifling space.

After five minutes of slow progress, Mayhew had a revelation. "This is our lives in essence," he spat. "Crawling through shit and piss towards an uncertain future."

"At least on this occasion you can keep your head above the surface," Launceston replied. "We should be thankful for that."

A little further on, Launceston came up hard against an obstruction. Feeling around in the dark, he realised it was an iron grille. Just as he informed the others, there was a loud click as a hidden switch was triggered and another grille slid into place behind Carpenter. Mayhew whimpered loudly.

"I dare you to panic," Carpenter growled.

"A cage . . . !" Mayhew began before fighting to calm himself.

Calmly, Launceston defined the shape of the grille with his hands. "We knew we would not be allowed free access to the palace. The Spanish are the spawn of hell, but they are not fools."

Mayhew's ragged overbreathing echoed in the confined space, but he knew better than to speak. Launceston withdrew one of the sachets of powder that Dee had given them before they left London and rested it on the point where the grille was bolted into the stone. "This is not as potent as the mixture Will carries, but it should suffice," Launceston said. "Press back and cover your faces. This will not be pleasant."

Fumbling to unfold the sachet, he dripped a small amount of liquid onto the powder from a hide pouch. The subsequent flash of light and heat threw them back against the rear grille, their heads ringing and their faces burning. When they had recovered, they found the grille hanging loose and it took only a little heaving from Launceston's shoulder to tear it free.

"Dee is a foul black magician," Carpenter said, "but I am glad he is our black magician."

They scrambled along the remainder of the tunnel and eventually emerged into a large pit. Overhead, light gleamed through a series of holes in the seat of the privy.

"Heaven," Carpenter gasped.

"At least heaven is not obscured by an arse," Mayhew muttered.

Iron rungs were fixed into the granite blocks lining the pit for workers to climb down to wash out the excrement when it backed up. At the top of the rungs, Launceston listened for anyone in the privy and then cautiously lifted the wooden seat. In the chamber beyond, there was water for washing.

"Hurry now," Launceston whispered, "or they will smell us long before they see us."

Stripping off and discarding their foul clothes down the privy, they washed themselves quickly before dressing in the guards' uniforms. A larger, empty chamber lay beyond, and then a quiet corridor running along the western edge of the palace. Launceston led the way with Carpenter bringing up the rear, ready to change direction at any moment if they heard approaching feet.

Eventually they located the large, steaming kitchens, almost empty now the evening meal had been prepared and served and most of the cleaning up had been completed. From just beyond the door, they watched as bowls and plates were carried, and spice and pickle jars returned to shelves. Waiting until the men had moved away from their vicinity, Carpenter selected a young scullery girl lazily mopping up a spillage not far from the door. Motioning Launceston and Mayhew to stay out of sight, he strode into the kitchen confidently, looked around, and then went over to the scullery girl. Fearing admonishment, she lowered her eyes and pretended not to see him.

In fluent Spanish, Carpenter said to her, "Please. Will you help me?"

The girl glanced across the kitchen to where her superior oversaw the storage of ingredients for the following day's meal.

"A moment of your time," Carpenter pressed.

As he had expected, the scullery girl eyed him suspiciously, and so he drew out the crucifix he had taken from the dead sentry and whispered dolefully, "My mother died this day. I would say a prayer for her, but I cannot be seen to be avoiding my duties. Is there a quiet place hereabouts? For only a moment?"

At the sight of the crucifix, the girl softened. Still glancing around, she took his hand and led him to a storeroom half covered in a white dusting of flour.

"Thank you," he whispered. As she made to go, he summoned her back and asked, "What is your name?"

"Chelo."

"You are a beautiful girl, Chelo."

She blushed.

"My name is Eduardo. I am new to the palace. I would have worked here sooner if I had known you were in the king's employ."

She blushed again, but didn't resist when he took her hand. "Perhaps you would find time to walk with me one day?"

She looked deep into his eyes, and as her pupils dilated, he knew he had her.

"Where are you from?" she began. "Your accent . . . ?"

"My mother is French. I grew up in the New World."

Her eyes widened with excitement. "Is it as they say? Dragons in the sea, and silver on the streets . . . and a city of gold—"

"All of that and more." He sealed the connection by kissing her hand. "But I hear there are wonders here too."

"Here?"

"An English spy held prisoner? You have heard of that?"

She sighed as if this were the most boring thing in the world. "Yes, we prepared food for him."

Carpenter restrained a triumphant grin. "And where is he being held?"

CHAPTER 42

Loosening his belt, Will cracked the stay of the buckle which was hollow inside and stopped with a small blob of wax. He placed this on one side, and then tore off the cuff of his shirt, which he wrapped around the door handle of his chamber cell. He had observed Dee's demonstration before he had left for Cádiz, but he still could not grasp how the combination of powder embedded in the cuff and the liquid in the buckle could have such an effect, and Dee had dismissed all his questions with irritation.

Removing the wax stopper, he turned his head away, covered his eyes, and poured the foul-smelling liquid onto the cuff, before throwing himself across the chamber.

The subsequent explosion deafened him. When he uncovered his head and looked around, he was confronted by a thick cloud of grey smoke that smelled as badly as the liquid, and when that cleared he saw the door was in tatters.

Outside in the corridor, one guard lay unconscious, another attempted to stem blood from a terrible wound on his leg, and a third staggered around in a daze. Deciding the dazed guard was the worst threat, Will put one arm around his neck, the other around his head, and twisted it sharply until the neck snapped.

The other guard made a pitiful attempt to stop Will, but the blood spurted whenever he removed his hand. Instead, he made to shout an alarm. Will slammed the heel of his hand under the guard's chin, throwing the head back to break his neck too. Before he had even hit the floor, Will had claimed a sword and a knife.

From the window, he quickly scanned the desolate landscape, but it was too dark to see if Launceston, Mayhew, and Carpenter were there. He trusted they would have followed him from Seville—they were good at what they did—but were they good enough to get inside such an intensely guarded palace-fortress? He had to presume he was on his own.

All he had done since Grace's abduction was allow emotion to rule him.

Launceston and the others had tolerated it out of loyalty to the leader of their team, but he knew they would each be secretly wondering why he hadn't taken the Silver Skull when he had it, forsaking the child and his plan to be kidnapped so he would be brought to Grace.

And now he was in danger of losing both Grace and the Skull. He cursed himself, cursed the Unseelie Court, and then cursed himself again.

As he expected, the explosion had drawn attention. Cries of alarm reverberated through the entire wing of the palace, and the sound of running feet rang on the tower's spiral steps. Will had hoped he would at least have had the time to reach the foot of the tower so he could slip into the maze of corridors and courtyards. Now he would have to fight his way out.

The pulse of the blood in his temple beat out the steady rhythm of the words in his head: no one would stop him.

He met the guards climbing the stairs head-on without slowing his step. Driving his sword through the heart of the first, he ploughed into the bodies, rolling across the top of them as they crashed against the stone, shattering limbs, spines, skulls. The knife flashed in his other hand, across throat after pale throat, and by the time he had passed the last guard the blood cascaded down the steps around him, and all above were dead.

How many guards and soldiers were in the palace? How many would he have to kill before he reached his objective?

At the foot of the tower, three more guards were on their way up, two with pikes, the third, a captain, armed with a sword. Instantly, he took Will on, parrying with some skill and attempting to return the attack, but Will had learned from the greatest swordsmen in Europe, and he had the advantage of height. There was no time for niceties. As the captain struggled to strike upwards, Will kicked his blade to one side and thrust his sword through the captain's throat. He fell backwards, frantically trying to stem the bubbling blood.

Something in Will's face scared the remaining pikemen—he could see the uncertainty and then fear flare in their eyes when they locked gazes with him. It was enough that they faltered in their attack. Will slashed his sword across the fingers of one so that he dropped his weapon, which Will promptly kicked towards the other. As the second guard struggled to bat the pike away, Will impaled him on his sword, and then finished the first with his knife for good measure.

With a bound, he was over the flailing bodies and into the corridor beyond. Cries rang out here and there, but in the confusion no one was really sure where the explosion had originated, or what it indicated.

Out of the confines of the tower, stealth was the key. Torches burned intermittently along the corridors, but in that austere place the gloom was never far away. Will kept to the shadows, moving from doorway to pillar, courtyard tree to arch, emerging in a flash of steel every now and then to slit a throat or run through any guard that got too near.

In room after room, he set fire to tapestries and furniture with the torches and lanterns he found. The blazes were not large enough to spread rapidly, but the smoke sweeping through the complex and the loud crackle of the flames would cause panic and confusion.

At first he attempted to hide the bodies, but soon he realised there were too many and it was slowing him down; they would find him soon enough. The corpses trailed behind him, too many to count as he progressed relentlessly towards the front of the palace where he presumed a carriage would be waiting to take Grace and the Silver Skull away from El Escorial.

At some point, the stream of deaths became an enchantment. He saw only sprays from opened arteries, bones revealed to the air, blown pupils; he smelled only iron blood and bowels released in the throes of death; he heard only final moans and desperate pleadings. And still he moved on.

Malantha and the Unseelie Court loomed darkly in his mind and he thought: *You have driven me to this. You have made me wound my own soul with each life I take. You will pay in full.*

Yet a part of him wondered if it was all inside him to begin with, and the Unseelie Court had, with their deft skill, only brought it to the surface to show him what he was really like: a brutal killer, as contemptuous of life as he believed them to be.

As he swept through the final courtyard, his fortune began to evaporate and even his skills could not keep him going. Cries rose across the entire palace as body after body was discovered, rising to become one long, furious alarm demanding his death. Boots thundered on stone, closing in from several directions at once. Within a moment, Will saw his way ahead was blocked by at least twenty men racing towards him with pikes and swords.

Cursing that he had been deterred when he was so close, he darted to his left into another corridor, doubling back on himself through the palace, no longer knowing where he was going. Concerned palace workers poked their heads from rooms, shrieking and withdrawing when they saw him run by trailing the blood of others.

His random course had also confused his pursuers who were unable to cut him off, and were forced to follow in his wake. All he had were impressions of grand rooms, the echoes of his boots, and the sound of a storm at his back.

Finally he was confronted by a knot of seven guards racing towards him from a branching corridor. Unable to get past them, he was forced to back against a wall to defend himself.

"Come, then!" he roared. "Who dies first?"

The guards hesitated until they realised their weight of numbers might crush him. But as they began to charge, one at the back suddenly pitched forwards coughing blood. A blade protruded from his throat.

As he fell to the ground, Carpenter slowly removed his knife and flashed a contemptuous glance at Will. Mayhew and Launceston stood with him.

Will joined them in falling upon the disoriented guards who were dispatched in seconds.

"Better late than never," Will said to Carpenter as he urged them back the way the others had come.

"You have led us on a merry chase," Mayhew said. "If you had only stayed in the tower we might have saved you."

"Instead of bringing the entire hordes of Spain upon our heads," Carpenter snapped.

"There was no time to lose." As they ran, Will briefly told them of the Unseelie Court's plans for the Silver Skull and Grace.

"Then we can end this here," Carpenter said.

The sound of guards approaching from all directions underlined the fragility of his words.

"The only end will be ours," Mayhew muttered. "We will never be able to fight our way out against all the king's men."

Will knew he was right. As they hesitated at a junction of corridors, unsure which way to go, Will fumbled for the handle of a door in search of other options.

"Not there," Carpenter cautioned, too late. As the door swung open, Will saw an array of bodies scattered around. Many were guards, but there were a number of the palace's workers, including a young woman who would not have posed any threat.

"Who did this?" Will asked. Even after all his slaughter, the bloodletting was shocking to him.

"I fear I lost control, a little." A feverish gleam lit Launceston's eyes.

"Are we no better than the ones we fight?" Will said with quiet intensity. The nearing pursuit shook him from his dull anger and he continued, "This is a matter for later. For now, hide beneath the bodies. Do not show your faces, but smear the blood upon you. If luck is on our side, it will buy us a few moments."

Leaving the door ajar, Will ran to the far side of the chamber where he pulled the body of a guard across his midriff and positioned the remains of a handmaiden over his face. As the running feet neared, the others scrambled into place, their stolen uniforms helping to disguise them. Mayhew was the last to settle a second before the door was flung open. Will heard the outraged comments from the guards, but as he had expected they did not investigate and within moments continued rapidly with their search.

When he was sure they were gone, Will levered the bodies off him, and quietly called for the others. Mayhew was shaken and on edge, but both Carpenter and Launceston remained focused.

"The carriage will be leaving in due course. We cannot afford to delay," Will said.

"And what strategy have you dreamed up that will get us out of this mess?" Carpenter asked. "Or have you finally completed the process of killing me that you started in the Muscovy snow?"

"A bold strategy," Will said. "Did you expect anything less?"

It was bold, it was dangerous, and it had the potential to bring down upon his shoulders the wrath of Walsingham, Burghley, and the queen herself, and would probably see him consigned to the Tower with an appointment with the block. Yet as the cries rang out through the echoing halls of El Escorial, he realised he had little choice. "To the basilica," he said.

Their ploy among the dead had bought them a little time. The guards who had passed the door were the last wave and the passages beyond were now silent. Flitting through the dark of the final courtyard, they reached the still sanctity of the basilica. In the bright glow of scores of candles, they were instantly revealed to the three guards waiting near the altar.

One shouted an alarm and hammered on the door beside the altar, while the other two approached cautiously. Carpenter took one down with his throwing knife, while Will and Mayhew dispatched the second. So swift he was barely seen, Launceston slid his knife across the throat of the one guarding the door.

"What lies behind the door?" Mayhew asked.

Without responding, Will tried the door, but it was locked as he anticipated. He motioned to Carpenter and Mayhew to use a heavy bench as a battering ram, and within minutes the door was torn from its hinges.

On his knees, head bowed in prayer, Philip did not deign to acknowledge them. Will could see he was preparing to meet his God, and ready to be a martyr to his religion.

"The king," Carpenter said incredulously.

Launceston caught Will's arm and whispered, "It is one thing to beard the Spanish on their home ground, but quite another to threaten the life of a monarch. You are an ordinary man. To challenge a king in such a manner goes against the established order. You could bring all of Europe down on England's heads. The queen will not take this lightly."

"If I had another path I would take it." Will strode over to Philip and said, "You must come with us."

Philip did not look up from his devotions. Will nodded to Carpenter and Mayhew, and after a moment's hesitation, they took Philip's arms and helped him to his feet.

"You are our passage out of here," Will said. "You have my word you will not be harmed."

Philip was unmoved. "England will burn for this."

"Where is that witch who has your ear?" Will hastily searched the quarters, but there was no sign of Malantha, and it was clear Philip would never betray her.

Containing his desire for revenge, Will led the way out of the king's quarters, through the basilica, and into the courtyard. They were brought up sharp by fifty or more of the king's men racing to defend Philip's residence. Coming to an abrupt halt, the blood drained from their faces when they saw the king in the hands of their enemies.

Drawing his knife, Will pressed it to Philip's throat. "Safe passage," he called, "or the king's death will be on your conscience."

Swords drawn towards the massed ranks of hateful eyes, Launceston, Carpenter, and Mayhew huddled in a tight knot around Will and Philip. Will could feel the tremors running through Mayhew and hoped they weren't visible.

With a snarl, one of the soldiers raised his pike, but the captain quickly thrust an arm across his chest.

"Safe passage and he will not be harmed," Will stressed.

Slowly, the ranks parted and Will and the others moved steadily through, eyes flashing all around for any hint of an attack. But Will knew they could not risk the king's death; grave repercussions would surely follow if any harm came to the monarch. Would he go that far? he wondered.

The soldiers closed around them, until they were an island in a sea of steel armour, threatened from every side by pikes and swords. Step by step they advanced, Will's knife never leaving Philip's throat, the entire courtyard enveloped in an anxious silence. The tension demanded release, but that would only result in slaughter.

Hold steady, Will thought. He cast an eye towards Mayhew, the most likely to crack and bring everything falling down, and then to Launceston, who still had the gleam of his death-hunger in his eyes.

As they came to the portico leading out of the courtyard, Will ordered Carpenter to collect several pikes. When he had them, they moved through the first set of doors, which Launceston slammed shut. An eruption of anger blasted from the other side as the soldiers threw themselves against the doors as one, but Carpenter had already rammed one of the pikes through the iron ring-handles; the doors bowed, but the pike held—not for long, Will knew.

With the clamour ringing at their backs, they now raced through the palace, hauling Philip along with them, and using the remaining pikes to block door after door. Will hoped it would give them enough time.

Emerging into the warm night, they saw a carriage waiting in the court-yard before the palace. The gates were already open. Beside it stood Don Alanzo and Grace. Cautiously holding the Silver Skull, opened on a hinge that was invisible when it was worn, the Don moved to fix it on Grace's head.

His gently persuasive voice floated through the still air: "Place this 'pon your head. You must do what I say. And we will release you from it when your task is complete." Yet Will could see the Don was reticent about what he had been guided to do.

"Grace, do not heed him!" Will called.

Whirling, Don Alanzo dropped the Skull as he went for his sword. Grace cried out and made to run to Will until the Don held her back with one arm.

"In case your eyes have failed you, we have your king here," Will said.

"And that will be added to the list of crimes for which you will pay," Don Alanzo replied. With a flourish, he brought his sword tip to Grace's breast. "Let us see where your loyalties truly lie." Don Alanzo scooped the Skull back up with his free hand and placed one foot on the step of the carriage.

Blood throbbed in Will's temples. He could feel the eyes of Launceston, Carpenter, and Mayhew upon him; and from somewhere unseen, too, he could feel the terrible regard of Malantha.

"Well?" Don Alanzo mocked. "Release the king or the girl dies."

"Give me the Skull or the king dies," Will responded.

"Then let us see whose life you consider more valuable." Don Alanzo pressed the sword tip against Grace.

"Kill the king," Will ordered. He couldn't bear to examine the devastation that flared in Grace's face.

Don Alanzo laughed, but the humour drained rapidly when he saw Will was not bluffing. Hesitantly, Carpenter drew his knife, and when Will gave the nod, moved in for the kill.

Eyes fixed on Don Alanzo as he estimated if he could save Grace before the killing blow, Will heard frantic activity at his back.

Carpenter's knife clattered across the flags. An instant later Carpenter was on his knees, his lips and nose bloody. Half turning, Will saw Philip flee across the courtyard to the palace. He was about to give chase when he was struck so heavily across the temple, it drove him to his knees, dazed.

Muffled voices rumbled through the dull haze in his head, and when he shook off the stupor, he saw Mayhew running to join Don Alanzo with Launceston in pursuit.

Mayhew, the traitor.

His head spinning, Will scrambled to his feet, just in time to see Don Alanzo thrust a screaming Grace into the carriage and bound in after her, with the Silver Skull safe under his arm.

Mayhew cried out, but the carriage began to move away. At the last, he flung himself onto the step, clutching the open window for dear life, and planted one boot into Launceston's chest to send him sprawling.

The carriage built up speed and rattled out of the gates and away across the dark Spanish countryside.

CHAPTER 43

"Leave me alone!" Mayhew shook his fist at Grace in a rage. Her tearstained face was filled only with contempt for him.

As the carriage raced away from the palace, Don Alanzo leapt forwards and drove Mayhew back into his seat, eyes blazing. "You do not speak to her like that!" he snarled. "You have no right to speak to anyone . . . traitor."

Mayhew felt like his heart would burst. The strain of keeping his traitorous nature undercover for so long had led him to the brink of self-destruction, but now a corrosive guilt had been added to the potent mix. He held his head in his hands and tried not to think about what he had sacrificed—his life in England, his countrymen, his queen, and his country itself—and he wondered how he would ever live with himself.

"But . . . I helped you," Mayhew said. Even he could hear the pathetic note in his voice. Why was the Spaniard treating him so badly? He had brought victory to Spain.

Don Alanzo studied him intently for several long moments, and Mayhew couldn't meet the intensity of his gaze. Then he said: "You are not a Spanish spy or I would know."

"No. I . . ." His shoulders sagged, and he could barely force out the words. "I help the Enemy. The . . . the Unseelie Court."

Don Alanzo glared at him with contempt. "You sold your soul for what easy gain?"

It was a question he could not easily answer. "If only you knew," he said, his voice breaking.

Don Alanzo eyed Grace askance, who was watching Mayhew with disdain. "She does not need to hear these things."

Mayhew nodded. "Agreed."

"Then there is some humanity in you after all," Don Alanzo sniffed. He turned his attention to the view from the window as if Mayhew was beneath his notice.

And the Spaniard was right, Mayhew accepted. He was a traitor, and a despicable human being. He deserved the loathing that would be inflicted upon him. He closed his eyes to hide the tears and sat back in the seat, pretending to sleep.

After a while, his head began to nod, and all the horrible images rose like spectres from his unconscious mind where he had locked them away for so long.

His father's funeral on a cold November day at their parish church in the village outside Hastings, the bitter air salty with the scent of the sea, stark trees black against the grey clouds, filled with crows, cawing their desolate chorus. At the graveside, he slipped his arm around his mother, whispering that he would look after her, provide her with a regular stipend from his new work under Lord Walsingham at the Palace of Whitehall. It was after he had privately agreed to work for the secret service, and three days before his induction into the true mysteries of existence, when he had still thought there was hope in the world . . .

Eight weeks later, and the snow was heavy on the roofs of the village, and the ground as hard as his heart had grown. The crows were still thick in the trees, but now he viewed them in a different light. A visit home after his assignment to the guard at the Tower, what at the time had appeared to be a short-term posting, filled with long hours of tedium. As he stepped through the door, he thought how thin and pale his mother looked, her skin slightly jaundiced, and when he hugged her he could feel her bones like hoes and trowels. "You are working too hard. You must rest more," he told her. She smiled weakly, wiser than he was . . .

Two months later, and he had missed three visits home because of the demands of his work. When he arrived at the cottage after dark, the parson waited, like one of the crows that never appeared to leave the surrounding trees. His mother was very ill, the parson said. He feared her time was short. She lay in her bed, delirious, calling out for his father, her own father and mother. She looked barely more than bones with skin draped over them. The rapid decline in such a short period shocked him, and he cursed himself, and the world, and wished for more and made deals with God. But she did not improve.

Under special petition from Lord Walsingham, he was given time away from his post to care for her in her final days. They were long, the nights longer, filled with tears, and anger, and her anguished cries as the pain gripped her. But she did not die within the week, as the parson had forecast, nor within two weeks, and by the end she was screaming in agony around the clock, and he clutched his ears, and then buried his head, and wept nonstop, until he was sure he was being driven mad by her unending suffering.

The desire to help her drove him on, but he could do nothing to relieve her agony, and finally his failure consumed him. He could bear to see her in pain no more. And then, after praying for her to live for so long, he prayed for her to die, soon, that moment, so her torment would be ended along with her awful cries, and that destroyed him even more; he had asked God for the death of his own mother.

But she did not die. And for a while he did go mad. He never left the house, and he did not eat for days, roaming from room to room cursing and yelling.

Then one night, when the moon was full, he saw from the window that the field beside the house was filled with statues, grey and wrapped in shadow. They watched, as the crows had appeared to watch. He ran to his mother, and prayed over her, but he was drawn back to the window time and again, and though the statues had disappeared, the shadows remained, flitting back and forth across the field in the moonlight.

The knock at the door came soon after. In the days following he could never remember the face, although at the time it burned into his mind, and he knew he would feel its eyes upon him for the rest of his days. But he recalled what passed between them. His mother would never die. She would remain in that purgatory of agony, and he would be with her for the rest of his days, never escaping her screams, cursed to watch her unending suffering.

He could not bear it, and he threw himself to the floor, and tore at his flesh, and for a while knew nothing.

When he had recovered a little, the honeyed voice told him there was hope; and he pleaded to know what it was, anything, he would do anything, and the voice said that was good. He would work for them, just for a while, and do the little things they asked, inconsequential things, and in the meantime they would give his mother balm, and when his time of service was done, they would ease her suffering into death.

For a while the requests were inconsequential; gradually they became greater, but he had already set off along the road, and so each new thing was just one tiny step further. When he discovered knowledge of the Palace of Whitehall and what was there, and then passed it on, it was nothing; there were no consequences. And when he revealed what he knew of the Tower, it was worse, but not much. But then he was helping them to overcome the Tower's defences that Dee had put in place, and released the chain of misery and death that still had not come to an end.

The carriage jolted over a rut and he stirred sharply from his reverie. As his eyes opened, he was shocked to see Don Alanzo looming in front of him, the Silver Skull open and gleaming.

"What—?" he began, but his question was cut short as Don Alanzo pressed the mask against his face and closed it with a clang. Instantly, his head swam with frightening images, things he had never seen and could never possibly have known. The sensation of movement all across his head unsettled him, until he felt a thousand points of agony as if insects were burrowing into him, through skin, and bone, and into his brain, and he wanted to scream, but could not utter a sound.

Dimly, he heard Don Alanzo saying, "Do as you are ordered and the mask will be removed. Resist us and be damned forever."

And he wondered if he was cursed to be a slave to others for all time, and if his suffering would never end.

rashing on horseback through the dense forest encroaching upon Lisbon on three sides, Will crested a ridge to look down on a scene that was at once breathtaking and chilling. In the bay on the estuary, edged with the silvery light of the moon amid pools of stark shadows, were around one hundred and thirty ships. The formidable fleet was so dense it was like another city floating alongside Lisbon, candlelight glimmering here and there aboard each ship, banners fluttering gently in the warm night breeze.

The Armada.

Somewhere in the teeming city, Don Alanzo would be meeting with the Armada's commander, the duke of Medina Sidonia, to secure a place for him and Grace on one of the ships about to depart. Will had to find him before the fleet sailed.

Weariness sapped him of any response beyond a dull relief that he had finally reached his destination after constant riding along dusty, deserted back roads, stealing a new horse whenever his mount tired.

It was May 8, and more than two week had passed since his escape from El Escorial with Carpenter and Launceston, close behind Don Alanzo's carriage. At their back, the still night had been shattered by the outcry as the king's men flooded from the palace to scour the surrounding countryside for the escaped spies. They had moved quickly across the desolate terrain, using the spoil-heaps and thickets for cover until they reached the village, where they escaped on three old nags, eventually exchanging them for other mounts along the way. Once they were sure they had left their pursuers behind, Will had instructed Carpenter and Mayhew to proceed to the location where they had agreed to rendezvous with the *Tempest*. Their orders were to carry the news of what had happened to whatever forces waited to confront the Armada. England's future hung by a thread and they all had a part to play.

Will took a moment to study the array of ships of different styles and strengths before wearily guiding his horse down the road winding around the hillside. At the foot of the hills, Lisbon nestled amid its walls, an ancient city whose narrow streets wound in confusion away from the quay. The architecture, like Cádiz and Seville, bore the influence of the Moors expelled by the Crusaders more than four hundred years earlier, the arches and geometric designs on the grander buildings, the minarets rising above the orange roof tiles.

For eight years now, Lisbon had been under Spanish rule following Philip's determined invasion. He knew how crucial the city was to his plans for his empire's dominance of Europe and the New World, as a hub for trade with Africa, the Far East, India, and the Spanish colonies in the New World. But thanks to the vast harbour in the estuary where the River Tagus flowed into the Atlantic, it played an even more crucial role as the home of the Armada.

As Will passed through the walls he left the fragrant pine-tinged air behind and plunged into a foul-smelling atmosphere where excrement and urine fought with rot in the dark streets. Instantly he could see something was wrong. Lisbon should have been awash with the riches of the New World, evident in the faces and the clothes of its citizens, in overflowing shops, and well-tended buildings, and streets filled with the heady air of exuberance he had encountered in Seville.

Instead an oppressive sense of decay hung everywhere. The narrow streets of the Alfama area were crowded with beggars calling to him and reaching out for his boots, sometimes clamouring so tightly around his horse he could barely continue forwards. Shops along the way were empty and closed, some boarded up. The area swarmed with prostitutes, some of them the roughest and most pox-ridden Will had ever seen; far from their stews, they competed in shrill voices for trade that often ended in violence. In the even darker alleys reaching from the main thoroughfares, Will glimpsed sudden movement and a flash of silver, heard cries cut suddenly short. He passed a body on the side of the street in a state of decomposition, unclaimed.

Will battened down his guilt at his failure. He had let the Skull and Grace slip through his fingers, and now he was sure Grace was trapped within that supernatural weapon. He couldn't bring himself to consider what that meant.

The one thing he could not shake from his mind was Grace's look of betrayal when he ordered the king to be killed in the full knowledge that Don Alanzo would respond in kind and kill Grace. It was an expression he had never seen before, as if all her hopes had been shattered in one moment.

The decision had almost destroyed him, but there was no way he could go back on it; what was done was done, and he would have to live with the consequences of his actions.

He channelled his feelings into a slow-burning hatred for Mayhew. So much misery would not have come to pass if not for him, and so many of his strange actions were now explicable. How the Unseelie Court had managed to breach the Tower's defences, where Mayhew's post had made him uniquely aware of its defences and its prisoner. How knowledge of Will's destination in Cádiz had fallen into Spanish hands before the soldiers tried to surround him near the cathedral. And the one that angered him the most, how Grace's secret hideaway at Hampton Court Palace had been brought to the attention of the Enemy. Her life would not be in danger now if not for Mayhew.

Will was happy to move away from the worst-afflicted region of the city and head towards the slopes leading up to the Castle of Säo Jorge overlooking the city. Once the royal residence, the homes of the city's wealthier inhabitants clustered close to its protection. Here the streets were quieter. Will eventually located the house he required in a long, white terrace of the well-kept homes of merchants, far enough away from the rich and important residents to avoid attention.

A gentle knock was answered by a man in his late twenties, strong, clean-shaven, and tanned, black hair framing an intelligent face. He matched the description that had been made available in the Palace of Whitehall.

"You are Luis Inacio dos Santos?" Will asked.

"I am," he said in heavily accented English and gave a formal bow. Once Will had announced the password, Santos admitted him into the gloomy interior. The Portuguese man carried himself with the strength and control of a soldier, but his face had the sensitivity of an artist. Both were true. Will knew he had been an acclaimed artist in Lisbon until the Spanish invasion, when he had fought in the resistance. The Portuguese lost in the face of Philip of Spain's overwhelming force, but resentment boiled away in the shadowy streets, and Santos was an easy turn for Walsingham's men. He hated Spain, and Philip, in a more visceral manner than any Englishman.

"You have a ship moored off the coast," Santos said. "Word came through this morning to prepare for the possible arrival of an English agent. Though," he added, "that word has been flying back and forth for months now. I sent missive after missive about the buildup of the Armada. Why was I ignored?"

"The queen has her favourites," Will replied, "and she does not always heed the most trustworthy voice."

"You must be exhausted after your journey. I can offer you food."

"A bite, but matters are pressing and I cannot rest." He explained to Santos about Don Alanzo and Grace.

"This afternoon word reached me of a new Spanish nobleman in the city, but I have no knowledge of where he stays or which ship he will be joining. You can afford at least a few hours' rest. This past hour also saw the arrival of a messenger from Philip's palace. He is believed to be carrying orders for Medina Sidonia to launch the Armada, but that will not take place until tomorrow at the earliest. The duke has waited two weeks for the order already. Another day will matter little."

Will wondered if the attack on El Escorial had prompted Philip—and Malantha—to move with haste. If preparations were not wholly complete, that could work in England's favour. "I cannot rest. If it is not possible to locate Don Alanzo in the city quickly, I must get aboard one of the ships," Will pressed. "The arrangements will take time, if that is even possible. Even though I speak Philip's tongue, or could pass as a French mercenary, the chances of discovery are high."

Laughing, Santos held up a hand to slow Will's anxious words. "These matters are in hand. Rest. The world will not end before dawn."

Although Will knew the truth of Santos's words, he couldn't shake an oppressive feeling of mounting doom, of secret plans coming together in the darkness. Yet after weeks with only a snatched hour of rest here and there, his eyes drooped quickly and he fell into a deep, dreamless sleep. He was woken by Santos later when the room was filled with the warming aromas of food.

Santos indicated a fine spread. "Red mullet from Setubal and mussels from Cabo da Roca. Goat cheese from Sobral de Monte Agraço, *zimbros* from Sesimbra, and pastries from Malveira. Cheese cakes and nuts, and for your pleasure, a bottle of Muscatel, also from Setubal. The best of Portugal, still, despite the Spanish occupation. Eat and drink your fill."

Santos's hospitality was as much a mark of his pride in his country and his defiance of Spanish rule, but Will was just as thankful. He ate hungrily, and when he was done, was ready with the questions that weighed upon him.

"What has happened to Lisbon?" he asked. "As I rode through, it was worse than the worst parts of London, filthy, seemingly poor. Where are the riches? Where is the food?"

"Another thing for which we must thank the Spanish," Santos said bitterly. "The Armada has brought more than thirty thousand men to Lisbon, all of them whoring, fighting, and thieving while the ships sit uselessly off our harbour for week upon week. They consume our food faster than we can replenish our supplies. Everything is scarce, and what is available is beyond the wages of the common man. We starve by the day. The Spanish run riot through our city, and the Portuguese have locked themselves behind their shutters, but even then there is no escape. In their filth and degradation, the Spanish sailors and soldiers grow diseased and ill. They desert by the score, and good Portuguese men are pressed to fill their spaces. Lisbon can take no more. The sooner we are rid of this damned Armada, the better."

"Do not wish it upon England," Will said, "but I understand why you are keen to help."

"And help you I shall, to all my power. A spy within the fleet itself may do little alone to turn the tide of battle, but still you may cause some damage in the thick of it. And if the worst happens, when the force lands on England's shores, you will have valuable information that may aid any resistance."

"If the Spanish set foot upon England, the hour will be dire indeed," Will replied. "But how will I disguise myself effectively among Spanish sailors for such a long sea voyage?"

Sitting back in his chair, Santos folded his hands together and smiled. "You will not be among Spanish sailors."

"Who, then?"

"Among your own kind. Englishmen."

Will eyed Santos incredulously.

"Not all your countrymen have the same pure motives as yourself. There are some two hundred Englishmen among the Spanish crews. Mercenaries, those driven by the passion of our Lord who believe this a crusade to return the one true religion to your land, priests who plan to become rich converting heretics, and exiles keen to reclaim their fortunes and their estates once rightful order has returned."

"A ship of traitors, then." Though unsurprised, Will was still angry that some were so eager to betray the land of their birth.

"Ships," Santos corrected, "for they are scattered among the fleet. I know for certainty eight are aboard the *Nuestra Señora del Rosario*. And there is rumoured to be one of great status aboard Medina Sidonia's flagship *San Martin*."

"The flagship? There is an Englishman in the command?"

"They call him Don William."

"Sir William Stanley," Will noted coldly. "The treacherous dog. I had heard he was in Dunkirk marshalling another part of Parma's invasion force. Stanley cares for nothing but himself. He betrayed the entire city of Deventer in the Netherlands to the duke of Parma. If he is here, he feels success in his blood. How did you come by this information? And how will I gain the necessary papers to find a berth without being press-ganged and ending up a slave at the oars of one of Medina Sidonia's galleys?"

Raising a candle to guide his way, Santos motioned for Will to follow him. As they climbed the flights of creaking stairs, he said, "It may be that your woman will be aboard the *Santiago*. *La Arca de las Mujeres* is the name by which it is commonly known."

"*The Ship of Women?*" Will translated.

"It carries the wives of many of the married officers, the only women permitted to sail with the fleet. No whores to distract the men. Though I have heard tell that one officer smuggled his wife on board disguised as a man, to provide him with comfort on the long nights at sea. Medina Sidonia does not want his men's fighting edge blunted by nights of carnal pleasure. But the *Santiago* is one of the most heavily guarded ships in the Armada. You will not get aboard it."

Will stored the information away as Santos led him up a final, short set of stairs to an attic room. The smell of blood and urine washed out the moment the door was opened. As Santos's candle drove back the dark, Will saw a man chained to the far wall on a bed of straw, his head hanging down so it was impossible to tell if he were alive or dead. As they walked in, he stirred and grunted, but he was barely conscious. Santos had clearly beaten him to get the information he required.

"Who is he?" Will asked.

"An English mercenary who goes by the name of William Prowd. I found him drunk in a bar and lured him back here on the pretence of more wine. He told me all I need to know, and I have his papers, signed by Medina

Sidonia's recruitment officer, so you will be able to slip on board." Santos collected the wine-stained papers from a stool and handed them to Will.

"Unless he has friends aboard."

"He tells me he travelled alone, as his regular acquaintances feared England's firepower, even against a fleet of this size."

Lifting the man's battered and bruised head, Will studied him for a moment while he thought. "There will be risks aplenty, but this will at least give me an opportunity. I thank you. Now I must disguise my appearance as much as possible, for I have unfortunately been the subject of several pamphlets published in London detailing my adventures, each of which came with an engraving, which, although it failed to capture my true heroic nature, could make me recognisable."

Santos guided Will out of the room, but did not close the door. "I will find you a razor, scissors, and dye. Now: have you everything I can give you to bring misery to the hated Spanish?"

"Your gifts and my own wits are all I need."

Santos's polite bow only just hid years of mounting hatred. "Then I must tidy up here. I will meet you downstairs shortly." He drew his knife and prepared to step into the attic room again before turning back briefly, his face haunted in the candlelight. "These times make monsters of all of us," he said. "I wonder sometimes where is the simple man who took joy from the art he created in the hills around Lisbon. I fear he is lost forever."

With that, he stepped into the attic room and closed the door behind him.

CHAPTER 45

"Take one more step and I will cut off your ears and your nose!" the Spanish officer barked in faltering English. One hand lay on the hilt of his knife, and he looked as if he wished to mutilate Will whether he complied or not.

Will came to a halt at the top of the rope ladder, on the brink of stepping onto the deck of the *Nuestra Señora del Rosario*, one of the most heavily armed ships in the Spanish fleet.

"Papers!" the officer demanded. Snatching them from Will's fingers, he cast an eye over the stolen documents while keeping Will's face in view. The cursory glance came to a sharp halt, and he read one section in detail, his brow knitting, before staring deeply into Will's eyes. When he drew his knife suddenly, Will was sure he had been discovered, and went for his own hidden knife. But then the officer jabbed the blade past him to indicate a clutch of three men further along the deck, and thrust the papers back into Will's hand with a contemptuous expression.

Playing his part, Will gave a sullen nod and climbed on board. Freshly clean-shaven, with trimmed hair dyed to turn it from black to dark brown, he was now William Prowd, a mercenary fighting man fresh from the campaign in the Netherlands. As such, he was not expected to be a seasoned sailor and could easily disguise his ignorance of the detail of the backbreaking work on deck. And with a supply of dye to keep his hair brown, he hoped he could survive for weeks, if necessary. By judgment or chance, Santos had done his work well.

But he was now trapped on a ship full of enemies who would take his life in a moment, amid a vast fleet filled with thousands more cutthroats en route to the fiercest battle the world had known. He would not be able to rest for a second.

The dawn had broken, clear and golden, with a light wind off the

Atlantic, the sticky scent of pine from the forested hills mingling with the tang of salt and the rich aroma of fresh fish from the small boats unloading their catch on the quayside. Amid the discordant screech of seagulls, Will had made his way to the ship early to avoid unnecessary scrutiny.

The *Nuestra Señora del Rosario* was moored on the far side of what the locals called the floating forest. It was a carrack, with a soaring forecastle that would prove a terrifying prospect for any would-be boarders. It was also the Spanish pay-ship, carrying the wages of every man sailing with the Armada, and as such Will knew it would be a prime target for England's pirates. The last thing he wanted was to be slain by his own countrymen within sight of home, if he survived that far.

The three men eyed Will suspiciously as he drew near. They were all English. Two were mercenaries like Will, happy to sell themselves to the highest bidder: Henry Barrett was a barrel of a man with enormous muscular arms that looked like they could crush bones, and a big belly, a shaven head, and protruding ears framing a face that had the half-lidded expression of someone on the brink of exploding into a rage; Jerome Stanbury was slight next to his associate but still muscular, with a hooked nose and lank grey-black hair hanging down to his shoulders. The third, Walter Hakebourne, was a coastal pilot who would guide the ship to safe harbour once they arrived in England. A small man, he appeared permanently anxious and on edge as if he expected an attack at any moment.

"Have ye heard the news?" Stanbury said. "Philip has sent his orders to sail. This day, May the ninth, is one for our journals, eh, friend? We will make good money out of this, for even when we reach England the Spanish will require much fighting and peacekeeping."

"How long till we are ready to depart?" Will asked.

"*We* can be ready in hours, for this is a well-run ship. It is under the command of Don Pedro de Valdes, one of the Armada's main commanders," Hakebourne stuttered. "But the rest of 'em? I would say two days."

As the day gradually warmed, they continued to speak about little of import in the curt manner of men who trusted no one: the poor quality of the food, their doubts about the management of the purchasing of provisions for the voyage, the inadequacy of many of the Spanish sailors. Guiding the conversation in an oblique manner, Will attempted to discover more vital information about Medina Sidonia's plans for the Armada, but it quickly became

clear that the men knew nothing, nor wanted to know. They were only interested in the money they were going to pocket, and were ready to do anything
asked of them.

A buzz began to spread across the other ships in the harbour, voices raised
cheerily, shouts and song, as news spread of the arrival of the king's orders and
the certain knowledge that the crews' long wait would soon be over. It was
the irony of their work; whenever they were at sea they craved the comforts
of port, but when on dry land, they could not wait to return to sea.

"This will be over in no time," Barrett grunted. "The Spanish officers
told Hawksworth that Elizabeth still persists with peace negotiations with
Parma, when Philip has no intention of seeing them concluded. There is no
time for England to get its defences in place. We will stride right up to the
door of the queen's bedchamber, knock politely, and ask for entry!"

They all laughed, but Will's mind was racing. "Hawksworth?" he asked.

Uneasily, they exchanged brief, flickering glances as Stanbury said, "Sir
Richard Hawksworth. You have heard tell of him?"

Will had. Hawksworth had spent his time in the shadow of the treacherous Sir William Stanley, but his reputation for deceit and cruelty was, if
anything, even greater. In the Netherlands, while helping Stanley complete
his betrayal of the city of Deventer to the duke of Parma for a substantial
purse of gold, he was rumoured to have sent his own brother to his death for
money. In a stew of traitors, cutthroats, and liars, Hawksworth would always
be the least trustworthy. More worrying to Will, Hawksworth had spent a
great deal of time at court, and while he had never met Will face-to-face, he
knew of his reputation, and perhaps other telling details too.

The mention of his name had certainly troubled the others for they had
grown bad-tempered, and there was still one thing Will wished to know
before they sloped off below deck.

"I have heard tell," he said, leaning in conspiratorially, "of strange things
occurring around this fleet. Of portents . . . and apparitions. I would not sail
with a fleet that is cursed."

Will knew many of the sailors and fighting men were superstitious, a
response to the closeness of death in their lives, but he was surprised by the
reaction. Barrett, Stanbury, and Hakebourne all went for the items they carried to ward off ill fortune: a rabbit's foot, medallion, and ring.

"I myself saw, two nights gone, mysterious lights under the waves after dark had fallen, moving from the shore to ship . . . several ships," Hake-bourne whispered.

"The beer turned to vinegar at an inn on the quayside after a drunken Spaniard cursed the Fair Folk." Barrett looked over his shoulder as if he expected someone to be standing on the ship's rail at his back.

"Spectres," Stanbury muttered. "Glimpsed in the evening mist, stalking the forests around Lisbon." He pointed an accusing finger at Will. "Do not mention them again."

Will didn't need to—he already had the answer he required: the Unseelie Court was accompanying the Armada to England. He was amid even more enemies than he had feared.

His question had cast a pall over their conversation and as they prepared to break up so Will could find his berth for the night, they were hailed loudly by a tall, flamboyantly dressed man with a pockmarked face. Will noticed he rarely blinked, so that he resembled one of the lizards he had seen basking in the sun on the rocks during his journey from El Escorial.

"Watch your back," Stanbury said quietly. "It is Hawksworth."

His heavy-lidded gaze flickered across those present before alighting on Will. Hawksworth's brow knitted briefly before he spoke, but his gaze kept returning to Will for unsettling periods. "I have just returned from a council of war on the flagship," he pronounced. Will knew Hawksworth was not one of the inner circle, however much he pretended, so he could only have been on the ship as an associate of Stanley, and was likely not privy to anything of importance. "You will have heard the order to sail has arrived, yes?" Hawksworth continued. "But the king also sent another missive, warning that English spies may attempt to sneak into the fleet. We must be on our guard at all times. You all have correct papers, yes?" He spoke to the group at large, but his eyes suggested he was only addressing Will.

Will showed him the papers, and that appeared to satisfy him, although as he swaggered away from the group he cast one final, curious glance at Will.

Soon after, Will was put to work in the hold securing siege guns and other weapons for the land war, which would be put to good use against vulnerable English towns along the south coast once the Spanish broke through the sea defences.

The Spanish officers worked the crew hard, but the sense of anticipation was high. The waiting and the boredom had started to prove self-destructive, and everyone was eager to put to sea, however much danger lay ahead. As they worked, Barrett and Stanbury bantered with a gallows humour, only falling silent whenever Hawksworth passed by. He appeared to do no work himself, and spent most of his time attempting to inveigle himself with the Spanish officers who showed little interest, and some irritation, in him.

As dusk fell, Will finally found his cramped sleeping space in the gloomy, noisy below-deck compartment. The crew slept on the bare boards with only one coarse dogswain blanket for comfort and a folded jerkin for a pillow. It was impossible to move without jostling another crew member, and the air was heavy with the vinegar-sour reek of sweat, and urine, and the ever-present stink of vomit from those who had consumed too much drink. After they'd eaten, the men turned to raucous sing-alongs or played cards, or told tales of their time at sea.

Much later, when he was sure his absence would not be noticed, Will crept on deck and examined the lights flickering across the floating city, mirroring the stars above.

Briefly, he considered swimming among the ships to try to find Grace and the Silver Skull and steal them away before they put to sea, but the chances of his discovery were high and of his locating *The Ship of Women* in such a mass were low.

Medina Sidonia's flagship, the *San Martín*, was moored close by, and throughout the day Will had surreptitiously watched the comings and goings on board for any sign of Don Alanzo, without any luck. But as he stood at the rail studying the ship, his attention was caught by familiar, unsettling movement—grey shapes flitting across the deck, insubstantial in the dark.

He watched the Enemy for long moments, trying to make sense of what they were doing on board, wondering how much the Spanish knew of the threat in their midst; for he knew the Unseelie Court would easily turn on their current allies once England was destroyed. Suddenly he became aware that one of the indistinct figures had come to a halt and was standing at the rail.

Looking at him?

Will ducked down and moved quickly away from his vantage point. Had he been seen? Worse, had he been recognized?

Returning to the seething mass of sleepers below deck, he tried to lose himself among the crew. The night was hot and uncomfortable in the crowded, confined quarters. Will slept with his knife in his hand, but the only disturbances came from sailors stumbling over him in the dark, and the resultant curses and kicks.

The next day passed with a sense of mounting anticipation as the fleet readied itself for war, and on May 11, Medina Sidonia took advantage of a light easterly wind and the Armada set sail downstream. But the long string of ships had barely passed the mouth of the Tagus when the wind turned and blew directly at them, and they were forced to drop anchor and wait. Storms raged up and down the coastline, and as Will watched the churning black clouds, he couldn't help but wonder if Dee had something to do with it. Rumours of his conjuring abilities had circulated the court for decades. Will had no idea how many of them were true, or if he was just a very clever and skillful man who was, like all in Walsingham's employ, good at portraying whatever face best served his purpose. Still, as lightning flickered and the crew grew irritated at the delay so early in their campaign, he wondered.

The wait dragged from hours into days and then weeks, the tension slowly escalating. Will took the opportunity to watch the constant stream of boats back and forth from Medina Sidonia's *San Martín*. He knew what they carried: intelligence reports from Philip's network of spies detailing the readiness—or lack of it—of the English forces. And the wind continued to blow, lashing the fleet with occasional bouts of stinging rain, and rolling the sea up into choppy waves of white-topped grey.

On May 27, Will finally caught sight of Don Alanzo aboard the *San Martín*, cloak wrapped tightly around him against the elements, deep in conversation with Medina Sidonia himself. Will kept his head down, working hard. But when he took the opportunity to glance back at the ship, he realized Hawksworth was watching him. He tried to pass off his attention as idle curiosity, pointing out the fluttering pennants and new gilding to a clearly disinterested Stanbury. When he glanced back, Hawksworth was gone, but he knew he would have to take more care.

That night, in the face of a fierce gale, Will and several others were sent up on deck to supplement the seasoned crew. As the deck bucked and heaved under his feet, he fought to stay upright, dragged to his knees time and again by sluicing water from the crashing waves. After an hour, the skin of his face burned from the lash of the rain and the spray and the bite of the wind. The officer barked orders in Spanish. Will had to feign ignorance, forcing him to attempt to give directions by pointing. After a while, he found it easier to leave Will alone and struggling to do what he could under the personal guidance of Hakebourne.

The other ships loomed like black castles in the dark on all sides, lamps glowing in their windows, as they fought their own battles with the gale. As Will gripped the rail in the face of one severe swell, he caught sight of a ship he had not seen before. It moved with a speed that belied the conditions, strange grey sails billowing; and as it sailed closer, Will was surprised to see there was no activity on deck to take the pressure from the straining rigging. It had an unsettling spectral quality, at times fading into the spray, at others seeming insubstantial even when the wind dropped. Flashes of greenish light came and went in the windows and on the forecastle, like the glows that burned over the marshes luring travellers to their doom. Will searched for some identifying banner or name, but there was none.

"What is that vessel?" he called to Hakebourne above the howl of the gale.

Hakebourne kept his eyes down as he tied a knot, easily bracing against the roll of the deck. "I see nothing," he shouted back.

"There!" Will indicated. "Astern!"

Hakebourne still did not look up. "Nothing," he replied, half turning his back on Will.

An atmosphere of dread followed the ship, and after a moment's study Will accepted that it could only be a galleon belonging to the Unseelie Court. Skimming the waves eerily, it appeared to be unaffected by the gale as it worked its way among the struggling Spanish vessels.

And then, as he watched, there *was* activity on deck, as though a veil had been drawn back to reveal the mystery behind it. These figures walked upright effortlessly, or stood easily in the rigging and on the mast, but it was the one who stood on the forecastle, arms raised to the heavens, that drew Will's attention.

Flashes of lightning burst among the clouds overhead, not lightning, but colours—red and green and purple. The rest of his crew continued to ignore them, but Will noticed their heads were all bowed, and where he could see faces they were strained. Their expressions only relaxed as the ship moved away into the deep dark, and not long after that the gale quickly dropped.

"It appears we are blessed, as the Spanish tell us," Will said to Hakebourne.

He only grunted in reply in a manner which suggested he thought they were more likely cursed.

And on May 28 the inclement weather finally cleared enough for the Armada to begin to make its way out of the Tagus and into open waters in its entirety. Each ship that passed Castle St. Julian was marked by the celebratory thunder of cannon fire, but it took until well past dawn of the next day for the whole fleet to leave the mouth of the river behind.

Standing on the rigging, Will could see the string of ships stretched for miles, a formidable sight for any enemy, but it was forced to move at the pace of the slowest hulk and that made progress excruciatingly slow for the Spanish officers.

After two days of sailing, the Armada was still south of the Rock of Lisbon, and it took thirteen more days to travel just one hundred and sixty nautical miles to Finisterre.

An outcry below deck drew Will's attention late in the afternoon. He found a knot of angry seamen gathered around the store of provisions, with a raging Barrett in the forefront.

"What is wrong?" Will asked.

Barrett flipped the lid off a barrel to reveal mouldy ship's biscuits heaving with maggots and worms. "The rice is the same," Barrett thundered. "And here." He opened another barrel from which Will recoiled at the foul stink. "Beef. Gone bad. All of it. And the fish too," Barrett added. He threw the barrel lid down so hard it shattered into pieces.

"All the provisions?" Will asked.

"Half of them. These damn Spaniards are like children. I should never have trusted them to mount an efficient campaign. They will poison us all with the food long before we engage in battle."

Will examined the biscuits. "These have been here a while?"

"Since the autumn," Barrett snapped. "All the delays to the Armada, and they sat upon their provisions. What were they thinking? There are already twenty men below, vomiting and fouling their quarters after eating this filth. The wine too has gone sour, and the water is undrinkable. I will have none of it."

Will saw an opportunity and fomented more anger among the gathered crew members before suggesting they take their complaints to Valdes. As the men stormed to the forecastle in search of the commander, Will held back, happy with the disruption he had caused. But as he waited, a hand caught his forearm. It was Hawksworth.

"Do I know you?" he asked. "Your face plays upon my mind. It would be ill mannered of me if we have fought beside each other in some campaign or other, or been in our cups in a tavern, and I did not recognise you."

"No, sir, I do not believe we have ever met," Will replied, with a contrite duck of his head. He made to go, but Hawksworth would not let him.

"That accent. Do I hear a hint of Warwickshire?"

"Sir, I have family in the Midlands, but I have not been home in many a year."

Hawksworth studied Will for a moment, and then asked, "And what campaigns have you been on?"

Will was grateful for the interruption of a Spanish officer ordering him to get back to work. He nodded to Hawksworth and trudged off, but could feel the traitor's eyes upon his back.

The fierce complaints spread from ship to ship as more and more provisions were found to be rotten, and Will did all he could to spread discontent. Medina Sidonia sent out requests for more supplies, from Philip, from anywhere in Portugal. All the time, men continued to fall ill with the flux, fouling their living spaces and bringing down the violent ire of those who slept near them. Barrel upon barrel of stinking food was tossed overboard.

Will watched the mounting chaos with a pleased eye, while searching for an opportunity to get to *The Ship of Women* to find Grace. His time would come, he was sure.

For four days, the fleet waited off Finisterre for victuals and fresh water to arrive, but there was never enough, and in the end Medina Sidonia called a council of war. Although initial orders demanded that no ship return to Spain under any circumstances, it was decided to put into Corunna to resupply.

Seeing his opportunity, Will volunteered for the shore crew who would oversee the collection and distribution of provisions across the fleet. It was a prime job, but the Spanish officers appeared happy to be rid of the Englishmen in their midst and, to Will's frustration, also assigned Hawksworth, Barrett, and Stanbury to the large team.

The coast of northwest Spain was a rugged expanse of sheer cliffs and sharp-toothed black rocks snapping against the crashing waves, but eventually it gave way to a pleasant crescent bay with the ragged spur of the Pyrenees rising up, purple and cloud-capped, in the distance. Perched over the bay was the fortress of Corunna guarding its walled city, built up by the Spanish over the years to deter any attack at the entrance to the peninsula, with a stout castle and a fort where a battery pointed seaward. Red, blue, and yellow roof tiles on the private homes glinted amid the gleaming white marble of the palace and public buildings so the city appeared to be studded with jewels in the morning sun. Along the seafront, peasants wound their way lazily with laden donkeys towards the market.

For most of the day, the lead ships settled into the harbour and dropped anchor, but by dusk nearly half the fleet—more than fifty ships—still waited at sea for daylight.

On the quayside, among the other crew members selected from the *Rosario*, Will waited for an opportunity to slip away, but Hawksworth watched his every movement with an unflinching eye. Every word Hawksworth said and every move he made reeked of suspicion, and Will had found himself waiting for the alarm to be raised and for him to be hauled off to the flagship and publicly executed. The strain of constant alertness was beginning to tell, and he had found himself sleeping fitfully, woken repeatedly by every slight noise in the filthy, stifling, overcrowded quarters.

Should he attempt to dispatch Hawksworth before the traitor acted, he wondered, or would that cause even more problems as the Spanish officers searched for the culprit?

His ruminations were disrupted by the sight of a storm sweeping in from the ocean. Lightning crackled in furious jagged bursts along the horizon, and as the wind gusted into the harbour, the ships bucked and rolled on the swell. The lanterns hanging outside the taverns swung wildly, the leaping shadows distorting the faces of those who waited. When the rain began to lash in horizontally, they gave up waiting for the officers who were supposed to be bringing their orders and fled into one of the taverns for shelter.

While the rest of the crew became progressively drunk on the local wine, Will stood at the window and watched the storm grow in intensity. The flashes of lightning revealed the ships at sea rising up on mountains before disappearing beneath a roll of black.

After a while other lights appeared in the sky, painting the roiling clouds in the colours that Will had witnessed over the ship with the grey sails. Was the Unseelie Court attempting to protect the fleet from nature's fury?

"Philip has sent his Armada against England knowing that his enemy has greater experience and more skilled commanders and refusing all the entreaties of his advisors." Hawksworth loomed at Will's shoulder, looking out across the harbour to the eerie wash of light. "Everyone told Philip not to send the Armada at this time," he continued, "but still he persevered. He stated his belief that God is on the side of the Spanish, and wherever weaknesses arise, God will help the Spanish overcome them. *The confident hope of a miracle*, he calls it. But consider this, Master Prowd. What if Philip does not put his faith in God after all? What if that sly king knows more than he says?"

Will watched the lights slowly die away until only impenetrable darkness remained.

"What if, instead, Philip has sided with the Devil, and England's sea forces face an infernal surprise that will destroy them? Out there, hidden among the fleet, is something beyond belief, waiting to be used."

"You know of these things for certain?" Will asked. Could Malantha have gifted the Armada with some secret weapon?

Hawksworth leaned in close so his hot breath warmed Will's ear. "Death waits ahead, and no one will be able to hide from its touch."

Clambering onto the deck of the *Santiago*, *The Ship of Women*, Will knew he had no more than five minutes to find Grace before the guards came hunting for him. On the gentle swell of the harbour below, the other men of the reprovisioning team struggled to prepare the barrels to be hauled up from the rowboat, red-faced and sweating in the heat of the day.

He was taking a tremendous risk. If he was found among the women he was likely to be flogged, or even killed by an officer defending his wife's honour, but it had taken a great effort to get assigned to the work group delivering provisions to the *Santiago* and it was unlikely he would get another chance.

At the rail, neither of the sentries paid him much attention, preferring to argue quietly over Medina Sidonia's decision to continue with the invasion despite the damage wreaked on the fleet by the storm. Will sensed they were both on the brink of desertion.

Easing out of their line of vision, he slipped quietly away. He tried to appear insignificant, but there were eyes everywhere. Medina Sidonia had posted infantry along the entire quay and throughout the city to prevent any more of the many desertions that had afflicted the Armada.

The mood across the fleet had been increasingly desperate since the storm. That night, the ships left at sea had been forced to run in the face of the tempest. Some suffered shattered mainmasts and rudders torn free, while others had limped to shelter further along the coast; thirty ships, including several galleons, had been missing for weeks.

Four days after the storm, Medina Sidonia had called another council of war. After a missive from Philip, the duke and his followers felt they had no choice but to wait in Corunna until the missing ships had been found, repairs had been carried out, and the entire fleet reprovisioned. The last ship hadn't returned until July 15.

For Will, the long wait was interminable. The Spanish commanders kept the men working hard under the hot sun, but his thoughts turned continually to Grace, the shadow that was falling across England, and the brooding threat of the Unseelie Court working their mysterious schemes just out of sight. Time and again he had been despatched into the dusty countryside as one of a team searching out wood for new barrels for provisions, until he thought he would go mad with the boredom.

At least the frantic repairs and reprovisioning provided some cover in the cluttered harbour. Everyone was even busier now the order to sail had been issued. When he saw an opportunity to search the Santiago, he took it with relief.

At the top of the steps leading below deck, Will glanced around quickly. No one was watching. He moved quickly into the stifling dark.

The *Santiago* was the oldest ship in the fleet, a six-hundred-ton hulk, flat-bottomed with a spacious hold, but clumsy at sea, and one of the drags on the Armada's speed and efficiency. Will had earlier glimpsed the women moving about on deck like ravens as they took the sea air in their black dresses and caps, but they had been ordered below rather than allow them to remain in full view of sailors who had been starved of comfort for so long. Yet in all the time he had been with the Armada he had never caught sight of Grace. Was she even there?

Below deck, the women had attempted to provide some comfort in their meagre quarters with bunches of dried lavender and muslin bags of rose petals everywhere. Sheets had been strung from ropes across the hold to provide a modicum of privacy.

When he appeared at the foot of the creaking steps, the curtains shifted as suspicious eyes inspected him. Puzzled mutterings rolled around the dark space and for a moment he was afraid the alarm would be raised, but from the glances he received from some of the younger women, he could tell they had been starved of comfort as much as the men. They flashed quick, nervous smiles and held his gaze a moment too long. Even the older wives occasionally let their gaze linger, though they maintained severe or sombre expressions and muttered angrily about his presence in their midst.

As the hull rang with the sound of barrels banging up the side of the ship, he realised time was running out and took the risk of asking one of the young wives where he could find an Englishwoman. Shyly, she guided him to the back of the living quarters where an area had been curtained off with several sheets of sailcloth.

Will pushed through the final sheet, and there was Grace, hugging her knees in one corner, a chain fastened to one ankle and affixed to the hull. She was not wearing the Silver Skull.

His relief palpable, he grabbed her and held her tightly for a moment. Her shock gave way to a rush of silent emotion, but after a moment she pulled back, her eyes blazing. She jabbed a finger towards him and fumed, "'Kill the king'?"

"Grace—"

"Have you come to finish the job? Where is your knife?" She thrust her chest towards him and framed her heart with her hands. "There. Does that make it easier?"

"Grace—"

"'Oh, yes, I will protect you, Grace. Until it comes to a hard choice and then I will blithely toss you to the wolves.'"

"You are alive, are you not?" he snapped.

"No thanks to you."

"Months apart and your first instinct is to scold me like a child? You are the most infuriating woman I know."

"I can give you your due reward once we are away from here. How will you free me from this chain?" With frustration, she gave it a yank then let it clatter to the boards.

"This is not the time," he began hesitantly.

She gave a sarcastic sigh. "Of course not."

"We are in the middle of the enemy's fleet. There is no chance of escaping with our lives at this time."

"Then how did you get here?"

"I am now William Prowd, a mercenary in the employ of Philip of Spain. Trust me, Grace. When the time is right—"

"Oh, yes, I trust you. Of course. When the time is right. In the meantime, I will continue to enjoy the indignities heaped upon me."

Will took a breath to steady himself. "Have you been ill treated?" he said, pronouncing every word carefully.

"Don Alanzo has treated me well, apart from chaining me like a dog." She sniffed.

Will took her face in his hands and examined her eyes. Deep within was a hint of whatever subtle control Malantha had exerted over her at El Escorial. Although she was not in the Unseelie Court's thrall at that moment, they still planned to use her in their plot, and then her life would be forfeit.

"What has happened to the Silver Skull?" he asked. "Don Alanzo intended to make you its bearer."

She explained how Don Alanzo had fixed the mask to Mayhew on the carriage ride from El Escorial.

"Then perhaps there is still some honour within him," Will said. "Now, I have but little time here before I am discovered. You must tell me quickly what you have learned during your time with Don Alanzo. He speaks with you?"

"He visits me to enquire after my well-being and if I have any needs, and on those occasions, we pass the time, if not as friends then as people who share a bond." Her face darkened. "A bond of suffering."

"Do you know where Mayhew is? Hidden on the flagship?"

She shook her head. "He was taken aboard a ship with grey sails. It appeared deserted. I have not seen its kind before."

"Then I must board that grey-sailed ship and see for myself," Will said, knowing exactly what that statement entailed. "Mayhew is the architect of much of the misery we have experienced. He will pay dearly for his crimes."

The clattering of the barrels continued, accompanied by a bout of shouting and cursing. Soon they would come looking for him.

"Don Alanzo did not tell me his plans," Grace continued, "but he was unguarded in some of his comments. He does not see me as a threat, and he knows there is nothing I can do until the Spanish plot bears fruition. There is some hidden weapon—"

"The Silver Skull?"

"No, another. Something that will be used when the Spanish fleet encounters our English ships. Don Alanzo appeared troubled when he realised he had mentioned it. It seemed to me that this was a secret even the Spanish officers did not know . . . something of which only Don Alanzo and a few others were aware."

"Spies are privy to many secrets denied the common man. That is our benefit and our burden," Will replied. "He said no more? What it was? Where it is held?"

She shook her head.

"Any more regarding the Spanish invasion plans?"

"No." After a brief pause, she added, "I asked him about Jenny."

Will flinched. "Why would you ask Don Alanzo about her?"

"I know your work is in some way connected to Jenny's disappearance, or so you think. If she was taken by Spanish spies, you would not tell me, for fear I would rush to Walsingham, or the queen herself, and demand we do all we can do to gain her return, even if it be war."

"And what did Don Alanzo say?" he asked.

"He sat down, here, and listened carefully to all my pleadings. He knew something, or he would not have listened."

"He knows nothing. Don Alanzo understands the world in which we operate, that is all."

"He told me he would make enquiries as to her well-being." Tears stung her eyes, and in them was a hint of accusation that Will had not done enough.

The clattering outside ended and silence descended on the ship. "I must go. We shall talk of this later," he said.

"And when will that be?" she asked tartly. "I would plan my swooning."

"Soon."

"I heard the order to put back to sea. Do you wait until we make land, which means England will have fallen, and our lives will amount to nothing? Or do we go down at sea under the weight of English cannon?"

"Trust me. I will do everything in my power to help you."

Relenting, she gave an exasperated nod. He squeezed her hand and an uneasy moment passed between them, before he stepped past the sailcloth and hurried back through the living quarters.

Back on deck, one of his fellows, a gruff Spaniard, angrily accused him of slacking. A fight brewed until the guards stepped in and urged the Spanish seaman over the side to the rowboat.

As Will waited to follow, a shadow loomed over him. It was Hawksworth; he'd been out of sight somewhere on deck, and must have arrived after Will.

How much did he see? Will wondered.

His answer came when Hawksworth leaned in and whispered, "I know who you are," before sweeping away across the deck.

CHAPTER 47

Sitting in tense silence on the rowboat back from the *Santiago*, Will watched the quayside for guards ready to arrest him, but every man was occupied with the frantic reprovisioning of the fleet. Why hadn't Hawksworth brought men to *The Ship of Women*? Why had he risked whispering to Will in the certain knowledge that Will could have slit his throat and attempted to make good his escape there and then?

Once the boat was tied up, Will uneasily joined the throng hauling barrels out of the warehouses while he tried to decide on a course of action. It was easy to lose himself in the swirl of noisy activity. New barrels were still being constructed amid a clatter of hammers, before they were lowered with grunts and curses into every available rowboat.

No one came for him. It made no sense, unless Hawksworth had a grander scheme in mind. But what could that be?

For the rest of the day, Will scanned his surroundings, the groups of stone-faced infantry, even the dark interiors of taverns and stores, but there was not even a furtive glance from the Spanish officers, no hint that anyone was the wiser about his true identity.

He was torn, but there was too much at stake to flee. Finally he decided to continue as planned and hope he could deny any allegation Hawksworth made. Once back on the *Rosario*, he acted as normally as possible, exchanging lewd banter with Barrett and Stanbury as he went about his allotted tasks. Occasionally, he caught glimpses of Hawksworth, but the traitor gave no sign that anything had passed between them. That puzzled Will even more.

Twilight brought a cooling breeze that eased the heat of the day. Will sat with the crew on the deck while the officers discussed Medina Sidonia's orders at the forecastle. After so long in Corunna, there was an eagerness to get back to sea although it was tempered by apprehension at what might lie ahead.

The gun to make ready sounded at midnight. Will dozed fitfully, in case

Hawksworth made his move during the night, and at dawn every crew member was up with the crack of the gun ordering them to sea. It was another very hot day, and it took until midafternoon for the fleet to assemble, and by the following dawn they were finally out of sight of Spain.

Will glimpsed Hawksworth regularly, talking to the officers or overseeing some mundane task, but he continued to give no sign that anything had passed between them. With each hour, the tense atmosphere magnified until Will wanted something to happen to end the unbearable waiting, though he knew he had to board the grey-sailed ship before his identity came to light.

He had noticed that the Unseelie Court ship regularly paused alongside the *Rosario*, as well as the flagship and some of the other important ships, for around fifteen minutes each night. Sailing with unnatural speed, it appeared to mark out a proscribed route among the fleet, as though following a ritual path.

Fifteen minutes to board the ship, find the Silver Skull, and escape was little time, but he made his preparations regardless. In the hold among the carpenters' tools, he had located the grapnels used by boarding parties and had secreted one on deck.

That night, while the crew members slept on their filthy blankets, he crept up into the salty night air, ready to mount vigil for the grey-sailed ship pulling aside. They were sailing under a bank of low cloud, drizzle coming in sheets. The *Rosario* bucked across a choppy sea, and with visibility poor the night crew were occupied. Across the water, Will occasionally glimpsed the lamps of the other ships in the fleet.

Huddled against the elements, he waited. Finally, he caught sight of the silhouette of a lightless galleon ploughing across the waves on a slanting path in the channel between ships. Its speed told him it was the grey-sailed vessel.

As he went for the grapnel, he caught sight of someone emerging from below deck. Ducking down at the rail, Will watched, stock-still, as the figure searched slowly while trying to keep out of view. At the foot of the steps to the poop deck, the swinging lantern revealed Hawksworth's profile, sword drawn, but kept low at his side.

"Prowd?" he growled.

Cursing under his breath, Will peered over the rail to where the grey-sailed ship had now moved alongside, keeping an exact pace with the *Rosario*. Although dark, Will could see there was no movement on deck, no one on the poop deck or forecastle, no lookout, no sound of orders being barked. To the casual eye, it could have been abandoned and drifting with the current if not for the purposeful way it had been steered alongside. *An illusion*, Will decided, like the Fairy House in Edinburgh, which always appeared empty from the street.

The ship was close enough to reach with the grapnel, but Will couldn't risk trying to move between ships with Hawksworth prowling around not far away. Nor could he risk a sword fight on deck, which would quickly draw attention and awkward questions.

After a moment's thought, he left the hook where he had hidden it and pulled himself onto the rail. Fleet-footed, he bounded up the rigging, the oily rope slick beneath his fingers. Away from the shelter of the deck, the wind tore at him and the rain lashed as the ship rolled across the swell. Hooking his arm through the rigging, he waited in the knowledge that Hawksworth would probably not think to look up.

In frustration, he accepted the moment had passed for the night. As he watched the grey-sailed ship, the hairs on his neck tingled as if someone was looking back at him. He wondered what really stood on that seemingly empty deck.

Below him, Hawksworth continued to prowl, sword ready to repel any attack, with all the balance and poise of a master swordsman. It appeared he had decided to eliminate Will himself, rather than hand Will over to the Spanish commanders. Will couldn't understand Hawksworth's thinking. The capture of a live spy who could be tortured to provide vital information was a prize that could be traded for a high reward. One dead body was proof of nothing.

Will drew his knife and waited.

Hawksworth moved steadily around, clearly puzzled that Will was nowhere to be seen. He'd obviously observed Will leave his sleeping space, and had decided he was either up to no good or that it was the best time to dispatch him quietly.

Edging around to the back of the rigging, Will held on in the face of the harsh wind. When Hawksworth was beneath, he dropped. Hawksworth's cry was lost to the gale as Will smashed him to the deck, and before the traitor could recover, Will propelled him into the rail, winding him. Lunging with his knife just at the moment when the ship bucked over a large wave, Will skidded on the wet boards, and he half went down, one hand keeping his balance.

Eyes blazing, Hawksworth brought up his sword with a skill that surprised Will. "Prowd," he snarled, "or should I say 'Swyfte'?"

Will couldn't wait for Hawksworth to raise the alarm. Using the momentum of the rolling ship, he threw himself forwards and plunged his knife into Hawksworth's gut. Hawksworth's eyes bulged with shock as if he was not expecting any attack. Blood splattered from his mouth.

"No!" he gasped.

Will whipped the knife out and sliced it across the artery at Hawksworth's neck. As the blood arced into the rain, the traitor slumped down against the rail, desperately trying to stem the flow, knowing it was already too late.

"You fool!" he said. "I am a spy, like you!"

"Lies at the last?" Will knelt next to Hawksworth so they would not easily be glimpsed, ready to use his knife again if Hawksworth attempted to call out.

"I worked both sides, but gave the last to Walsingham." Hawksworth's clothes were now sodden with the blood.

"He said nothing—"

"Walsingham never says anything!" More blood ran from his mouth. "The Spanish were close to uncovering me. My time was short, and I needed your aid. Together, we both could have escaped when we engage the English fleet. I have details of Parma's invasion force . . . locations . . . numbers . . ." He coughed, grew weaker.

"You are the fool! Why did you not identify yourself?" Will demanded.

"I had to be certain. And now it is too late! We spend so long pretending . . . we waste our lives on lies . . . we are always slain by our own deceit. All of us."

His final breath rattled from his throat, and his chin slumped onto his chest. Briefly, Will bowed his head too, so that they resembled reflections of each other, one alive, one dead. His guilt quickly turned to anger at the stupidity of the confusion, both of them hiding behind masks, both mistrusting each other.

When Will was sure no one was watching, he lifted Hawksworth to the rail and pushed him over into the sea. In the wind, and the crash of the waves against the hull, the splash was not audible. The body went under and was gone.

The grey-sailed ship still kept apace with the *Rosario*, but as he watched, it gained speed, pulled ahead, and then sailed across the prow and away into the dark towards the *San Martín*. Will stifled the bitter sting of failure with the knowledge that he no longer risked discovery, and could return the following night to try again.

But as he walked towards the steps that led below deck, he thought he glimpsed a dark shape waiting there, quickly disappearing down as he neared. Had someone seen him dump Hawksworth's body? Worse, had someone overheard their exchange?

He hurried in pursuit, but when he reached the sleeping quarters, no one stirred. There was only the sound of the waves on the hull, a steady, deathly beat like the slow tick of a clock.

CHAPTER 48

"The time of reckoning has come," Launceston said as dispassionately as if he were preparing for a saunter along the shore. Eerily motionless, he looked out to sea where the ships waited.

Beside him on the quayside at Plymouth, the setting sun warmed Carpenter's face, the brassy light blazing across the jumbled rooftops cascading towards the sea. "Call it what you will," Carpenter replied. "We are likely sailing to our deaths, and death at sea is not like death on dry land, the brief, honourable pain of a sword thrust or the creak of old age. It is lungs bursting with water, and madness as breath is sucked away, or roasted alive in hellish fires, or limbs left splintered by cannon, your blood leaking into your shit and piss."

"Death is death," Launceston said simply.

Everywhere was unnaturally quiet at the end of the working day as the doors of the warehouses clattered shut and the merchants bid each other a quiet farewell, hurrying away with the workers from the sail-lofts and the other businesses that served the great ships. The delivery carts rolled off lazily amid the fruity aroma of horse dung. The taverns and stews around the harbour were deserted, most of their regular drinkers now aboard the ships, others hiding away in their homes in case they were pressed into service.

"If these are our last days, Robert, we should live them to the full," Carpenter mused. "Be the men we want to be, or dream we are, or give voice to the whispers in our hearts. What say you?"

Launceston considered this for a moment, and then nodded. "You speak sense, but for some of us that is not such an easy task."

Clouds of midges danced in the lazy heat, and as the shadows lengthened, the sounds of boots clattering at a steady pace over the cobbles drew towards them from the direction of the dark, mazy streets descending the steep hill to the dock. A confident, upright man emerged, striding purposefully, his hands clasped behind his back, his chest puffed out, and his head held high as if he was being watched by everyone he passed. His brown moustache and beard were carefully trimmed for the occasion and his hair swept back from his forehead. His features would have been familiar to almost all Englishmen and Englishwomen from the surfeit of pamphlets in circulation to mark the great successes of England's bravest adventurer, navigator, and sea captain.

"Sir Francis Drake," Launceston said, adding, "Does 'vice admiral' fit him better than 'privateer' these days?"

"No one can doubt what he has done for England, whatever his title."

Drake had dressed in his finest clothes, a new doublet in deep brown with gold stitching at the shoulders, a high white collar, and a black collarbone protector held in place by a gold chain. He walked up to them with a pronounced swagger and enquired, "Walsingham's men?"

"Yes, sir," Carpenter replied. "We are to accompany you aboard the *Revenge* in case the knowledge we have gained of the Enemy . . ." He corrected himself. ". . . the Spaniards, may be of some use in the coming battle."

"Very good," Drake replied. "Good men are always welcome aboard my ship."

"It is true, then," Carpenter enquired. "The Armada has been sighted."

"Fifty Spanish ships, off the Scilly Islands this very dawn, seen from the lookout of the *Golden Hind*, assigned to patrol the western approaches to England. The captain, Thomas Fleming, raced to tell me himself. This day, July twenty-ninth, will never be forgotten, for it is the day that the sleeping beast of England was woken."

"As we had heard," Launceston said. "The Spanish race up the Channel to engage us at their leisure."

With pride, Drake looked to his ship, the *Revenge*, resting elegantly on the gleaming waves amid the other great ships. "I have spent the afternoon at Plymouth Hoe, studying the weather for any change in the direction of the wind. I have said my goodbyes to my Elizabeth, and now I am ready."

"Should there not be more haste?" Carpenter ventured.

"More haste?" Drake repeated superciliously. "Nothing could be done until the tide had turned. Besides, these are Spaniards and we are Englishmen. I could put out tomorrow morning and still whip them like dogs."

News of Drake's arrival at Sutton Harbour spread quickly in whispers along the narrow streets. Soon groups of old women and men gathered to see the great hero, shooing the clutches of excited children racing and playing along the harbour's edge.

Drake briefly moved among them, bragging about the natural prowess of Englishmen, and by the time he left they were all cheering and pumping his hand.

"He plays his part well," Launceston observed, "like Will."

"I am not so sure it is a role with Drake," Carpenter replied. "He believes his own legend."

A rowboat took them out from the quay to the *Revenge* in the lee of St. Nicholas' Island. Drake's eyes never left his ship as they neared. "How can the Spaniards even hope to win this war?" he said. "They circulated full details of the strength of their Armada, hoping it would strike fear into us and encourage the powers of Europe to support them. All it did was give us a tactical advantage." He waved his hand towards his ship. "Thirteen years old, forty-three guns, firing shot of nine pounds to sixty pounds in weight. What fine firepower for an Englishman! Thanks to the Spanish, we now know that their most heavily armed vessel, the *San Lorenzo*, has forty guns, and sixteen are but sakers or minions firing only four or six pound a shot." He laughed, his eyes gleaming.

Carpenter watched him closely. He'd heard the stories but had never encountered Drake before, and he wondered if his bravado rang true. Whether it did or not, Drake's confidence was infectious. The black mood that had gripped him since he had disembarked the *Tempest* lifted slightly.

A hundred feet long at the keel, but appearing even larger, the *Revenge* grew more imposing as they neared. It was weather worn and its green and white chevrons had faded slightly, but that only gave it the appearance of a seasoned warhorse. Carpenter could smell the sticky bitterness of the fresh tar that turned the keel a shining black.

On deck, the crew waited in small groups to greet Drake. Drake never met their eyes, but Carpenter could see they were comforted by his presence. The great cannon gleamed, the gun crews standing at the ready. As if in silent prayer, he glanced up the mainmast to where the sails were furled at the yards, gave an approving nod, and then began his final inspection.

As the last glimmer of the setting sun lit the waters ablaze, the wind from the sea turned, and with the tide on the ebb, the signal gun fired. Slowly but steadily, the *Revenge* and the other great English galleons began their journey down Plymouth Sound. Night fell.

Once they were in open water, the crew scaled the rigging like monkeys to unfurl the sails. Carpenter knew this was a crucial time. The Spanish could have been waiting to bear down on them, but the topmen reported no ships ahead, though the danger would remain until first light. Drake gave the order for all lanterns to be extinguished, and they moved forwards as part of the night.

Launceston stood at the rail, his deathly pallor unnerving some of the crew who bowed their heads and muttered prayers as they passed. Carpenter thought a strange mood had come upon him.

"Will they strike now, coming out of the dark before our journey has even begun, like the death we spoke of ashore?" he mused.

Carpenter didn't know what to say, and left him there to watch Drake as he strode proudly across the still-warm deck, the master of his world.

When dawn came, the seas were still empty and the tense mood lifted slightly. The fleet of fifty-four ships led by Lord Howard of Effingham sailed out into mist and squalls.

At three p.m. that day, an exuberant Drake summoned Carpenter to the poop deck. "Would you like your first sight of our enemy?" he said gleefully.

Carpenter peered into the drizzle, but could see nothing, even when the rain cleared briefly. He eyed Drake to see if he was finding humour at the expense of a man who had not earned his sea legs. He was surprised to see Drake watching him deferentially.

"I, and all England, owe you a great deal," he said. "You have turned the tide of this war."

Carpenter was lost for words. From behind his back, Drake handed him a long tube of shaped beechwood, bounded by brass hoops. A second tube slid in and out of it, and there was glass in the end.

"What is this?" Carpenter asked, still unsure if he was to be made a joke.

Drake pressed the tube to Carpenter's eye and positioned him. Spanish sails loomed up in Carpenter's vision, shocking him so much he almost dropped the device. He lowered it, but could no longer see the sails.

"They are far away," he stuttered, "beyond my natural sight. Yet this device lets me see them. Is this some of Dee's magic?"

Drake laughed. "It is Dee's magic, but not in the way you mean. It is called a tele-scope. This arrangement of glass draws closer that which is distant. No supernatural power there, only human ingenuity."

Admiring the tele-scope, Carpenter said, "I never knew we had such a thing. How is that?"

"No one knows. No one will know, for many years to come. It is a secret, and you would know about those things. There is plenty that never reaches the ears of the common man, am I correct?"

Carpenter nodded. "But what has this to do with me?"

"As I heard it from Lord Walsingham, Dee worked upon a type of this very device, in years gone. He heard whispers and talk among his kind . . ." Drake smacked his lips in disapproval. ". . . that some Italian painter had drawn designs for this tele-scope many centuries past, and so he set about building one. He struggled to find the right glass, until word reached him of another similar design, being studied by the tsar's magicians."

Carpenter's brow furrowed. "In Muscovy?"

"The tsar's device did not work either, but he had a different part of the puzzle. And so two brave spies were sent to retrieve his invention—"

"This is what Will brought back!" Carpenter said, examining the simple tube. "I thought it was some great weapon."

"You do not understand its importance," Drake said. "Only a true seaman would. This tele-scope will turn the tide of battle. We can study the Spanish ships from afar, watch their preparations, their direction, and we can be upon them at the point of *our* choosing."

Carpenter was too stunned to speak.

"I heard you paid a great price for the recovery of the item that led to this great thing Dee has made," Drake continued. "Know you, then, that every scar you bear marks a thousand . . . nay, ten thousand English lives that have been saved this day. Saved by you, Master Carpenter. Your sacrifice will keep England free."

Dumbfounded, Carpenter could barely respond to Drake's praise. He made his way down the steps from the poop deck, his mind struggling to reconcile the bitterness that had encysted his heart since Will had abandoned him with the new knowledge of what had been won.

As he gathered his thoughts by the rail in the salty spray, he decided this new information had to be conveyed to Launceston, whom he had not seen since dawn had broken. He searched the length of the deck, and then plunged into the stifling, near-deserted confines below, his puzzlement growing by the moment. Eventually, he had exhausted all possibilities apart from the section of the hold containing the sail stores, timber, carpenters' tools, and all the items necessary to keep the great ship afloat.

When he called out, his voice was lost beneath the symphony of sound that filled every ship, the constant boom of waves against the hull and the chorus of creaking as every board flexed to cope with the pressures upon them. His view obscured by canvas hanging like drapes amid piles of timber, he worked his way through the obstacles, pulling back sheet after sheet.

As he drew back the final covering, he was convulsed with shock. Had he suddenly stepped into hell? As red as the Devil, Launceston loomed over a sticky mess, his knife still dripping. When he looked at Carpenter, fires blazed in his eyes, and it took a second for him to focus. With a faint, dreamy smile, he said softly, "What wonders to behold."

It took Carpenter several seconds to comprehend what lay before him. "Is . . . is that the cabin boy?"

Launceston examined the mess, and appeared to see it for the first time himself. His smile now had the sheepish cast of a man caught out drunk before night had fallen. "Do not judge me, John," he said.

"Judge you?" Carpenter ran a hand through his hair as his thoughts reeled with all the possibilities that now lay ahead.

The knife slipped from Launceston's slick fingers and he stood up, his expression haunted. "I have . . . unnatural desires, John. I know my shortcomings, and I fight every day to keep them under control, but what you said . . . about being who we are . . . in the shadow of death—"

"I did not mean *this*!" Head in his hands, Carpenter crashed onto a pile of timber. "I must think. Damn you! This will destroy everything!"

"We are who we are. Our natures rule us, for better or worse. What makes me like this makes me a valuable tool for England, and the queen, and Walsingham." He released a deep, juddering breath.

As Launceston's words settled on him, Carpenter glared. "They know?"

The earl did not respond directly. "I do not wish to be this way. My life is filled with torments," he said, his voice breaking. "This business makes us monsters to deal with monsters. I wish only the peace of a summer afternoon, but this is my world now, and always." With disgust, he looked down at what lay at his feet. Tears sprang to his eyes and streamed down his cheeks. "Help me, John," he pleaded.

After a moment, Carpenter stood and rested a hand upon his shoulder. "We must dispose of all this before it is discovered. And get you cleaned up." Carpenter reeled. He had always sensed Launceston was not like other men, but he had turned a blind eye to the extent of the darkness lurking within. Did that make him complicit in Launceston's atrocity? The notion sickened him.

"Thank you, thank you," Launceston muttered pathetically.

"We are in this together," Carpenter said with a sigh as he saw the magnitude of what lay ahead. "Damn you, Robert. Damn you."

CHAPTER 49

reeping on deck when the sun had set, Will feared it was his last chance to board the grey-sailed ship. Since he had killed Hawksworth, every attempt had been thwarted by events beyond his control, and now, with battle looming, he had to risk all.

Hawksworth had been missed the day after Will had disposed of the body, but it was presumed he had either thrown himself overboard in a fit of despair or had fallen; it was not an unusual occurrence. Will had spent the first few days brooding over the stupidity and confusion that had led to Hawksworth's death, but he knew it was one of the risks of his profession where every face was a mask. Soon the dark thoughts were washed from him, as he was sucked into the feverish preparations for the coming battle. Day after day the crew engaged in dry runs of the battle procedure under the urgent eyes of the clearly unsettled commanders. Fearful faces turned towards the grey horizon in every free moment, and rumours spread beneath deck like fire. Increasingly frustrated by the lack of opportunity to reach the Unseelie Court ship, Will could only wait. And then, that night, he seized his moment.

The night was clear, with a large swell, but there was no more rain, which would make his task easier. Below, the crew grabbed fitful hours of sleep in preparation for what would likely be an eventful day.

Locating the grapnel, Will waited patiently at the rail for the grey-sailed ship. Along the coast of England, beacons blazed, warning of the threat off the shore and calling the nation to war. It was Saturday, July 30, and the Armada was at anchor at Dodman Point in a state of heightened anxiety after sailing east along the Channel.

Earlier, he was convinced his final opportunity to find Mayhew and the Skull had slipped through his fingers. As the Spaniards watched the beacons, an English pinnace had swept across the bows and fired a single shot. But it was more to mock than threaten and the pinnace disappeared as the *La Rata*

Santa Maria Encoronada returned fire to no avail. The English fleet was sighted, but they did not attack. Medina Sidonia and his Spanish commanders had made sure they had the weather gage, the best position in relation to the wind and coastline. They would wait out the night before battle commenced at dawn.

Finally, Will caught sight of the grey-sailed ship making its strange, circuitous journey around the fleet with what appeared to be increased urgency. Once it sailed alongside, he clambered onto the rail, braced himself against the rigging, and spun the grapnel before letting it fly. It fell short, splashing into the waves. Quickly, he hauled it in and adjusted his next throw for distance. This time it caught in the rigging of the grey-sailed ship. Tightly fastening his end to the *Rosario*'s rigging, he gripped the rope firmly and then swung his legs up, crossing his ankles over the top to hang like one of the monkeys that performed in the market on Cheapside.

He'd left some slack, but his fear was that one or other of the ships would sail away and tear the rope free, plunging him into the black waves. Ignoring the blast of the wind, he shimmied along the rope. At the midpoint between the two ships, the swell swung the rope wildly and it took all his strength to hold on. Beneath him, the waves grasped for his back, driven high by the furious confusion of battling currents, two inches beneath him, one, his clothes soaked by the spray.

Gritting his teeth, he forced himself slowly up the curve towards the grey-sailed ship, one hand at a time. His fingers slid on the slick rope, his heart beating out every second the journey took.

By the time he reached the rail, his limbs were shaking from the strain. With a final effort, he hauled himself over the rail and onto the deck. The roll of the ship made him land harder and more noisily than he intended, and he quickly hid in the lee of the quarterdeck.

The stillness was unsettling. A strange odour hovered over everything, sickly-sweet but with a florid bitterness beneath, like mould on an apple in the autumn orchard. After a moment he heard the tramp of boots, which paused above his head and then moved towards the steps. Someone was investigating the dull sound of his landing.

Drawing his knife, he waited in the shadows against the steps as the ship pitched and yawed, seawater sluicing across the boards. From his hiding place, Will could not see who approached—a lookout? The helmsman?—and he only had the noise of the boots to estimate the position. When the figure loomed at the foot of the steps, he brought his knife up and across the throat. He had a glimpse of long brown hair and blazing eyes, and then as hands went to the open throat, Will spun him around and pitched him straight over the rail into the sea.

Once he was below deck, the constant roar of the sea retreated, but the sickly orchard smell was stronger. He could hear nothing beneath him apart from the steady heartbeat of the pumps keeping out the seawater. On either side, the quarters appeared empty. The crew would be in the berth, resting among the cannon. Will did not want to risk disturbing them and bringing every one of the Enemy upon him.

All depended on where Mayhew was being held. Would they be cruel enough to imprison him in the vile conditions beneath the waterline, with the rats and the stench? He was too valuable for that. That left the officers' quarters, the captain's own quarters, the brig, or the infirmary, if the Unseelie Court needed such things.

As he progressed, distorted sounds faded in and out of the unsettling silence, reminding him once again of the Fairy House—voices chanting in an incomprehensible language, mournful pipe music.

The door to the officers' quarters was ajar. Inside a group of figures sat around a long table, heads bowed, their faces hidden in the half-light. Although they appeared to be communicating with each other, all was quiet. He could see four, guessed there could be as many as ten.

Slipping by, he continued to the great cabin and the captain's cabin. The door here was also partly open. Inside, flickering lanterns cast shifting shadows as a male swayed around the room soundlessly in what appeared to be some kind of ritual. His movements reminded Will of the pattern the ship defined on the sea. A bitter aroma filled the air, incense or burned herbs, and there was the occasional gleam of objects, a chalice, he thought, a knife with a cruelly curved blade.

In the bowels of the galleon, it was darker, and damper, the sour stink rising from below the water level. Outside the door to the berth, he felt an uncomfortable pressure upon him from the other side. Blood trickled from his nose and a dull buzz echoed in his head.

Beyond more deserted officers' quarters, he found what would have been the infirmary and mess on an English galleon. Here the door was locked, and no sound came from within.

Removing the velvet pack of locksmith's tools all Walsingham's men carried with them, he got to work. He was not an expert lock-pick like some in the service, but after a moment he heard the tumblers turn with a dull clunk. Hesitating a moment to see if there was a response from the other side, he slowly swung the door open.

A slow-pulsing white light forced the shadows back, holding them at bay for a second before they swooped back in. It came from a glass globe just large enough to be contained in two hands, resting on a small table. Inside the globe was another that opened and closed like an iris, releasing the steady beat of light. It was of such a unique appearance, it had to be of some importance, but Will could not guess its purpose. Three more of the globes stood on plinths on the boards beneath the table, but no light emanated from them.

Wary of triggering an unseen alarm, he studied the room before taking a step inside. In the glare beyond the globe, the gloom held a figure lying on a mat on the boards, asleep or drugged. The glint of silver told him it was Mayhew. Beside the door was an open-topped barrel. From the salty smell, it appeared to contain only seawater, but as he reached towards the surface to test the liquid, an eel-like creature about as thick as his arm burst from the depths, snapping for his fingers. He withdrew his hand just in time, but he had glimpsed teeth like needles. He had never seen its like before.

Time grew short. He intended to kill Mayhew and cut off his head, as he had done with Don Alanzo's father, dumping the Silver Skull into the sea to be lost for all time. But as he took three steps towards the prone figure, he suddenly found himself facing the door.

The disconnection left him reeling. He tried to approach Mayhew again, but the same thing happened. Finally, he decided the inexplicable turn must have been caused by the pulsing globe. It was a protection device of some kind, either working its influence upon his mind and disorienting him, or physically spinning him around in the blink of an eye. Whatever, he could not get near to Mayhew, nor could he approach the globe to destroy it.

In frustration, he retraced his route to the steps where he grabbed one of the lanterns that illuminated the passageway. The sounds in the ship came to him more clearly, as if the longer he spent there, the more attuned he became to the peculiar qualities that existed on board. A carpet of rats scurried away from his feet as he descended to the lowest level, the orlop deck, the store for the spare sails, rigging, timber, and carpenters' tools, the galley, magazine, and brig. Amid the foul smell of bilge in the damp and the dark, he swayed across the rolling deck to where the grey sails hung. Any second now the ship would start to sail away and he would be trapped aboard.

Stacking the timber to create a pit, he used the lantern to set fire to one of the sails within it. Leaping flames rapidly filled the deck with thick smoke.

In the right conditions, the fire would send the ship down to the bottom of the Channel, and Mayhew and the damned Unseelie Court with it. At worst, he hoped it would cause enough damage to make it worthless to the fleet.

As he pounded up the steps, rapid activity erupted in the berth. He only just made it past the door when it was thrown open and bodies rushed out on the trail of the rising smoke.

On deck, he saw the ship had started to sail away. Without stopping, he leapt over the rail and grabbed the now-taut grapnel rope, swinging his feet up to shimmy along it. The rope strained beneath his fingers as the two great ships pulled apart. Below, the waves surged hungrily towards him.

Fearing a break at any moment, he dropped his legs and used his arms alone to power him on. He didn't slow until he grabbed hold of the *Rosario*'s rigging and released the grapnel rope into the churning water.

The grey-sailed ship had come to a halt, the smoke swirling in the wind. With satisfaction that he had struck a decisive blow, Will settled against the rail to watch the mounting conflagration. A second later he heard movement at his back. Barrett was there, and Stanbury, and several others drawing closer.

"Spy!" Barrett snarled.

Will had a second to guess Barrett had seen him dispose of Hawksworth's body, and then a fist laid him flat.

He came round to the silver of a new day, wrists bound behind him, head still ringing, a light breeze caressing his bruised face. As his vision cleared, he saw he was on a forecastle, looking down at a crew gathered in a crescent. They stared back at him with hateful eyes. At the front stood Medina Sidonia and several of the other Spanish commanders; it appeared he had been transported from the *Rosario* to the *San Martín*. Nearby, the grey-sailed ship listed, although no fire damage was visible from his vantage point. He guessed he had been under observation since he had killed Hawksworth, and his boarding of the grey-sailed ship had been the final condemning evidence against him.

Don Alanzo stepped before him. Though he attempted to remain aloof, a deep hatred burned in his eyes. "You are like a disease, infecting the very heart of our glorious empire," he said quietly. "But we have a cure."

"Your empire is already black and corrupted. Your sister knows the truth, Don Alanzo."

In a blaze of anger, Don Alanzo made to strike Will, but caught himself. "Your part in this business is now done." He paused. "By business, I mean life."

"So, an execution at sea. Do I not have the right to be heard?"

"A spy has no rights."

"I hope you feel the same if you are ever captured on English soil." He nodded towards the grey-sailed ship. "Should you ever reach England. Without your dogs, you are a toothless opponent."

Don Alanzo's cheeks flushed. "Our allies are already at work repairing their vessel. You have caused a delay, not an end."

"With England's ships so close, a delay may be more than enough."

Don Alanzo held Will's gaze. "I know the inner workings that drive you." A shadow crossed his face, and for a moment Will understood him too. "You have no regard for your life, and there is little I can do that will cause you pain," he continued. "But you must know punishment for your crimes before you die . . . for your crimes against Spain, and against my family. Against me."

"There is nothing you can do—" Will was cut short by the flash of a familiar face in the crowd as Barrett and Stanbury dragged Grace to the front. Her frightened eyes looked up at him in desperation.

"Leave her alone!" he snapped.

"I had no wish to harm her. You did this. You brought her to misery. Let that stain your conscience as you die."

"There is much of the Unseelie Court in your cruelty," Will said.

Don Alanzo winced, but there was still some joy in his eyes at the pain he was causing Will.

"Do not kill her," Will pleaded.

"I will not. She is vital to our allies' plans, and therefore to our plans. But I can protect her no longer. I allowed her to sail on *La Arca de las Mujeres* to keep her safe from harm. You have forfeited that right. She will be taken from here to that ship . . ." He indicated the grey-sailed vessel. ". . . and she will travel with our allies."

"No!" Will cried. He tried to throw himself at Don Alanzo, but a guard caught his arms and flung him to the deck. "No man or woman can abide being among them for any period. Their very presence is corrupting. She could be driven mad, or worse. You know this!"

"On your head," Don Alanzo said quietly.

Grace cried out as Barrett and Stanbury roughly dragged her towards the rail to transport her by rope to the grey-sailed ship. In fury, Will renewed his efforts to reach Don Alanzo and felt the pommel of the guard's sword crash against the back of his head, plunging him into unconsciousness once more.

When he came round again, Grace was nowhere to be seen. He was leaning against the rail, a rope wrapped around him and stretching across the deck, the other end trailing over the side into the water. Two teams of men waited on either rail so he could be pulled tight against the barnacled keel.

"We have no time to waste here, or I would relish inflicting suffering on you," Don Alanzo said. "Your death will be quick, but your suffering no less for haste."

"Do it, then." Will's head was hazy from the punishment of two blows. "I have damaged your plans. My life is a fair price if it brings you to your knees."

Don Alanzo ignored Will's taunting. He appeared calmer now that he could see Will's end was close. "You are not a seafaring man. Nor am I. Punishment at sea has its own particular flavour, I am told. What you are about to undergo has proven effective in the Dutch navy, according to the mercenaries aboard."

Will's gaze followed the trailing rope. "Keelhauling," he said.

Don Alanzo nodded. "Pulled tight and fast, the rope will drag you down, under the water, and along the keel. Barnacles affixed to the keel will slice through clothes, and tear off skin, and the bloody prisoner that emerges on the other side of the ship is thereby made repentant. Pulled slack and slow, the prisoner hangs beneath the keel, and drowns. Either way, you will not survive this ordeal."

Unbidden, the terrible, shattering sensation of drowning Will had experienced in the Fairy House flashed across his mind. With all his will, he fought back the wave of terror. "Come, then. I would not delay your encounter with my countrymen. Your own reckoning awaits." He cast one eye towards the grey-sailed ship, and tried not to think of Grace.

At Don Alanzo's nod, Barrett and Stanbury lifted Will onto the rail, and then steadied the rope trailing from his back. On the other side of the deck, four sailors prepared to drag him under.

"And so the debt to my father is paid," Don Alanzo began. "This day—"

"Do not torture me with prattle." Will flashed Don Alanzo a defiant grin, and leapt from the rail. He took pleasure in Barrett's angry cry as the rope burned through his hands, and then he hit the water. The cold shocked the last of the wool from his head. His lungful of air would not last long. The two teams of sailors both now had the rope taut, dragging him directly beneath the ship where he was held tight against the barnacle-encrusted hull.

The air burned in his lungs, and however much he tried, he could not escape the haunting sense-memories of his torture in Edinburgh.

With a tremendous effort, he ignored the panic pricking his thoughts, the flashes of what would happen the moment he exhausted his breath, the water rushing into his lungs, the feeling of being trapped. By will alone, he calmed himself.

Pressing his right arm against the keel, he released the trigger on the hidden blade in the leather forearm guard under his shirtsleeve. He prayed he would have the opportunity to thank Dee for his ingenuity.

Twisting, he rubbed his restraining rope against the blade, which quickly frayed and broke under the sharp edge. He drifted down from the keel, towards the dark depths.

His lungs burned. He could not last much longer without another breath. On deck, they would realise the rope had broken and would be watching out for him. Kicking out for the stern, he surfaced just beyond the rudder before his lungs burst, and trod water. They would not be able to see him from above, but one of the other ships might spy him if he waited too long. From above came the calls of his enemies as they hung over the rails searching the water.

With difficulty, he rubbed the bonds at his wrists along the edge of the rudder, and after several attempts, the wet ropes loosened until he was able to wriggle his hands free.

Gulping air, he continued underwater beneath the next ship. The rest of the fleet was visible all around, but they would be too distracted preparing for the battle to see him in the water. After a brief rest, he carried on, surfacing for air at every ship, until he reached open water.

He was free, but adrift in the middle of the English Channel. How long could he survive before exhaustion dragged him down to his death?

CHAPTER 50

"God's teeth, the Spanish are slow-witted rabbit-suckers." On the forecastle of the *Revenge*, Drake watched the Armada in the first light of dawn through his tele-scope. "We are at war. Did they expect us to sit back and wait for them to attack?"

"What could have distracted them?" Carpenter mused.

"Ha!" Drake laughed. "Their topmen have finally seen us. Now there will be a commotion aboard their ships, and Medina Sidonia's prayers will amount to naught!"

Closing his tele-scope with a snap, Drake set about ordering his men to prepare for battle, boosting their spirits with loud bragging and comical contempt for their enemy.

If Carpenter had doubted whether Drake's skills matched his arrogance, he was convinced now. During the night, Drake, Howard, and the other commanders had left five ships floating in easy sight of the Armada. It had fooled the Spanish into thinking the entire fleet was steady, while eighty ships were taken upwind to claim the weather gage. The English now had the advantage.

Launceston waited calmly by the rail, as though the horrors of the previous day had never happened. But at times Carpenter saw the earl's eyes flicker towards him; a bond had been forged, however much Carpenter was repulsed by it. If Drake guessed what had happened, he showed no sign of it; the word had gone out that the cabin boy must have fallen overboard during the dark sail from Plymouth harbour.

"If they had had Drake's tele-scope they may have got an early warning in the grey light," Launceston mused. "We should give thanks that Walsingham and Dee see a greater picture than you or I."

"I will give thanks if we survive this damnable thing," Carpenter growled. "I am not meant to feel the world rolling beneath my feet. Dry land for me, and soon!"

"Look. It begins." Launceston indicated a squadron of eleven English ships streaming west and then tacking between the Armada and the Eddystone Rocks at a speed that must have startled the slow-moving galleons.

"Our race-built galleons," Launceston noted approvingly. "None faster."

"Stop speaking some foreign language," Carpenter snapped. "Race-built? Is this some salty-haired sailor's argot?"

Launceston allowed himself a faint smile.

A signal flag went up on the mizzenmast of the lead ship, and instantly barking orders rolled out across the waves as the gun ports snapped open. The cannon on each ship in turn blasted the Spanish before the squadron raced back to the fleet, untouched.

At that moment, Carpenter and Launceston both noticed a curious sight and leaned across the rail to get a better look. Against the wind and the currents, a grey-sailed ship was limping away from the fleet, its starboard side blackened by fire. It was soon lost behind a wall of vessels, and before Launceston and Carpenter could question what they had seen, the Armada responded to the attack.

As Medina Sidonia fired his signal gun, the Spanish ships sailed into their prearranged battle order: a crescent, with a short spike in the centre, stretching several miles across. To an uneducated eye, the floating city looked imposing, a mass of white sails painted with the red cross of the Crusades, the water barely visible between them.

But Launceston waved a lazy hand towards the mass and said, "See—they create an illusion. The warships are all on the outside of the formation, but inside . . . useless hulks, transport ships . . . Their number is much less than it appears."

"Nevertheless," Carpenter said, "a single piece of shot will take me apart."

The *Disdain*, Lord Howard's personal pinnace, sailed out to fire one shot at the Spanish: a challenge; and in response Medina Sidonia raised the Spanish royal standard ordering his fleet to battle.

"Is Swyfte out there, somewhere, aboard one of those enemy ships, I wonder?" Carpenter said as he watched the dense fleet begin to attack. "What irony to be blown to pieces by your own countrymen after risking so much." He struggled with his conflicted emotions and then said, "Let us go below deck. It will be safer there, until we are needed."

"Are you sure?" Launceston asked with an odd tone.

Flushed, his eyes blazing, Drake was consumed by the moment. As the *Revenge* raced towards the fray, it seemed to Carpenter that the fleet's vice admiral was overcome by a religious fervour.

On the gun deck, the master gunner watched tensely as the vessel clipped across the swell into position. His hand held high, he waited, and then released it with a bellow. Carpenter was not prepared for the shock of the devastating noise as the gunfire rolled in continuous thunder from the bow chasers, to the broadside cannon, to the stern chasers, and finally to the windward guns, flash after flash of red flame, acrid black smoke rolling out of the gun ports. He staggered back, clutching his ears at the pain of the volume.

From outside the stifling world of smoke and fire came the shriek of the shot tearing through the air, and the splash where it fell short or the thunderous boom and crack of disintegrating wood where it met its target. There were screams, too, louder and more shocking than the destructive boom of the cannon fire.

As each cannon fired, it was hauled back in and prepared for the next shot. With all the ships in the fleet, the noise never stopped. On the gun deck, it seemed to Carpenter that there was mad confusion as men ran back and forth with shot, stoking powder, cursing as they burned themselves on red-hot metal, diving out of the way of the recoil.

"This is hell . . ." Carpenter choked, motioning for Launceston to follow him out.

In the open air, his ears still rang and he wondered if he would be permanently deaf. Staggering to the rail, he saw the Spanish return fire, but their response was leaden and they released only one shot for every three that came from English ships.

Launceston indicated movement among some of the ships. "They are fleeing downwind," he said. As some of the ships broke rank, they caused confusion among the others, crowding them as they tried to continue their attack.

Drake saw his moment and sent the *Revenge* to attack the wing where the squadron's flagship was unsupported. Drake was joined by another ship, the *Triumph*. "Frobisher," Launceston said with an approving nod.

The Spanish flagship faced the attack alone and saw its rigging and forestay and part of the foremast disintegrate under Drake's attack. As the *San*

Martín continued to hold its ground, Drake marched by and announced loudly, "It tries to draw us in. It is a trap, but we Englishmen are too clever for that!"

"He acts as if he is taking the air along Plymouth harbour," Carpenter bellowed above the roar of cannon fire. "Does this madness not trouble him in the slightest?"

Leaning on the rail, Launceston studied the bodies floating in the water, some so blackened and torn they could barely be identified as human. In one area, near the Spanish ships, they were so thick it seemed possible to walk across them without getting wet feet.

For the next three hours, the English taunted the Spanish, attacking then sailing out of reach of a response, before both fleets continued eastwards. The slow speed of the Armada, barely more than that of a rowboat, was a source of amazement to Carpenter, until Launceston pointed out that the fleet had to move at the speed of the slowest ship to keep the formation intact.

Beside them, observing through his tele-scope, Drake said, "They appear to be protecting a grey-sailed ship. Why is that so important they would risk the loss of so many other vessels?"

"That ship must be vital to their strategy in some way," Launceston replied.

Drake mulled over this puzzle for a moment before pacing the deck to check on his crew, but Launceston and Carpenter both remained focused on the mystery of the grey-sailed ship, and in their hearts they knew who was aboard.

"That ship may have sustained some damage," Launceston said, "but if the Spanish continue to protect it, then its threat remains. What is it they plan? And when will they strike?"

CHAPTER 51

Exhausted and cold, Will struggled to stay afloat as the world exploded in fire and thunder around him. Fragments of shattered hulls and broken masts had been his support for hours as he was caught up in the fleeing ships, but his legs had grown numb with the cold and his fingers could barely grip. Acrid smoke drifted continually across the water so it was impossible to tell the time of day, with flashes of flame seen dully here and there through the dense bank.

In that twilit place, his existence was reduced to surviving from one moment to the next. Hulls cleaved out of the smoke, the currents pulling him under, dragging him along in the wake, so he moved continually with the Armada. Sizzling English cannonballs crashed into the water all around with a hiss and a cloud of steam. Body parts washed by, white hands reaching dismally, boots and hats, sodden letters to loved ones, never to be read. How he still lived was beyond him.

After he had noticed the grey-sailed ship limping away, his concern for Grace had kept him going in the maelstrom that began the moment the battle started. The shore was tantalisingly close—sometimes he even thought he could see the people of Devon lined along the cliffs watching the battle— but every time he struck out the ferocity of the fight drove him back. And so he had been sucked into the churning heart of the conflict.

Nearby the *Revenge* and the *Triumph* attacked the stricken flagship of the Spanish squadron on the Armada's wing. Through the heavy smoke generated by the English guns, a carrack swept towards Will en route to aid the flagship. For a second, he remained frozen by the familiar outline: it was the *Rosario*, bearing down on him like death.

With drained limbs, he searched for the reserves of energy to swim out of its path, but at the last he faltered and the ship struck him a glancing blow. Dazed, he went down, swallowing water, and for a moment he was back in Edinburgh, dying slowly.

As the dark reached up for him, he finally found enough strength to strike out for the surface. Gulping air, he clawed onto some flotsam, his head still dull and drifting from the blow. The thunder of the gunfire receded, became muffled, disappeared, and there was only the sound of his ragged breathing and the blood in his head. Half-seen images faded in and out of the smoke.

The confusion of Drake's attack, Spanish ships careering recklessly. The *Rosario* colliding with another ship, shattering her crossyard and spritsail, the carrack losing all control and slamming against another, destroying her bowsprit, halyards, and forecourse.

Nearby, a tremendous explosion blasted Will from his stupor. On the *San Salvador*, a ship Will had helped reprovision, the stern powder store had exploded upwards through the poop deck and the two decks of the sterncastle. Amid the plume of smoke, timbers were driven up to the mast-tops before cascading down on the closest ships. Will dived down as the wreckage rained all around, streaming trails of white bubbles plunging within inches of him where the timber fell.

Surfacing with a gasp, he saw bodies raining down too, limbless, blackened. In the background, the *San Salvador* blazed like the sun, thick black smoke turning the day into night. Men on fire dived into the sea; others chose drowning over the conflagration. At least two hundred were lost, Will estimated.

In the middle of the confusion, a sudden squall hit the flailing *Rosario*. As her foremast shattered, men with axes ran to cut it loose from the rigging, but it was too late: the carrack was crippled.

In the chaos of the listing vessel, men plunged overboard, fighting to stay afloat amid the bodies and the burning wreckage. Clinging on to his pathetic pieces of timber to stay afloat in the tossing sea, Will watched many drown.

One sailor struck out strongly for a section of broken crossyard. Another reached it first, but as he struggled to climb across it, the other dragged him off and held him under until he drowned. The act of brutality came as naturally to the survivor as breathing, and as he turned his head, Will saw the heavy-lidded, lizard expression of Barrett. Shock flared briefly when he recognised Will, but then a sly glance told Will all he needed to know as the swell brought them towards each other.

With the flames burning all around and the black smoke heavy on the water, there was only the two of them, locked on a course of destruction. Grinning, Barrett drew his knife.

In a surge of grey-green water, they clashed like the waves breaking against the Eddystone Rocks. Barrett stabbed wildly. His strength ebbing, Will avoided the first blow and caught Barrett's wrist at the second. In their struggle, they were dragged off their respective supports and splashed into the rough water. They went down quickly as they wrestled for advantage.

Cheeks and eyes bulging, Barrett's face was a mask of fury, but the water impeded his attempts to stab, and instead he tried to grip Will's throat. The water grew black around them, the shimmering grey light far above.

Back and forth they rolled, ineffectually, sinking ever deeper, until Will's lungs burned and he knew his last moments were upon him. A deep clarity descended. He thought of Grace, of Jenny, and knew he could not die there.

Pressing his forearm against Barrett's throat, he triggered the hidden blade. Blood gouted out in a black cloud. In a frenzy, Barrett gulped mouthfuls of seawater. The last thing Will saw as he struck out for the surface was Barrett's eyes rolling up white as he sank down into the depths.

On the surface, Will filled his lungs and found the crossyard that Barrett had abandoned. His fingers slipped on the wet wood and he could only hold on weakly. All around, the gunfire gradually dimmed as the battle came to an end for the day, and he knew he would have to seize the chance to escape the madness or he would not survive the night.

On every side, the sea was thick with bodies and wreckage. Will eyed the carnage and death for a moment, and then with resignation dragged the nearest corpse towards him. Once he had fished some of the rigging out of the water, he drew another corpse and bound the two together. Looping the rope around, he caught three more corpses and fastened them tightly with the last of his strength. Once the makeshift raft was complete, he crawled on top of the cold bodies and, with one arm trailing in the water, paddled slowly away from the burning ship.

The urge to close his eyes and sleep was powerful. Half aware, he realised Medina Sidonia had given the signal to leave the *Rosario*, and the Armada sailed on, leaving Will's former shipmates lost to despair that they had been abandoned so easily. Will knew why: compared to the grey-sailed ship, the rest of the fleet was dispensable. It was a harsh message to broadcast to the Spanish ships, and would be bad for morale. It also revealed how effectively the Unseelie Court had mesmerised the Spanish commanders: the Enemy was more valuable than the thousands of human beings under Medina Sidonia's command.

On the heaving seas, the Armada eventually faded from Will's view. As the smoke gradually dispersed, he slipped in and out of consciousness, and eventually realised night had fallen.

Overhead, a crescent moon shone brightly. It took him a while to realise ships were once again all around him, just silhouettes against the night sky. They were under battle conditions—no light shining. In the gloom, he could just make out the pennants festooning the vessels and the Cross of Saint George, dark against the white background.

Home, he thought weakly.

Hailing the ships, his voice was frail at first, but eventually found its strength. He was answered by a booming cry, and when he responded in English and identified himself, there was rapid activity on deck.

That was all he remembered.

For a time he swam through darkness to an island where grey figures slowly drew towards him. They whispered terrible things that filled him with dread, but on awakening he could recall none of the words, only the sickening way it made him feel.

"Ho! You have slept the sleep of the dead! Or the just! One or the other, I cannot recall." The booming voice filled the cabin the moment Will's eyes flickered open.

His wild hair and beard a fiery red, Captain John Courtenay strode around the cabin, passionate and intense. Will sensed he was the least thing on the captain's mind.

"I am on the *Tempest?*"

"For two days now."

"Two?" Will replied incredulously.

"You were plucked from the water by the *Triumph* aboard a merry raft you had constructed, and Frobisher delivered you here."

"Then, it is . . . August second?" Will struggled to rise.

Courtenay eyed him askance and said, "It might do well to rest longer after your ordeal."

"There is no time to rest. I have much to tell, and there is much we must do. The Enemy plots—"

"As always."

Almost falling backwards, Will steadied himself before taking a step. His legs felt like lead, his head light. "The Armada?"

"There have been victories, small perhaps, but each one adds to the pile. The capture of the *Rosario* and all the riches it contains. We drove the Spanish fleet past Torbay, and yesterday held them off from Weymouth in a fight more vehement than ever has been seen at sea. The *San Martín* itself was riddled with gunfire, the royal standard in tatters, and was only saved at the last by a line of Spanish galleons."

Breathing deeply, Will staggered to the door, acutely feeling every ache and pain. "And today?"

"Today is Wednesday." Courtenay clapped his hands loudly. "Today is the defence of the Isle of Wight and the Solent."

"You are in the vanguard of the attack?"

"My orders were to stay away from engagements, unless our firepower was desperately needed. We have greater business than a few Spanish bastards. The Enemy has not yet shown their colours. But you and I know they will, and then we must be ready. But first, if you are insistent upon putting your feeble limbs to the test, come and meet old friends."

Courtenay led him out of the cabin and onto the deck, bright in the morning sun. On the blue sea all around, the English fleet were becalmed amid a flourish of coloured pennants and flags, while across the Isle of Wight and the Hampshire coast trails of black smoke drifted high, beacons summoning the militia to the defence of the nation. Watching the activity at the foremast were Launceston and Carpenter.

Trying to disguise the weariness in his face, Will left Courtenay and lurched over. Carpenter scowled when he saw Will, looked away, and then marched over to meet him. Will was surprised when Carpenter shook his hand, although his expression showed no warmth.

"We will never be friends, but I understand you more," Carpenter said. "I am glad you survived the perils of the damned Spanish. Hiding out among our bitter enemy is the kind of bravado that will carve your name into history."

Will was puzzled by what might have led to this change in attitude, but did not question it. "I would thank Medina Sidonia personally for his hospitality some time."

They joined Launceston, who nodded in his usual aloof manner as if it had only been an hour since he saw Will last. "This weather ensures there will be little more fighting this day. We drift slowly eastwards." With a faint air of disappointment, he added, "It is quieter here. On the *Revenge*, there was action aplenty. And death too."

"Why did you return to the *Tempest*, then?" Will asked.

"Courtenay may be mad, but he is a haven of sanity after the *Revenge*," Carpenter growled. "Any more of Drake's bragging and I would be heading for Bedlam, and lock the door myself."

"Then the fighting begins again tomorrow." Will looked towards the eastern horizon. "But our task is harder even than that faced by Howard's brave band. Somewhere in that sprawling fleet lies a grey-sailed ship, which purports to be the architect of all our misery. The Enemy will be working hard to repair the damage I wrought, and soon it will be brought into play. The Spanish seek to hold out until it is ready, for they know it could mean victory for them and destruction for England. We must prepare ourselves, for this business is only going to get more dangerous."

CHAPTER 52

In a red glare, the last of the setting sun illuminated the forest of masts of the Spanish ships at anchor just off Calais, tightly packed into their defensive crescent formation. In the middle of that mass, there was no chance of Will identifying the grey-sailed ship, even with its distinctive outline, but he studied them with Drake's tele-scope nonetheless.

"Why do you fear this ship so?" Drake asked. "It is only more Spanish rabble, yes?"

"No. These allies of Spain have Dee's wit and cunning, and the information I have gathered suggests they hold a great weapon."

"Great enough to threaten us?" Drake said with gently mocking disbelief. "Time and again our tactics have shown the Spanish up to be the children they are. We drove them away from the English coastline and their last chance for a bridgehead or a haven, where they could replenish their diminishing supplies of food, water, and munitions. Pursued them across the Channel, where they were at the mercy of the open seas, and now they wait for Parma's aid. If they had a great weapon, surely they would have used it by now."

Will was not convinced. The Unseelie Court was expert at misdirection and subtle manipulation, and when they seemed least of a threat was when they were at their most dangerous. With the plans Howard, Drake, and the other commanders of the English fleet had concocted for that night, he expected the sleeping beast to be woken.

"And if we do see that ship, it will be blown out of the water by good English cannon." Drake sniffed as he reclaimed the prized tele-scope that had been such an aid in marshalling his strategy over the last week.

Will showed no reaction, but his dilemma consumed him. Drake's suggestion was the correct one, but how could he stand by and watch Grace die, even if it meant victory? Ever since she had been taken, he had swung between the old Will, who had existed in study and good humour before the

Unseelie Court had entered his life, who would put the survival of his friends above any abstract notion of loyalty to country; and the man he had become, corrupted by a world where there appeared to be no right or wrong, only survival in the face of unspeakable threats, and where terrible things had to be done for good ends.

It was Sunday, August 7. The *Revenge* was at anchor at the head of a fleet that appeared to be sleeping. At the rear, the *Tempest* was ready to be called into battle if the Unseelie Court showed its hand, but Will, Carpenter, and Launceston needed to be in the forefront for what they expected to be a decisive night.

The English fleet was upwind of the Armada, with the floodtide in their favour. It was a strong position, but a little further along the coast in Dunkirk, Parma had gathered his invasion force, ready to join the Armada in barges sent from ports along the Flemish coast. No one on the English side knew the level of preparedness of Parma's army, nor their numbers, but it was clear they had been in regular contact with Medina Sidonia. Everything might have been different if Will had not killed Hawksworth, but that matter had passed and they had to deal with the situation before them.

All was not yet lost. Dunkirk was blockaded by Justin of Nassau and his ragged but fierce Dutch Sea Beggars, but that would crumble if Medina Sidonia sent ships to drive the Dutch away. If the Spanish broke through the English fleet with Parma's army, England was only a few miles away. There were so many vagaries, and everything was crucial; and the Unseelie Court had yet to show its hand.

Drake turned his face to the last of the sun, and for the first time Will saw none of the braggart and only the devout man who was prepared to sacrifice everything for his God and his country. "I must lead the men in prayer," he said, "and impose upon them what is at stake for their families and their country if we fail this night."

After Drake had departed, Will joined Carpenter and Launceston. They were both introspective as they prepared themselves for the night ahead, although Will noticed a strange fire in Launceston's eyes. Without conversation they toured the ship, watching the stern-faced men working silently and pensively at their stations, stacking the shot and the powder on the gun deck, preparing the water to dampen any fires on board, eyeing the rigging and the sails on the main deck ready for the order to sail. In the infirmary, the ship's surgeon had his tools already laid out.

And then it was only a matter of waiting for the tide to turn.

From the rail, Carpenter studied the eight ships that had been selected. "I do not know which is the worst death," he mused. "Frozen in the forests of Muscovy, or burned alive in an inferno. But there is one common factor in both." He eyed Will.

"You say I am some pariah, leading you to mishap?" Will replied wryly.

"I say nothing. But if you see a connection, perhaps there is some truth in it."

"Fire or ice, heaven or hell, we are always caught between two sides, John. The only debate that concerns me is wine or beer, and we can decide that in the Bull when we are safely back in London."

"Fair comment." Carpenter shook Will and Launceston's hands in turn. "For England, for the queen."

He left quickly, but Will thought he saw a surprising glimmer of the Carpenter he had known before their experiences in Muscovy. Will envied the peace Carpenter appeared to have found.

They were each transported to one of the three central ships in the formation of eight where they watched the tide turn and waited for midnight. By the time the moon glimmered silver on the water, the ships were pulling at their anchors in the strengthening tide. The creak of timbers drowned out any noise the few crew members made as they completed their final preparations.

When midnight came, Will glanced to his left to Carpenter and to his right to Launceston and gave the nod. Across the eight vessels came the dull thud of the crew chopping the cables that held them fast, and within seconds the ships were caught in the tide and moving downwind towards the Armada in complete silence.

Relieved that the waiting was over, Will moved quickly around the deck where clutches of men waited with flints. Their apprehensive eyes flickered towards him. Acknowledging their bravery, he nodded to each in turn and then checked on the helmsman, who had set the course for the heart of the Armada and was busy lashing the helm in place. In the holds, more men waited, cupping their hands around smouldering match. Here the smell was almost too much to bear—pitch, brimstone, gunpowder, and tar—and the men coughed and covered their faces with scarves.

"On my mark," Will said loudly, counting the steady beat in his head, as he knew Carpenter and Launceston would be too. The ship built speed, the waves crashing loudly against the hull. Eyes white in the gloom, the men all turned their faces towards him as he raised his hand.

"Now!"

Along the hold, match plunged into pitch and flints were struck. Sparks glowed like stars, flames flickered, caught, surged into life, and after a moment smoke quickly began to fill the dark space. Will waited until the last man had dashed to the steps and then followed onto the deck where tiny pockets of fire were already whipping up in the night wind.

Their faces lit orange, the men waited anxiously against the rail.

"Well done! Heroes all!" Will called. "Your work here is over!"

Relieved, some of the men leapt directly into the sea as the flames surged at their backs, while others swung on ropes to the escape skiffs towed alongside.

Will turned to see an amazing sight: castles of fire growing larger on either side as each of the eight ships sprang alight, all at full sail. Red and gold danced across the black water, and the ruddy halo surrounding every ship made it impossible to see what was happening away in the dark. Deafened by the roar of the fire rushing along the boat from stern to prow and licking up the rigging towards the sailcloth, Will barely heard the cries of alarm from the Spanish lookouts. Heat roasted his back and neck, but still he was determined to wait until the last, scanning the waters ahead.

As expected, pinnaces moved out from the Armada at speed towards the flanks. Hurling grapnels, the Spanish sailors struggled to overcome the flames. Will knew they would be gripped with fear that the ships were packed with gunpowder and stone like the "Hellburners" used at Antwerp three years earlier, but the English did not have the resources to duplicate that feat.

As they fought to steer the two outer ships towards the beach, Will saw Carpenter and Launceston both dive into the water, satisfied that the main body of the fire ships would reach the Spanish fleet. But just as he was about to follow, another pinnace sailed rapidly towards the fire ship alongside his own and held station between the two English ships. On board, the Spanish sailors parted to make way for a man cloaked and hooded as protection against the fire. Clutching a bag against his chest, he swung onto the grapnel rope now strung between the two vessels and began to make his way towards the burning ship.

Intrigued by the sailor's clear insanity and puzzled by what he could possibly be intending, Will steadied himself with one foot on the rail and watched.

The sailor crossed the gulf between the two ships rapidly, but as he landed on the burning deck, his hood fell away and Will saw it was Don Alanzo.

On the brink of throwing himself into the water, Will paused, realising that here was unforeseen danger. Don Alanzo would not risk his life without reason. From his bag, he pulled an object Will instantly recognised it: the shimmering globe from the cabin of the grey-sailed ship, though at that moment it remained dull and lifeless.

Will didn't wait to see what Don Alanzo was attempting as he hunched over the globe amid the raging fires. Plucking a grapnel that one of his men had used to lower himself into a skiff, Will hurled it across the water where it caught in the Spanish pinnace's sail. Without a second thought, he swung across the gulf.

Relieved to feel the cool night wind after the blazing heat of the fire ship, he heard the rip of the sail before he landed heavily on the pinnace deck. The four Spanish sailors were taken by surprise. Will had thrown two overboard before the remaining two rounded on him. He drew his sword, but rather than face him, the frightened sailors both chose to abandon ship.

Reclaiming the grapnel, Will made it catch on the fire ship's rail. As he swung out against the hull and began to climb, he had the strangest sensation that the vessel was starting to slow. Glancing back, he saw it was true. The pinnace and all the other fire ships were now slightly ahead.

The heat was like a furnace as he pulled himself over the rail and onto the deck. A sheet of flame roared up the rigging and ignited the main topsail and the main course sail. Ribbons of burning sailcloth fell to the deck all around so that it appeared to be snowing fire. Pitch blazed across the deck in channels to the quarterdeck where flames licked out of the door to the officers' quarters.

Don Alanzo had pulled his hood back up to protect him against the heat, and Will saw now that his cloak had been soaked in seawater. Acutely aware he had no such protection, Will drew his sword and advanced quickly.

The Spanish spy was hunched over the globe, which now emitted the slow-pulsing white light. As he caught sight of movement from the corner of his eye, he drew his own sword in a flash. When he saw it was Will, his shock quickly gave way to malice.

"Are you charmed? What does it take to stop your foul heart beating?" he snarled.

"More than you have at your disposal."

The ship came to a juddering halt, almost throwing Will from his feet. Don Alanzo laughed at Will's puzzlement, and then nodded slowly as Will's eyes fell upon the globe, now pulsing with even greater intensity. Slowly but steadily, the fire ship began to move backwards, towards the English fleet.

"And so the world turns on its head, and what was a threat to us now becomes a spear driven into the heart of our hated enemy. With allies like ours, nothing can ever be as it seems," Don Alanzo mocked.

"Yes, you think you are on the road to heaven when you are sliding down to the pits of hell."

Will lunged with his sword, but Don Alanzo parried easily. The ship gathered speed as it moved towards the English fleet. Wind drove sheets of flames at Will and his opponent. It was a nightmarish arena even for two such master swordsmen. The raging heat seared Will's face and hands, and brought stinging tears to his eyes that blurred his vision as he attempted to attack. With his left arm thrown across his face to shield him from the heat, Don Alanzo was pushed off balance, each thrust a fraction awry.

Ducking and thrusting, Will tried to get close to the glowing globe, but Don Alanzo continually maneuvered himself in the space between. Whatever the nature of the object, Will could see it was no longer operating as it had in the cabin. Neither he nor Don Alanzo was affected by the globe; its power was seemingly directed into the ship itself, forcing it ever backwards.

The intense heat sapped Will's energy. Blazing chunks of wood falling from the yardarm and flames racing across the deck from the burning pitch left him little room to maneuver.

A wall of flame now enclosed them. Even if the English ships had their lanterns alight, Will would not have been able to see them. If the fire ship crashed into the fleet, all would be lost. The ships were so tightly packed that the fire would spread rapidly from one to another.

Thick smoke snaked around both of them. The air was now so hot it burned his throat and lungs every time he inhaled, and the fumes from the brimstone made his head spin.

Bounding back and forth among the flames, he and Don Alanzo performed an intricate ballet. Despite the conflagration drawing closer by the second, he could see in the Don's fierce eyes that he would not desert his post. His hatred for Will's slaying of his father burned as brightly as the fires, and

Will was convinced his opponent was prepared to go to his death as long as he took Will with him.

The fire forced them into closer combat, making every sword-stroke even more difficult to direct. Will's blade tore through Don Alanzo's steaming cloak. The Don's missed Will's cheek by a hairbreadth. But whatever thrusts and feints he executed, Will could get no closer to the globe.

Smoke rose from where their clothes were singed by the fire, and their skin reddened, and their breath shortened, but still they fought on.

Will had a sudden shocking vision that he was in hell, that his entire life had prepared him for that moment, and that fire would be all he saw forevermore.

And then the air was torn by a resounding crack that sounded like the ship itself was splitting in two. The main mast cracked near the base, falling towards them in a cascade of flaming sail, rigging, and yards. Throwing himself sideways, Don Alanzo slammed hard on the smoking deck.

As the mast rushed towards him, Will propelled himself beneath the falling fire. His boot crashed hard against the globe and it shattered in an explosion of light with a sound like a child's cry. Will continued his motion in a tumble that took him mere inches away from the mast's thunderous impact. Flames soared up with a whoosh and the deck crumbled beneath it. Kicking out, Will launched himself towards the rail as the boards fell away beneath him.

Behind there were only flames. Don Alanzo had either been consumed by the fire or fallen into the gaping, blazing hold.

Will's clothes were alight, flames licking up his back. Placing one foot on the rail, he dove. A trail of fire followed him into the black water.

After the tremendous heat, the cold water was a shock. Striking back to the surface, he saw the fire ship now headed back towards the Armada where the other fire ships were already causing chaos among the Spanish fleet. Upwind, the signal cannon set the English ships in motion.

The battle had begun.

CHAPTER 53

A drift in the high swell of the night tide, Will struck out towards the distant cliffs of Calais, but the sea was too strong. The blazing beacons of the fire ships cast a ruddy glare across the water, and for a while he thought it was the last sight he would see.

"Swyfte! Swyfte!"

His name was barked over the surging waves and the wind, but whoever called was hidden by the rolling swell.

"Here!" he yelled back.

A moment later a skiff crested the swell. Carpenter leaned over the prow, searching the water, Launceston and another seaman rowing behind. Carpenter hollered when he caught sight of Will, and they quickly fished him from the sea.

"We saw you dive from the fire ship," Carpenter said. "You prevented it from sailing into our fleet."

Shaking the saltwater from his hair, Will observed, "You came back for me, John."

He waited for Carpenter to claim the moral high ground, but he wouldn't meet Will's eyes and only said acidly, "Could we leave England's greatest hero to drown?"

"You have my thanks, John, and you, Robert." He glanced towards the soaring flames. "Together we led the start of the battle here, but there is much more to do. Let us head back to the *Tempest*, for I suspect those grey sails will soon hove into view."

A series of tremendous explosions tore through the night. Near the Armada, the cannon aboard one of the fire ships had exploded, blasting hot metal and burning wood into the scattering pinnaces and small boats. Columns of fire rose from the water, reminding Will of the Templar chamber in Edinburgh.

The fires of heaven and hell.

One by one the fire ships' guns exploded, raining burning fragments on the Armada's front line. Confusion was already rife among the Spanish fleet as ships raced haphazardly to escape the coming inferno, with most breaking free of the constrictions of the bay for open sea. There were collisions, torn rigging, shattered yards as the panic escalated. Many commanders ordered the mooring cables to be severed by the crew so they could sail away rapidly without anchor, a desperate act that would hamper them regaining any stable position. The defensive crescent formation fragmented across its entire length.

"Damn them!" Carpenter raged. "The Spanish have the luck of the Devil."

Vessels avoided the path of the fire ships by ten feet here, a foot there, but none of the Spanish fleet caught alight. Still blazing thirty feet into the air, the remnants of the fire ships came to rest in succession on the shore.

Will shrugged. "A bonfire of Philip's ambitions would have been a good sight, but the confusion itself is enough. We have increased our advantage."

They sculled the skiff back to the English fleet where they could hear the jubilation rising up from every deck. After the protracted fight along the channel, they had finally destroyed the Armada's formation. The ships were scattered to the four winds.

On board the *Tempest*, Courtenay roamed the deck, singing his bawdy shanties at the top of his voice. As the men cheered, and as Launceston looked faintly baffled by the attention and Carpenter embarrassed, Will leapt onto the rail and grabbed the rigging for support.

"This night we have struck a blow against the forces that wish to stop every Englishman living free, but it is only the start," he announced to the crew. "A battle like no other awaits us, and we must not rest until every Spaniard is sent fleeing back to their homeland with the fear of all hell in their hearts. No one asks you to lay down your lives. We ask only for the steel in your arms and the fire in your hearts, the courage to stand proud and fight hard for your families, for all who wait in their homes praying you will keep them safe. The flame we ignite this night will burn on through history, a beacon to all oppressed, a promise of hope to those who live in fear and shed tears of despair. For right! For England!"

The crew joined in Will's rallying cry. When he leapt to the deck, they mobbed him and slapped his back as he pushed his way through to Courtenay.

"England's greatest spy," Carpenter noted archly as he passed.

"He plays his part well," Launceston replied.

Will flashed them a grin. "We all play parts, friends. Mine just has greater purpose than most."

Courtenay stood at the forecastle watching the dying fires on the beach. Soon only embers would be left of the great ships.

"Tell your topmen to look out for grey sails," Will told him. "The ship may be hiding because repairs are still under way, or it may be biding its time to emerge with the greatest impact. We must not be blinded by the illusion of this small victory. The darkest hours lie ahead."

Will and the others snatched a few hours' sleep, and at first light they were awoken by the blare of trumpets and the boom of Howard's signal gun. Anchors broke water next to all of the hundred and fifty ships in the English feet, sails unfurled into the morning wind, and within the hour they were away in pursuit of the enemy. Word went from ship to ship that as a mark of Drake's brilliance in the campaign he would be allowed to lead the attack on the Spanish.

Medina Sidonia pursued his scattered vessels along the coast in a desperate attempt to bring his Armada back together. With a southwesterly propelling them at speed, the *Revenge* spearheaded the English squadrons in pursuit, through the Straits of Dover and into the North Sea.

Will never took his gaze from the horizon in his lookout for the grey-sailed ship, but the first ones he saw were Spanish, seven miles off Gravelines, a small port in Flanders under Spanish control. At the rear was Medina Sidonia's *San Martín*. Will knew the Spanish commander would realise he had no options. Trying to flee would doom his fleet on the sandbanks and shoals that lined the coast, the sea-marks removed by his Dutch enemies. All he could do was turn and fight.

Courtenay clapped his hands in eager anticipation. "What a day for blood!" he bellowed.

With the Spanish in such disarray, the English were not afraid to confront them at close quarters. The battle began at nine a.m. as the *Revenge* closed on the *San Martín*, and within seconds the air was thick with shot from both fleets. Even the constant sound of the sea was lost beneath the rolling thunder of guns never silenced.

Drake held his fire until he was within fifty yards of his opponent and then released the bow guns followed by the broadsides. Medina Sidonia responded in kind, the shot tearing holes in both ships.

"Sea warfare is madness," Carpenter hissed to Will. "Give me a knife in a dark room every time. Two swords at most, but definitely on land."

"Drake is not mad." Will watched the furious battle. "He has his flaws, but he is a brave man. He has thrown himself into the forefront to take the Spanish guns."

The *San Martín* came off worse. The Spanish seamen were not trained to reload the cannon rapidly, unlike their English counterparts, and as increasing amounts of damage were inflicted on the Spanish flagship, their ability to respond diminished rapidly. Chain-shot ripped through rigging and sail. The four-inch-thick planking just above the waterline shattered under Drake's heavier guns.

After his initial attack had weakened the vessel, Drake pulled away to lead his squadron in pursuit of the other Spanish warships, leaving Frobisher and the *Triumph* to continue the slow destruction of the *San Martín*.

Courtenay bellowed his orders as he strode about the deck, and the *Tempest* set off behind the *Revenge*.

Seeing their flagship in a desperate state, other Armada warships sailed to protect it, and with some luck managed to re-form their defensive crescent formation. The English fleet swept in to pound the wings relentlessly. The *Revenge* fired continuously into the dense mass of Spanish ships, almost without aiming. The barrage was so intense the smoke from the guns blocked out the sun, and the air was filled with a constant rain of exploding wood. The gunfire was so loud that every conversation had to be carried out at a bellow, but still the screams of the dying and wounded Spanish sailors rose above it. Will could see its chilling effect on all the seamen aboard the *Tempest*; though it was the enemy, the suffering left no one untouched.

The *Tempest* sailed into the thick of the battle where there was little room for maneuver, the way ahead obscured by dense smoke, the ships so closely packed in the ferocity of their combat that it was possible to see the death throes of the enemy.

In the galleasses, hundreds of slaves chained to the oars fell where they had sat for days, under fire from arquebusiers or shot from the English galleons. On one warship, the Spanish commander's head exploded in a mist of blood and bone from a piece of random shot. Another commander's hand disintegrated, a third lost his leg at the knee. Some resembled pincushions from the shards of wood rammed into their bodies after the cannon blasted apart the hardwood of their ships. They staggered back and forth across the deck, all sense lost. Blood sluiced across the boards as deeply as seawater at the height of a storm.

Carpenter was increasingly sickened by the intensity of the sea battle. "Every fight I have seen on the waves since I joined the fleet has been worse than the previous one," he said in a low tone of horror. "This is slaughter not fit for animals."

"And they would do the same to us if they had the opportunity," Will replied. "We do what we have to, to survive. There will be shouts of glory for whoever wins this day, but we here on both sides know there is none in it."

For nearly nine hours the battle raged, as the *Tempest* roamed the perimeter of the dense mass of Spanish ships searching for the true Enemy. The smoke was so thick even the topmen could not see far ahead. Launceston had been entranced by the parade of atrocities and the sickening gush of blood, but in a shift of smoke caused by the explosion of a powder store, a movement caught his eye, and he pointed beyond the immediate carnage. "There!"

Hoving into view through the drifting smoke, beyond the fire of the explosions, were grey sails.

"Captain Courtenay!" Will yelled. "The chase is on!"

Bloody John ordered the helmsman to change direction as the crew scrambled on deck. The *Tempest* shifted course in pursuit of the grey-sailed ship, already lost to the dense smoke.

The Spanish ships were too concerned with basic survival to give the *Tempest* any attention. Through the collapsing enemy formation it swept, past tightly contained dramas of death and destruction where ships fought one-sided duels.

Speeding to the forecastle, Will, Carpenter, and Launceston searched the drifting acrid clouds for another sign of their prey. Finally, they broke through to a clear stretch of sea. The grey-sailed ship raced ahead with near-supernatural speed and maneuverability. It far exceeded the capabilities of any other vessel present, yet it was still falling short of the peak performance Will had witnessed on the journey from Spain.

He could just make out that repairs were still under way on the blackened side that he had damaged with the fire. New timbers had been fitted, but there was a faint list to the vessel, like a wounded beast limping to its lair to recover. Whatever trouble he had caused, it had prevented the grey-sailed ship from following its ritual protective route among the fleet, and, perhaps, stopped it releasing whatever weapon it carried on board. He wondered how different things would have been if it had been in any state to take part in the fight off the Isle of Wight, and then near Calais.

"Your requirements, Master Swyfte?" Courtenay asked.

"First, try to contain it against the other ships, and then we shall see how it withstands a broadside or two."

"And then prepare to board?"

Will hesitated, not wanting to inflict the toxic contact with the Unseelie Court on the *Tempest*'s crew. "There is nothing worth plundering aboard that foul vessel, Captain."

"We should send it straight to the bottom," Carpenter said. "Silver Skull and all."

Will couldn't argue with him, but the thought of Grace still aboard chilled him. "We will decide on our future options as the situation unfolds, Captain," he said, not knowing what he would do if he was forced to choose.

Nodding his agreement, Courtenay called for the master gunner to prepare his men on the gun deck. The *Tempest* ploughed through the swell, but the grey-sailed ship easily remained ahead en route to the English fleet attacking the southeastern wing of the Armada formation.

"Why now?" Will mused. "They have held their cover in the most desperate circumstances and not used their weapon." The answer struck him the moment he had finished speaking. "Unless their repairs have now ensured enough speed to escape whatever carnage their weapon wreaks."

As he spoke, he glimpsed a glimmer of movement as something small and writhing passed over the grey-sailed ship's rail and fell into the sea. In the water, a shadow grew rapidly as though whatever had been dumped there was increasing in size at a phenomenal rate. Within moments a black tube of water barrelled towards them, a furrow of white surf breaking the surface.

"In the name of God, what is that?" Carpenter breathed.

An anxious cry to the helmsman echoed behind them. They turned to see Courtenay hanging over the rail to peer into the sea, his face white and strained. Leaning hard on the wheel, the helmsman began a barely perceptible shift in the *Tempest*'s course, but it was just enough to miss the projectile thrusting beneath the surface. There was a crash and a quick grind as it skimmed the edge of the keel, and a split second later the *Tempest* lurched over at an alarming angle. Everyone on deck was thrown off their feet. Catching Carpenter's sleeve, Will prevented him from going over the rail, but others were forced to clutch on for dear life.

As the wake passed, the *Tempest* righted itself with a crash that sent seawater washing across the deck.

"What is that?" Carpenter raged.

From the drawn expression on Courtenay's face, Will realised he knew the answer. As Will raced towards the captain, the truth revealed itself before his eyes. The projectile continued in a direct line from the *Tempest* towards another English ship that Will couldn't identify. Rooted by the impending collision, he watched agape as the projectile arced out of the water and over the vessel. It smashed through the foremast and dragged it into the sea on the other side. Seamen scrambled across the boards to hack at the rigging with axes before the ship could be hauled down to the depths.

"What is . . . that?" Carpenter gasped a second time.

The projectile was long, black, and sinuous, glistening like an eel, but a man's height across and as long as two galleons. When Will caught sight of the head and the needle-teeth arranged around the circular mouth, he knew it was the thing he had seen in the barrel in the cabin on the grey-sailed ship, now grown unbelievably large.

"Sea serpent." Courtenay had joined them. His gaze never left the white wake tearing into the thick smoke. "I have encountered their kind before, out in the stormy Atlantic returning from the New World. The damnable beast almost took me, and the entire ship, down to the bottom. Nothing can stop them. They tear ships into matchwood and consume every good man as they swim through the drink."

"This is the Enemy's weapon," Will said, "stalking silently beneath the waves to destroy the fleet."

From deep in the smoke, they heard another crash of splintering wood, followed by cries that rose above the thunderous guns.

"Engrossed in the noise and fury of battle, no one will know it is there until too late," Carpenter said. "This will turn the tide of the battle."

"Then we must stop it," Will said.

"How?" Carpenter said. "What weapons have we that could strike dead a thing like that? Even if we could catch it. Musket and arquebus fire is too small. The big guns would never land a shot 'pon it at the speed it moves."

Will quickly turned over the options and then said, "I have a notion. Leave that to me." To Courtenay he said, "Your job is to get us close enough to attack the beast."

"Close enough is too close," Courtenay replied. "But no man ever gained glory with faint heart. Ambition and risk go hand in hand."

Will searched the sea for the grey-sailed ship, but it had already disappeared into the smoke. Launceston read his mind. "If we lose the Enemy ship, misery may lie ahead. They still have the Silver Skull."

"If the serpent destroys our fleet, the Spanish will regroup, collect Parma's army, and England will fall. Come, we have our course. Let's to it."

As the *Tempest* sailed through the smoke, they encountered the remnants of a galleon slowly taking on water. The hull was torn in two, shattered masts trailing in the water like oars. Seamen clung to the wreckage. Several were dead, chunks of them torn away.

Amid the boom of gunfire, the sound of cracking wood emerged from the smoke to reveal the location of the sea serpent. It had settled on the fringes of the Armada's southeasterly wing where several English ships attacked. More wreckage, another damaged ship that had lost its rudder and drifted directionlessly.

Finally they emerged from the smoke. The serpent's wake was clear on the swell, a large V flecked with foam near the point. As it prepared to attack another ship, its head broke the water. The circular mouth flexed. Yards from the ship it submerged and then erupted from the sea in a cascade of white foam, crashing through the ship's rigging and bringing down the mainmast as the terrified crew fled the deck. Splashing into the swell on the far side, the wake continued forwards before beginning a wide turn for another attack.

"Is it . . . growing larger?" Carpenter asked. "Soon it will be able to ensnare an entire ship in its coils."

"Draw its attention!" Will shouted to Courtenay. "We must deflect its attack!"

Courtenay ordered the helmsman to continue the course that would put the *Tempest* between the serpent and the damaged ship. The northwesterly filled the sails and sped them on.

"You are sure this is the correct course?" Launceston asked in a blithe manner that hid the doubt he obviously felt. The same emotion was clear in the faces of the seamen who flashed unsettled glances Will's way.

"I thought you would thank me for easing the boredom of a sea journey," Will replied.

The preparations he had ordered were hastily brought together and delivered to the deck, but were not yet ready for use.

"Brace yourselves!" Courtenay barked.

Gripping the rail and the rigging, the crew steadied themselves as the *Tempest* plunged into the serpent's path. At the last, it submerged, but the wake threw the ship's prow towards the sky, the stern almost plunging beneath the waves.

Muscles straining, Will held tight. A sailor with a pox-marked face lost his hold on the rail and flew backwards with a cry. He missed Will by an inch and slammed into the cabin door with bone-breaking force.

For a second, it felt as if the ship was going over. Silence gripped all those who clung on, eyes screwed shut as they waited for the momentum to continue. But then the ship crashed back, swamping them with water.

"This is the sturdiest ship in the fleet, but we cannot maintain this punishment," Courtenay yelled.

"Then pray we do not have to," Will replied. He eyed the seamen working on the preparation and received a curt nod in return. "Get us near to the beast. We must draw it out of the water to attack us."

"Now we are all to be sacrificed to your mad scheme?" Carpenter asked.

"All schemes are mad until they succeed, John. Think of the stories you will be able to tell once we are back in Bankside."

Carpenter's derisive snort followed him as he ran for the rail. With Courtenay's bellowed directions from the forecastle, the helmsman's maneuvers kept the serpent within view. Predicting its movements in relation to the most vulnerable ships on the fringe of the attack, they tracked the beast. Each time they tried to divert it, the encounter brought them close to sinking. Will could see the crew growing increasingly rebellious.

Finally, the wake turned towards them. "There, we have it," Will muttered. He ordered his team to ready themselves.

Expressions fixed and grim, the eyes of everyone on board turned towards the furrow in the water driving towards them. No one moved, not a word was uttered.

Seconds before the serpent broke the surface, Will yelled, "Now!"

A flint was struck and the barrel of pitch and brimstone ignited. As the beast erupted from the water, his men flung the burning barrel directly into the creature's mouth. An explosion of flame showered the serpent with the sticky, blazing liquid, driving it into wild convulsions. The lashing tail slammed against the *Tempest*'s hull, but somehow no serious damage was done. The ship tipped one way, crashed back down, continued on, the crew rooted by the fear of what would transpire next.

But as they all moved to the rail, they saw the creature's thrashing begin to slow, and eventually it grew still and hung dead in the water amid a smell like burned leather. The crew cheered, but Will quickly silenced them.

"Celebrate our victory, by all means, but this is no time to rest. We must return to the hunt for the grey-sailed ship!"

Emboldened by the serpent's death, the crew returned to their posts with gusto. The helmsman guided the *Tempest* back towards the fray, but they could all see that as the evening drew on, the worst was over.

The Spanish continued to fight, even though the English assault had whittled away their capabilities, their ships, and their men. Even with their guns silenced, some sailed bravely to try to aid their fellows that were in more immediate danger. All around them the water was no longer visible amid the wreckage, the bodies, and the frothing crimson blood.

Even the weather began to support the English. The northwesterly drove their ships on and pinned the Spanish back. Their defensive formation had collapsed, their ammunition mostly spent with only arquebus and musket fire being returned. Some of their ships were reduced to floating piles of timber that barely echoed their former shape. Many crewmen abandoned ship and attempted to escape in small boats.

"We have won," Carpenter said with clear relief. "Now it is just a matter of clearing up the dregs."

"We will never win until the Unseelie Court is destroyed," Will replied. Searching the dying embers of the battle for any sign of grey sails, Will's thoughts turned once more to Grace: what would the Enemy do with her now the Spanish had been defeated? Would they simply spirit her away, never to be seen again?

Like Jenny.

Launceston, whose attention rarely left the carnage like a hungry man at a feast, indicated a pattern of shifting lights visible through the pall of smoke. Will instantly recognised the colours he had seen over the grey-sailed ship. As he turned to search for the outcome, the *Tempest* was buffeted by a strong wind. Black clouds churned in the southwest, rushing towards them.

"What—?" Carpenter began.

"Unnatural," Will replied, turning to Courtenay, but the captain had already seen the approaching squall and ordered his men to trim the sails. The rain hit soon after, so intense they could barely see ten yards beyond the ship. As the gale battered the *Tempest*, the crew fought to hold steady, but in the middle of the battle there was chaos. Ships were blown into one another, ensnaring rigging and bringing down masts. The surviving Spanish vessels attempted to use the weather to flee their destruction.

For half an hour, the squall continued in full force. Courtenay's expertise kept the *Tempest* clear of any collisions, but he couldn't drop his concentration for a moment.

As the clouds cleared, they saw the remaining Spanish ships sailing north away from the battle, struggling to resume their crescent formation. The hearts of the crew fell with the knowledge that the core of the Armada lived on, but everyone knew they were out of ammunition and sailing into dangerous waters. The English fleet began pursuit to finish the work they had started.

The smoke of battle had now cleared, and in the light of the setting sun, the topmen caught sight of their prey. Their hail drew Will's attention to grey sails heading west.

"They have abandoned the Armada?" Carpenter said. "What, they flee now?"

As Will weighed the tactics of the Unseelie Court, he mentally plotted their course until a chilling realisation dawned upon him. "They sail for England," he said, voicing his thoughts to himself. "With the Silver Skull aboard."

"They had given up the fight?" Carpenter suggested.

"No. No!" Will became animated. "Consider: the English fleet is now being drawn away from our waters. The militia line the coast awaiting Parma's invasion force. The queen will be protected, but aside from those soldiers, London's defences are now wide open. We have been distracted from their true objective."

"The Armada . . . the entire might of Spain's empire . . . was merely a distraction?" Carpenter said incredulously.

"They have sacrificed the Spanish on the rocks of their own vanity. The empire . . . all the lives lost mean nothing to the Unseelie. The conflict simply served to draw our might, and our attention, away from where it was most needed."

"London?" Carpenter looked to the ship disappearing towards the horizon.

"The seat of our nation. The core of our defences against them. The queen."

"All a manipulation." Carpenter's quiet voice was filled with disbelief at the extent of the deceit, but gradually the magnitude of the repercussions filled his face. In silence, the three of them stood at the rail as the *Tempest* gave pursuit, but the grey-sailed ship was faster, and soon it had disappeared from view.

CHAPTER 54

In the hour before dawn, a sepulchral silence lay across the Palace of Whitehall. Up past midnight with Walsingham, Burghley, and her other advisors discussing the fleet's fortunes against the Armada and the strategy for the coming days, the queen had finally retired to her chambers. In a display of confidence at the success of her forces, she had already made plans to spend the next day hunting in Epping Forest, while waiting for news of the battle off Gravelines, but it was clear to everyone who saw her that she remained uneasy.

Nathaniel and Marlowe had spent the early evening drinking in the Traveller's Rest in the shadow of the walls surrounding the palace complex. For most of the night, Marlowe had tried to cajole the owner to stage a play he had been writing, to no avail. Nathaniel had paid little notice, his attention drawn to the anxiety that blanketed the other drinkers. The mood was subdued, the conversation barely rising above a murmur. No entertainment had been planned for the inn-yard, and trade was sparse, though Nathaniel had heard there was brisker trade in the church across the street. The gossip raced back and forth: the Spanish had been defeated; the English fleet had been destroyed, and the Spanish were at that very moment landing along the south coast; death and destruction drew nearer.

The same air of apprehension hung over the entire palace, from the kitchen staff to the queen's maids, from the gardeners to Walsingham himself. Marlowe had questioned the spymaster on more than one occasion as the evening drew on, but Nathaniel was not allowed to be privy to the conversations; whatever the response, it did not raise Marlowe's mood. A dismal air surrounded him as if he had received a portent of his own death; Nathaniel wondered if it was just the way of writers.

"We are like children, wrapped in a mother's skirts," Nathaniel complained as they wandered through the formal gardens filled with the perfume of night-scented stock. Moonlight glimmered off the diamond-pane windows of the long north range where the gallery looked over the courtyard before the queen's residence. From beyond the jumble of buildings to the west came the dank, florid smell of the summer river, the cries of the watermen long since ended.

"Do not yearn for conflict and danger, Nat. These moments of peace are few and far between," Marlowe replied.

"But men are putting their lives at risk in the defence of England even as we speak. In defence of our lives, Kit, yours and mine, and we do nothing but wander through the gardens at night out of boredom. Does that not irk you to the very heart of your being?"

"We keep watch. We are ready if needed—"

Shaking his head forcefully, Nathaniel tried to allow his anger to erase his fears for his master, and also for Grace. He felt powerless, and the more he learned about the world Will inhabited, the less he understood. There were more dark shadows than he had ever anticipated, and though he feared he knew what lurked within them, he was not sure he wanted to know the truth. Already he had trouble sleeping, his nights haunted by grey figures flitting through the dark, and things that should not exist under the eyes of God.

Gentle pipe music, lilting and entrancing, drifted over the peaceful palace grounds. Nathaniel paused and cocked his head, a smile leaping to his mouth unbidden. "Do you hear that? Such beautiful music. Who would play at this hour?"

Marlowe shrugged. "I hear nothing." He trudged along the path beside the low box hedge.

"At least you have some purpose here. A spy. What can I offer, apart from keeping you company?"

"I am not a swordsman like Will," Marlowe said. "My strength lies in getting in my cups with cutthroats and gambling with rogues. Petty thievery and low deception." The note of bitterness in his voice was potent. "Choose a writer to live in a world of lies! Walsingham knows men well."

Nathaniel came to a slow halt as he heard the music again, faint, caught on the wind; it came and went in a strange manner, and while its melody was enchanting, he now heard a more disturbing tone beneath.

Catching it for the first time, Marlowe paused too. Nathaniel was puzzled by the troubled expression that crossed his associate's face. "What is it?" he asked.

Marlowe waved a hand as if it was nothing, but Nathaniel could see it was important to him. As Marlowe put his head back to sniff the air, Nathaniel realised he could smell a rich perfume, slightly sickly, drifting across the gardens.

"Come," Marlowe whispered. He broke into a light-footed run until he reached the passageway that cut through the long range of buildings into the courtyard in front of the banqueting house. The flags were lit by the moon. All was still. From the shadow of the passageway, Marlowe studied the courtyard intently, taking in the chapel in the far corner and the haphazard collection of buildings to his right where an archway led through to the palace's private wharf on the river.

"It is empty," Nathaniel began until Marlowe silenced him with an insistent wave of his hand.

Ahead was the Lantern Tower where the Silver Skull's Shield had been stored, and from which all but a chosen few were denied access. At the top of the tower, a green light pulsed, so faint it would have been easy to miss, but now that he had seen it, it was impossible for Nathaniel to take his eyes off it.

He had no idea what could cause such an odd hue, but it had the feel of a beacon, calling, or warning, he was not quite sure.

Marlowe turned to him and hissed, "Something is amiss—exactly what I do not know—but I feel it in my gut. There is danger nearby."

Nathaniel let his gaze wander over the empty square, and realised he too could feel whatever was troubling Marlowe.

A surprising flash of sympathy crossed Marlowe's face. "Nat, it would be good if you stayed away from here—"

"No!" Nathaniel interjected. "You would send me away now when I may actually prove I have some use in this world beyond fetching and carrying for my master?"

"There are things that you should not see, or know exist. Once in your head, they can never be put out, and this life goes from being a joy to a burden that you would be rid of soon. That is the nature of our business." He searched Nathaniel's face and grew sad. "I can see you will not be deterred. You are a brave man, Nat. But take my advice: whatever you see, put it out of your head the moment your eyes fall upon it. Ask no questions, neither of yourself, nor of me. Simply accept, and move on." Marlowe delivered his speech even though it was clear he didn't believe it was possible. "Do you understand?"

Nathaniel nodded, not understanding at all.

"Good. Then no more talk." He drew his knife and watched.

After a moment, a solitary figure wandered into the centre of the court-yard and looked around with an air of confusion. Nathaniel was shocked to see it was Grace.

Marlowe made to silence him as he called her name quietly, but Nathaniel was so relieved to see her he darted out into the moonlit square and threw his arms around her. She was stiff and unyielding, and when he looked into her face, he saw a blankness that reminded him of a child's doll.

Quickly, he pulled her into the shadow of the row of buildings and said quietly, "Grace? Are you well?"

She continued to stare blankly until a tremor crossed her face and she blinked once, twice, lazily. When she looked at him, her eyes had a dreamy, faraway look like someone deep in their cups, or on the edge of sleep.

"Nat," she breathed. "Oh, it is so good to see you. It has been . . . how long has it been?" A puzzled furrow crossed her brow, quickly gone, and then her lazy smile returned. "I have had the strangest dream, Nat. Of life aboard a magical ship, taking me to great adventures across a sparkling sea beneath the light of the moon. Of friends, whispering comfort in my ear, and joy. Oh, Nat! The kind of joy you never experience once you are grown." Closing her eyes, she continued to smile at her memories.

"How did you get here, Grace? Where have you been?" he probed gently. He could see she was not herself, and wondered if she had taken one of the potions that the cutpurses sometimes used to dull the senses of their victims in the stews on Bankside.

Ignoring him, she wrapped her arms around her and swayed gently in the breeze.

In the entrance to the passageway, Marlowe beckoned furiously. Nathaniel tried to guide Grace towards him, but she resisted.

"No, Nat. I have work to do. For my friends." Her voice had the singsong lilt of some melody only she could hear. "I led them to the guards so they could come in . . ." Her brow furrowed again, as though at an unpleasant memory, but nothing dark would stay with her. "And now I must show them through the maze of the palace. They need me, Nat. I cannot deny my friends."

"That is not a good idea, Grace," he began, but he could see she was not listening to him. Gradually, she pulled away and drifted across the courtyard, his presence already forgotten.

Nathaniel ran back to Marlowe and said, "She has helped her captors to enter the palace."

"We must alert the guards, then. To the gatehouse."

As they made to move, Marlowe suddenly grabbed Nathaniel and dragged him back into the passageway. Pressed against the wall, they saw grey shadows shimmer from the archway that led to the gate, following in Grace's wake towards the range of buildings on the other side of the courtyard.

Blinking to clear his eyes, Nathaniel wasn't sure if he was seeing moon-shadows, so insubstantial did they appear. His attention was diverted by a cloaked and hooded figure walking slowly, head and shoulders bowed as if consumed with despair. More shadows followed, slightly more substantial this time; Nathaniel felt his eyes were clearing, although he could not explain the strange effect.

Once the courtyard was empty again, Marlowe motioned for them to leave the passageway. They ran along the wall around the edge of the court-yard, hesitating every now and then in case more of the intruders appeared. As they edged through the archway to the gatehouse that lay next to the river entrance, they were overwhelmed by a smell of rot.

The gates hung wide revealing the path that led to the warehouses along the river and the wharf. Two guards lay on the cobbles in the entrance, the moon illuminating skin that was blackened and suppurating. Nathaniel retched at the vile stink that rolled off the bodies and chewed on the back of his hand to control his gag reflex. As he edged closer, he saw large boils had risen up around the guards' necks and a thick white foam covered their lips.

"Plague!" he gasped, throwing himself back against the wall of the arch. "But . . . but the guards were well earlier. And plague does not strike one dead so quickly!"

Marlowe led him away several paces and whispered, "Steady yourself, Nat. This plague is not natural. It comes from a weapon the Enemy has under their control—"

"The Spanish have a weapon that can bring disease?" Nathaniel gushed anxiously.

When Marlowe didn't reply, Nathaniel knew his worst fears were confirmed: there was another enemy, beyond the Spanish, and he knew instinctively what it was. Marlowe struggled to find words to continue the conversation and so Nathaniel interjected, "What kind of weapon does this thing, Kit? I have not heard the like of this anywhere."

"I told you—no questions. We can talk of these things later. Right now we must raise the alarm." Nathaniel followed him into the gatehouse, but they'd barely gone three steps over the threshold when the foul smell told them all they needed to know. "Damn them!" Marlowe snapped.

"They are slaying every man they encounter. Is there no protection from this weapon?"

"Dee searches for some defence, but as yet has found none. If used gently, without the protection of the Shield, I am told it has a range—like an arquebus. Stay beyond that range and you will be unharmed."

Nathaniel nodded his approval. "Good. That we can do." He hesitated as a thought struck him, and then said, "The queen! If these guards are dead, the others may be taken by surprise. We must protect her!"

"We are also charged with protecting what is held in the Lantern Tower. That will be the Enemy's first port of call."

They ran from the gatehouse back across the courtyard and into the range of buildings that led to the banqueting rooms. Through the windows, they could see the maze of buildings that surrounded the queen's residence, the Black Gallery and the Tryst Rooms on the far side, and in the foreground the row of stone houses next to the Lantern Tower. Nothing moved in the immediate vicinity.

But as they continued down the corridor, they heard the sound of a guard's challenge ahead. Slowing, they came to a corner and peered around cautiously. At the far end of the great hall, a guard levelled his sword at the hooded intruder, demanding to know his business.

The figure did not respond. For a moment he hesitated, until the guard prodded him with the sword, and then he held out his hand. Dropping the sword, the guard cried out, his hand leaping to his throat. Horrified, Nathaniel watched boils burst from the man's neck, his skin blackening and mouth foaming white, his eyes rolling until he fell to the ground, convulsing a little before he died. The whole process took barely a minute.

"So quick," Nathaniel whispered.

Once the guard had fallen, Nathaniel became aware of figures across the hall, as if they had just stepped out from behind some unseen curtain. If they were the shadows he had glimpsed earlier, they now had substance, though he could see none of their faces. Still indistinct, they appeared to swathe themselves in shadows that were thrown by no obvious light source.

Grace was among them, still entranced. Two of them guided her towards the door on the far side of the hall, the others loping behind. Not a sound echoed; it was as though the hall was filled with ghosts.

Peering through a window, Nathaniel saw the intruders fanning out across the palace complex. "They are everywhere. We cannot confront them all. What do we do?"

"Stealth, Nat," Marlowe whispered. "There is nothing to gain by revealing ourselves yet. An opportunity will present itself." Marlowe did not sound convinced, and Nathaniel could see on his face his anxiety as he searched desperately for an answer. Motioning for Nathaniel to follow, Marlowe dashed across the great hall to the door.

"It is down to you and me now, Nat," he said grimly. "The two of us, to save England and the queen."

CHAPTER 55

The desperate rhythm of pounding hooves matched the pulse of the blood in Will's head. Under the light of the moon, he drove his horse along the sun-baked lanes, over the marshland where lights burned ominously, and past the peaceful fields where the corn waved in the night breeze, with Carpenter and Launceston alongside.

Over the long hours that the *Tempest* pursued the grey-sailed ship, the three of them had remained in constant council. There was no doubt in their minds that the Unseelie Court would head directly for the Palace of Whitehall, to secure the Shield so they could unleash whatever plan they had nurtured since the Silver Skull had been taken from the Tower.

As they entered the Thames estuary, Will ordered Courtenay to put them ashore before they reached Tilbury. The grey-sailed ship would take the most direct route, slowing to navigate the upper reaches of the river to London Bridge before the Enemy moved to smaller boats to reach the palace. They had a chance to make up some time on the faster ship.

Parched by the dust, they finally reached the city walls during the hour before dawn. Admitted by the night watch, they thundered through the deserted streets to the west where the palace sprawled hard against the river. As they neared, Will's attention was caught by the inexplicable and troubling faint green halo around the Lantern Tower.

Dead guards littered the eastern gateway, features ravaged by disease. Without slowing to examine the corpses, Will, Launceston, and Carpenter continued to the yard next to the Black Gallery.

"No sounds of resistance," Will whispered. "The guards have been surprised and defeated before they could sound the alarm."

Carpenter indicated through the archway to figures making their way among the adjoining buildings. "Our arrival was noticed," he said. "The palace is overrun. Is it too late?"

"Courtenay will soon be here to raise the alarm and seal off the palace, as ordered." Will directed them towards the Black Gallery. "Till then we must do what we can."

"They will try to hunt us down, but their attention is elsewhere," Launceston said, once they were inside. "That will help us evade capture."

At the stairs to the Tryst Rooms, Will said, "We must go our separate ways. I will attend to the Lantern Tower. The Unseelie Court will attempt to break through the defences Dee has put in place. You must protect the queen at all costs."

Carpenter and Launceston raced up the stairs to take the route through the connecting buildings to the queen's quarters. The lock at the entrance to the Black Gallery turned with a clank as Will ran into the map room, locking the door behind him. He proceeded through Dee's personal library to his workshops and then out into the warm night.

Over hundreds of years, the random development of the palace had left a confusing ground-plan for those unfamiliar with its maze of passageways, courtyards, gardens, and buildings, grand and mundane. For Will, it provided ample shadowed doorways and dark places as he attempted to make his way to the Lantern Tower unseen.

The faint glow around the tower's summit still troubled him. He had heard the rumours of unearthly noises emanating from the tower at night, but he had always put that down to a widespread suspicion of Dee and his work.

He took a circuitous route to the range of buildings where the tower stood. Carpenter had been correct: the palace was overrun. Figures prowled through the quiet buildings and searched the open spaces. They ignored the sleeping servants and the members of the court, but culled all armed men as soon as they came upon them.

Unable to help, Will was sickened when he saw a good man's throat slit, a nightwatchman run through before he had even seen his opponent. He tried to estimate the numbers, but they were constantly and rapidly moving. Of the Silver Skull, there was no sign.

Whenever his fears for Grace surfaced, he mercilessly drove them from his mind and concentrated on reaching the tower. On more than one occasion, he had to double back through the deserted kitchens or into the banqueting house to approach from a different direction. Once he had to take refuge in a store filled with an odd mix of carpenters' materials and unwanted items from one of the ships moored at the palace wharf—fishing nets, grapnels, sailcloth, and barrels of pitch. He hid behind a pile of dirty rope while footsteps paused briefly at the door before moving on.

Afterwards, as he stalked along a dark gallery listening for fugitive footfalls, he was overcome by a disturbing sensation of being watched. The feeling grew so powerfully he was convinced someone was hiding in the gallery, but he could find no one among the furniture or behind the tapestries. Finally, as he prepared to leave with every hair on the nape of his neck prickling, he glanced into a large mirror. Instead of his reflection, he saw Malantha, watching him as though she stood in the room with him. Instantly, he was jolted back to the strange mirror that stood in the ritual room in Seville. He smashed the mirror with his sword hilt, but even in the glittering shards he could see her hateful gaze multiplied a hundred times. He hurried out before he was discovered, but the unsettling sensation stayed with him.

When he reached a window overlooking the courtyard that surrounded the Lantern Tower, he saw he was too late. Before the door at the foot of the tower, three shadowy figures watched a fourth who knelt over one of the pulsing glass globes, although this one glowed with a dull, ruddy light like a blacksmith's forge. The kneeling figure busied himself with some unseen activity before the globe. Whatever he was doing, the quality of its light altered repeatedly.

Will Dee's defences hold? Will wondered.

Four more figures entered the courtyard from the direction of the river. At the forefront, Cavillex strode purposefully towards the tower, a barely restrained look of triumph on his face.

The globe flared darker. The door opened.

CHAPTER 56

arpenter and Launceston sprinted along the echoing corridors of the upper floors as they wound their way towards the queen's rooms. From the windows, they watched the Unseelie Court dispatching guards with brutal efficiency, peering into rooms, darting through doorways, moving steadily towards the royal residence.

"Hold," Launceston insisted as they crept along the Blue Gallery. He called Carpenter back to a view over the lawns and paths that lay in front of their destination where Grace was pointing to the queen's chambers. Her head was bowed slightly, a dreamy smile on her lips. Beside her, Mayhew stood with his hood removed so that the Skull gleamed brightly in the moonlight.

"She is entranced," Carpenter said. "She cannot help herself."

"Still, she guides them—she knows the palace better than Mayhew. If the opportunity arises, she may need to be removed from the game."

"Save your bloodlust for Mayhew, Robert. That damned traitor deserves to be carved like a side of beef." Carpenter glared at the Silver Skull for a moment, all his secret loathing now directed towards his former ally.

No guards waited at the queen's door, and there were no bodies. The door itself was slightly ajar.

Fearing the worst, Carpenter pushed it open, his sword drawn. The windowless antechamber was dark and empty. They waited a second until their eyes adjusted to the gloom and then entered, but no sound came from the bedroom beyond. At the doorway, they hesitated, fearing the consequences of breaking into the queen's chamber at night, despite the seriousness of the occasion. Finally, Launceston grabbed the handle and flung the door open.

A flickering candle on a side table illuminated another empty room. Carpenter and Launceston exchanged an uneasy glance when they saw the bedclothes had been torn back roughly.

"We are too late," Carpenter said. "They have her."

Acting as if he had not heard, Launceston stood deep in reflection.

"The Unseelie Court is on its way! We must leave or they will trap us here!" Carpenter insisted.

"If the Enemy had already arrived, the guards would be dead at the door," Launceston mused. "No, they left to investigate the attack. Perhaps they were directed by . . . someone."

"Then where is the queen?" Anxiously, Carpenter glanced back towards the antechamber, already imagining Enemy footsteps drawing nearer.

Launceston turned slowly, and then allowed his attention to focus on the candle. Its flame bent in a draft, although the windows were shut and heavy drapes drawn across them. Striding quickly to the candle, he followed the direction of the draft to the oaken panelling marked with the queen's initials. Along one edge was a dark vertical line. With his fingertips, Launceston eased open a hidden door.

"A secret passageway," he said. "Not sealed tight amid a hasty exit."

"Enough talk." Carpenter thrust Launceston into the passage and closed the door behind them with a soft click.

The passage was dry and dusty. Rats scurried ahead of them. They continued in the dark for a little way, wishing they had brought the candle with them, until a soft glow appeared ahead. Swords raised, they edged forwards slowly.

From the dark, a figure clattered a sword against Launceston's weapon. The fight was brief and the attacker driven back, until the half-light washed over them.

"Marlowe!" Carpenter exclaimed.

Relief flooded Marlowe's face and he lowered his sword. "Thank all the powers there are," he breathed. "I am more dangerous with a quill than a sword. I thought this was the end of me."

He led them along the passageway to a series of windowless rooms. In the first, Nathaniel waited with Walsingham and Dee, their faces drawn. Through the half-open door to the adjoining room, they could just make out the queen, seated on a chair, her head bowed, her face as white as Launceston's in the gloom. Without her red wig to cover her grey stubble she was a picture of age and impotence far removed from the regal figure they had all seen in public.

"She would not have you see her like this," Walsingham said quietly. He closed the door a little more, but there was only one light and he did not want to plunge her into darkness.

"Is it as bad as we fear?" Dee asked.

"Worse. The Enemy has the run of the palace," Carpenter replied.

Walsingham hung his head dismally. After a moment, he said, "The queen would already be lost if Master Marlowe and Master Colt had not raised the alarm. There is still hope—"

He was interrupted by a loud crash echoing from the queen's bed-chamber, followed by more as the furniture was thrown roughly around.

"Trapped," Launceston said. "How long before they find the passage?"

CHAPTER 57

Scrambling out of the window, Will pulled himself up onto the roof. The lichen-crusted tiles threatened to crumble beneath his boots and pitch him to the courtyard far below. The door to the Lantern Tower hung open, and though Cavillex had ventured inside, Will knew it was the place Dee mysteriously treasured most and he would have installed a series of doors and defences.

The tower was one of the newest constructions within the palace complex, erected rapidly not long after the beginning of Elizabeth's reign by her decree and under Dee's strict design. Around the top of the tower, beneath the conical tiled roof topped by a weather vane, ran decorative battlements to give the tower gravitas. Will hoped the stone was secure enough to take his weight.

A golden dawn dispelled the gloom that would have made his task impossible. Weighing the grapnel he had recovered from the store of unwanted ships' items in which he had hidden, he steeled himself, and then whirled it around his head before loosing it. His first attempt didn't even reach the tower. The second time the grapnel bounced off the stone wall with a resounding clang that he feared might draw attention. The third attempt failed too, and the fourth. A quarter of the way up the tower, the globe's ruddy glare was visible through one of the windows.

On the fifth occasion, the grapnel caught on the battlements, slipped a little, and then held tight. Wrapping the oily rope around his wrists, he put all doubts out of his mind and launched himself off the roof.

The battlement held. Bracing against the impact, he steadied himself and began to climb rapidly. One floor below the top, he swung in an arc to crash through one of the arch-shaped windows. Jagged glass tore the skin on his hands and arms, and he tumbled into a bone-numbing landing on the stone steps. Scrambling to his feet, he drew his sword. Above him, the way was barred by a heavy oak door marked with a series of Dee's sigils. From beneath it, the familiar green light gently pulsed.

The stairs spiralled down to another floor, and from somewhere below that he could hear the sound of Cavillex talking in a language he didn't recognise. As he prepared to descend, an odd feeling convulsed him: his thoughts twisted like the eels they hauled from the muddy waters of the Thames, and his stomach knotted and heaved. Blood dripped from his nose.

Cavillex, he thought. But the notion did not seem correct.

Before he could consider what it meant, a door crashed open below. Bounding down the steps, he found himself in a room that covered the entire floor of the tower, and on a table in the centre was the Shield.

As he made to grab the artefact, a trapdoor into the room burst open. A queasy feeling of dread filled the space. As his senses skewed, shadows flew, accompanied by a distorted noise that reminded Will of crows in a winter sky. The dank, underground smell of loam. He knew what was coming, and however much Dee prepared him to deal with the disorienting qualities of the Unseelie Court, he was never ready.

Grey figures surged. Will caught only the briefest impression of hateful eyes and churchyard faces amid a pooling dark before he was enveloped in a furious battle.

His perceptions slid around the room's new occupants. All he could do was slash and lunge with his sword in wild abandon, feeling some blows parried, others tearing through bodies. One of the Enemy fell at his feet. Another thrust a blade that tore open the flesh on Will's neck. The Enemy were faster than most men, their stamina greater, and though Will's sword-skill was more refined, the fight was unequal.

Briefly, Will glimpsed Cavillex, red-rimmed eyes flaring, his contempt too strong to contain, but it felt like the dark was closing in from every side. Somehow he managed to keep himself between the Shield and his opponents.

Three of the Unseelie Court moved around him like ghosts at twilight. But they were substantial. He laid one down with a thrust through the heart, but the other two surged forwards from opposite sides. Will parried the first, rolled quickly out of the way of the other.

As the second drove a sword towards his chest, Will dropped to his knees and flipped backwards. When he came up, he caught the toe of his boot under a stool, thrashing it viciously into his opponents' faces. The crunch of shattering bone echoed across the room and one of them went down. As the other attacker sprawled over the falling body, Will laid open his throat with the tip of his sword, following through with two heart-thrusts to end their lives.

Another attacker ran forwards. Will didn't even attempt to confront him. Stepping to one side at the last moment, he rammed his hand at the back of his enemy's head, propelling it into the window, and through it. As the broken glass ripped open his opponent's face, Will heaved both elbows onto the back of the neck, driving the shards at the base of the window through the throat.

The elemental fury that consumed Cavillex was so potent Will could barely look at him. "How honourably you kill." The voice, like stones dropped on a coffin, echoed from all parts of the room.

"There is no honour in any of this," Will replied. "Only survival."

As Cavillex stalked forwards, Will levelled his sword and said with a humourless grin, "We have business, you and I."

"Why, we have been in business for a long while," Cavillex said enigmatically. A bone white hand gestured towards the Shield. "You transported that item to the place where we needed it to be."

Will laughed, but Cavillex's oppressive aura sucked any humour from his voice. "You try to make a cake out of crumbs."

"I make the truth out of shadows . . . shadows to you. What safer place for the Shield than here? If we had kept it in Edinburgh, you would not have let us rest. With it here, we could go about our work untroubled, knowing the item we valued most was ready for us when the time was right."

Another manipulation. Was he that easy to direct?

"You always do our bidding," Cavillex said, as if he could read Will's thoughts. "You, your fellows. We know what makes your hearts beat faster. We understand your fears and sadnesses. We see the crack in the door, ready to be pushed wide." The weight of his attention became unbearable. "We run you, like you run the animals in the field."

Keeping his sword trained on Cavillex, Will fumbled blindly until his fingers closed on the Shield. "You could set the Silver Skull loose, destroy all of London, perhaps all of England. Why do you need the Shield?" he asked.

"Because we do not wish to destroy all." His presence sucked every glimmer of light from the room. Will felt as if he was standing in the deepest dungeon. "Dartmoor looms large in the minds of my people. And there are greater punishments than death, as you well know." An icy smile, challenging Will to deny it.

A clatter rose up from the stairs. Cavillex didn't look, but his smile grew broader as if he knew exactly who was coming. Without taking his eyes off Will, he gave a languorous summons with the fingers of his left hand, and the Silver Skull climbed through the trapdoor.

"Mayhew. You are a traitorous bastard—" Will began emotionlessly, until he was interrupted by another figure behind the Skull.

"Grace." His eyes flashed to Cavillex. "If you have harmed her—"

"She has not been harmed. See?" Pale fingers eased under Grace's chin to raise her head. She blinked dreamily, her gaze finally alighting on Will.

"Will . . . it is so good to see you," she said.

"Our entrance to the palace would have been much more difficult without her help," Cavillex said.

Other members of the Unseelie Court bustled into the room, surrounding Grace. It was impossible for Will to get to her. Backing away until his heel was on the first step of the flight he had descended, Will moved his sword back and forth, ready for the first attack, but he could never overcome the weight of numbers.

"We shall go from this room, and take your queen and infect her with a disease that will eat away her skin, her bone, her senses, yet keep her alive," Cavillex said. "She will suffer unimaginable agony, without respite."

Will thought he saw Mayhew flinch.

"Once we have her, we will release a plague across all London," Cavillex continued. "An entire city will die in a moment. With the Shield, we will be untouched by the whirlwind of disease unleashed by the Silver Skull, and we will walk through it, alongside your queen so she can see the corpses rotting in the street. Then we will take her to our home, to live on with the memory, and the pain."

Will was stunned by the cruelty of Cavillex's scheme; the unnecessary death and suffering, purely because their supremacy had been challenged.

"Your nation will be crushed by the magnitude of the blow struck against you," Cavillex added. "And that will only be the beginning of your country's agonies."

Will examined the Shield in the palm of his hand. "So, without this artefact you cannot unleash the full fury of the Skull and survive. You will be corrupted too, here at the heart of the whirlwind."

Will backed up the stairs another step. "The cost of this item is high," he said, holding the Shield up so Cavillex could see it. "How many of your lives will buy it?"

"You are a lesser creature and you have already taken too many of our lives," Cavillex replied. He gently led Grace forwards. "As you value life so lightly, your friend's death will be meaningless to you."

Will hid his concern. "If you wish to barter the girl's life for this trinket, think again. That route has already been tried. My loyalty lies with queen and country . . . and seeing the destruction of your kind."

"You misunderstand. I do not barter. We will take the Shield from you when we slaughter you. The loss of this girl's life is a punishment for your brutality. The sight of her dying—the consequence of your actions—will be the one you take with you to the grave."

Will stepped forwards, but the other members of the Unseelie Court closed around Grace. He would never reach her.

"You claim to be the injured party, but slaughter comes easily to you. If you kill without regard, if you murder your own, even, over arguments about religion and politics, if morals do not guide you, then how can you expect us to act any differently?" Cavillex continued.

"You have forced us down to your level."

Cavillex's laughter was harsh and mocking.

"Again, this is about survival," Will said. "We do not have the luxury of morals or gentility when we are being preyed upon." Even as Will spoke, he could hear the hollow ring to his words.

Tired of Will, Cavillex turned to Mayhew and said, "Make her die, now, in a way that will scar his mind forever."

In Mayhew's hesitation, Will saw a chink and acted quickly, "Do not do this, Mayhew. Grace is an innocent. Kill her and you will be damned for eternity."

"He is already damned," Cavillex said lightly. "That is the least of his concerns."

"Mayhew," Will pressed. "Do not ally yourself with these monsters. Whatever rewards they have promised you, they are not enough to tempt you to turn your back on your fellow man, or on your own humanity."

"Do you think we bribed him with gold? You truly do not understand us," Cavillex said. "We know every part of you. We understand your weaknesses, your flaws, and we play them like a musician plays his instrument. A personal weakness makes you its mare, and it rides you hard, and you cannot throw it off, whatever you do. None of you are that strong. The only way he will be free of his torment—the only way he will be free of the mask—is to do my bidding." He pointed a slender finger at the Silver Skull and then directed it to Grace. "Kill her. Now."

Mayhew turned his face to Will as if offering his apologies, and then raised his hand to Grace's forehead.

"No, Matthew," Will pleaded. "Grace does not deserve this."

Mayhew hesitated for the briefest moment, and then planted his hand on the nearest member of the Unseelie Court. In the swimming dark, Will glimpsed convulsions, boils, blackening skin, eyes growing thick with pus, a foaming mouth. Mayhew turned to the next, and another, both hands reaching out.

The inhuman shrieks were so loud Will thought his ears would burst. As the shadows whirled, he had the impression of Cavillex throwing himself away from Mayhew towards the trapdoor. The red-rimmed eyes, with no glimmer of humanity in them, would haunt him forever.

"You do not know us as well as you think," Will called after him. "Our weaknesses do not define us."

As the Enemy fell around Mayhew, Cavillex lashed out. Will caught the glint of a blade driving towards Grace, and with an instinctive lunge yanked her out of its path. The blade continued into Mayhew's chest.

Cavillex's voice set Will's teeth on edge: "Some part of our account will be balanced this day. Your queen will die." And with that, he was gone.

Still gripped by the Unseelie enchantment, Grace stood blissfully as Mayhew lay beside her in a growing pool of blood. "Take care of Mayhew in his final moments," Will called to her, unsure if it would have any effect. He paused briefly beside Mayhew and whispered, "At the last, you did right." And then he was down the steps in pursuit of Cavillex, for the life of the queen.

CHAPTER 58

Only the musket-shot crack of Cavillex's boots disturbed the dawn stillness of the palace as he swept into the range of buildings that would eventually lead him to the queen's quarters. Will was close behind.

Through the windows, he could see the grey shadows of more of the Unseelie Court patrolling the palace grounds, oblivious to the drama that was unfolding. If Cavillex gained the opportunity to raise the alarm, there would be nothing Will could do to protect the queen, or himself, or any of them still alive there.

But Cavillex appeared consumed by a furious rage, driven by the deaths of his associates and the failure of his intricate plan, his only thought revenge of the most brutal kind.

Rounding a corner, Will caught up with Cavillex among three more of the Unseelie Court. Cold faces snapped towards him, black eyes devoid of all compassion; his mind squirmed under their attention. Doubling back quickly, he bounded up the stairs to the next floor and took an alternative route.

As Cavillex passed the foot of another flight of stairs, Will flung himself off the steps with no thought for the stone flags below. The force of the impact drove Cavillex to the floor. With his knife, Will fought like a wild animal, every moment of suffering and misery he had endured driven into each stab. The blade plunged into muscle and bone, tore through features and chest, arms and guts. Blood flowed, but he couldn't tell if it was his own.

It felt like he had a fox under his hands. Cavillex thrashed and fought, writhing from Will's grip. Finally, he broke free and threw himself on top of Will, gripping Will's head in his hands. Pressing his face close, Will swam in deep shadow and those hideous red-rimmed eyes. They burned deep into Will's mind, turning over his thoughts, driving into his memories, abusing the most private part of him.

Throughout his body, he felt a sickening change: muscles knotting, every fibre straining, and he remembered the scarecrow in Alsatia that had once been a man.

With a tremendous effort, he brought the knife up hard into the side of Cavillex's neck. The inhuman shriek made Will's thoughts fizz. Cavillex lurched up, catching Will with a sharp backhand as he staggered away, clutching at his wound.

Dazed, Will sprawled across the flags, but he could already feel the pains deep in his body diminishing. By the time he had recovered, Cavillex was gone, but blood trailed in his path.

When Will reached the queen's chambers, Cavillex was already ransacking the room with three other members of the Unseelie Court. They rounded on him instantly, more animals then men. Will had a second to realise Elizabeth was not there before he was forced into such a furious ballet of parrying and thrusting he could only act on instinct.

A loud crash echoed across the room, but Will couldn't afford to divert his attention for an instant. Driven back by the intensity of the onslaught, he fought for his life, seeing only steel and cold eyes and mouths that snapped and snarled like the beast that had attacked in the frozen Russian forest.

But then one of his opponents fell forwards, a blade protruding from his chest, and another clutched futilely at his throat, across which a knife had been swiftly drawn. The third was so distracted by the sudden slaying of his associates he was unprepared for Will's thrust through his chest.

Carpenter and Launceston stood over the bodies, already turning to confront Cavillex, who stood by an entrance to a passageway behind the panelling. He could barely stand from the injuries Will had inflicted on him.

Cavillex snarled something in his unsettling language and darted into the dark space.

"The queen!" Carpenter exclaimed.

Will bounded past him into the secret passageway. Cavillex was already lost to the dark, his urgent movements echoing back. Careering into a room, Will found Cavillex wrestled against a wall by Nathaniel. His friend attempted to stop Cavillex reaching Elizabeth, who cowered in a corner next to Walsingham and Dee.

"Nat! Leave him!" Will barked, too late.

Leaning in, Cavillex whispered into Nathaniel's ear. As Cavillex unburdened his secret horrors, Nathaniel's eyes became glassy. The blood drained from his face and a fixed expression of dread gripped him. Swaying for a moment, he slithered to the floor, head in his hands.

Though terribly wounded, Cavillex still managed to give Will a look of triumph.

Lost to rage, Will beat Cavillex so hard bone shattered and blood flew under his knuckles. He was about to draw his sword to run Cavillex through when Carpenter grabbed him forcibly and pulled him away.

"Wait," he said. "There are worse things than death." His unconscious echoing of Cavillex's words brought Will up sharp. Carpenter indicated Launceston standing in the entrance to the passageway, ghastly in the gloom. "Let Robert spend some time with him."

"What?" Will began. "Why—?"

"Trust me," Carpenter whispered. "This is my gift to you, to draw a veil over our past disagreement. Launceston has a . . . specific touch."

Not understanding, but his anger now spent, Will allowed Carpenter to guide him away so he could turn his attention to Nathaniel, lying broken on the floor, his eyes fixed on a point far beyond the walls of the room.

Will knelt next to him. "Nat. What have I done?"

He was half aware of Launceston stepping by him, grabbing the beaten Cavillex, and thrusting him into the room at the back. The door closed. The lock turned.

Walsingham helped Will to his feet. As Dee quickly led out Elizabeth with all the concern and affection of the man who had tutored her since she was a child, Walsingham said, "There is still time. We may be able to aid your assistant, if we act quickly. Leave him with me. Go, and run these foul creatures from the palace. Kill as many as you find."

Will was reluctant to leave Nathaniel, but he understood Walsingham was right. Flashing one deeply concerned glance at his friend, Will entered the passageway with Carpenter, but he couldn't escape the memory of Miller, hanging from the rafters, slain by a whispered word. Some slight comfort came to him as he stepped out into the queen's chamber. Echoing along the passageway from the secret rooms came Cavillex's agonised cry, continuing unbroken until Will had left the rooms far behind.

They scoured the palace grounds, but they could find no sign of the Unseelie Court. It was as if Cavillex's invading force had vanished with the coming of the dawn.

While Carpenter went to liaise with Courtenay and his men who had sealed off the palace from the rest of London, Will returned to the Lantern Tower where he found Grace slowly coming out of her daze. She blinked and looked around, not knowing how she had come to be there.

Will was relieved, for it meant she would not recall her time with the Unseelie Court. There was still hope for her sanity. He had protected her, as he had vowed, though as much by good fortune as by his own actions.

"Every fighting man needs luck," he whispered. Confused, she made to ask him what he meant, but he took her in his arms and held her tightly. She nestled into him, and he could feel her emotions acutely, but all he could think of was Jenny and how it should have been her he saved.

After a moment, he pulled away to examine Mayhew, lying dead on the floor. The Key had been taken, and without it the Skull and the Shield were worthless. He felt oddly relieved. Cavillex's words returned to him: if they could not act to some higher standard, they would deserve to be destroyed, as the Unseelie Court deserved it.

"Oh," Grace said. "He has left a message." She indicated the wall, where Mayhew had used the last of his life to carve an inscription in the plaster with broken, bloody fingernails.

"*Bury my mother*," she read. "What does that mean?"

CHAPTER 59

cross London, the church bells were ringing. In the dead August heat, Will waited in the shade of a soaring elm, trying to ignore the powerful stink of the filthy slums that sprawled along the Thames to the east of the Tower. Majesty and vileness, side by side; that was London, that was his life.

Nearby, Leicester strutted back and forth, revelling in the attention of the thousands of men waiting in their ranks or on horseback, playing the hero in his mind, though he had not been called on to fight. On the ridge overlooking the river, the camp at West Tilbury was a splash of colour, red, gold, and blue pennants fluttering on the slight breeze, flags flying proudly above the white pavilions erected to shield the nobility from the noonday sun.

Eschewing the crowds lining both banks of the river and hanging from the windows of the houses with the best views, Will had opted for a period of quiet contemplation while he waited for the queen to arrive. There was much to consider.

Somewhere in the far north, the Spanish were drowning, fighting devastating seas, ships sunk and torn apart, men washed up on beaches to be slaughtered by the local people. The price that nation had paid—and would pay—for the poor judgment of their leaders was great. But here at home, the English ships were returning to port lauded, every man aboard a hero. A new day was dawning.

As the queen's barge arrived in a blare of trumpets on its triumphant journey along the river from the Palace of Whitehall, the sense of anticipation mounted. Following the causeway across the foul-smelling marshes where clouds of flies buzzed, she made her way to the camp on a white gelding. Cannon fire proclaimed her arrival.

Led by the Earl of Ormonde carrying the sword of state, and with two pages dressed in white velvet, one carrying her helmet on a cushion the other leading her horse, she strode along the ranks, a silver breastplate shining over a white velvet gown, her auburn wig a blaze of fire, sparkling with diamonds and pearls. The men cheered loudly, and shouted their devotion to Elizabeth and to England.

Will was not moved. Whatever he saw, he knew there was always another face beneath. Walsingham had already given him a glimpse of the carefully rehearsed speech the queen planned to deliver at Tilbury the following day. It was designed as much for the ears of the Unseelie Court as it was for her own people, or Spain. The Enemy would be listening. They were always listening.

"My loving people," she would begin, "we have been persuaded by some that are careful for our safety to heed how we commit ourselves to armed multitudes for fear of treachery, but I assure you, I do not desire to live to distrust my faithful and loving people. Let tyrants fear. I have always so behaved myself that under God I have placed my chiefest strength and safeguard in the loyal hearts and goodwill of my subjects.

"Therefore, I am come amongst you, as you see at this time, not for my recreation and disport but being resolved in the midst and heat of the battle to live or die amongst you all and to lay down for my God, and for my kingdom, and for my people, my honour and my blood even in the dust.

"I know I have the body of a weak and feeble woman, but I have the heart and stomach of a king, and of a king of England too, and think foul scorn that Parma or Spain or any prince of Europe should dare to invade the borders of my realm; to which, rather than any dishonour shall grow by me, I myself will take up arms. I myself will be your general, judge, and rewarder of every one of your virtues in the field. I know already for your forwardness you have deserved rewards and crowns and we do assure you, in the word of a prince, they shall be duly paid you."

Let tyrants fear.

The Unseelie Court would never rest, but a gauntlet had been thrown down. England would meet them head-on.

Will was soon joined by Walsingham, who had travelled on the second barge with the queen's closest advisors, out of place in his sombre black gown yet seemingly untouched by the oppressive heat. He stood beneath the elm next to Will, hands clasped behind his back, and watched the queen inspecting her loyal soldiers with an air of gentle pleasure.

"I would say it went well," he mused.

"Apart from the death and the suffering."

Walsingham sniffed. "There is always that."

Relenting, Will nodded. "Yes, we won a great victory."

"And you played a great part in that, Master Swyfte."

"And the others: Carpenter, Launceston." Pausing, he remembered the young man who had joined Walsingham's band so proudly only to encounter things he never dreamed existed and which stole his life from him. "Miller. They should not be forgotten."

"Oh, they will be. As will you."

Will eyed Walsingham askance.

"Your task is to move behind the skin of history, not upon its surface." Walsingham continued to follow the queen's progress, nodding approvingly whenever the cheers rose up again. "Your work is by design invisible, and it will remain that way. If it were made public, it would detract from the glory of the queen and the true heroes of England."

"I have a public face now."

"Yes. We created the great William Swyfte to provide comfort for the people of England, so they knew they were always cared for, protected from the many hardships that assail this world by someone greater than them. But that will only continue in stories told by the fireside or in the taverns, and soon those stories will die. There will be no public record of the part you played this day, you or any of your band."

"The pamphlets—"

"Will be destroyed, one by one, over time. When the accounts of these days are written in years yet to come, it will be a story of the heroism of honest Englishmen. It will not be a story of deceit and trickery, however great the sacrifices made. That would not do justice to the legend of England. It is your destiny to be forgotten. You must come to accept that."

Will shrugged. "I care little what happens when I am gone."

"There will be rewards in this life, for you and your associates. Launceston will go unpunished for his unnatural urges. Riches, women, drink. Enjoy it."

"Forever unknown," Will said reflectively. "I find some comfort in that, oddly." A thought that had troubled him for a while surfaced, and he asked, "Tell me of Dartmoor and what happened there."

Shaking his head slowly, Walsingham said, "We keep our secrets dearly, Will, all of us. You must never speak of Dartmoor again."

Leicester continued to strut around, trying to catch the queen's eye, but her attention was clearly upon her new favourite, Robert Devereux, the earl of Essex, who rode at her side. In the shadow of great affairs, humanity's true motivation was apparent, Will saw.

"This day has seen the beginning of the end of the Spanish empire, and the ascendancy of our own," Walsingham noted.

"The world we inhabit is nothing but madness and brutality. And England's empire will be built upon it," Will replied.

"Then so be it. Better our madness and brutality than theirs."

"The Unseelie Court has been pressed back, but they will not be defeated."

"No, they will always challenge us. That is why we must always be vigilant. But as our strength grows across the globe, so will our ability to resist them, on every front, in every land. And here at home, Englishmen and Englishwomen will finally find peace."

As Walsingham turned his face to the sun for the first time, Will saw tears glistening in his eyes, and the shift of deep, repressed emotions in his face.

"Not an ending, then," Will said.

"A beginning, of many things." Taking a deep breath, Walsingham steadied himself, then began with surprising sympathy, "I have some troubling news. About your assistant."

Before Walsingham had even finished speaking, Will was speeding from the camp, and beyond the palisaded embankments to where his horse was tethered.

London seethed in the heat as Will raced through the rutted, dusty streets to Bishopsgate. The church spire was visible above the rooftops, but he could hear the screams echoing through the alleys long before he saw the three stone buildings of the old priory around the cobbled courtyard and the gardens beyond. The dusty, smeared windows were now obscured by bars, the stone worn, tiles missing from the roof, and grass sprouting among the cobbles. Two open sewers ran on either side, filling the air permanently with the stink of human excrement.

Will hammered on the door until the keeper came, a big man with a large belly, long, grey-black hair, and a three-day stubble on his chin, a substantial ring of iron keys at his belt. He eyed Will suspiciously until Will introduced himself, and then the keeper clapped Will on the shoulder and proclaimed the glory of England over Spain.

Will had no time for niceties and demanded to be taken to Nathaniel. With a shrug, the keeper complied. Will could hardly make himself heard above the screams that rang from behind every door and in the long, vaulted cellar where the inmates of Bethlehem Hospital prowled in their own private worlds, clawing at the dank walls or kicking the filthy straw in a frenzy. Everywhere smelled of dirty clothes, urine, excrement, and vomit.

Noticing Will's pained expression, the keeper said, "This is Bedlam. There is never quiet here."

He led Will to a quieter annexe and unlocked a door that led into a windowless room. After Will's eyes adjusted to the dark, he saw there was only a bed within. Nathaniel squatted in a corner, hugging his knees.

"The dark is good for those distraught from their wits," the keeper noted, "and they must be kept free from all distractions. It is best for him," he added, seeing the dark look cross Will's face.

"Has he spoken?" Will asked.

"He says nothing. He eats if we feed him, but there is nothing left of him." He shrugged. "He will not recover."

Turning on the keeper, Will flung him against the wall and pressed his face against the keeper's. "Do not beat him—"

"They must be beaten, for their own good!"

"Do not beat him, or I will return and deal to you tenfold whatever you deal to him," Will snarled. He threw the keeper from the cell in a rage.

Pausing for a moment to control his churning emotions, he squatted in front of his assistant. "Nat, it is Will," he began quietly. "Your Master . . . Your friend."

No reaction crossed Nat's face, and when he did not move, Will placed a hand on his arm to check he was still warm.

"I have failed you, Nat," he continued. "There are times when I fear everyone close to me will be destroyed." As he watched his friend, the weight inside Will grew until he felt it would crush him. "I will not abandon you," he whispered.

CHAPTER 60

Stark slabs of exposed granite sparkled silver under the full moon hanging over the uplands, where the brackish streams trickled down through gorse and sedge, catching the light like jewels. It was a warm night, sweetly scented with the aromas of a country summer. Across the vast expanse of desolate grassland, not a light twinkled; all human life could have been extinguished.

Dusty from his long journey, Will let his rapid heartbeat subside, his breathing slow, and he listened to the singing of the breeze in the grass. Turning slowly, he surveyed the empty Dartmoor landscape. Alone in the world. From the moment Jenny had walked out of his life, nothing had changed.

Long nights of agonising had followed long days visiting Nathaniel in Bedlam, turning over all he knew, letting unseen connections slowly rise from his memories, until finally he had made his decision.

Ahead of him, the standing stone towered against the starlit sky, almost twice his height. Beardown Man, the locals called it; a reminder of when giants walked the Earth, some said, a warning from the Devil of the fate that awaited all sinners, others averred. Will thought the latter was probably closer to the truth, according to the legends that had grown up around Devil's Tor, where he stood, the ghostly sightings, the ethereal music playing on summer nights, the noises deep in the earth.

"Here I am, then," he announced. "Come to me!"

Only the sighing of the wind replied.

For long minutes he stood waiting, and then made his way to a lichen-covered boulder where he sat patiently. They would come in their own time, when they had shown it was not at his bidding.

An hour passed slowly, until thin strands of pearly mist drifted across the grassland. For no reason that he could discern, the skin on his arms became gooseflesh.

When the mist had passed, figures stood like statues here and there across the tor, their faces turned towards him, all lost to shadow. None moved; none spoke.

After a moment, a figure caught his eye, striding towards him through the grass past the threatening sentries. Tall and slender, he wore grey-green robes with a strange design in gold filigree, like the symbols of an unknown language, faintly visible whenever the moon caught them. His age was indiscernible. His cheeks were hollow and dark rings lay under his pale eyes, but his long hair was a mixture of gold and silver. Trinkets and the skulls of mice and birds had been braided into it so that he made a soft clacking rhythm as he walked.

He came to a halt before Will, his emotions unreadable. "Few dare to call to us," he said in a dry voice.

"You know me?" Will asked.

The stranger paused thoughtfully, and then said with a wry smile, "I know of your kind."

"And you speak for the Unseelie Court?"

"Ah," he said, still smiling, "*unholy.* Yes. You may call me Deortha. I am . . . an advisor." With his right hand, he appeared to be plucking words from the aether that Will could comprehend. Finally, with a nod, he settled on, "I am the Court's equivalent to your Doctor Dee."

"You know Dee?"

"Oh, yes." Deortha gave a strange smile.

"A sorcerer, then. An alchemist. A wise man."

Deortha's pale eyes twinkled in the moonlight. "You have a request of us?"

"How do you know?"

"You would not be here otherwise."

"What you are is anathema to humankind," Will began. "You are the madness in the night. The shadow on the family hearth. In the very nature of your being, you tell us that however much we order this world to make it sane, it is not, and will never be, and we are nothing. We have no control."

Deortha nodded wryly.

"Some who come too close to you are burned to ashes, like moths approaching a lantern's flame." Will watched Deortha's face closely for any hint of manipulation, or sign of an impending attack. He knew his own life hung in the balance the moment he set foot on the tor. "My friend is one of those. His wits are gone. He could not cope with the secrets that lie behind your eyes."

"Unlike you. You would revel in the knowledge of our secrets," Deortha challenged.

Will ignored him. "My own people cannot help him. You have at your disposal great things unknown to us . . . charms . . . potions . . ." Will shrugged. "Can you help him?"

A faint glint shone in Deortha's eyes, quickly gone. Will knew he had bared his throat for an attack.

"And why should we aid you?" Deortha asked.

"I killed several of your own. I helped bring about the death of Cavillex, one of your leaders. Help my friend regain his wits, and I will give myself to you for whatever punishment you see fit."

"Are you sure you are prepared to lay yourself open to our attentions? Our punishments are fierce."

"Nevertheless, that is my offer."

"Even though you will never see your kind again? Even though you will plead for a death that will never come?"

"I am ready."

Deortha was intrigued. "If you are ready, then those punishments have no value."

"Tell me about Dartmoor," Will said.

# CHAPTER 61

ive carriages trundled along the rutted, muddy ways in the last light of the sun. The gale had finally blown itself out. From the window of the second carriage, Walsingham watched the shadows pool over the bleak Dartmoor uplands, the sense of apprehension mounting with each second of the day that passed away.

"You are still convinced this is the correct course?" he asked.

On the opposite seat, Dee kneaded his hands together, an anxious tic that had begun to irritate Walsingham as the journey from Plymouth drew on. "I am not convinced of anything in this world," he replied. "We fumble around, making what progress we can in the pitch dark of our existence, and hope for the best."

"Hope for the best," Walsingham repeated, with a crack of anger born of his uneasiness. "How do we know they will not try to trap us?"

"We do not."

"And we take the queen into this danger, regardless?"

"Elizabeth made the decision herself. There is too much at stake for England to let an opportunity like this slip by. She has courage. You cannot deny her that merely because she is a woman." Dee cast a critical eye over Walsingham.

"She could be dead by the time the sun rises. As could we all."

"I hope . . . I hope I have done enough to convince them of our intentions," Dee said, now tugging at the hem of his cloak.

"I hope so too, Doctor." Walsingham had always considered himself a good captain steering a steady course through the turbulent seas of his life, but at that moment he could barely contain his fears.

Promising more rain, the lowering clouds brought the dark in too soon. The carriages came to a halt four miles east of Yelverton on the western edge of the moor, and the guards busied themselves lighting lanterns to guide the way.

Wrapped against the autumn chill, Elizabeth held her head defiantly erect as she climbed down from the carriage, though Walsingham could see the fear in her eyes.

"Is all ready?" she asked him.

Resisting the urge to express his own doubts, he nodded and bowed.

"Then let us be done with this business. I dream of a warm fire." She strode out across the moor with the guards hurrying to keep up.

After ten minutes of steady walking, they came to the cairns and menhirs standing proudly against the darkening sky. Elizabeth cast a contemptuous look at the ancient monuments and said to Walsingham, "This is the place?"

"It is. It was chosen carefully. The preparations have been made."

"And now?"

"We wait."

Darkness came down hard. Around the standing stones, the lanterns flickered in the harsh wind, offering little comfort. Finally, the moon broke through the clouds and they were there.

Walsingham almost cried out in shock, but the queen, to her credit, showed no sign of surprise. She rose to greet the arrivals. Forty of them stood on the edge of the circular indentation next to the standing stones, more than he had anticipated. His apprehension increased. Most of them had the look of armed guards, like the tight knot that surrounded Elizabeth, but two males carried themselves like aristocrats, heads held at a haughty angle, their clothes refined, though with a hint of decay. And at the front was the Faerie Queen. Her beauty was so potent it took his breath away. Brown hair tumbled in ringlets around her shoulders, and her flawless skin appeared to shine with a faint golden light. Her hazel eyes flashed with sexual magnetism. She wore a clinging gown of a green that appeared to reflect the night-dark grass all around. But beneath her appearance, something unsettling waited. Watching her, feeling the power she radiated, Walsingham dreaded what lay ahead.

"I am Elizabeth." She strode forwards confidently to address her counterpart.

"I know you are." The Faerie Queen smiled seductively, her voice mellifluous.

"We meet here as equals," Elizabeth said firmly.

The Faerie Queen gave a slight bow, but did not show any sign of agreement.

"You have preyed on my people for a great many years," Elizabeth continued.

"As you have preyed upon the animals of the field." The Faerie Queen caught herself, and smiled slyly. "We have been like shepherds, guiding you over the rough ground of your existence. At times you may have encountered . . . difficulties. At times we were not as cautious in our dealings as we should have been. You yourself know this. Your encounters among your own kind have proved . . . turbulent."

"England will no longer tolerate . . ." It was Elizabeth's turn to catch herself.

"The time for predators and victims is past," she continued, choosing her words carefully.

"I come to you as one queen to another," the Faerie Queen said. "Our intermediaries have agreed on the terms of our meeting. Members of the High Family are here to observe." She indicated the two aristocratic males who both gave thin-lipped smiles in response. "There is an opportunity for a new relationship between our two nations. Peace, even."

"Would you have responded so positively if our strength had not increased? Our defences? Our ability to challenge you for the first time?" Elizabeth asked.

Walsingham winced; the words were too bald, and he was afraid they would only drive the Enemy into an unnecessary confrontation.

The Faerie Queen's eyes flickered towards Dee. "You have gained a great deal indeed under the auspices of your wise and honourable counsel." Smiling, she gave Dee a respectful bow. He nodded in return.

"I feared you would use this opportunity to attack us," Elizabeth stated.

The comment stung the Faerie Queen. "We are an honourable people."

"You can afford to be," Elizabeth responded.

"Now!" Walsingham called.

From their hiding places in covered trenches, the fifty-strong army rose up as one, their pitch-covered arrows ablaze in an instant. As Elizabeth's guards rapidly guided her away from danger, the soldiers fired into the mass of startled Enemy. Many caught ablaze, their cries terrible to hear. Others retreated in the face of the onslaught.

A small group of soldiers grabbed the Faerie Queen and dragged her to Dee, who forced the contents of a small phial into her mouth. As her eyes flickered shut, the Enemy attempted to reach her, but the English soldiers blocked their path and drove them back with more arrows. The Enemy retreated into the slight indentation in the grassy ground next to the standing stones. Walsingham could see they were already preparing an assault that would no doubt be devastating.

The thin covering on the ground gave way beneath their feet and they plunged into a gaping hole, one of the pits the local tinners had used for lodeback work. The mine was not deep, but it would serve the purpose.

From their hiding place, the soldiers dragged the barrels of pitch and sulphur, setting them alight and flinging them into the pit one after the other. The screams that rose up would haunt all present for the rest of their days.

When the flames soared so high the soldiers were forced to back away from the edge, the dreadful cries finally died away.

Shielding his eyes from the blaze, Walsingham announced to Elizabeth, "You said you dreamed of a warm fire."

"Enough!" she said with restrained fury. "This night has blackened the history of England! Oh, how can I live with the memory of our treachery!"

Chastened, Walsingham replied, "The ends will justify the means." He gestured to the unconscious Faerie Queen, her wrists and ankles now bound under Dee's direction. "She will be our prisoner for all time, locked away at the top of the Lantern Tower where she will serve as the crux of Dee's magical defences for our country. The Enemy will be kept at bay, their power muted."

Elizabeth did not appear convinced.

"This dark night will fade against the golden days that lie ahead," Walsingham pressed. "England . . . finally free of the grip of an Enemy that has hounded our people for sport, slaughtered them, mutilated them, defiled their lives, and spoiled their dreams. The English people have always deserved peace, and now they will get it."

"I do not share your conviction, Lord Walsingham." She glanced back at the burning pit and then quickly averted her gaze. "I fear this night will echo down the years forever, and none of us will know sleep."

CHAPTER 62

For a moment, Will was convinced he could smell smoke on the wind, but it was just the enchantment of Deortha's words.

"You understand now," Deortha concluded.

In his pale eyes, Will saw the depth of emotion, and understood so much that had troubled him: what was kept in the room at the top of the Lantern Tower; why the Unseelie Court had risked so much to attack the Palace of Whitehall, and why they needed the Shield as protection when they unleashed the Silver Skull's plague; the comments Cavillex had made in Edinburgh about Dartmoor; and why the Enemy was so determined to destroy England.

"This madness will never end," Will said. "Each atrocity drives worse from the opponent in a spiral of horror."

"It will end," Deortha said firmly, leaving no doubt as to his meaning.

"No one can win," Will pressed. "There is no good here, no evil. Everything is tarnished. Do we even remember why we fight?"

"*We* remember."

"We continue this war, then, like the dogs tearing chunks off each other in the pits in the inn-yards of Bankside?" His bitterness made the words catch in his throat.

"What your kind did that night can never be forgotten, or forgiven," Deortha said coldly.

"And what you did to England for generation upon generation—"

"Then you understand fully. There can be no peace. We are too much alike."

Will felt as desolate as the dark landscape stretching out into the night.

"There is worse to come," Deortha continued. "Cavillex's death is a bitter blow to the High Family, which has already suffered greatly in this conflict.

His brothers and sister burn with the desire for vengeance. Your nation will soon fear the heat of their response."

"It never ends," Will said to himself. "Then grant my request. Help my friend and let them take me and punish me for their brother's death."

For the first time, Deortha's laughter was filled with clear contempt. "You think you are a fair exchange for a member of the High Family? If all your countryfolk were put to death, and your nation burned to the ground, it still would not make amends. You mean . . . nothing."

Will set his jaw. "Then you will not help me?"

Deortha considered for a moment and then said, "I will help." His smile chilled Will.

"The conditions?"

"You must make a choice. Aid for your friend . . . or an answer to the mystery that consumes your nature: what happened to your lost love."

Will was stunned, not only that Deortha had offered such a dilemma, but that he knew about Jenny. The slyness around his eyes showed that he was aware exactly what effect his offer would have.

Hiding his shock, Will replied, "Why? You refuse to take me for punishment, perhaps death, yet you gladly offer help if I make a simple choice?"

"Choose."

He could see Deortha revelling in the agonies that consumed him. Knowing the truth about Jenny had been the only thing that mattered for so long, it consumed him, drove him on to do everything he did; how could he turn has back on what might be his only chance? Yet how could he knowingly consign Nathaniel to the horrors of Bedlam? He saw the elegant cruelty in Deortha's dilemma: either answer had the potential to destroy him, not in sudden brutality at the hands of the High Family, but gradually, over years, with a slow magnification of pain that would eventually consume him. He was responsible for Nathaniel's suffering. He was responsible for never knowing the truth that would finally give him peace.

"I choose . . . my friend," he snapped.

"Very well." The triumph in Deortha's face sickened Will. "There are worse things than death," Deortha continued wryly, as though he knew the phrase had been uttered before. "For the rest of your days, you will be haunted by the knowledge of this night, as we are haunted by the knowledge of that other night. You could have solved the mystery that wrenches your heart. You could have found the one answer that will allow you to sleep at night. Perhaps you could even have brought your love back to you."

"Enjoy your small victory," Will said. "What I have achieved for my friend is worth my own suffering."

"At this moment," Deortha agreed. "In a week's time? A year's? At the end of your days, lying on your deathbed, knowing your entire life has been wasted by the never-knowing?" He shook his head.

"You think you know our ways so well," Will replied. "But you do not understand hope. I have hope that I will find my Jenny, and I will do everything I can to bring that about."

"Exactly." He smiled one more time, and then motioned for Will to wait. At some point Will could not define, he disappeared from view, and when he returned he held a small phial. "Give this to your friend. One drop, on the tongue. He will forget his contact with the flame of our being, and he will recover. And should it happen again," he added knowingly, "administer one more drop. It will only work for him."

Taking the phial, Will held it tight in his palm, afraid Deortha was going to snatch it back once he had finished his taunting.

"You make all your choices with such a poor vision," Deortha said. "You see a week ahead, at best a year. We are long-lived. Our plans move cautiously over years, decades, generations. Connections that are invisible to you fall into relief only when seen from our perspective. You cannot fight us when your reactions to our schemes are based only on the here and now. Who is to say that the things you do are not aiding us? That everything you consider a victory is only a step we expected and factored in to our plans, leading inexorably to our ultimate victory?" He nodded and added pointedly, "Enjoy this moment."

Weighing Deortha's words, Will looked down at the phial in his hand, and when he looked up the Unseelie Court was gone. Yet something glinted in the grass in the moonlight, a meaningless object Deortha had dropped in the warm glow of his cruel victory.

For a moment, Will stared at it, barely believing, and then he plucked it up and made his way back across the moor.

CHAPTER 63

The stage was set, the players ready in costumes of green and gold and scarlet, trying on their expressions for a good fit, their true selves long since forgotten. Yet their private conversations carried subtle, conflicting notes. The dress rehearsal was a pivotal point, the end of the prelude. They were filled with the apprehension of how their performances would be received, yet also jubilant at a new start filled with possibilities.

The yard at the Bull Inn was flooded with early morning sun and crisscrossed with cooling shadows cast by the pennants that had been strung haphazardly from window to window overhead. They were only one of many marks of celebration at the news still coming in of the wrecking of Spanish ships in storms all around the northern coasts of England, Scotland, and Ireland.

All yawns and lazy smiles, doxies hung from windows to watch the players run through their final preparations. Scents of honeysuckle and rosewater mingled with the sour aroma of beer drifting from the shadowy interior of the inn.

Leaning against the cool stone in the shade, his arms folded, Will watched the proceedings. It was going to be a hot day.

Marlowe sauntered over in a brighter mood than Will had seen him in for a long while. He was accompanied by a young man who shyly left before he was introduced to the great hero of England.

"One of yours?" Will nodded to the players running through their lines.

"A shine on the speeches here and there. Nothing more." A dismissive shrug. "I am filled with passion for a greater work. The one we spoke of? A man who makes a deal with the Devil for rewards which only prove fleeting."

A chill ran through Will, but it quickly dissipated in the summer warmth. "I am sure it will be well received, Kit."

Shielding his eyes, Marlowe studied the players approvingly. "I feel better times lie ahead, Will. With the Spanish so roundly defeated. The

Enemy pushed back once more. We can get on with our own lives, and there is much I wish to do with mine. Great plays to write. I see years of productive activity lying ahead." Embarrassed, he looked to Will and laughed. "You will think me an impostor."

"I am glad your spirits are high. You deserve some pleasure." Will watched Marlowe's young friend squeezing into a dress before he made his entrance on stage; a role upon a role upon a role. "I will speak with Walsingham," he added, "and smooth this disagreement that lies between you."

"No one has any control over Walsingham."

"I do." Will ignored Marlowe's probing gaze; he was still considering how to use the information he had gained from Dartmoor, and how far he could go with it before he became a liability.

They were interrupted by a carriage thundering into the inn-yard. Onlookers scattered as it came to a halt near the stage, much to the annoyance of the players. Nathaniel climbed out and then offered a hand to Grace.

Marlowe flashed Will a glance.

"He is well," Will said, but offered nothing more.

Two players involved in a furious argument dragged Marlowe away to give them better lines, and he left Will with a wink. Will was pleased to see him at peace; he hoped it would last.

His troubled emotions surfaced thick and fast as he watched Nathaniel and Grace approach, fear of what lay ahead for both of them and doubts about whether he could continue to fulfil his vows and keep them safe. Briefly, he wondered if he was like the Unseelie Court, a too-hot flame that burned all those who came close. But for now they were safe, and after the threat that had hovered over them, that was a victory he could cherish.

"The end of a long night, or the beginning of a long day?" Nathaniel eyed Will and then the open door to the inn.

"Neither, Nat. I am enjoying the sun and the peace of a day away from my duties."

Nathaniel made a disbelieving face. "The Spanish defeated, the country in the mood for celebration, and you are not already three drinks ahead? Something is amiss."

"There is time enough for that. I have been contemplating hiring a new assistant. The old one has a sharp tongue and I feel he mocks me when my back is turned."

our front only," Nathaniel said indignantly. "I am not a spy—I am ... in my ways."

"And we are all thankful for that, Nat," Grace said warmly. "No news of Jenny?" she asked Will hopefully. She paused, her brow wrinkling as she struggled with the gap in her memory. "Have I asked you this recently?"

He smiled. "No, not recently. Do not worry, Grace. The physician says the blow to your head has left you in good health, if a few memories short. You will soon make new ones. And the answer to your question is, not yet. But I continue my endeavours."

"It warms me that your love for my sister was so strong it still burns brightly even after she has gone. But sooner or later you must let someone else into your life, Will. You deserve warmth, and comfort, and your love returned by a good woman."

I deserve Jenny, he thought.

His smile and a nod were enough for her. Pleased, she took her leave and went to tease Marlowe who was caught in a huddle of bickering players.

"You will break her heart, Will," Nathaniel cautioned.

"What do I do, Nat? I must protect her from harm. I cannot keep her at arm's length to do that. She mistakes my care for love and will not hear any different."

"She may be right, though. She loves you—"

Will's cautionary glare stopped him in his tracks.

"Yes, yes, I know. There is only room for one woman in your heart." Nathaniel shook his head in frustration. "Do not complain to me in your bitter, lonely old age. You work a cold business in sour times. You need some warmth to stop your heart becoming as hardened as the world you inhabit."

"You are like an old wife, Nat." Will feared his friend spoke true, but in his hand he clutched at hope. He unfurled his fingers to reveal the glint of gold.

"What is that?" Nathaniel asked.

"Something I found on Dartmoor."

"A locket?"

Jenny's locket. Within it was a fresh rose petal, a mark of a love that had not died in all the years apart.

Although the High Family would be invigorated by their loss and there would be no respite in the long battle, he now had a hope that he scarcely dared believe.

On stage, the players put away their true selves. Intricate layers of trickery and emotion unfolded in the subtle spin of their words. The crowd laughed at the conceits, applauded the deceits. At the side of the stage, Marlowe nodded in approval at how the players danced to the strings he pulled.

Will clapped a hand on Nathaniel's shoulder. "Our Lord Walsingham muttered something about more work, in France. In Krakow. And in fair Venice. And on the Spanish Main. No rest for the swords of Albion, ever. But for now the sun is shining, and time runs away from us. There is wine to be drunk, and women to be romanced. Whatever lies ahead, the here and now is good, Nat, and we must make the most of it. Let us celebrate our great victory and drink to a world made right."

ABOUT THE AUTHOR

A two-time winner of the prestigious British Fantasy Award, Mark Chadbourn has published his epic, imaginative novels in many countries around the world. He grew up in the mining community of the English Midlands, and was the first person in his family to go to university. After studying Economic History at Leeds, he became a successful journalist, writing for several of the UK's renowned national newspapers as well as contributing to magazines and TV.

When his first short story won *Fear* magazine's Best New Author award, he was snapped up by an agent and subsequently published his first novel, *Underground*, a supernatural thriller set in the coalfields of his youth. Quitting journalism to become a full-time author, he has written stories which have transcended genre boundaries, but is perhaps best known in the fantasy field.

Mark has also forged a parallel career as a screenwriter with many hours of produced work for British television. He is a senior writer for BBC Drama and is also developing new shows for the UK and US.

An expert on British folklore and mythology, he has held several varied and colourful jobs, including independent record company boss, band manager, production line worker, engineer's "mate," and media consultant.

Having traveled extensively around the world, he has now settled in a rambling house in the middle of a forest not far from where he was born.

For information about the author and his work:

www.markchadbourn.net
www.jackofravens.com
www.myspace.com/markchadbourn